ANALOG

A CYBER-DYSTOPIAN NOIR

VOLUME ONE
DEATH BY ALGORITHM

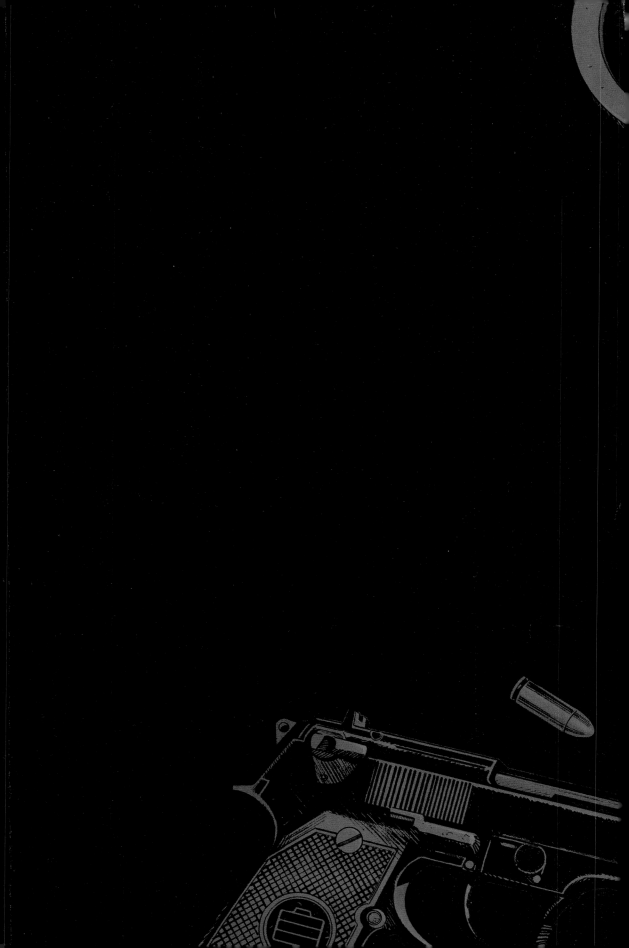

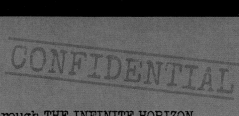

I first became aware of Gerry's work through THE INFINITE HORIZON, which he created with Phil Noto.

His first Image book was a stunning work of frightening prescience. He and Phil predicted the MAD MAX-adjacent apocalypse in the Middle East years before it really came to pass. When I was paging through the trade and saw Gerry thank our mutual friends David Mandel and Kelvin Mao, I asked for an introduction. Dave and Kelvin obliged, and it has since led to a long and fruitful creative relationship and friendship between Gerry and I. I ended up adapting INFINITE as a feature screenplay and we sold it on spec to Warner Bros. A happy ending.

Some years later at a whisky event (Gerry and I also share a deep and abiding love for the water of life — particularly any made in the Islay region of Scotland), I became aware of ANALOG, which he created with the talented newcomer David O'Sullivan. Gerry was predicting our future again! This time it was about our relationship with the internet and the mushrooming digital world we all find ourselves living in whether we like it or not. I saw another movie. Very clearly. ANALOG was an incredible, searing cyberpunk view of our soon-to-be future. I had to have it.

Mustering what little dignity I had remaining as a screenwriter, I begged Gerry to trust me again. Maybe it was the Islay whisky, but trust me he did. And now this incredible book you hold in your hands is being developed as a feature film by us, Lionsgate Entertainment, and the virtuoso action director Chad Stahelski, who you will all know for creating the JOHN WICK series. We hope the film gods are with us on this, because it's a good one.

If Gerry keeps predicting the future the way he has, we're all going to have to follow him to Las Vegas. Or into a fallout shelter. Whichever makes more sense.

Or, at the very least, maybe we can ask him when the New York Giants are going to have a winning season again.

Ryan Condal
Los Angeles
August, 2018

IMAGE COMICS, INC. • **Robert Kirkman:** Chief Operating Officer • **Erik Larsen:** Chief Financial Officer • **Todd McFarlane:** President • **Marc Silvestri:** Chief Executive Officer • **Jim Valentino:** Vice President • **Eric Stephenson:** Publisher / Chief Creative Officer • **Corey Hart:** Director of Sales • **Jeff Boison:** Director of Publishing Planning & Book Trade Sales • **Chris Ross:** Director of Digital Sales • **Jeff Stang:** Director of Specialty Sales • **Kat Salazar:** Director of PR & Marketing • **Drew Gill:** Art Director • **Heather Doornink:** Production Director • **Nicole Lapalme:** Controller • **IMAGECOMICS.COM** • **Deanna Phelps:** Production Artist for ANALOG •

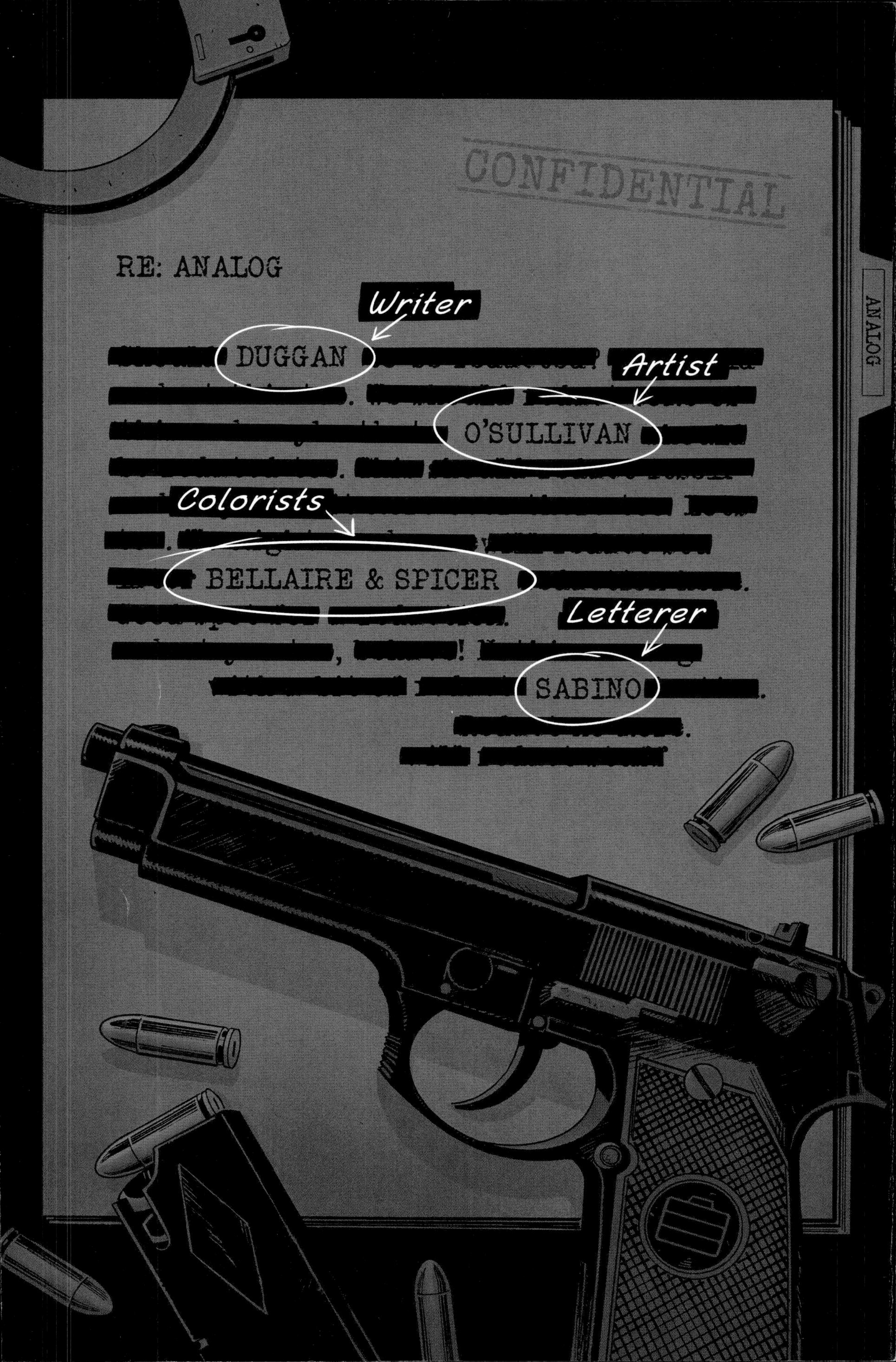
CONFIDENTIAL
RE: ANALOG
Writer
DUGGAN
Artist
O'SULLIVAN
Colorists
BELLAIRE & SPICER
Letterer
SABINO
ANALOG

CHAPTER 1

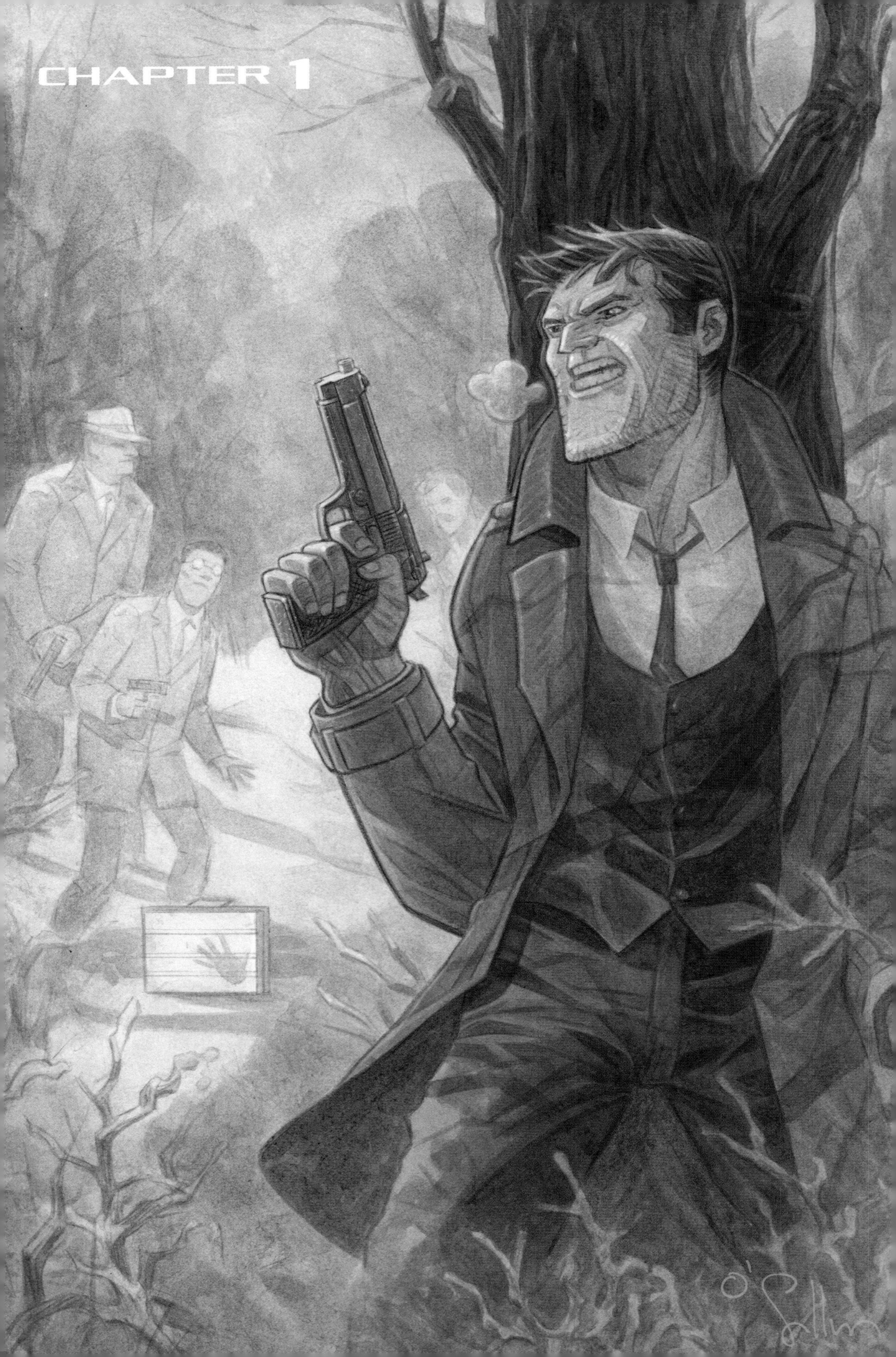

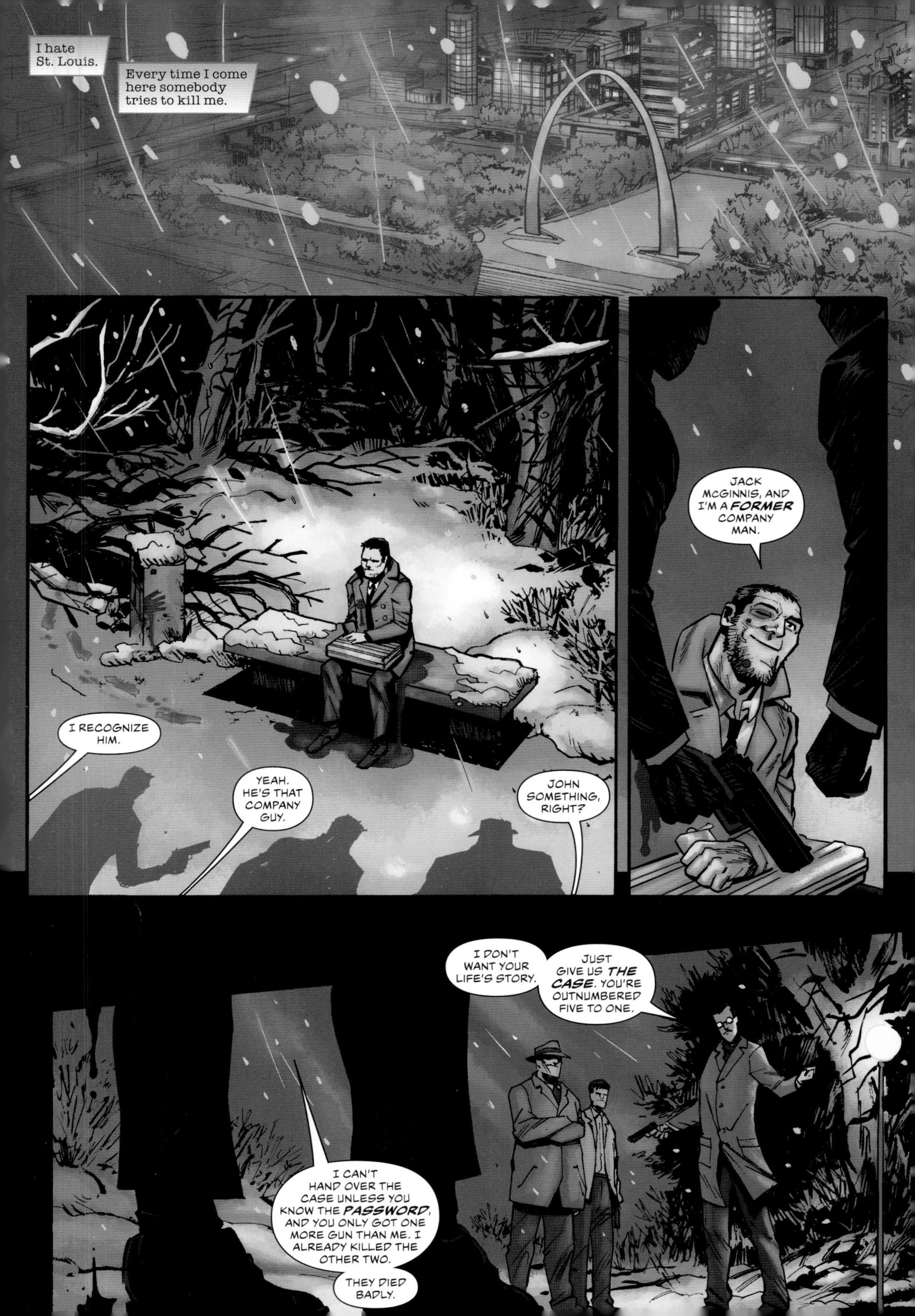
I hate St. Louis.
Every time I come here somebody tries to kill me.
I RECOGNIZE HIM.
YEAH. HE'S THAT COMPANY GUY.
JOHN SOMETHING, RIGHT?
JACK McGINNIS, AND I'M A FORMER COMPANY MAN.
I DON'T WANT YOUR LIFE'S STORY.
JUST GIVE US THE CASE. YOU'RE OUTNUMBERED FIVE TO ONE.
I CAN'T HAND OVER THE CASE UNLESS YOU KNOW THE PASSWORD, AND YOU ONLY GOT ONE MORE GUN THAN ME. I ALREADY KILLED THE OTHER TWO.
THEY DIED BADLY.

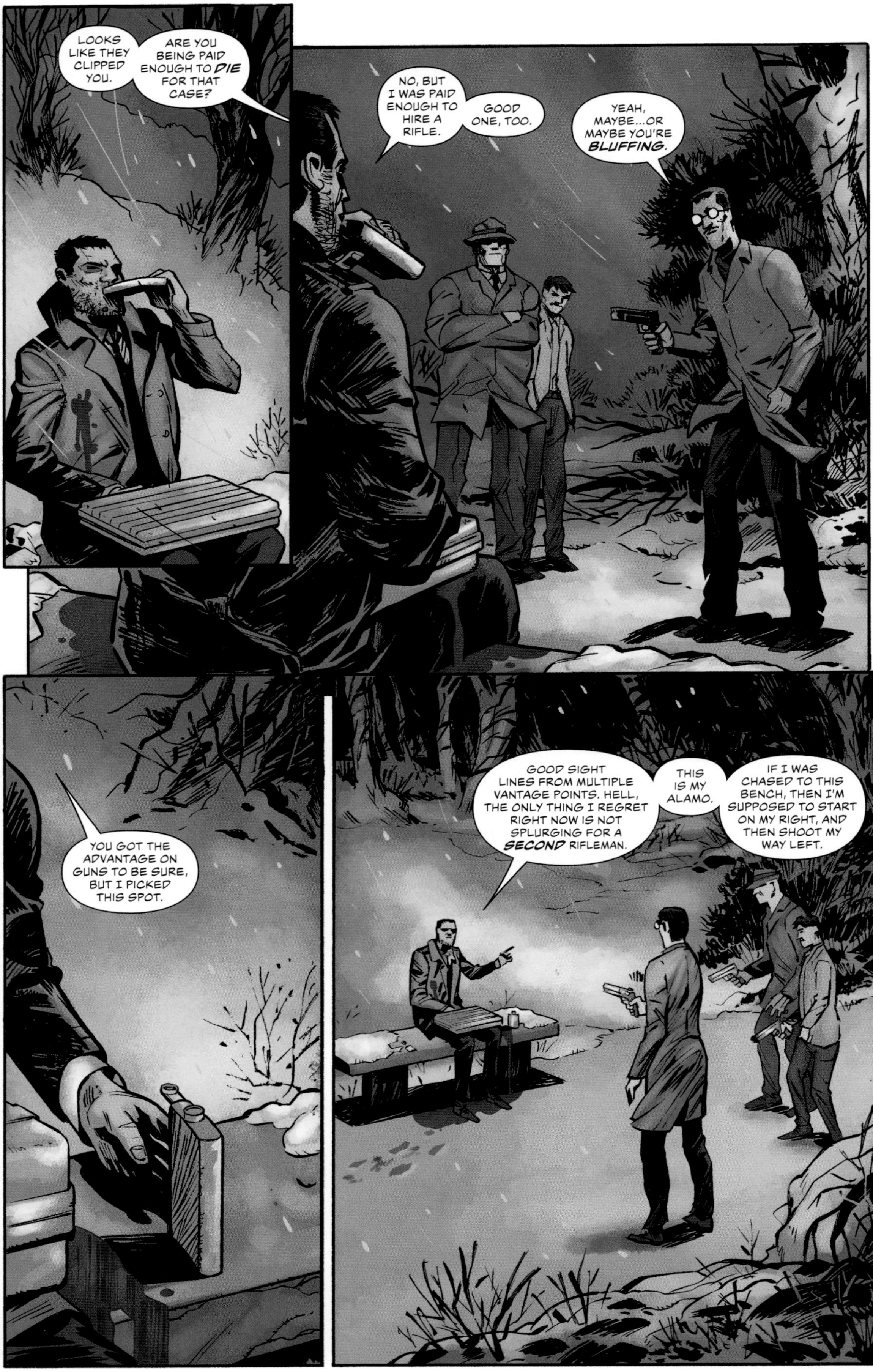
LOOKS LIKE THEY CLIPPED YOU.
ARE YOU BEING PAID ENOUGH TO DIE FOR THAT CASE?
NO, BUT I WAS PAID ENOUGH TO HIRE A RIFLE.
GOOD ONE, TOO.
YEAH, MAYBE...OR MAYBE YOU'RE BLUFFING.
YOU GOT THE ADVANTAGE ON GUNS TO BE SURE, BUT I PICKED THIS SPOT.
GOOD SIGHT LINES FROM MULTIPLE VANTAGE POINTS. HELL, THE ONLY THING I REGRET RIGHT NOW IS NOT SPLURGING FOR A SECOND RIFLEMAN.
THIS IS MY ALAMO.
IF I WAS CHASED TO THIS BENCH, THEN I'M SUPPOSED TO START ON MY RIGHT, AND THEN SHOOT MY WAY LEFT.

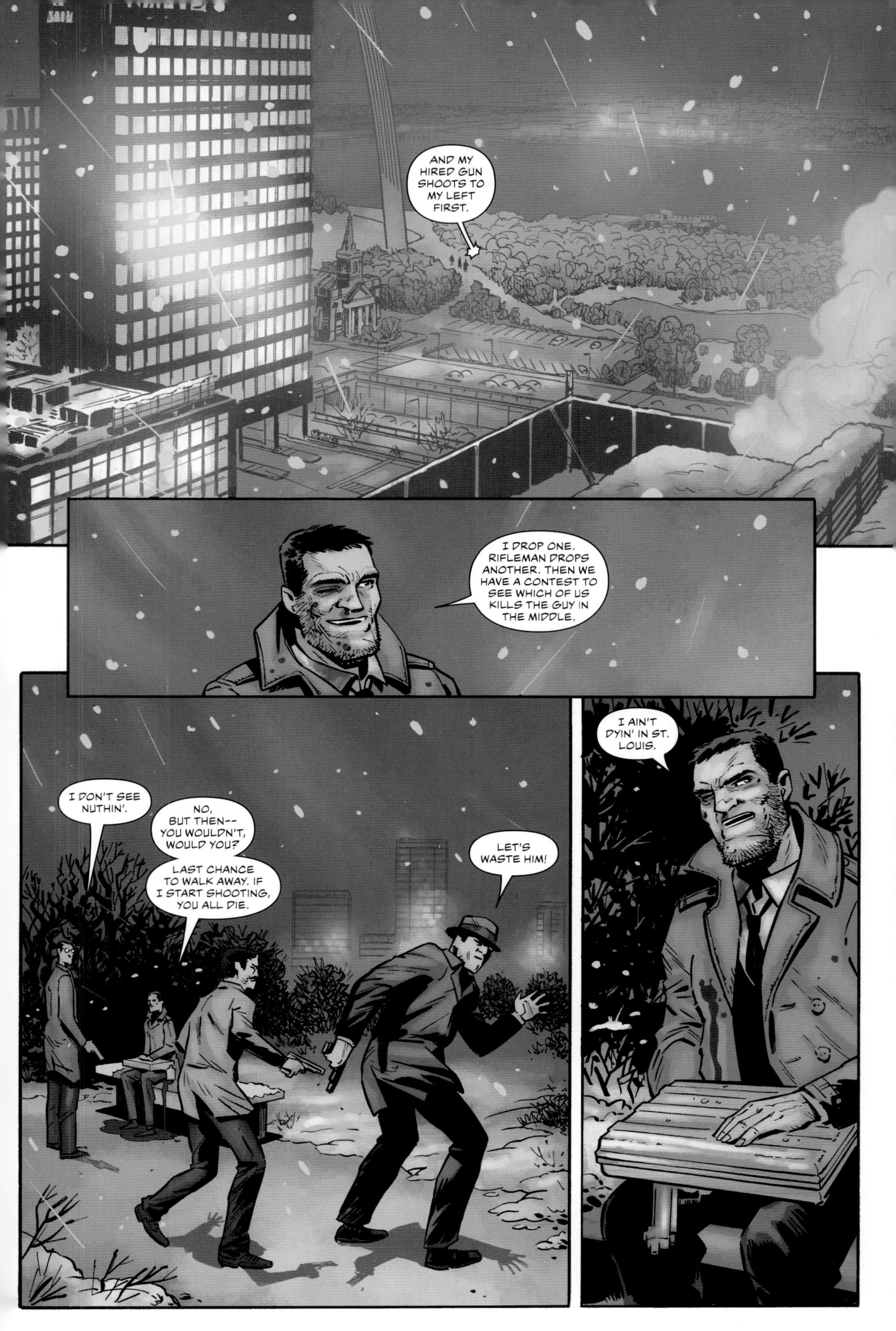
AND MY HIRED GUN SHOOTS TO MY LEFT FIRST.
I DROP ONE. RIFLEMAN DROPS ANOTHER. THEN WE HAVE A CONTEST TO SEE WHICH OF US KILLS THE GUY IN THE MIDDLE.
I DON'T SEE NUTHIN'.
NO, BUT THEN-- YOU WOULDN'T, WOULD YOU?
LAST CHANCE TO WALK AWAY. IF I START SHOOTING, YOU ALL DIE.
LET'S WASTE HIM!
I AIN'T DYIN' IN ST. LOUIS.

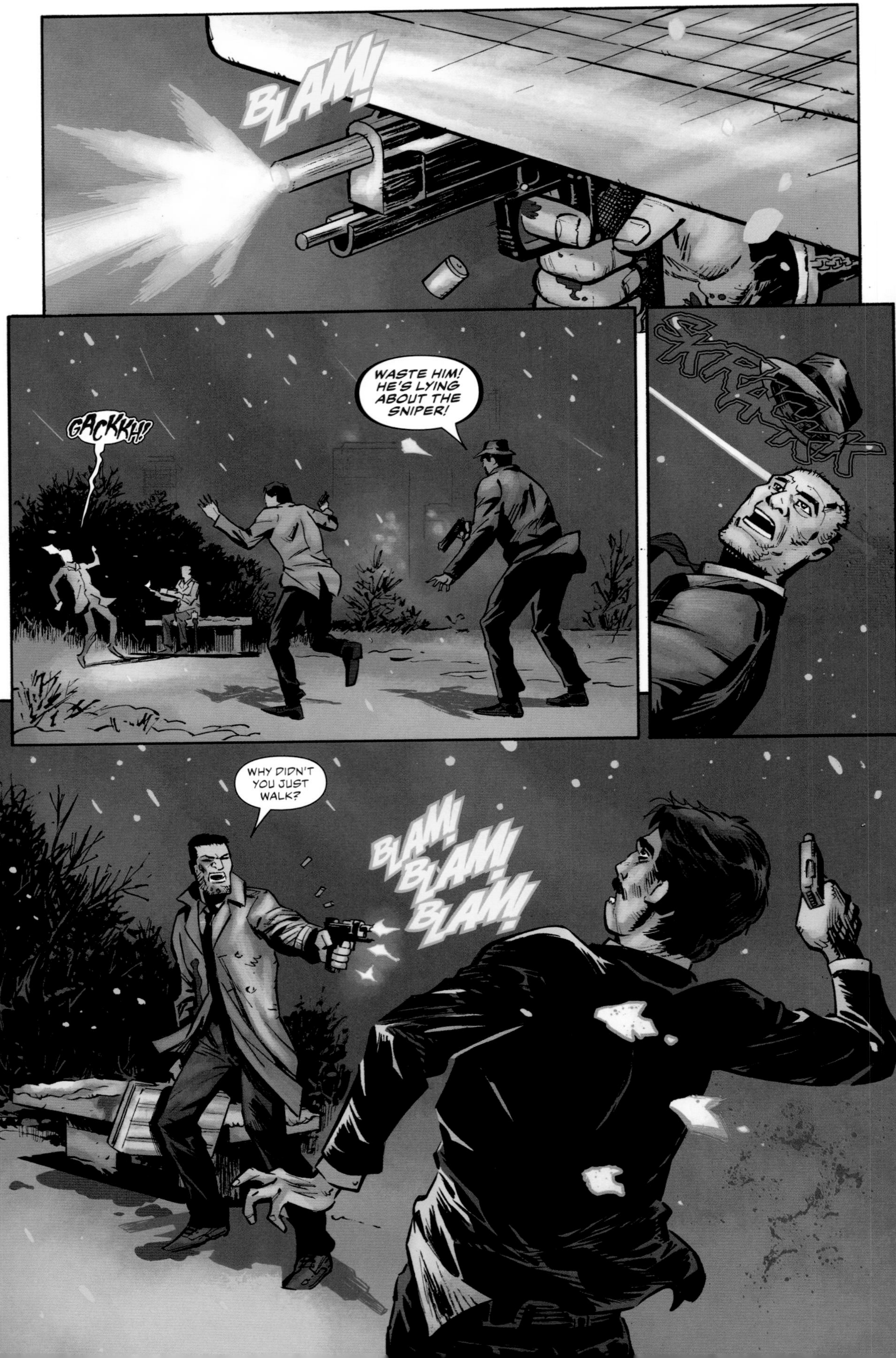
BLAM!
GACKKH!
WASTE HIM! HE'S LYING ABOUT THE SNIPER!
WHY DIDN'T YOU JUST WALK?
BLAM! BLAM! BLAM!

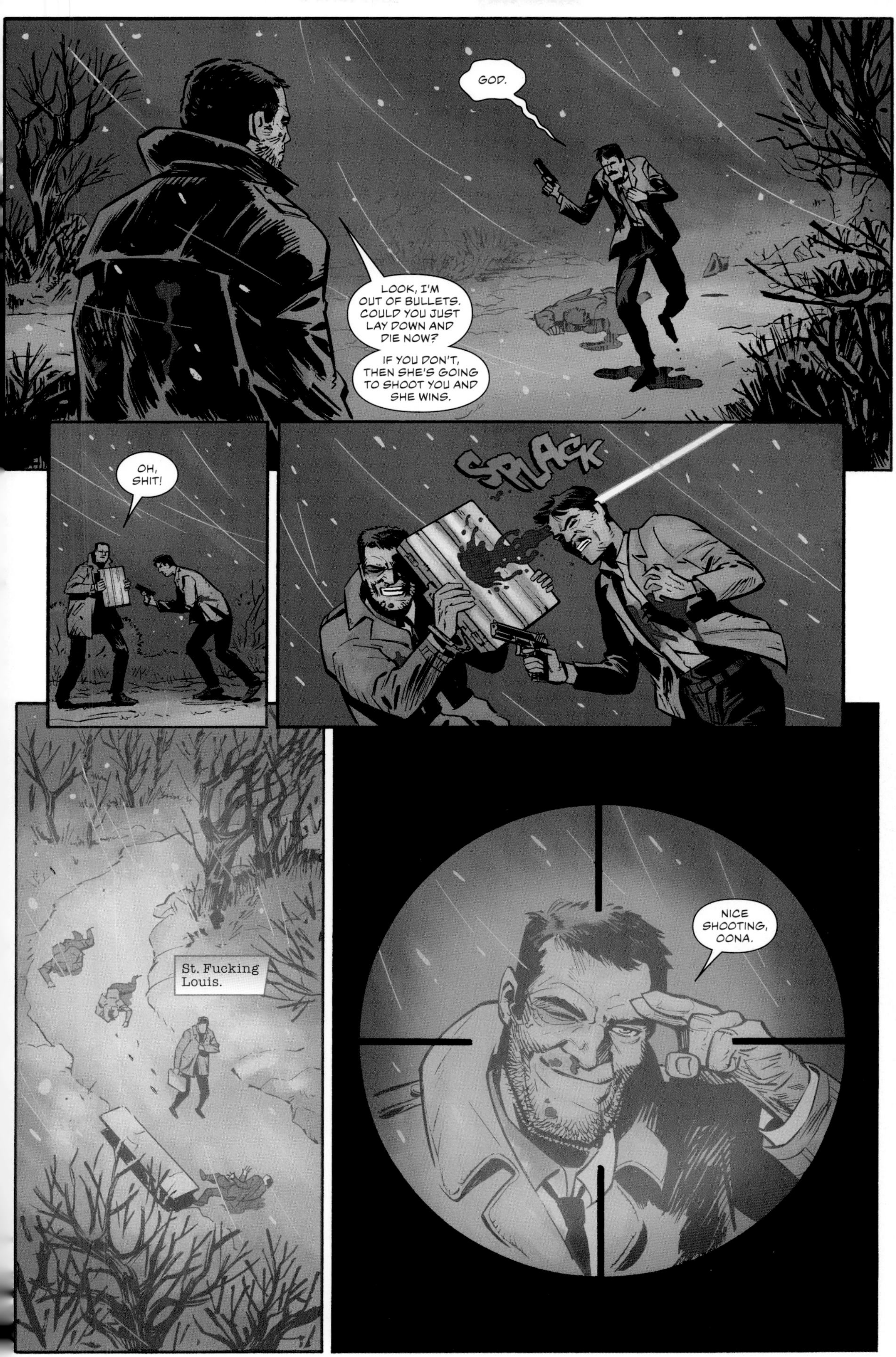
GOD.
LOOK, I'M OUT OF BULLETS. COULD YOU JUST LAY DOWN AND DIE NOW?
IF YOU DON'T, THEN SHE'S GOING TO SHOOT YOU AND SHE WINS.
OH, SHIT!
SPLACK
St. Fucking Louis.
NICE SHOOTING, OONA.

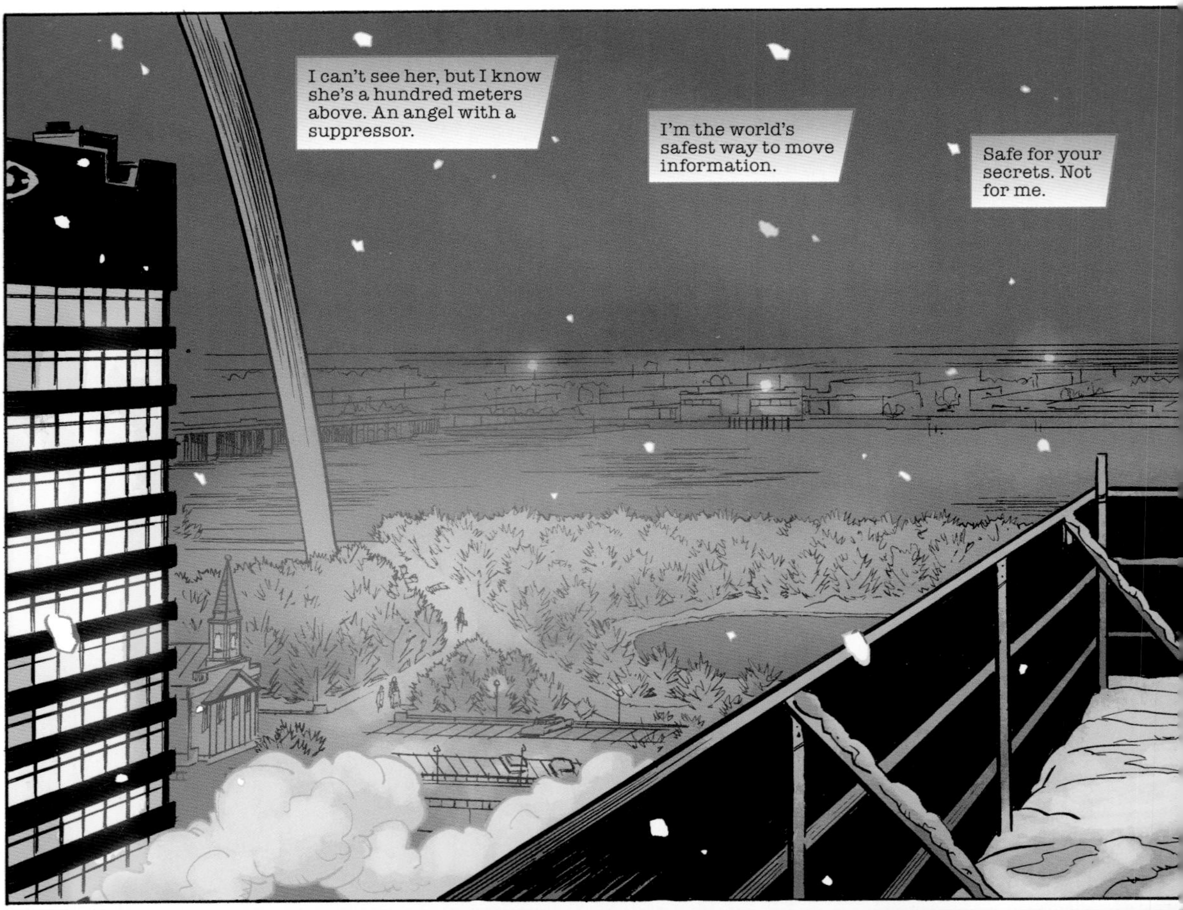
I can't see her, but I know she's a hundred meters above. An angel with a suppressor.
I'm the world's safest way to move information.
Safe for your secrets. Not for me.

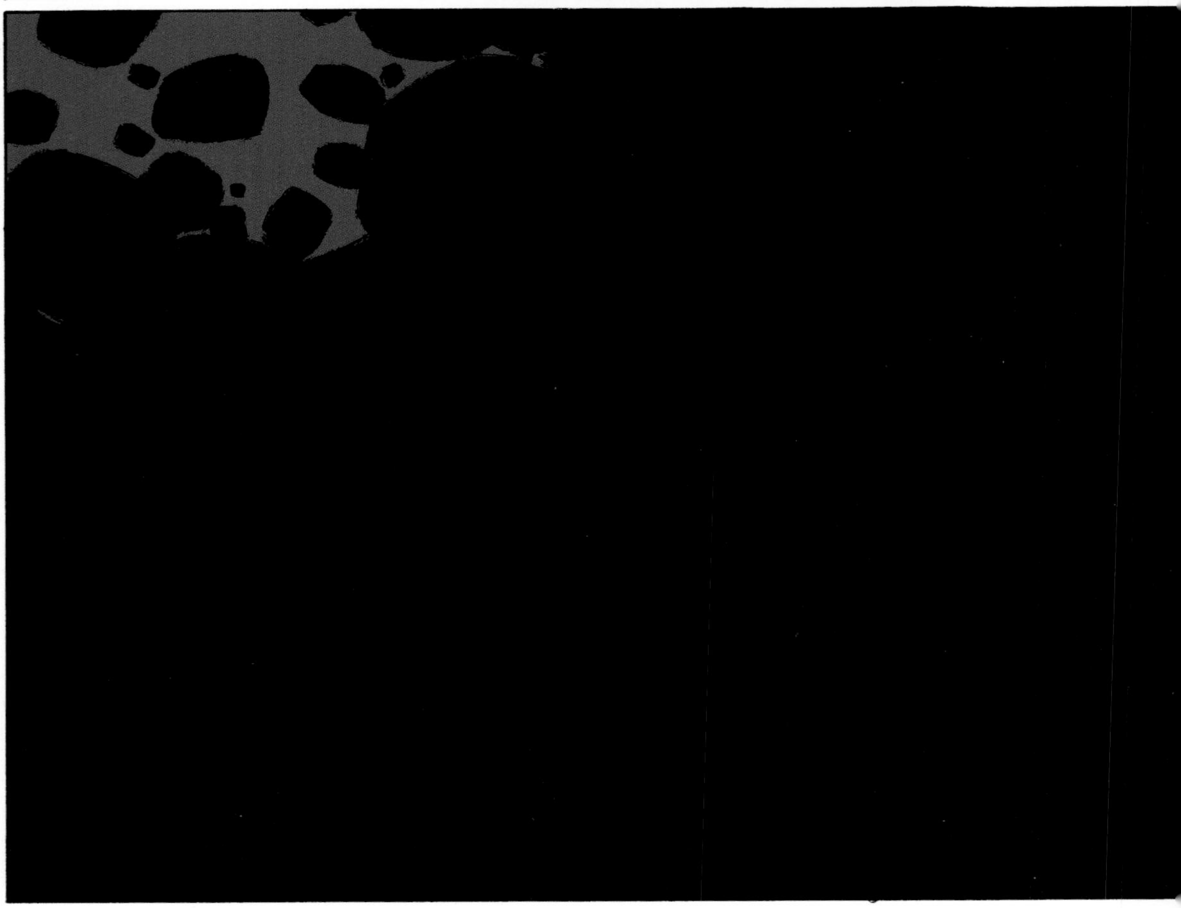

My name is Jack McGinnis, and I'm a **Ledger Man.**

GERRY DUGGAN
WRITER

DAVID O'SULLIVAN
ARTIST

JORDIE BELLAIRE
COLORIST

JOE SABINO
LETTERER

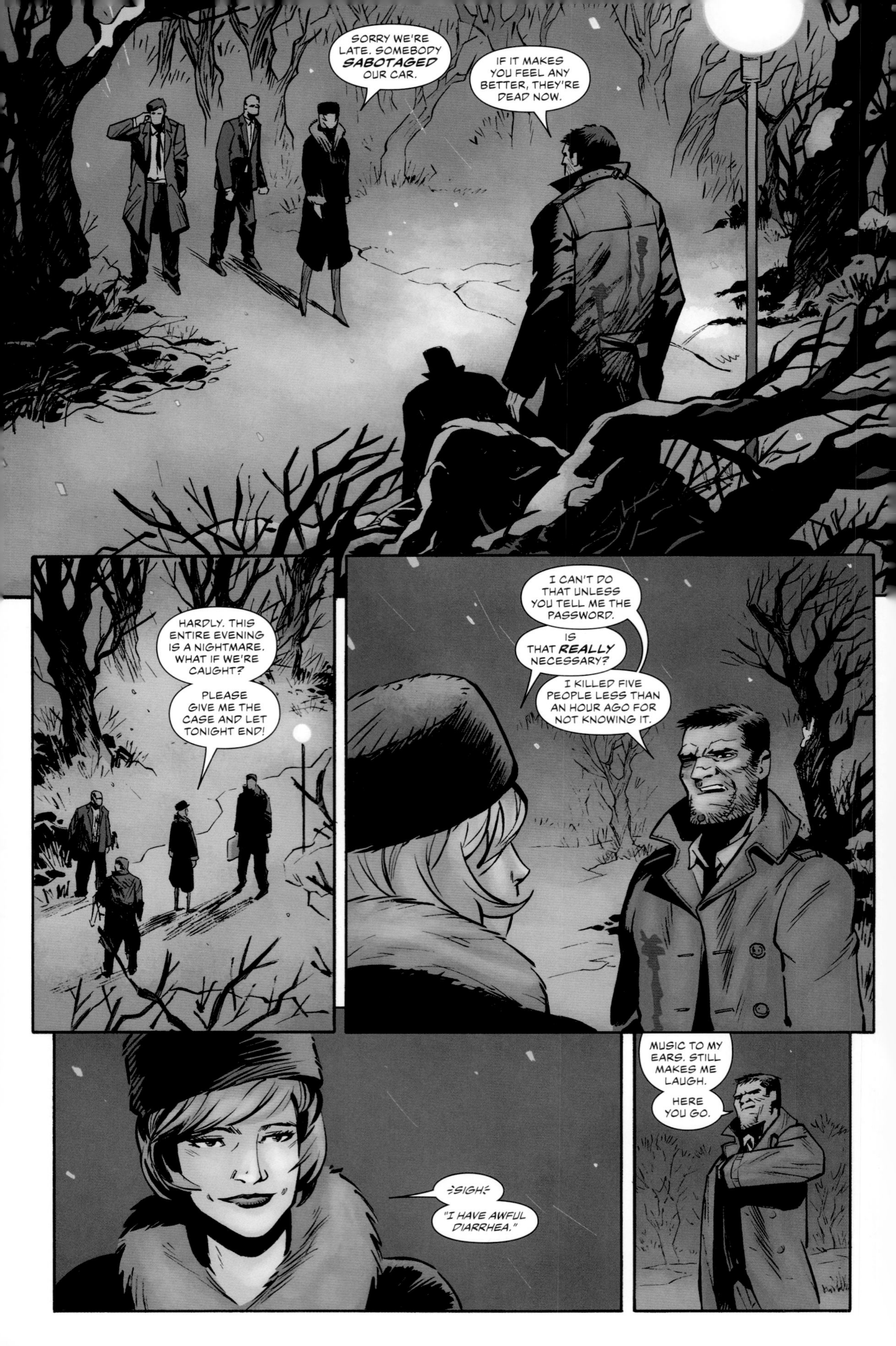
SORRY WE'RE LATE. SOMEBODY **SABOTAGED** OUR CAR.
IF IT MAKES YOU FEEL ANY BETTER, THEY'RE DEAD NOW.
HARDLY. THIS ENTIRE EVENING IS A NIGHTMARE. WHAT IF WE'RE CAUGHT?
PLEASE GIVE ME THE CASE AND LET TONIGHT END!
I CAN'T DO THAT UNLESS YOU TELL ME THE PASSWORD.
IS THAT **REALLY** NECESSARY?
I KILLED FIVE PEOPLE LESS THAN AN HOUR AGO FOR NOT KNOWING IT.
SIGH
"I HAVE AWFUL DIARRHEA."
MUSIC TO MY EARS. STILL MAKES ME LAUGH.
HERE YOU GO.

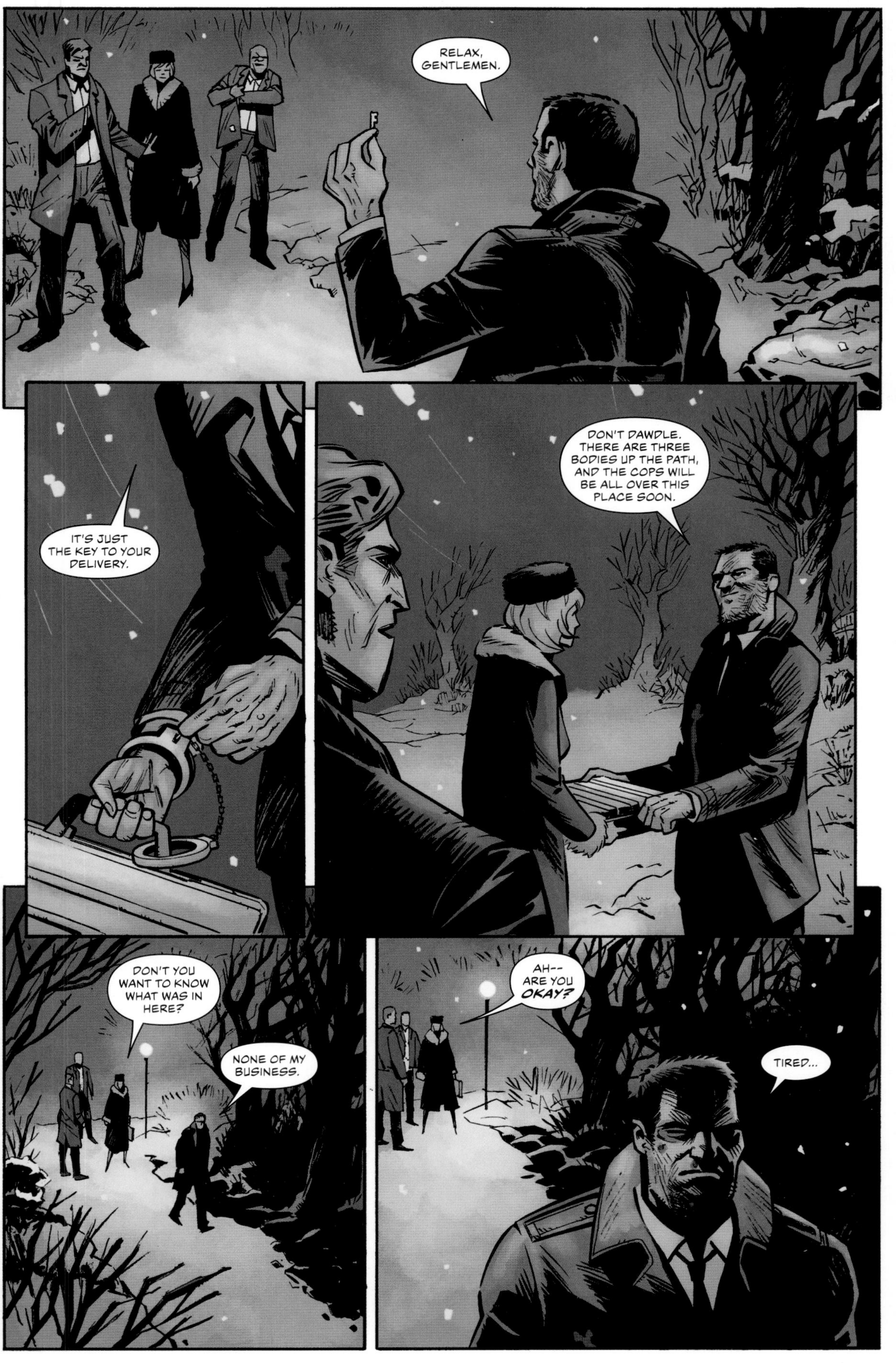
RELAX, GENTLEMEN.
IT'S JUST THE KEY TO YOUR DELIVERY.
DON'T DAWDLE. THERE ARE THREE BODIES UP THE PATH, AND THE COPS WILL BE ALL OVER THIS PLACE SOON.
DON'T YOU WANT TO KNOW WHAT WAS IN HERE?
NONE OF MY BUSINESS.
AH-- ARE YOU *OKAY?*
TIRED...

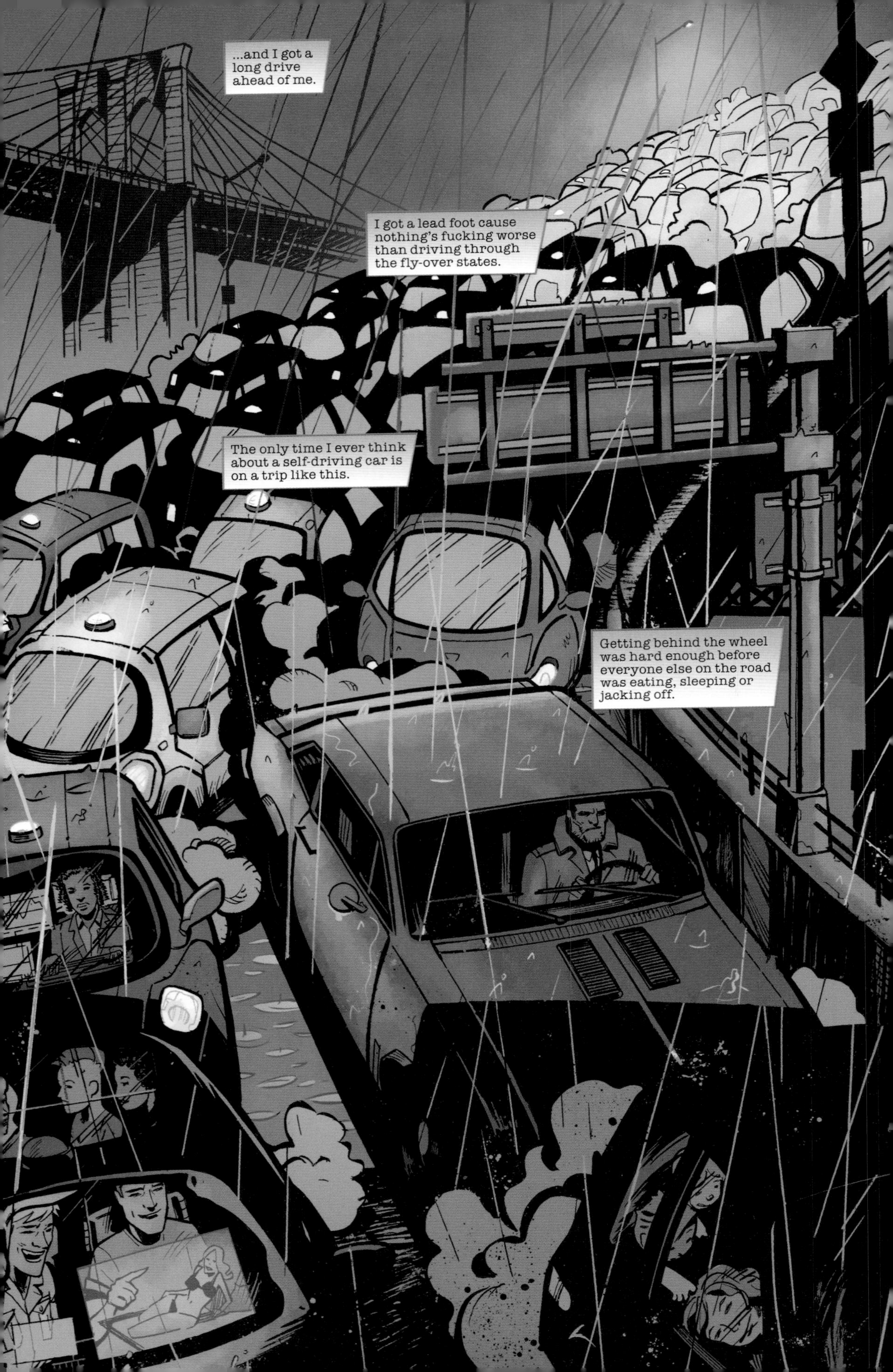

...and I got a long drive ahead of me.
I got a lead foot cause nothing's fucking worse than driving through the fly-over states.
The only time I ever think about a self-driving car is on a trip like this.
Getting behind the wheel was hard enough before everyone else on the road was eating, sleeping or jacking off.

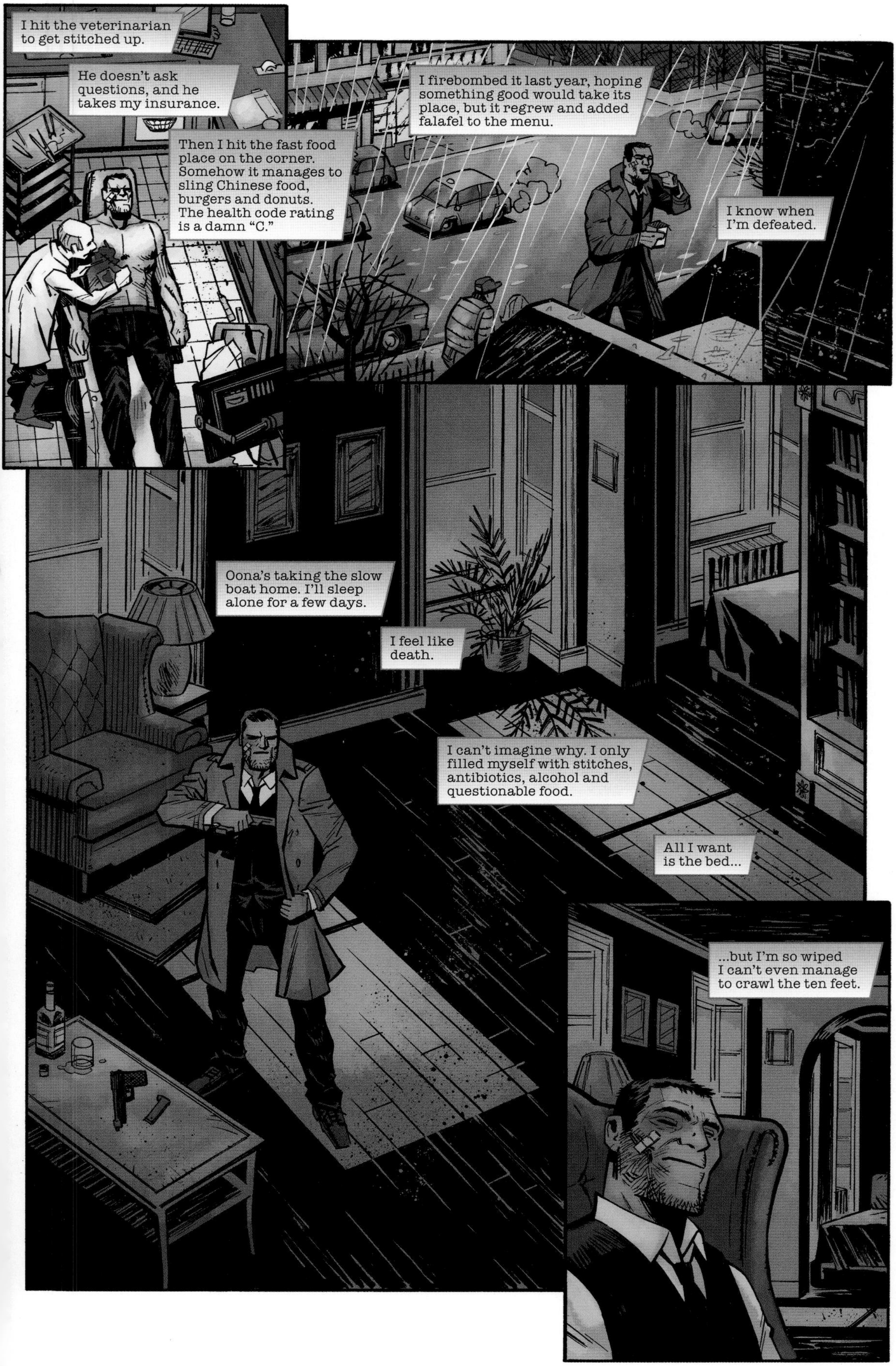
I hit the veterinarian to get stitched up.
He doesn't ask questions, and he takes my insurance.
Then I hit the fast food place on the corner. Somehow it manages to sling Chinese food, burgers and donuts. The health code rating is a damn "C."
I firebombed it last year, hoping something good would take its place, but it regrew and added falafel to the menu.
I know when I'm defeated.
Oona's taking the slow boat home. I'll sleep alone for a few days.
I feel like death.
I can't imagine why. I only filled myself with stitches, antibiotics, alcohol and questionable food.
All I want is the bed...
...but I'm so wiped I can't even manage to crawl the ten feet.

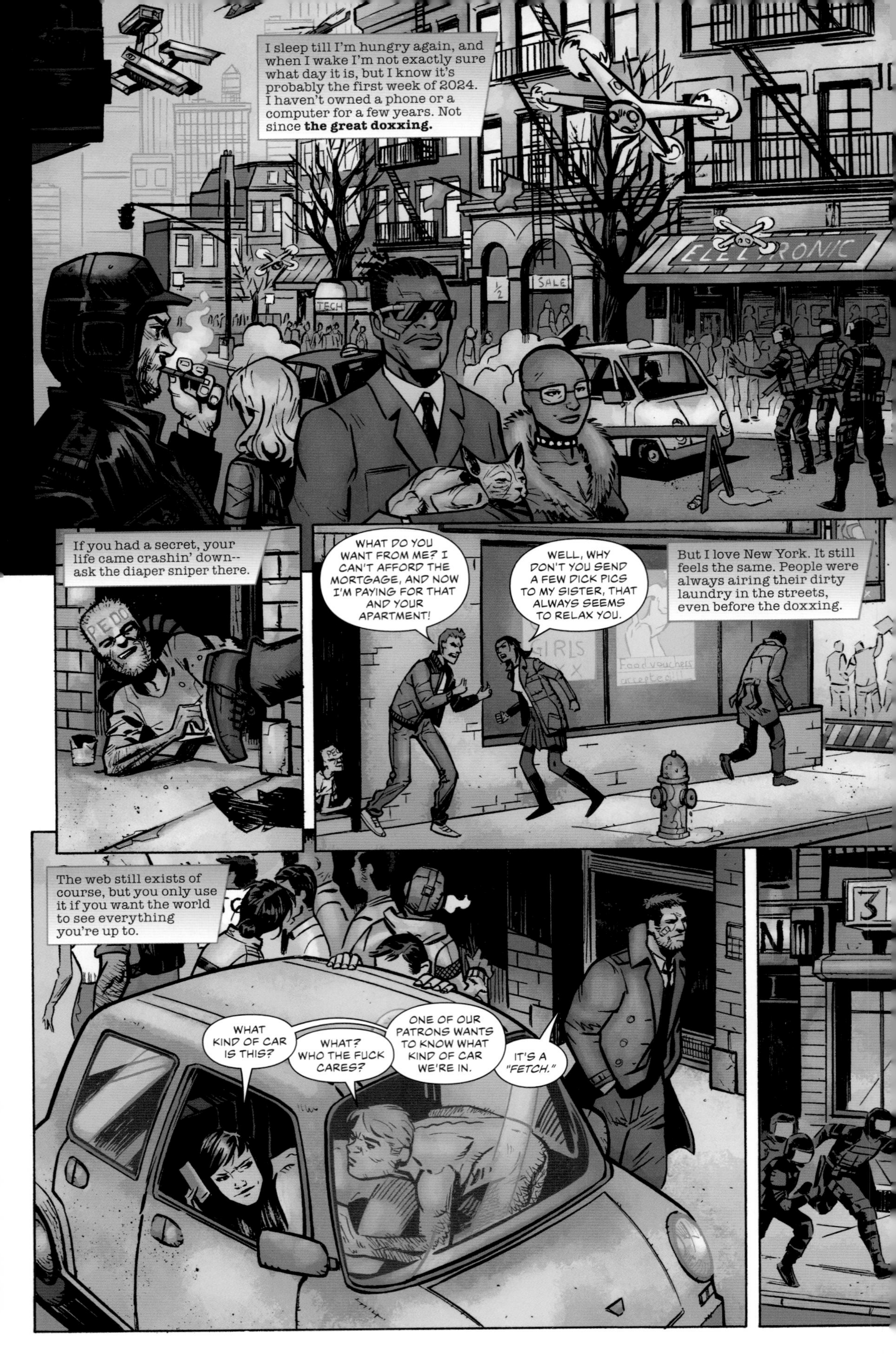
I sleep till I'm hungry again, and when I wake I'm not exactly sure what day it is, but I know it's probably the first week of 2024. I haven't owned a phone or a computer for a few years. Not since **the great doxxing.**
ELECTRONIC
TECH
1/2
SALE
If you had a secret, your life came crashin' down--ask the diaper sniper there.
PEDO
WHAT DO YOU WANT FROM ME? I CAN'T AFFORD THE MORTGAGE, AND NOW I'M PAYING FOR THAT AND YOUR APARTMENT!
WELL, WHY DON'T YOU SEND A FEW DICK PICS TO MY SISTER, THAT ALWAYS SEEMS TO RELAX YOU.
But I love New York. It still feels the same. People were always airing their dirty laundry in the streets, even before the doxxing.
GIRLS
XXX
Food vouchers accepted!!!
The web still exists of course, but you only use it if you want the world to see everything you're up to.
WHAT KIND OF CAR IS THIS?
WHAT? WHO THE FUCK CARES?
ONE OF OUR PATRONS WANTS TO KNOW WHAT KIND OF CAR WE'RE IN.
IT'S A "FETCH."
3

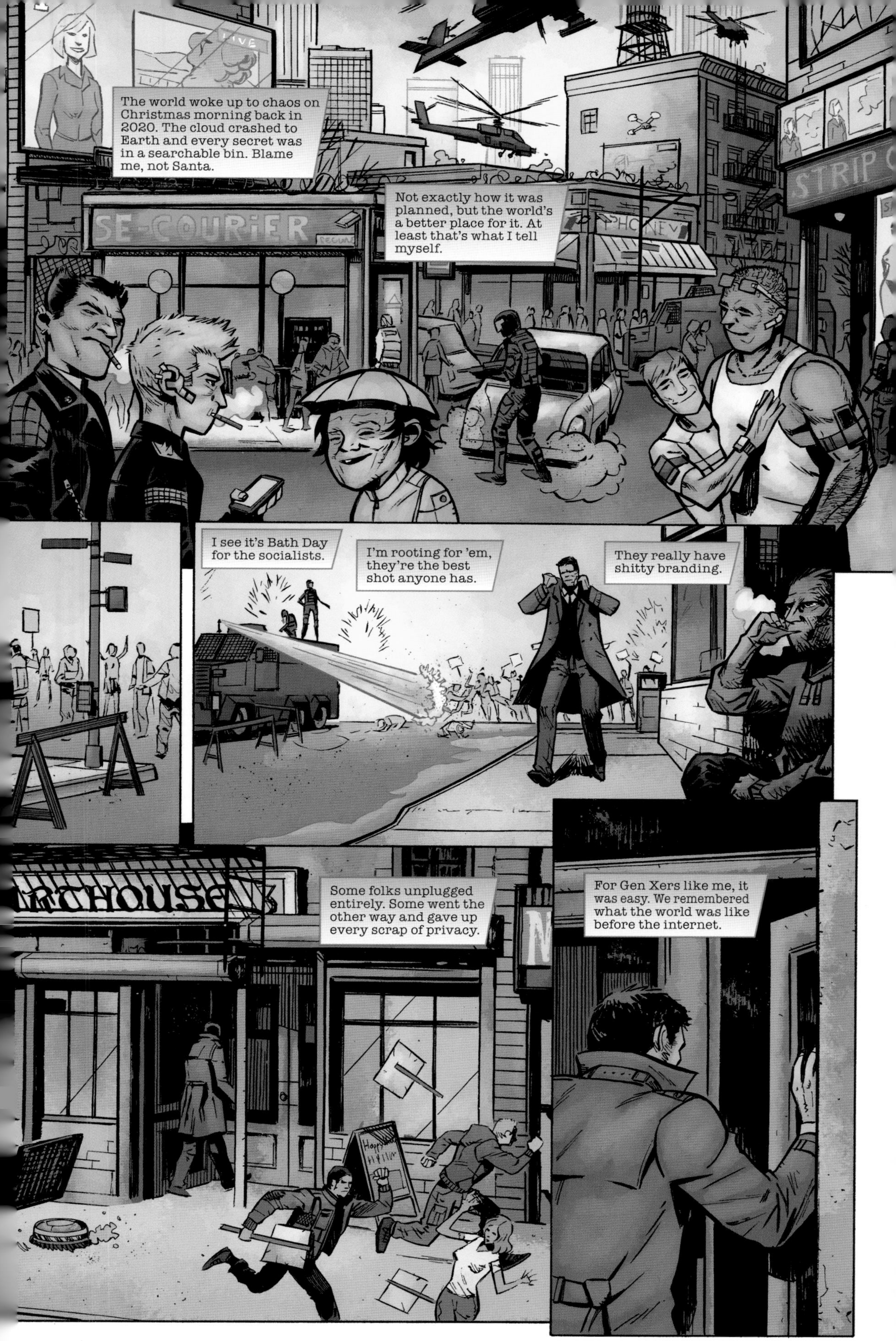
The world woke up to chaos on Christmas morning back in 2020. The cloud crashed to Earth and every secret was in a searchable bin. Blame me, not Santa.
SE-COURIER
Not exactly how it was planned, but the world's a better place for it. At least that's what I tell myself.
I see it's Bath Day for the socialists.
I'm rooting for 'em, they're the best shot anyone has.
They really have shitty branding.
Some folks unplugged entirely. Some went the other way and gave up every scrap of privacy.
For Gen Xers like me, it was easy. We remembered what the world was like before the internet.

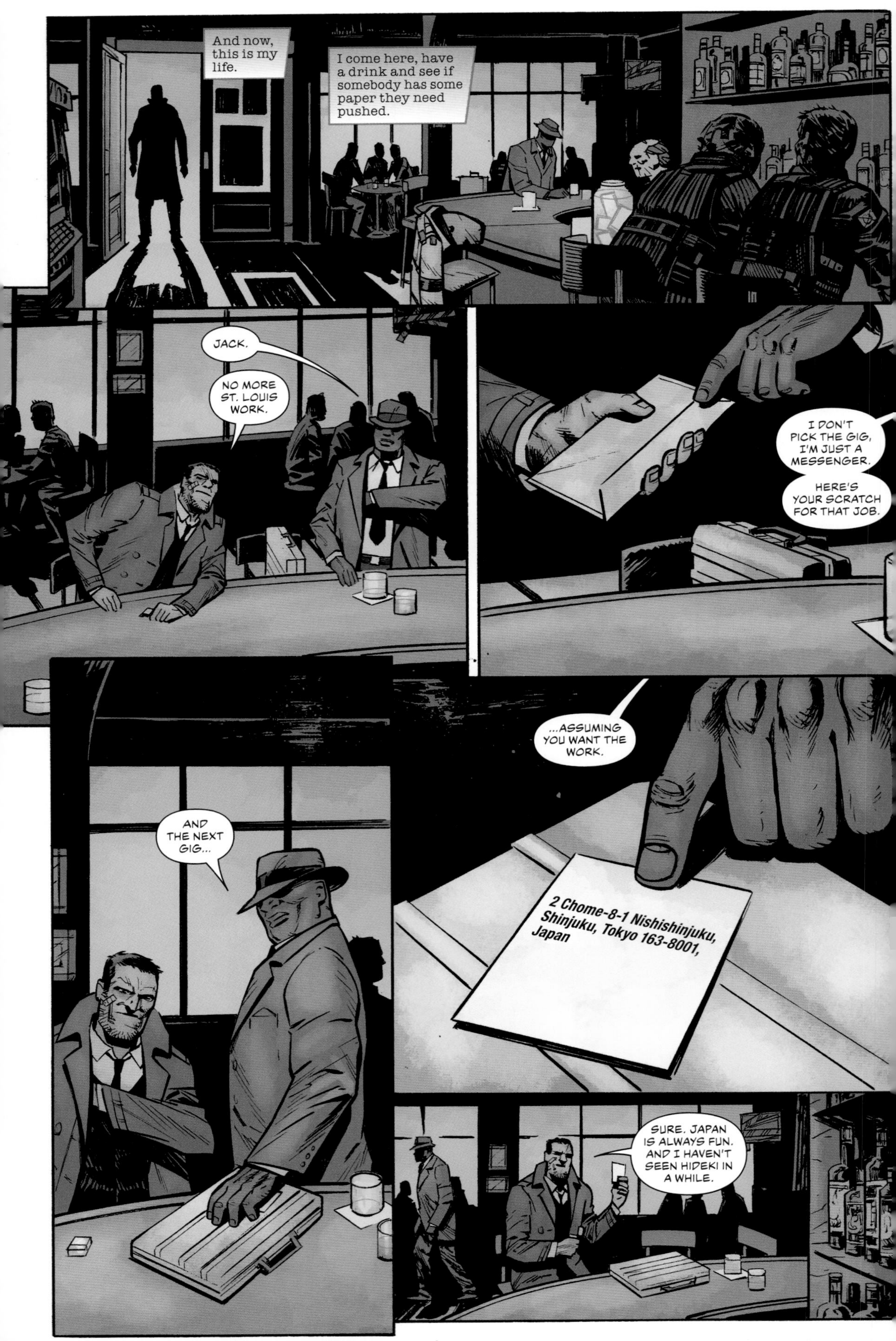
And now, this is my life.
I come here, have a drink and see if somebody has some paper they need pushed.
JACK.
NO MORE ST. LOUIS WORK.
I DON'T PICK THE GIG, I'M JUST A MESSENGER.
HERE'S YOUR SCRATCH FOR THAT JOB.
AND THE NEXT GIG...
...ASSUMING YOU WANT THE WORK.
2 Chome-8-1 Nishishinjuku, Shinjuku, Tokyo 163-8001, Japan
SURE. JAPAN IS ALWAYS FUN. AND I HAVEN'T SEEN HIDEKI IN A WHILE.

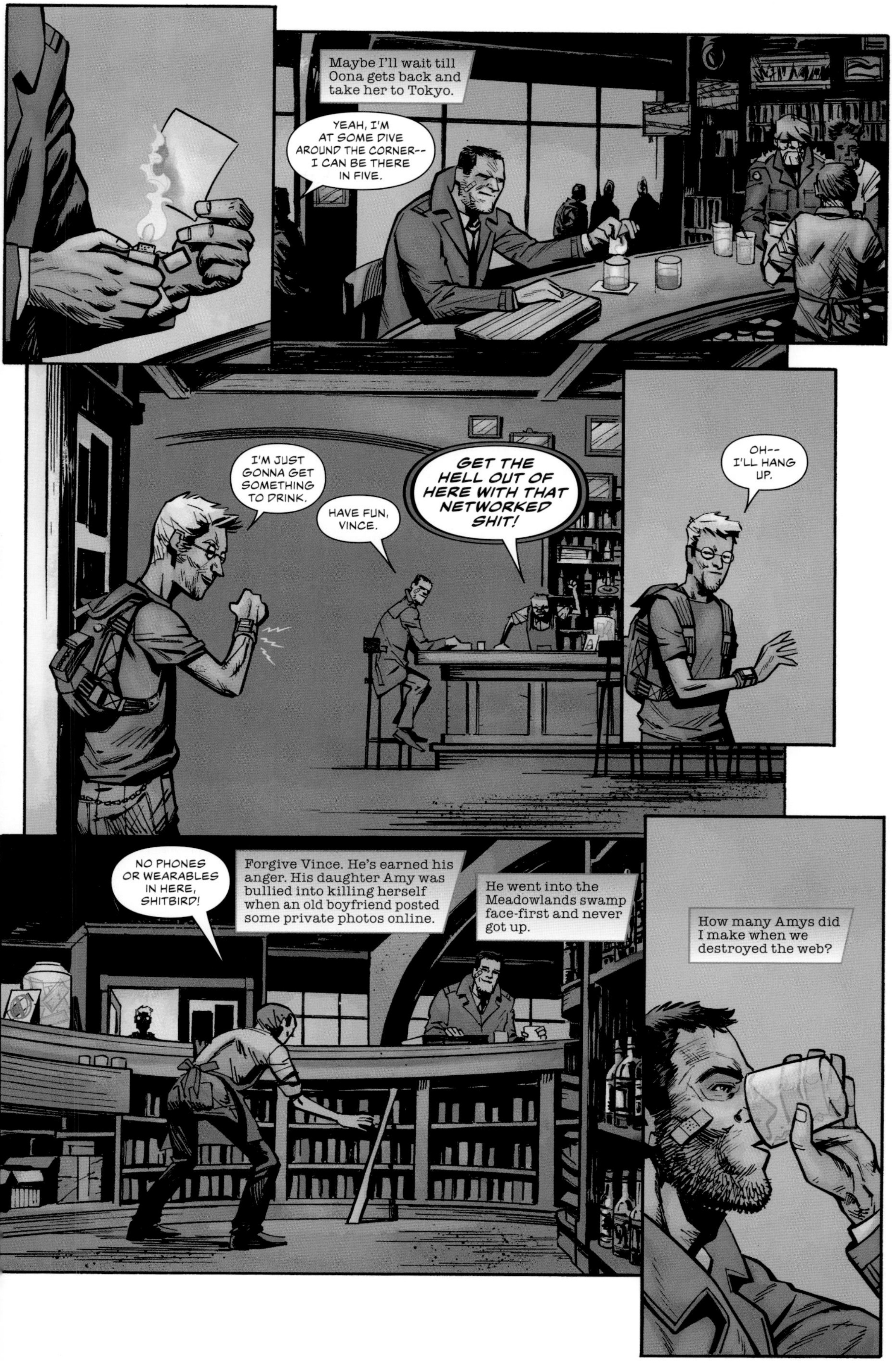

Maybe I'll wait till Oona gets back and take her to Tokyo.
YEAH, I'M AT SOME DIVE AROUND THE CORNER-- I CAN BE THERE IN FIVE.
I'M JUST GONNA GET SOMETHING TO DRINK.
HAVE FUN, VINCE.
GET THE HELL OUT OF HERE WITH THAT NETWORKED SHIT!
OH-- I'LL HANG UP.
NO PHONES OR WEARABLES IN HERE, SHITBIRD!
Forgive Vince. He's earned his anger. His daughter Amy was bullied into killing herself when an old boyfriend posted some private photos online.
He went into the Meadowlands swamp face-first and never got up.
How many Amys did I make when we destroyed the web?

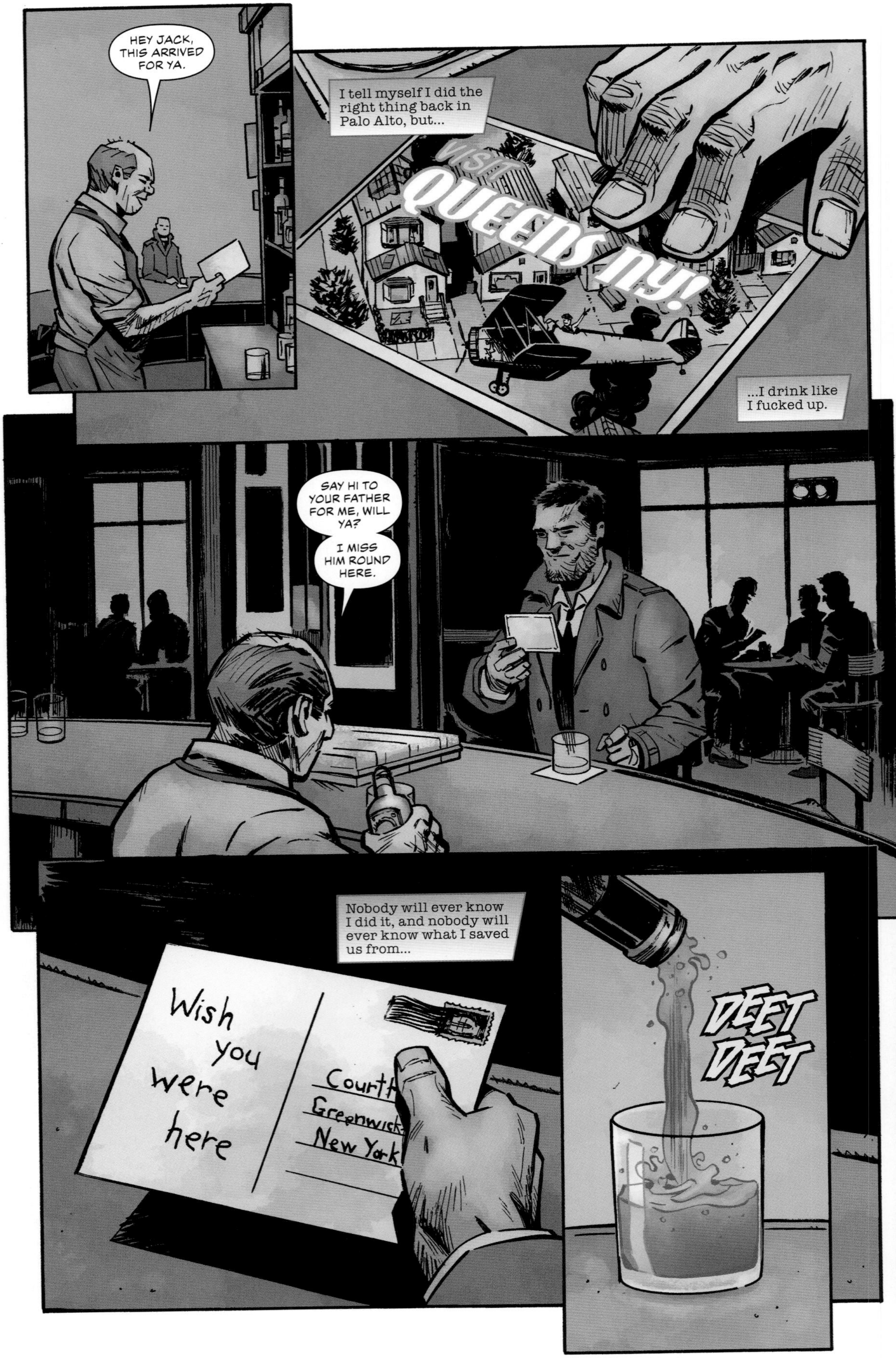
HEY JACK, THIS ARRIVED FOR YA.
I tell myself I did the right thing back in Palo Alto, but...
VISIT QUEENS NY!
...I drink like I fucked up.
SAY HI TO YOUR FATHER FOR ME, WILL YA?
I MISS HIM ROUND HERE.
Nobody will ever know I did it, and nobody will ever know what I saved us from...
Wish you were here
New York
DEET DEET

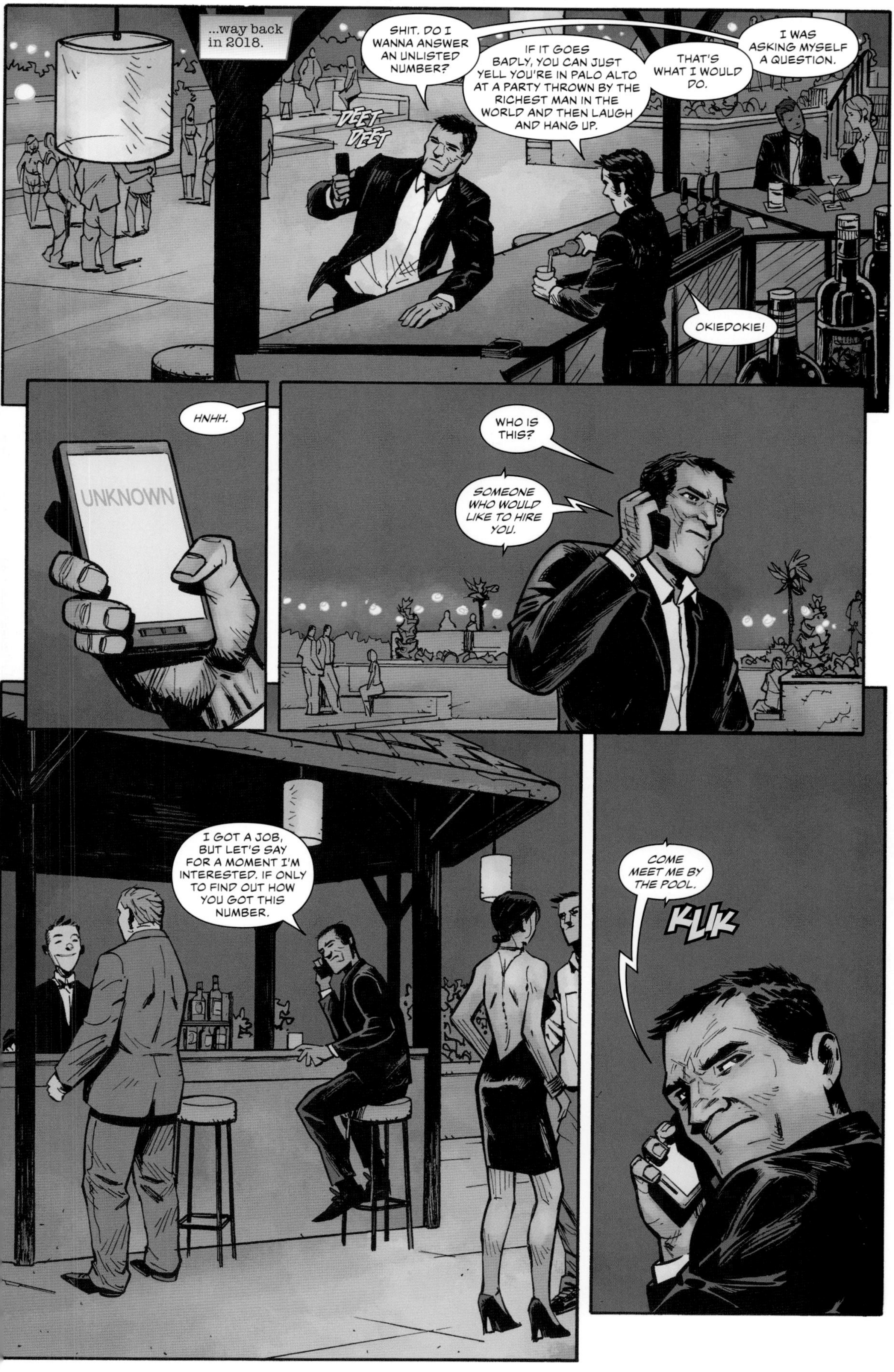
...way back in 2018.
SHIT. DO I WANNA ANSWER AN UNLISTED NUMBER?
I WAS ASKING MYSELF A QUESTION.
IF IT GOES BADLY, YOU CAN JUST YELL YOU'RE IN PALO ALTO AT A PARTY THROWN BY THE RICHEST MAN IN THE WORLD AND THEN LAUGH AND HANG UP.
THAT'S WHAT I WOULD DO.
DEET DEET
OKIEDOKIE!
HNHH.
UNKNOWN
WHO IS THIS?
SOMEONE WHO WOULD LIKE TO HIRE YOU.
I GOT A JOB, BUT LET'S SAY FOR A MOMENT I'M INTERESTED. IF ONLY TO FIND OUT HOW YOU GOT THIS NUMBER.
COME MEET ME BY THE POOL.
KLIK

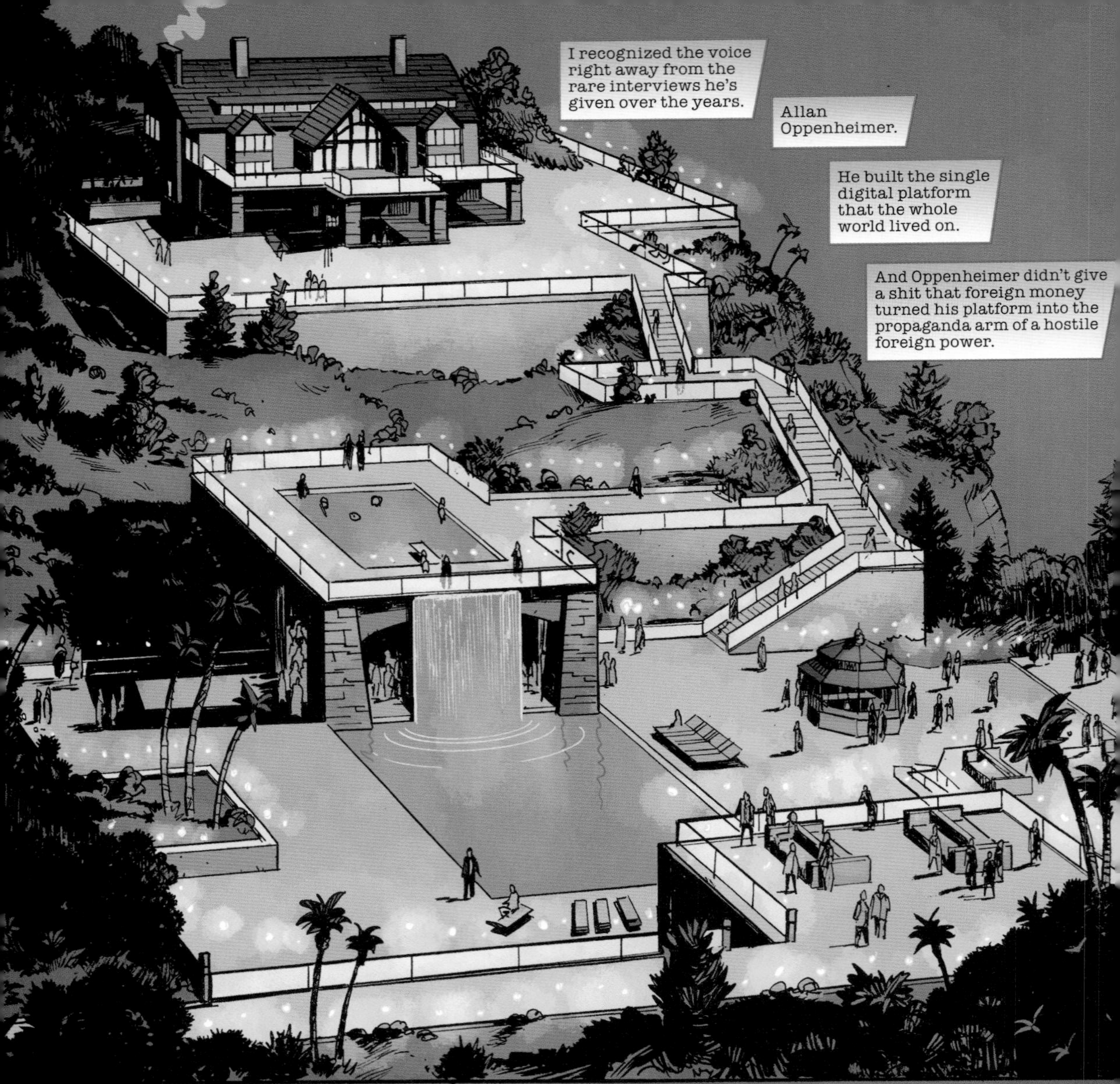

I recognized the voice right away from the rare interviews he's given over the years.
Allan Oppenheimer.
He built the single digital platform that the whole world lived on.
And Oppenheimer didn't give a shit that foreign money turned his platform into the propaganda arm of a hostile foreign power.

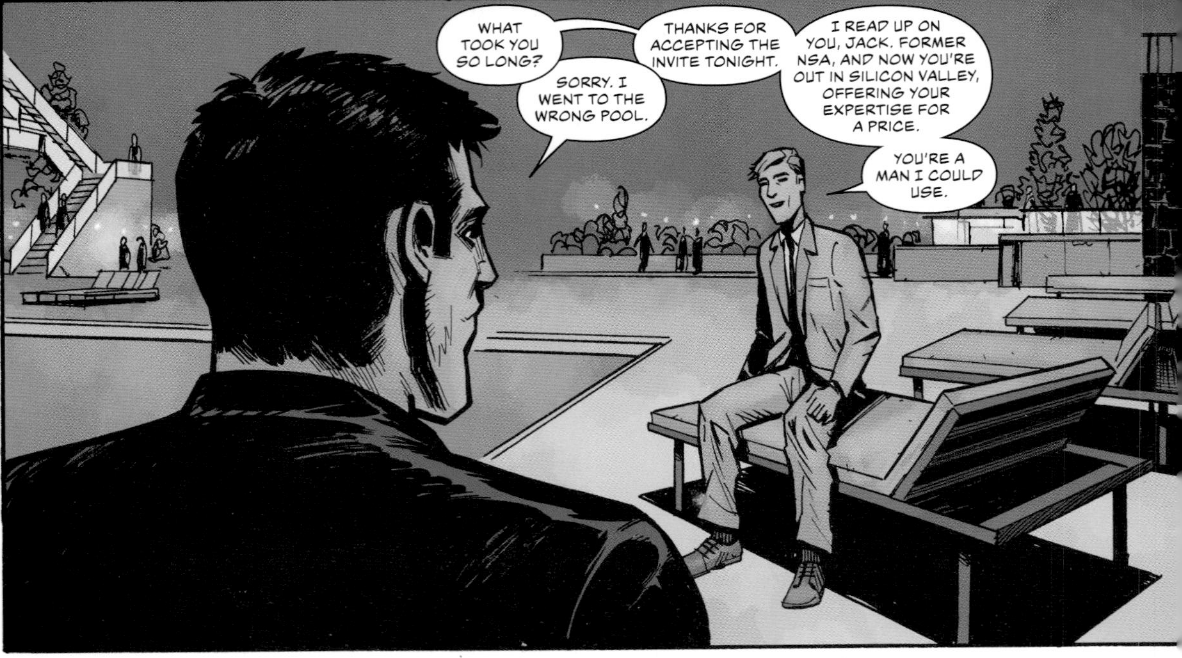

WHAT TOOK YOU SO LONG?
SORRY. I WENT TO THE WRONG POOL.
THANKS FOR ACCEPTING THE INVITE TONIGHT.
I READ UP ON YOU, JACK. FORMER NSA, AND NOW YOU'RE OUT IN SILICON VALLEY, OFFERING YOUR EXPERTISE FOR A PRICE.
YOU'RE A MAN I COULD USE.

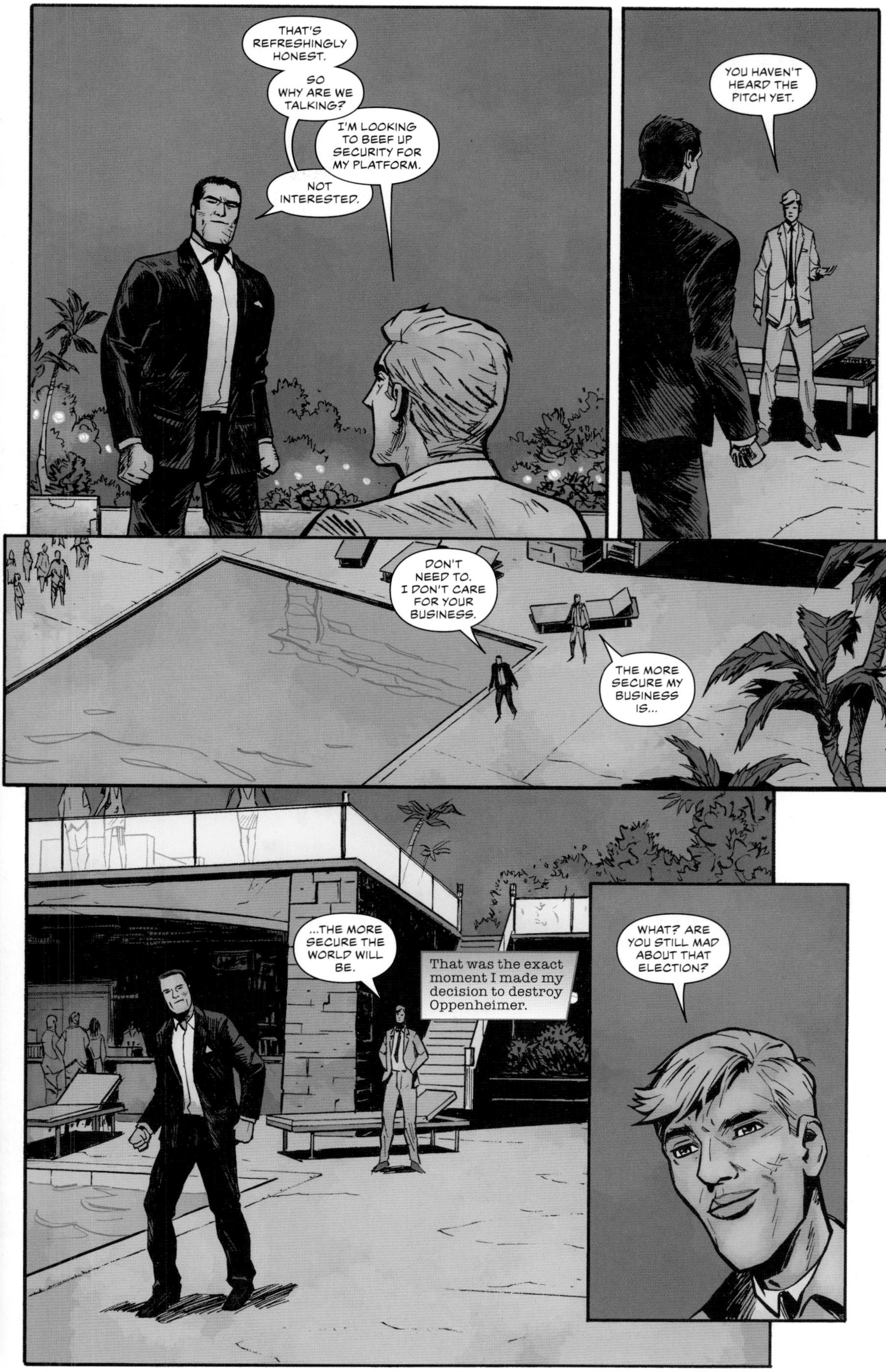
THAT'S REFRESHINGLY HONEST.
SO WHY ARE WE TALKING?
I'M LOOKING TO BEEF UP SECURITY FOR MY PLATFORM.
NOT INTERESTED.
YOU HAVEN'T HEARD THE PITCH YET.
DON'T NEED TO. I DON'T CARE FOR YOUR BUSINESS.
THE MORE SECURE MY BUSINESS IS...
...THE MORE SECURE THE WORLD WILL BE.
That was the exact moment I made my decision to destroy Oppenheimer.
WHAT? ARE YOU STILL MAD ABOUT THAT ELECTION?

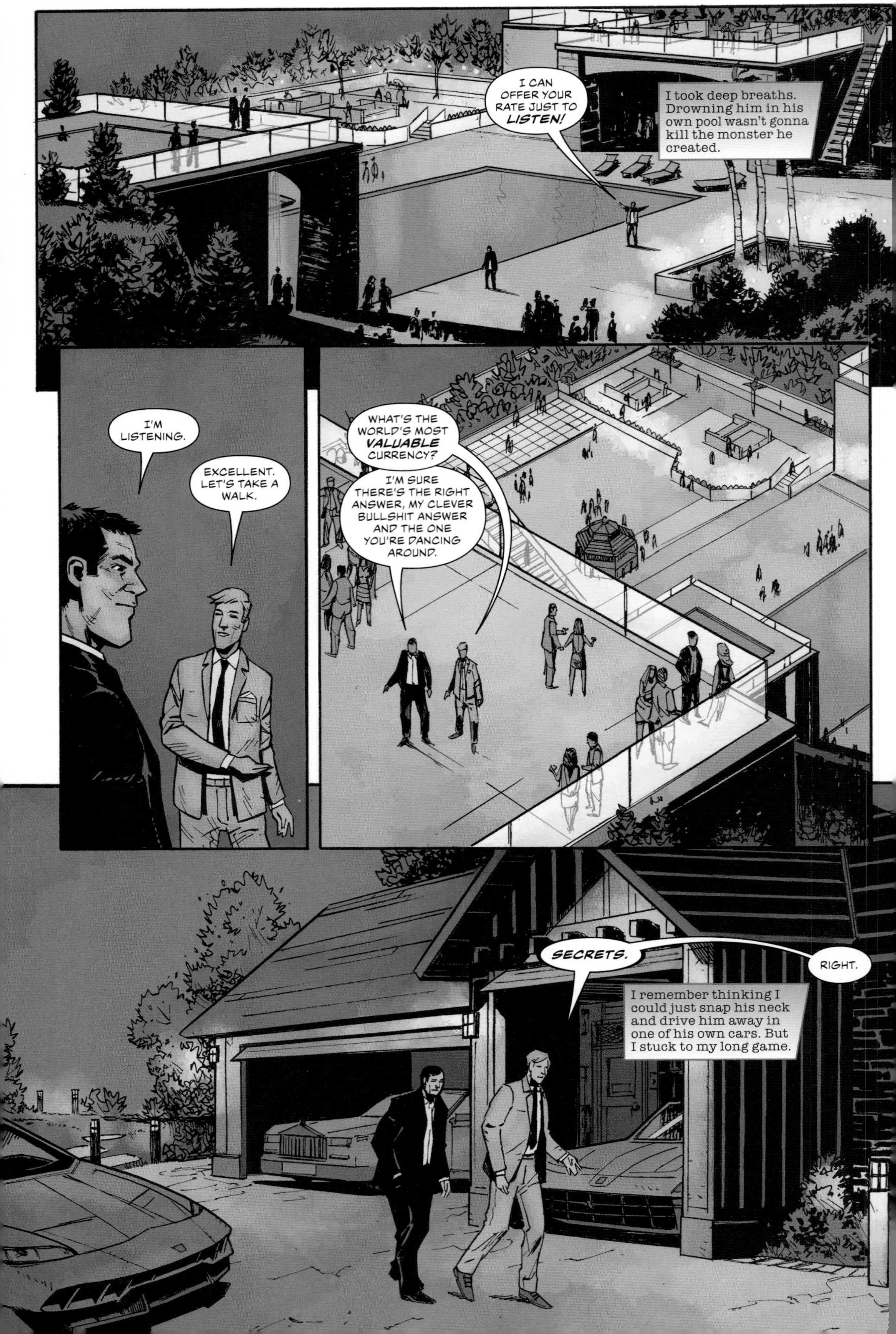
I CAN OFFER YOUR RATE JUST TO LISTEN!
I took deep breaths. Drowning him in his own pool wasn't gonna kill the monster he created.
I'M LISTENING.
EXCELLENT. LET'S TAKE A WALK.
WHAT'S THE WORLD'S MOST VALUABLE CURRENCY?
I'M SURE THERE'S THE RIGHT ANSWER, MY CLEVER BULLSHIT ANSWER AND THE ONE YOU'RE DANCING AROUND.
SECRETS.
RIGHT.
I remember thinking I could just snap his neck and drive him away in one of his own cars. But I stuck to my long game.

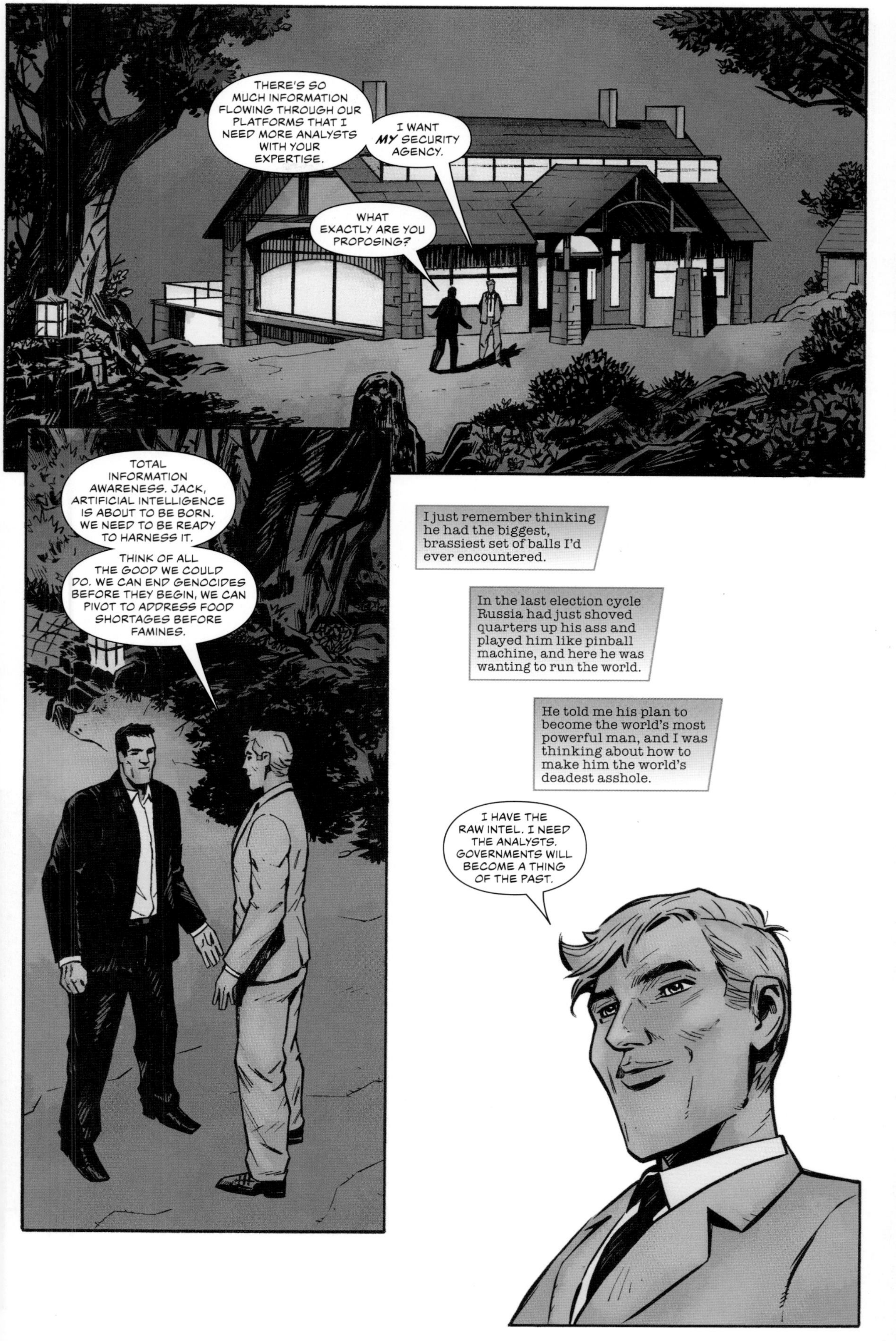

THERE'S SO MUCH INFORMATION FLOWING THROUGH OUR PLATFORMS THAT I NEED MORE ANALYSTS WITH YOUR EXPERTISE.
I WANT *MY* SECURITY AGENCY.
WHAT EXACTLY ARE YOU PROPOSING?
TOTAL INFORMATION AWARENESS. JACK, ARTIFICIAL INTELLIGENCE IS ABOUT TO BE BORN. WE NEED TO BE READY TO HARNESS IT.
THINK OF ALL THE GOOD WE COULD DO. WE CAN END GENOCIDES BEFORE THEY BEGIN, WE CAN PIVOT TO ADDRESS FOOD SHORTAGES BEFORE FAMINES.
I just remember thinking he had the biggest, brassiest set of balls I'd ever encountered.
In the last election cycle Russia had just shoved quarters up his ass and played him like pinball machine, and here he was wanting to run the world.
He told me his plan to become the world's most powerful man, and I was thinking about how to make him the world's deadest asshole.
I HAVE THE RAW INTEL. I NEED THE ANALYSTS. GOVERNMENTS WILL BECOME A THING OF THE PAST.

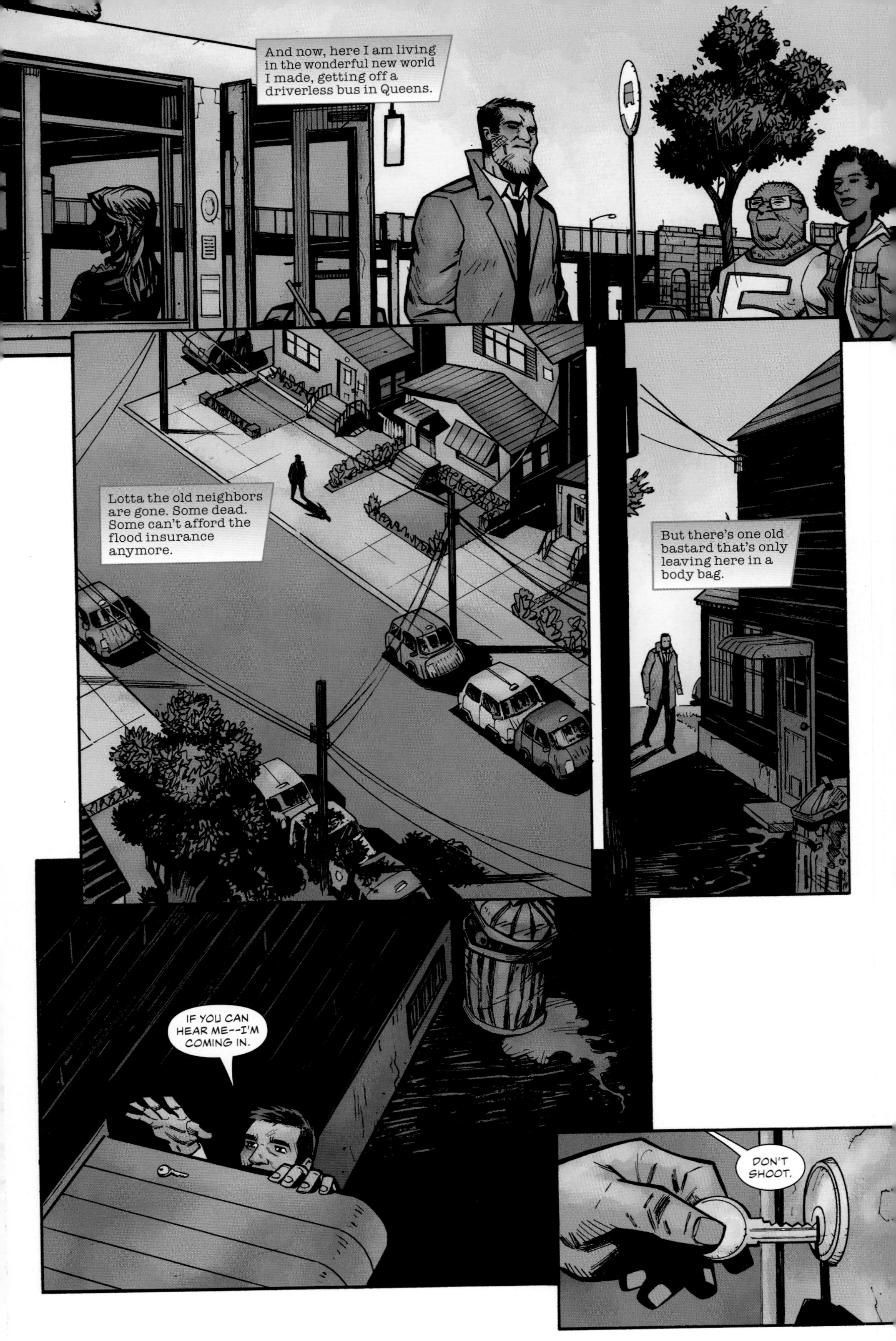
And now, here I am living in the wonderful new world I made, getting off a driverless bus in Queens.
Lotta the old neighbors are gone. Some dead. Some can't afford the flood insurance anymore.
But there's one old bastard that's only leaving here in a body bag.
IF YOU CAN HEAR ME--I'M COMING IN.
DON'T SHOOT.

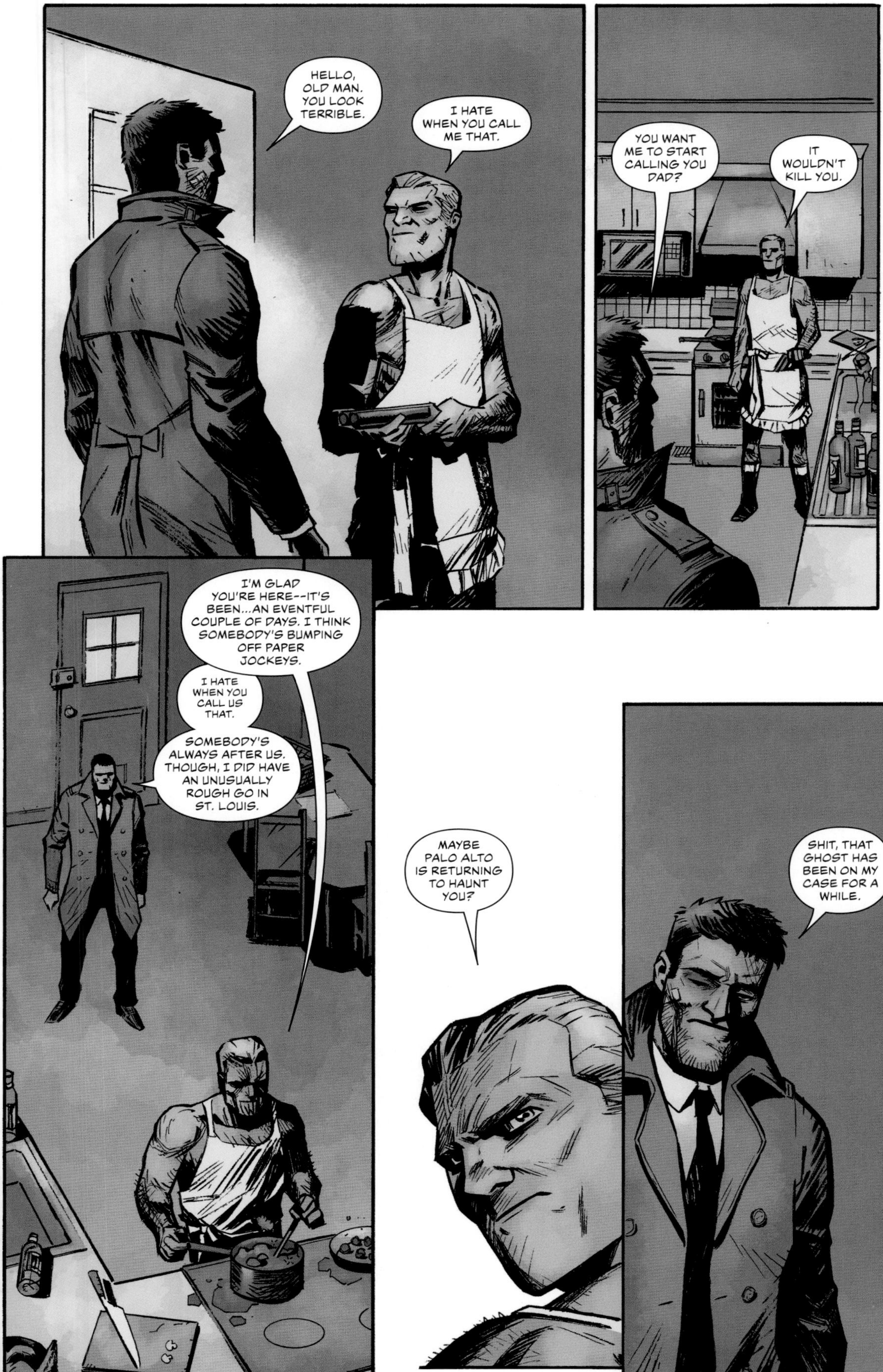
HELLO, OLD MAN. YOU LOOK TERRIBLE.
I HATE WHEN YOU CALL ME THAT.
YOU WANT ME TO START CALLING YOU DAD?
IT WOULDN'T KILL YOU.
I'M GLAD YOU'RE HERE--IT'S BEEN...AN EVENTFUL COUPLE OF DAYS. I THINK SOMEBODY'S BUMPING OFF PAPER JOCKEYS.
I HATE WHEN YOU CALL US THAT.
SOMEBODY'S ALWAYS AFTER US. THOUGH, I DID HAVE AN UNUSUALLY ROUGH GO IN ST. LOUIS.
MAYBE PALO ALTO IS RETURNING TO HAUNT YOU?
SHIT, THAT GHOST HAS BEEN ON MY CASE FOR A WHILE.

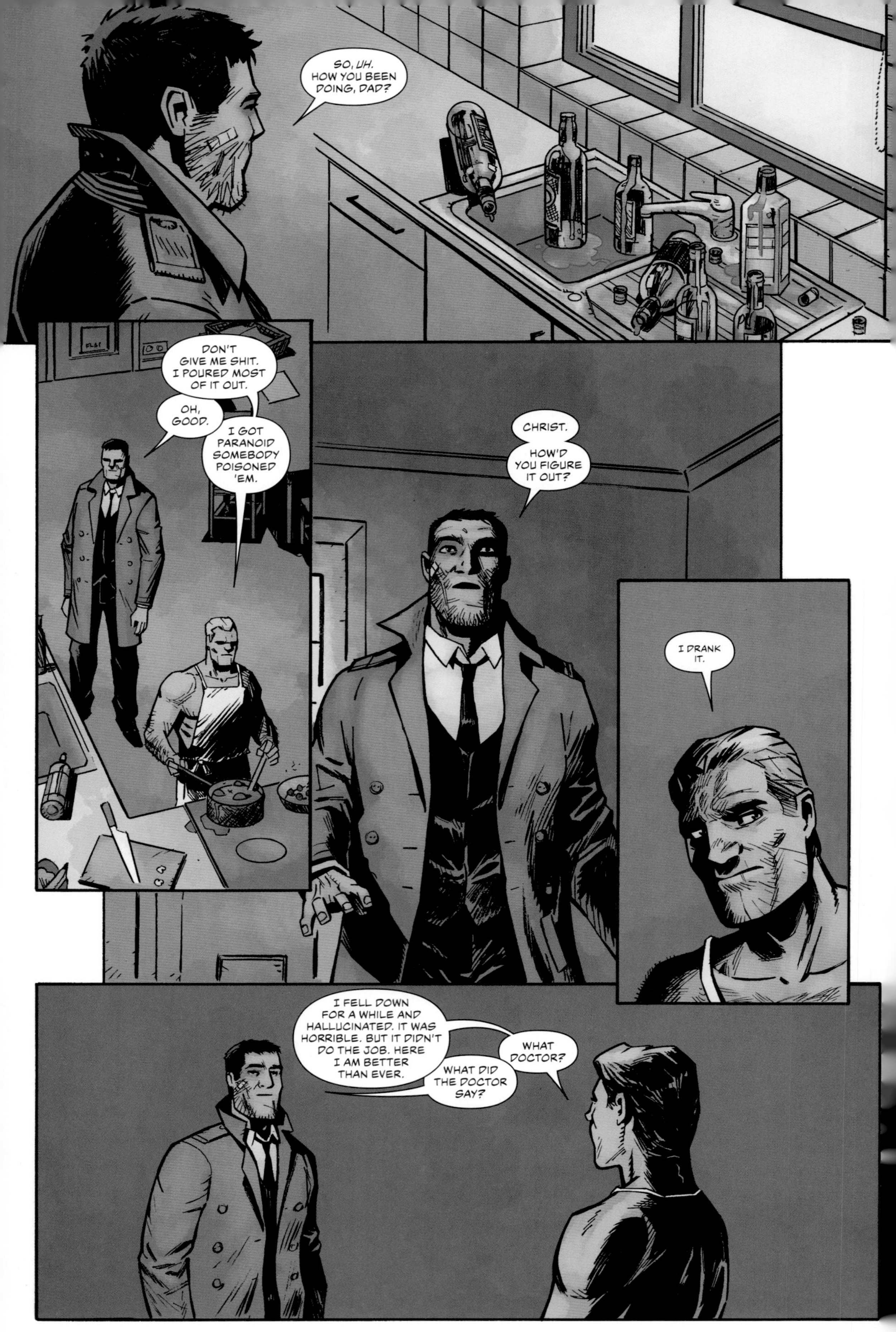
SO, UH. HOW YOU BEEN DOING, DAD?
DON'T GIVE ME SHIT. I POURED MOST OF IT OUT.
OH, GOOD.
I GOT PARANOID SOMEBODY POISONED 'EM.
CHRIST.
HOW'D YOU FIGURE IT OUT?
I DRANK IT.
I FELL DOWN FOR A WHILE AND HALLUCINATED. IT WAS HORRIBLE. BUT IT DIDN'T DO THE JOB. HERE I AM BETTER THAN EVER.
WHAT DID THE DOCTOR SAY?
WHAT DOCTOR?

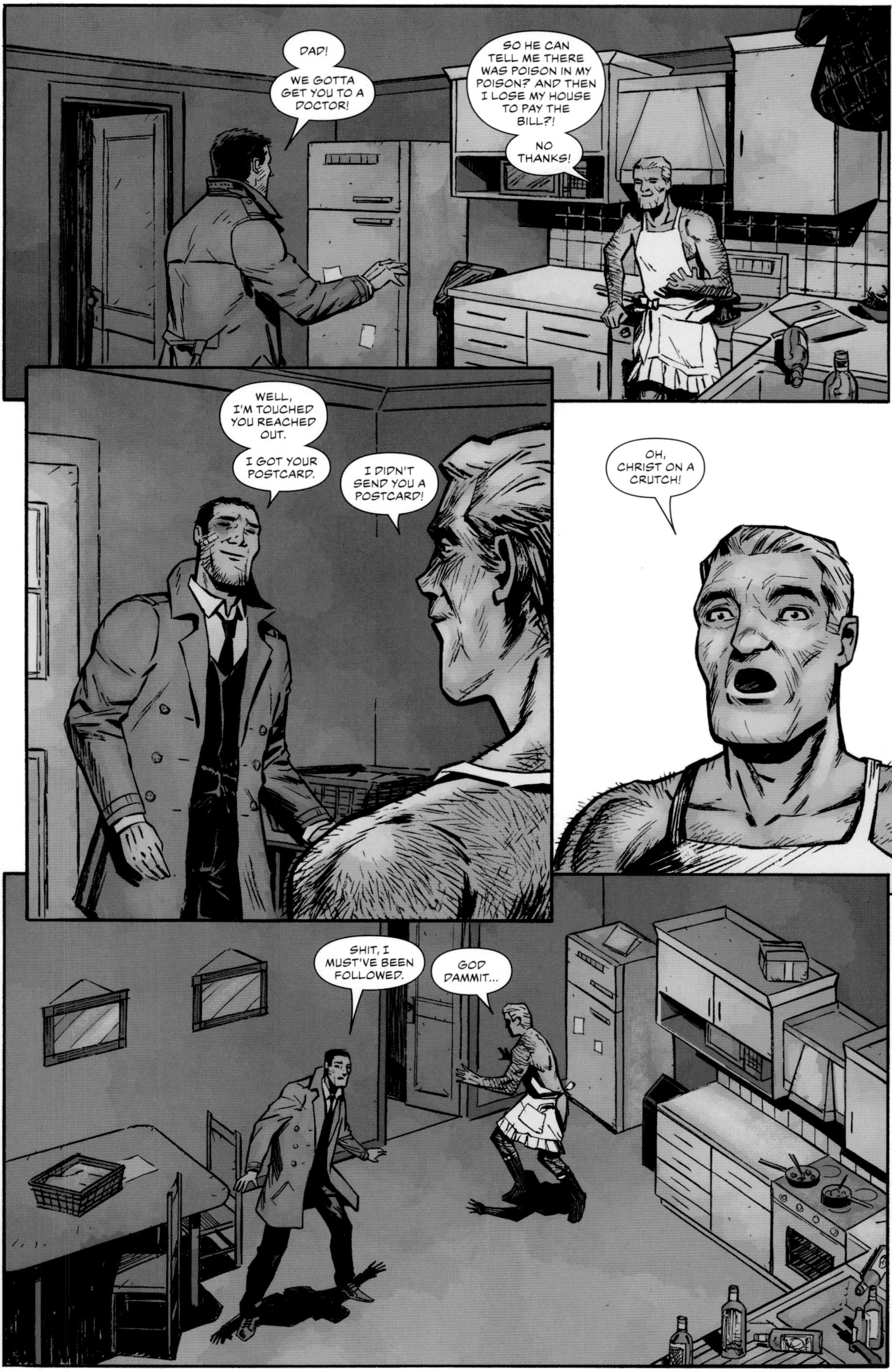
DAD!
WE GOTTA GET YOU TO A DOCTOR!
SO HE CAN TELL ME THERE WAS POISON IN MY POISON? AND THEN I LOSE MY HOUSE TO PAY THE BILL?!
NO THANKS!
WELL, I'M TOUCHED YOU REACHED OUT.
I GOT YOUR POSTCARD.
I DIDN'T SEND YOU A POSTCARD!
OH, CHRIST ON A CRUTCH!
SHIT, I MUST'VE BEEN FOLLOWED.
GOD DAMMIT...

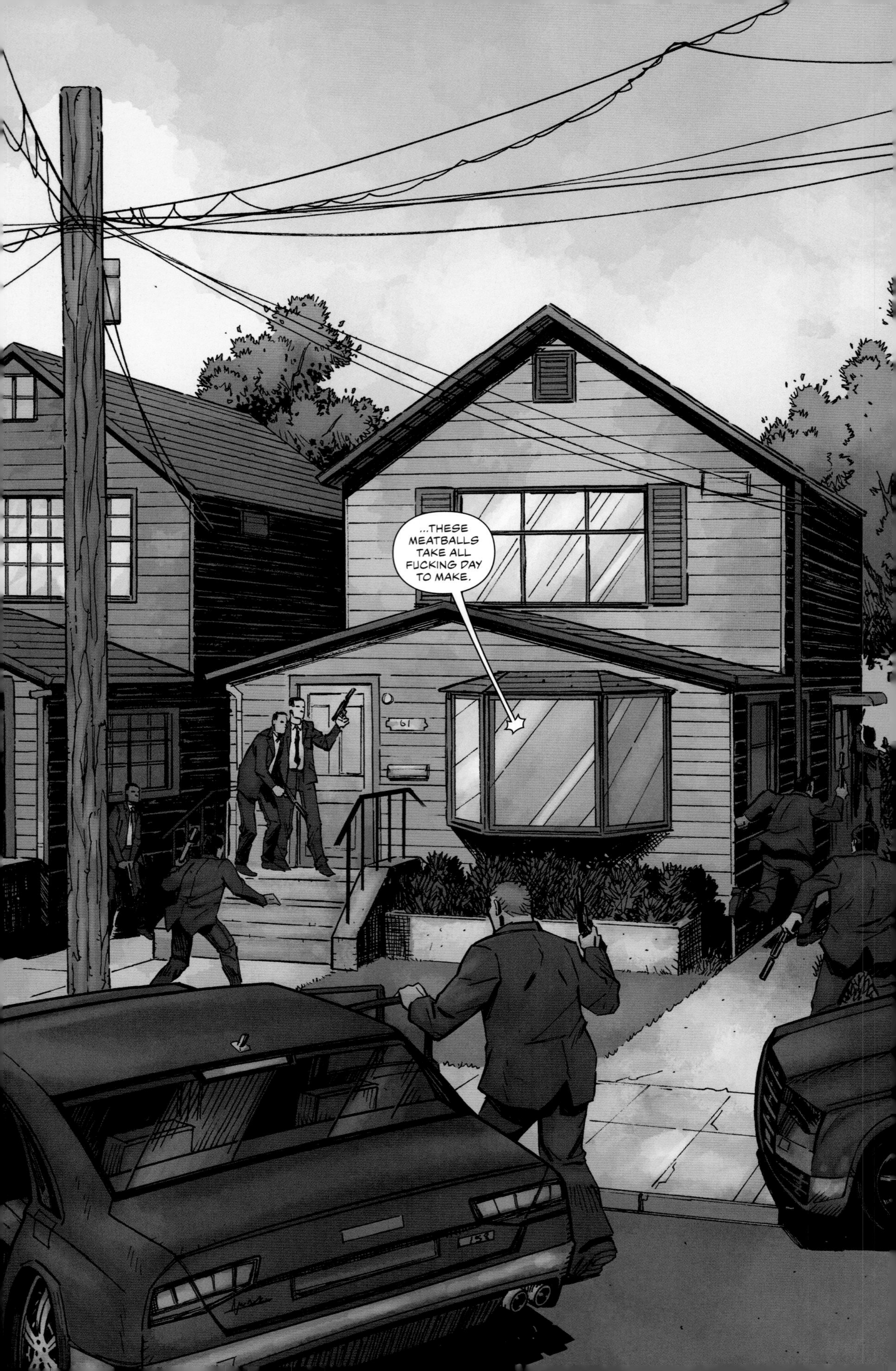
...THESE MEATBALLS TAKE ALL FUCKING DAY TO MAKE.

CHAPTER 2

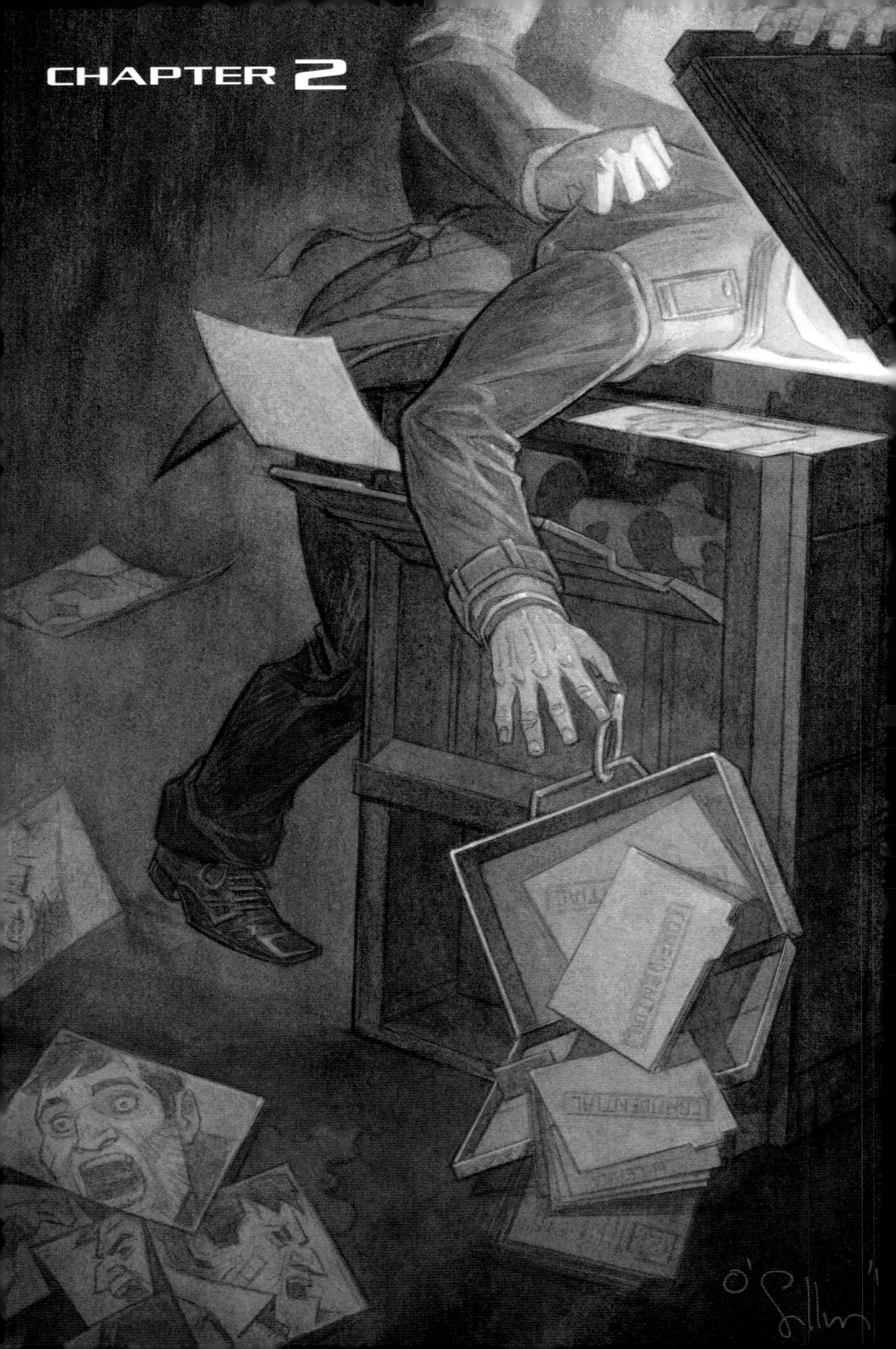

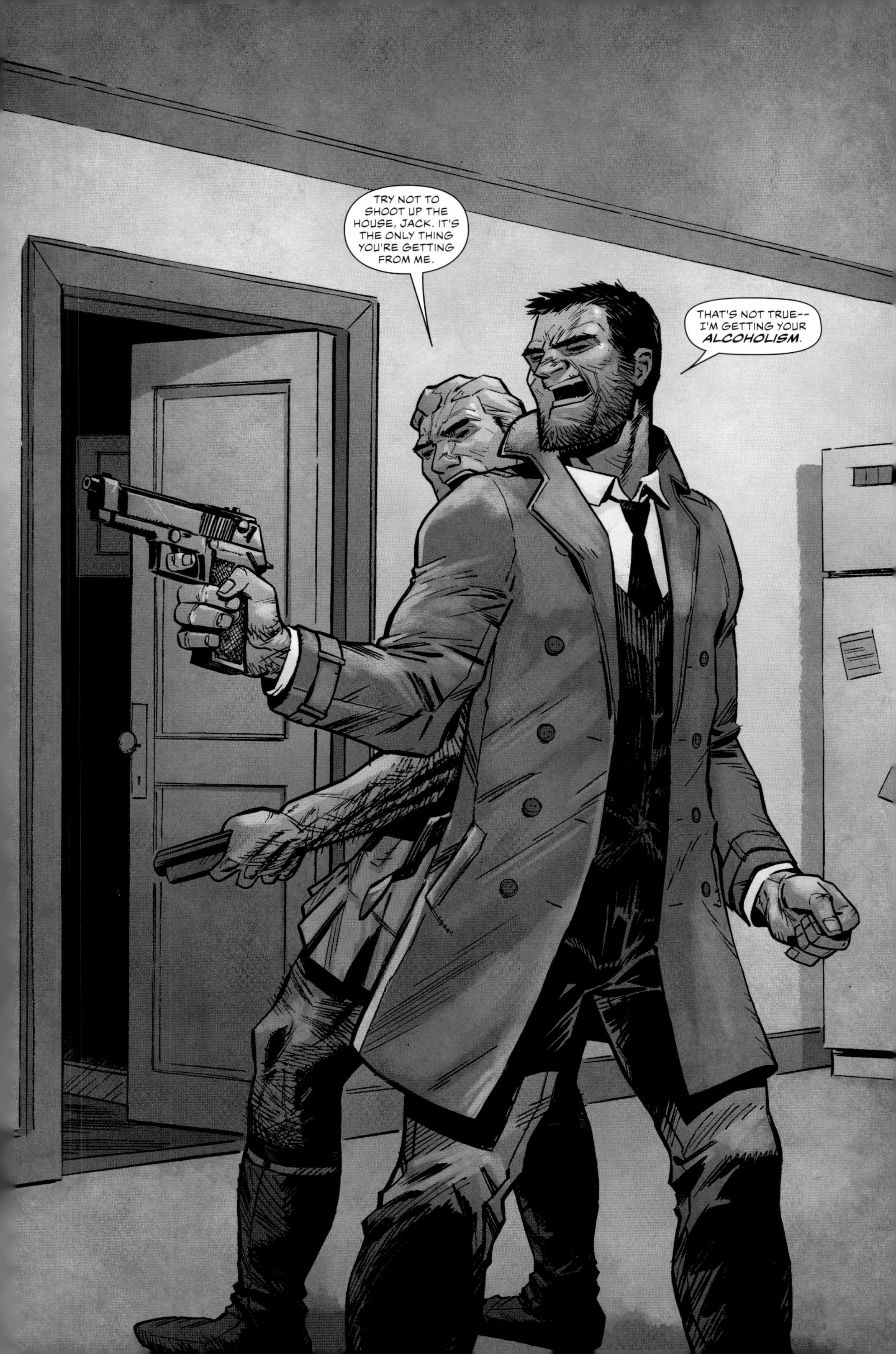
TRY NOT TO SHOOT UP THE HOUSE, JACK. IT'S THE ONLY THING YOU'RE GETTING FROM ME.
THAT'S NOT TRUE-- I'M GETTING YOUR *ALCOHOLISM*.

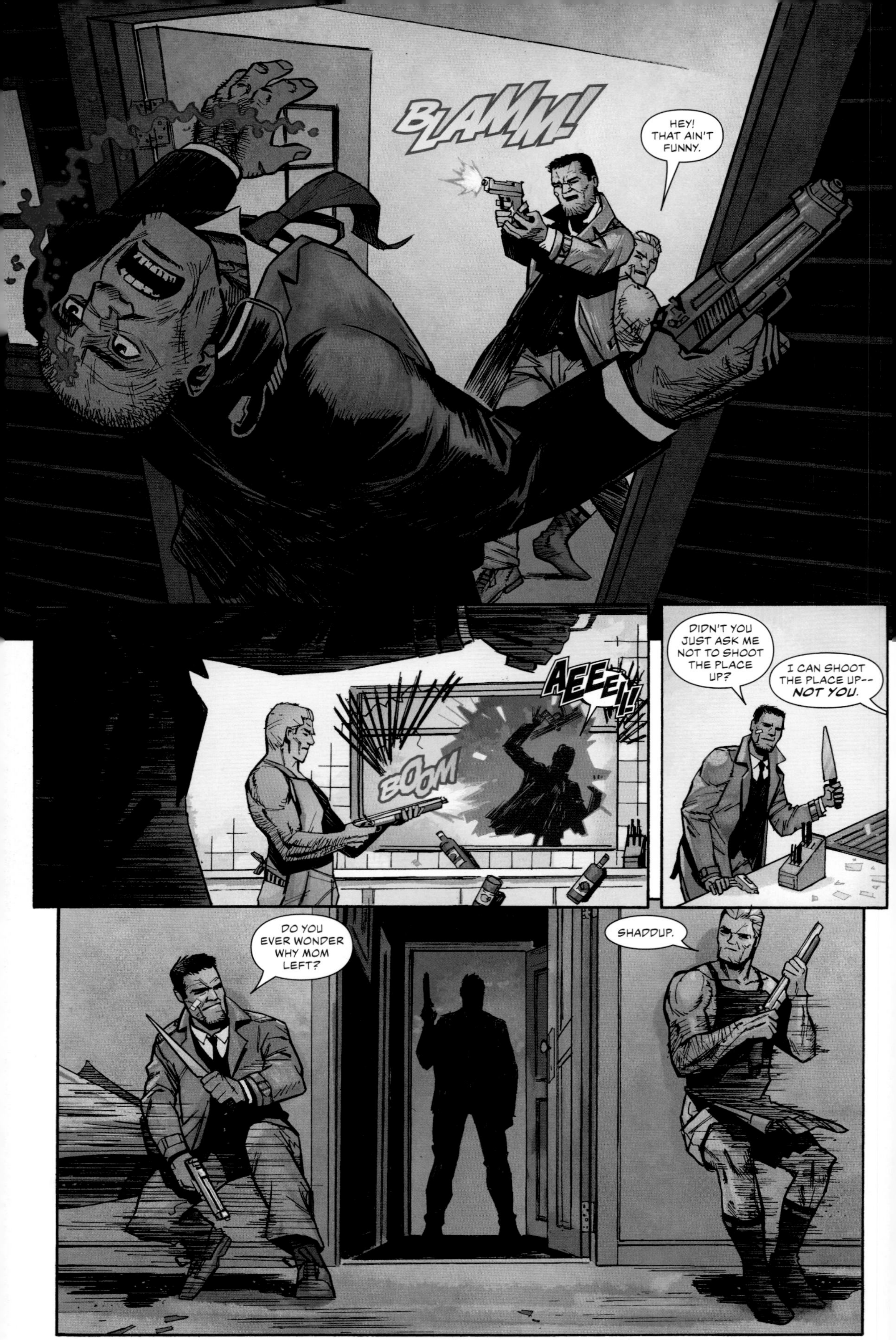
BLAMM!
HEY! THAT AIN'T FUNNY.
AEEEII!
BOOM
DIDN'T YOU JUST ASK ME NOT TO SHOOT THE PLACE UP?
I CAN SHOOT THE PLACE UP-- NOT YOU.
DO YOU EVER WONDER WHY MOM LEFT?
SHADDUP.

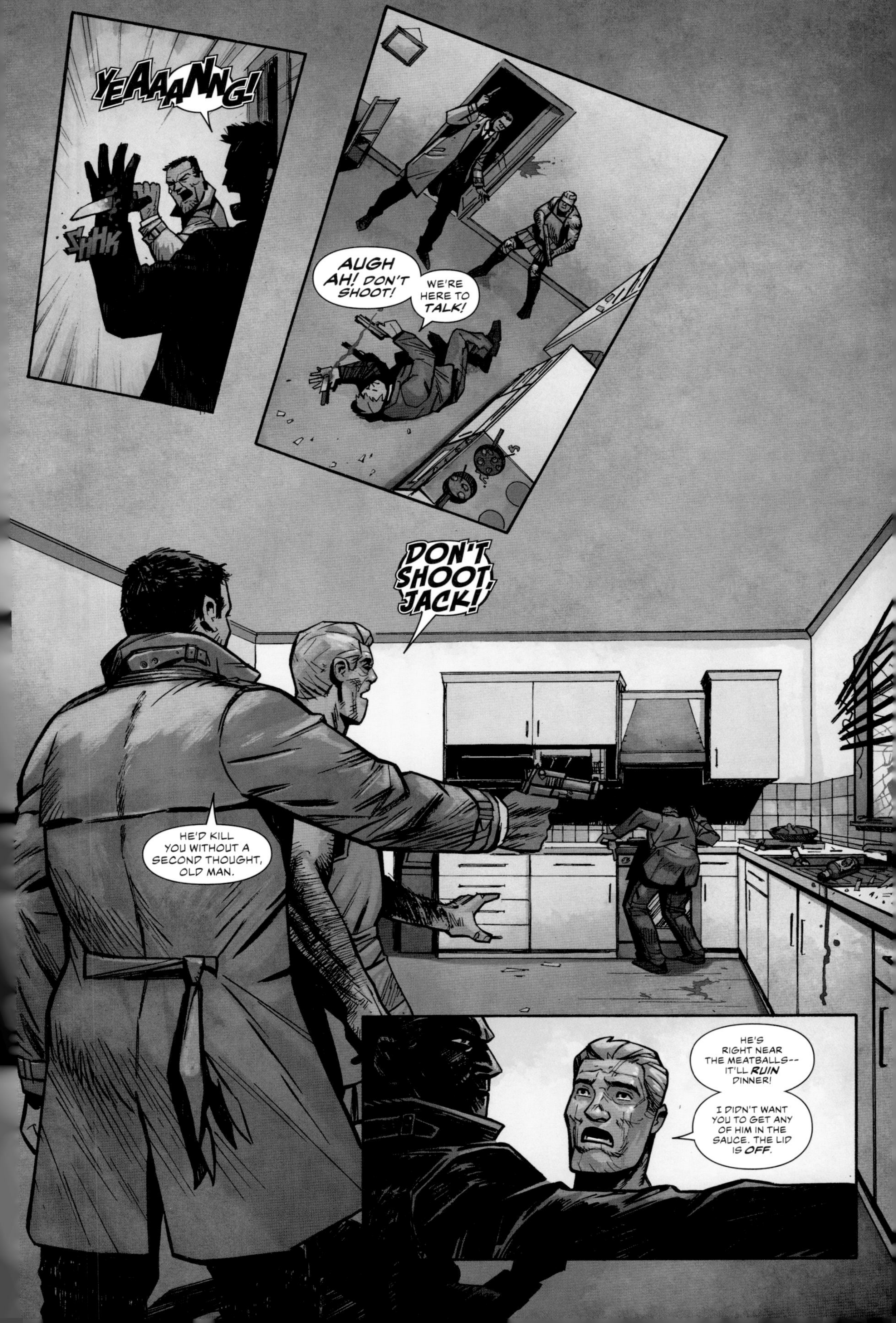

YEAAAANNG!
SHHK
AUGH AH! DON'T SHOOT!
WE'RE HERE TO TALK!
DON'T SHOOT, JACK!
HE'D KILL YOU WITHOUT A SECOND THOUGHT, OLD MAN.
HE'S RIGHT NEAR THE MEATBALLS-- IT'LL RUIN DINNER!
I DIDN'T WANT YOU TO GET ANY OF HIM IN THE SAUCE. THE LID IS OFF.

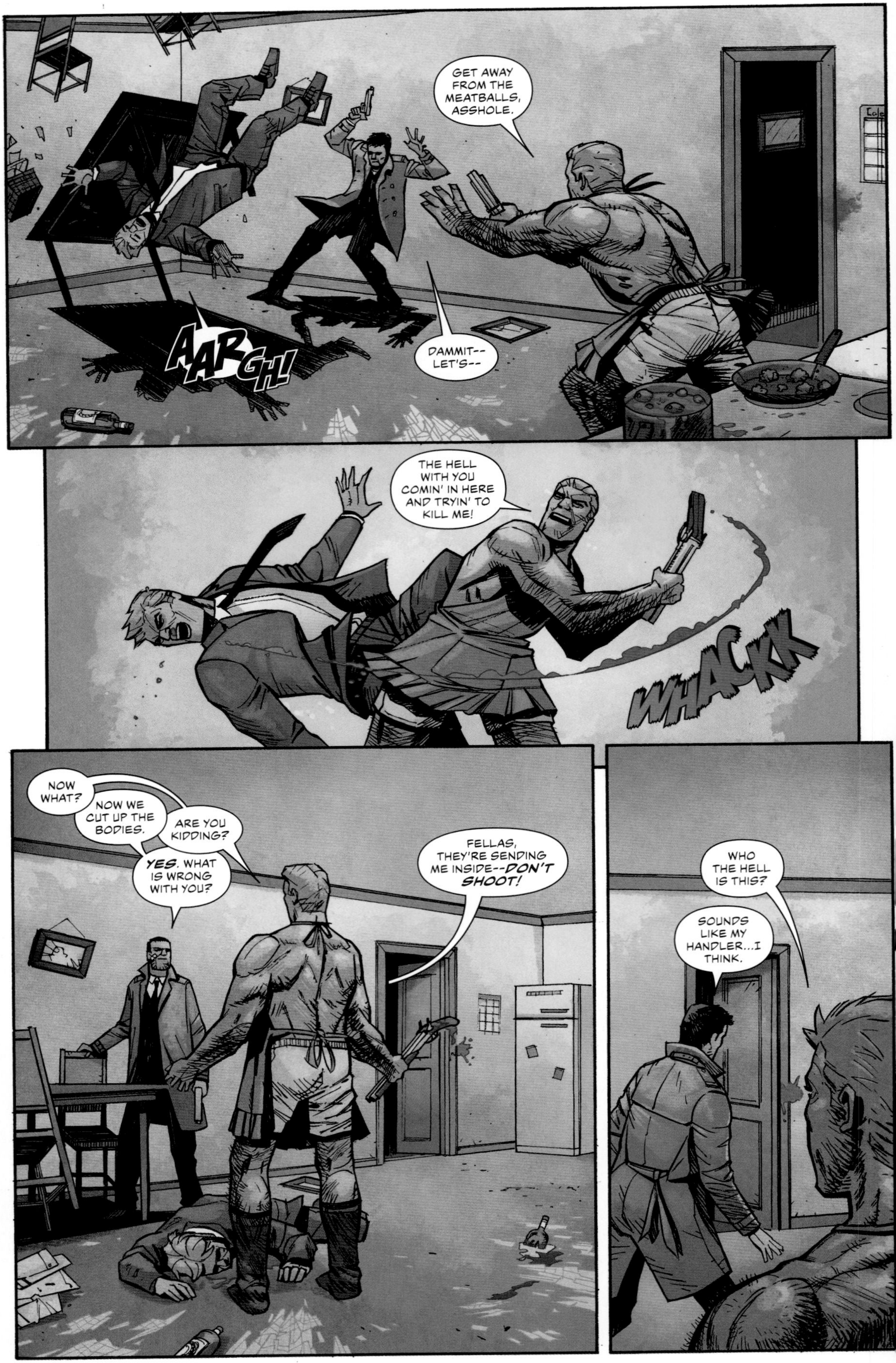
GET AWAY FROM THE MEATBALLS, ASSHOLE.
AARGH!
DAMMIT-- LET'S--
THE HELL WITH YOU COMIN' IN HERE AND TRYIN' TO KILL ME!
WHACKK
NOW WHAT?
NOW WE CUT UP THE BODIES.
ARE YOU KIDDING?
YES. WHAT IS WRONG WITH YOU?
FELLAS, THEY'RE SENDING ME INSIDE--DON'T SHOOT!
WHO THE HELL IS THIS?
SOUNDS LIKE MY HANDLER...I THINK.

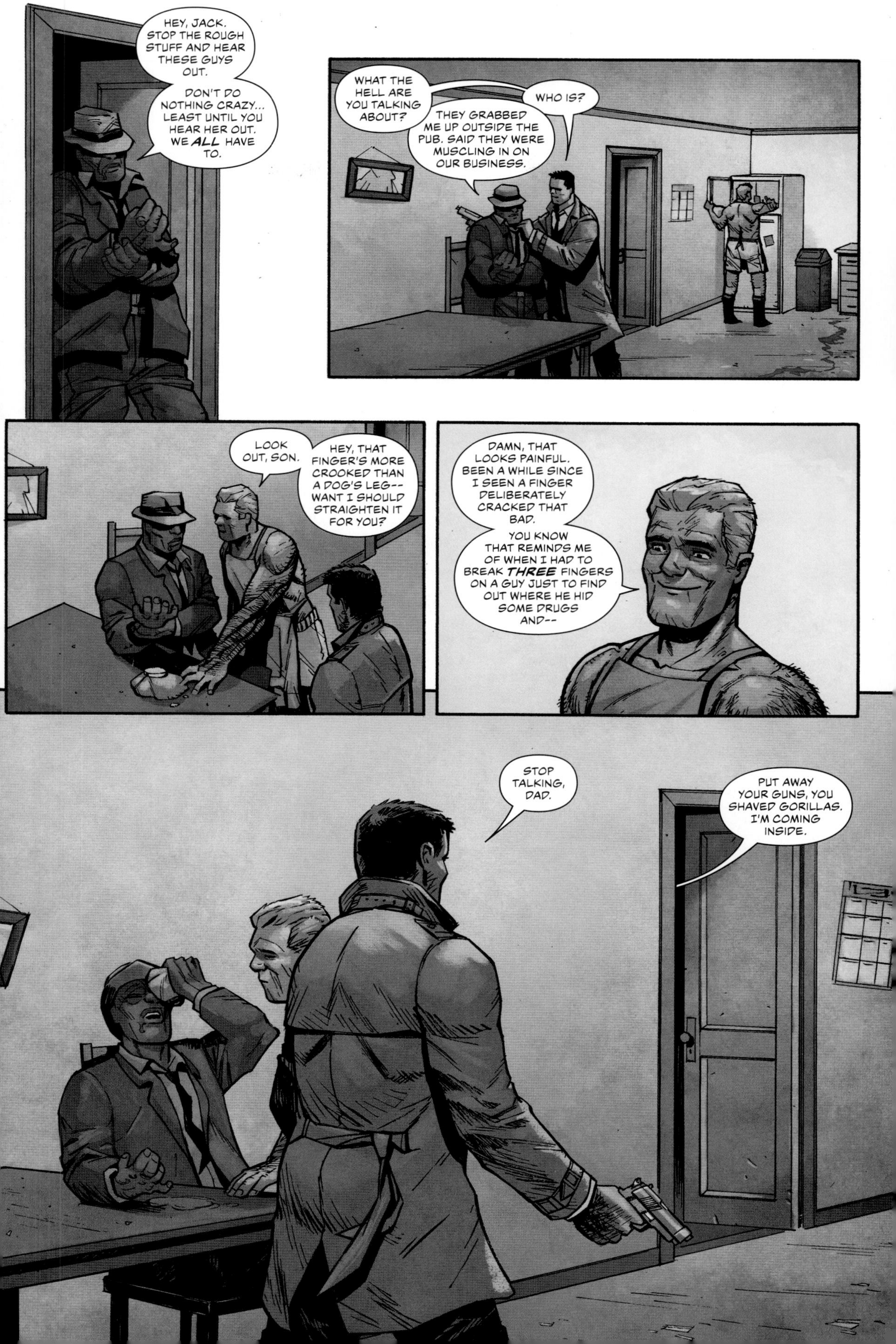
HEY, JACK. STOP THE ROUGH STUFF AND HEAR THESE GUYS OUT.
DON'T DO NOTHING CRAZY... LEAST UNTIL YOU HEAR HER OUT. WE ALL HAVE TO.
WHAT THE HELL ARE YOU TALKING ABOUT?
WHO IS?
THEY GRABBED ME UP OUTSIDE THE PUB. SAID THEY WERE MUSCLING IN ON OUR BUSINESS.
LOOK OUT, SON.
HEY, THAT FINGER'S MORE CROOKED THAN A DOG'S LEG-- WANT I SHOULD STRAIGHTEN IT FOR YOU?
DAMN, THAT LOOKS PAINFUL. BEEN A WHILE SINCE I SEEN A FINGER DELIBERATELY CRACKED THAT BAD.
YOU KNOW THAT REMINDS ME OF WHEN I HAD TO BREAK THREE FINGERS ON A GUY JUST TO FIND OUT WHERE HE HID SOME DRUGS AND--
STOP TALKING, DAD.
PUT AWAY YOUR GUNS, YOU SHAVED GORILLAS. I'M COMING INSIDE.

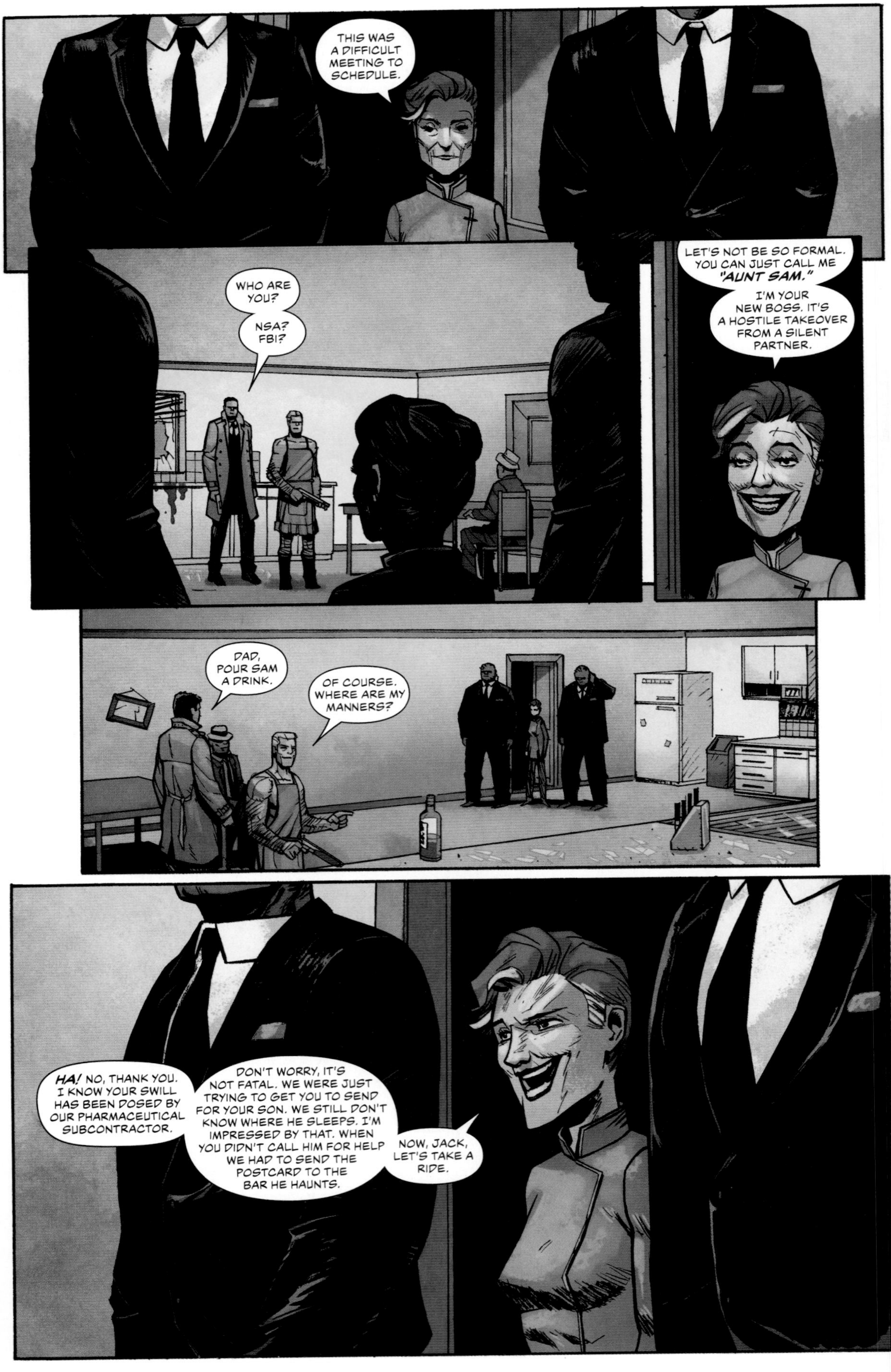
THIS WAS A DIFFICULT MEETING TO SCHEDULE.
WHO ARE YOU?
NSA? FBI?
LET'S NOT BE SO FORMAL. YOU CAN JUST CALL ME "AUNT SAM."
I'M YOUR NEW BOSS. IT'S A HOSTILE TAKEOVER FROM A SILENT PARTNER.
DAD, POUR SAM A DRINK.
OF COURSE. WHERE ARE MY MANNERS?
HA! NO, THANK YOU. I KNOW YOUR SWILL HAS BEEN DOSED BY OUR PHARMACEUTICAL SUBCONTRACTOR.
DON'T WORRY, IT'S NOT FATAL. WE WERE JUST TRYING TO GET YOU TO SEND FOR YOUR SON. WE STILL DON'T KNOW WHERE HE SLEEPS. I'M IMPRESSED BY THAT. WHEN YOU DIDN'T CALL HIM FOR HELP WE HAD TO SEND THE POSTCARD TO THE BAR HE HAUNTS.
NOW, JACK, LET'S TAKE A RIDE.

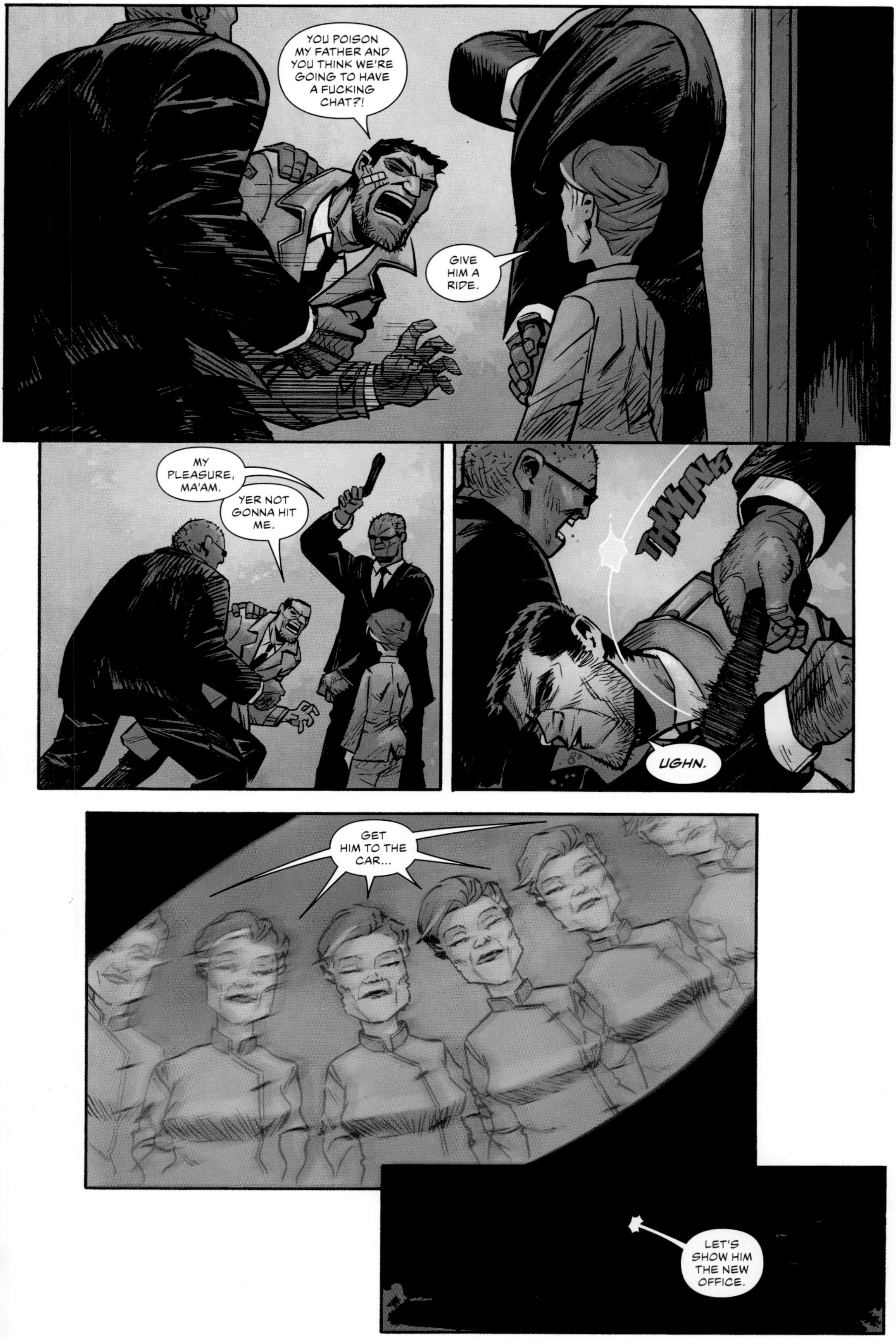
YOU POISON MY FATHER AND YOU THINK WE'RE GOING TO HAVE A FUCKING CHAT?!
GIVE HIM A RIDE.
MY PLEASURE, MA'AM.
YER NOT GONNA HIT ME.
THWUNK
UGHN.
GET HIM TO THE CAR...
LET'S SHOW HIM THE NEW OFFICE.

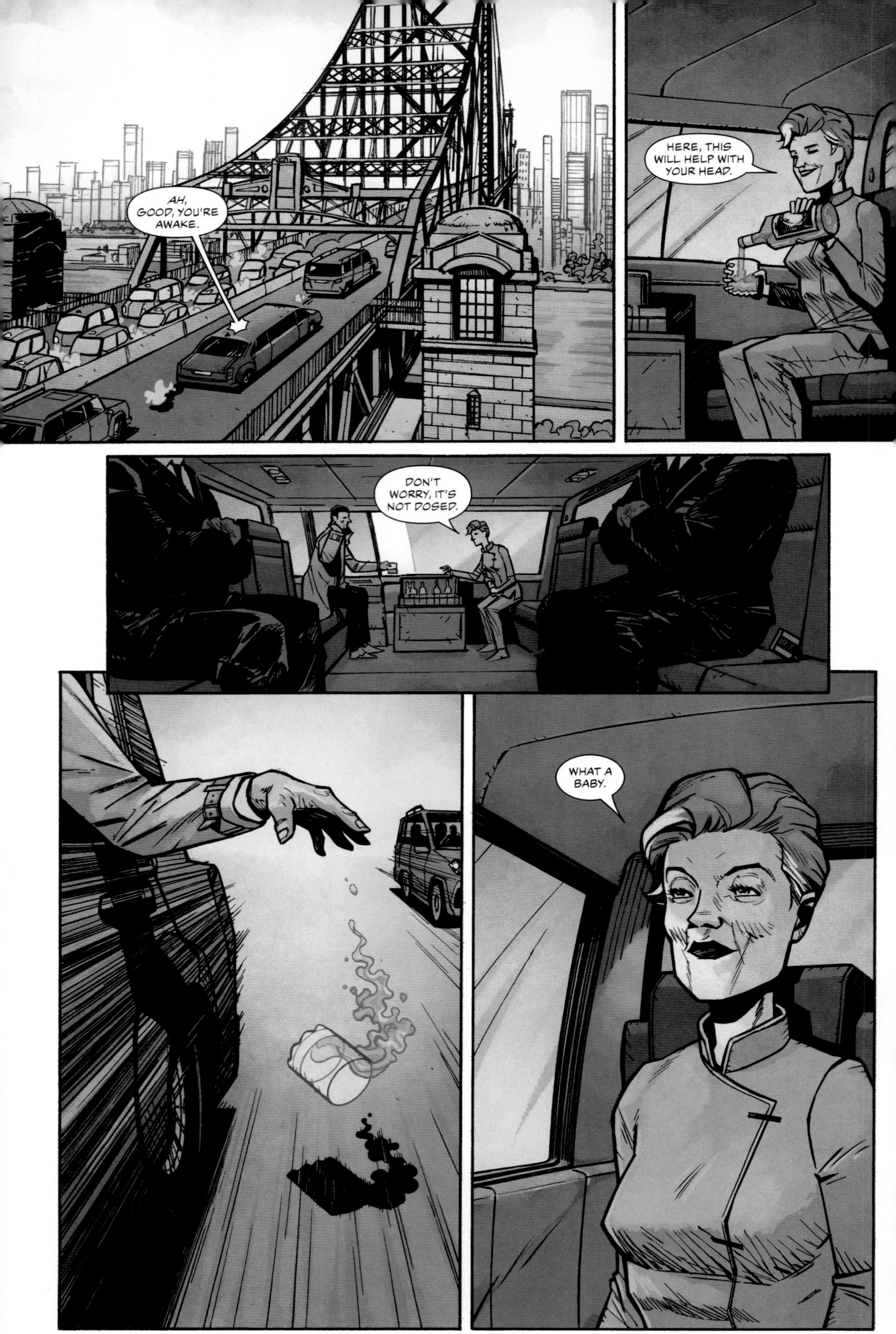

AH, GOOD, YOU'RE AWAKE.
HERE, THIS WILL HELP WITH YOUR HEAD.
DON'T WORRY, IT'S NOT DOSED.
WHAT A BABY.

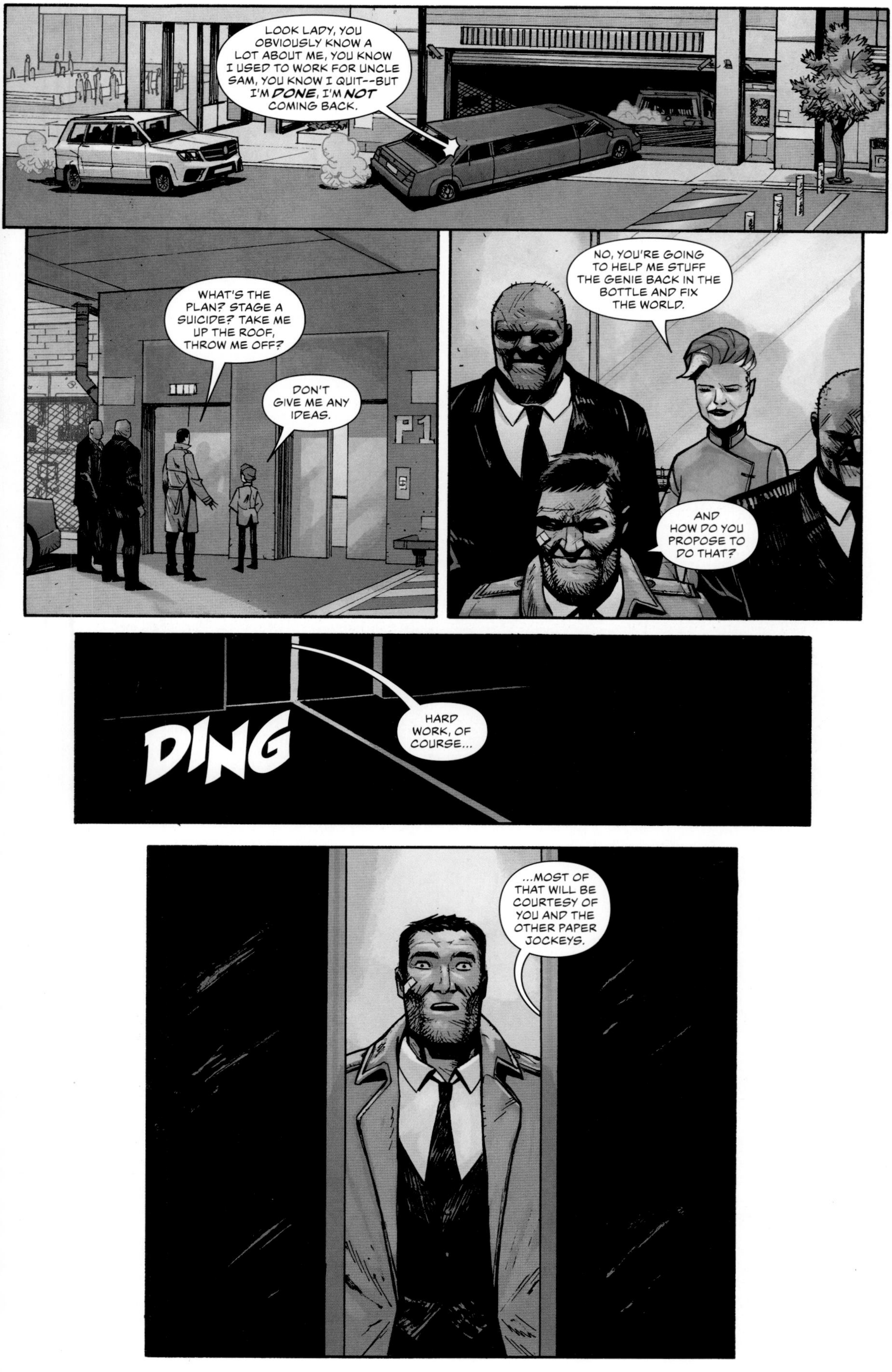
LOOK LADY, YOU OBVIOUSLY KNOW A LOT ABOUT ME, YOU KNOW I USED TO WORK FOR UNCLE SAM, YOU KNOW I QUIT--BUT I'M DONE, I'M NOT COMING BACK.
WHAT'S THE PLAN? STAGE A SUICIDE? TAKE ME UP THE ROOF, THROW ME OFF?
DON'T GIVE ME ANY IDEAS.
P1
NO, YOU'RE GOING TO HELP ME STUFF THE GENIE BACK IN THE BOTTLE AND FIX THE WORLD.
AND HOW DO YOU PROPOSE TO DO THAT?
DING
HARD WORK, OF COURSE...
...MOST OF THAT WILL BE COURTESY OF YOU AND THE OTHER PAPER JOCKEYS.

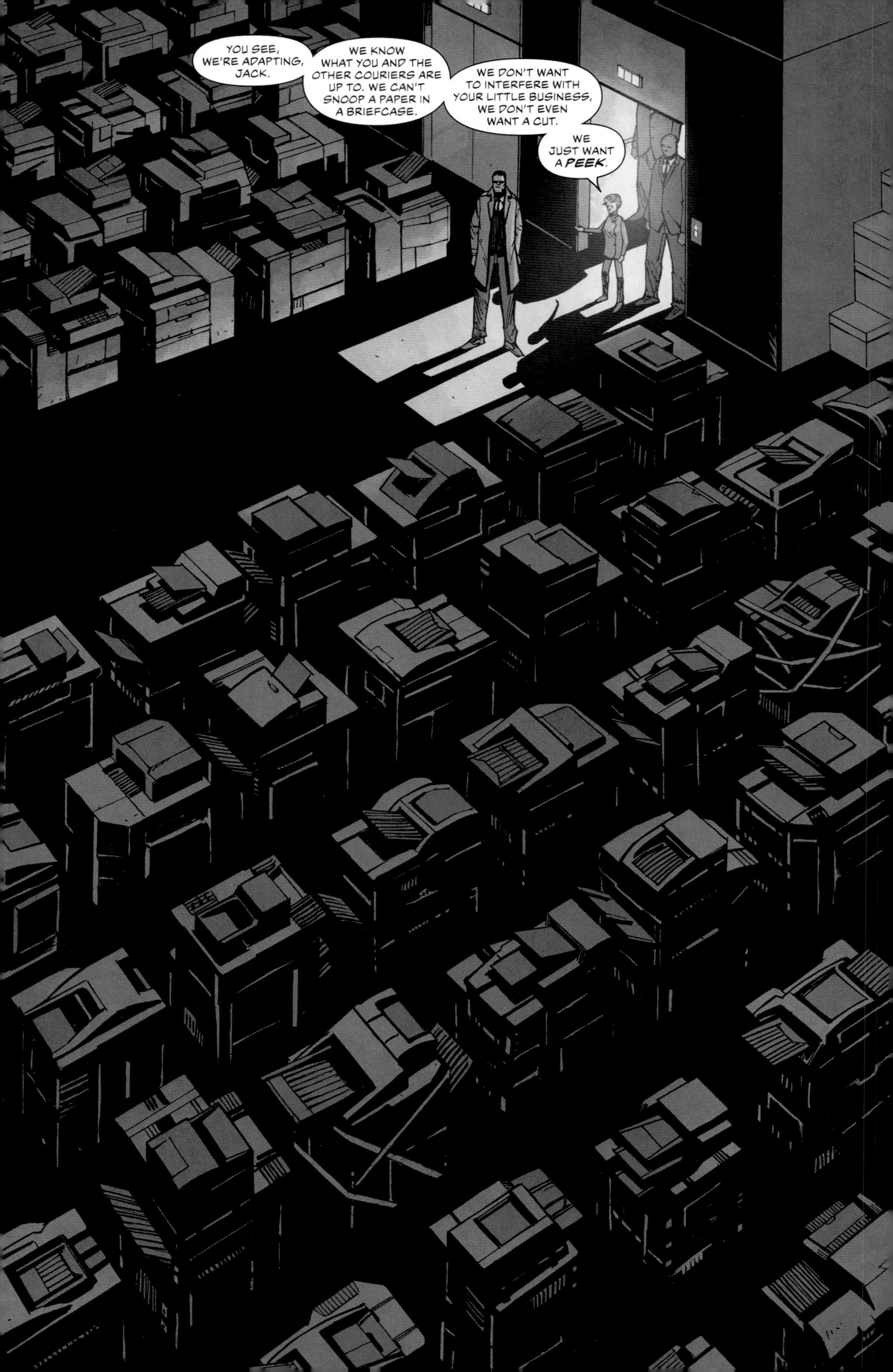
YOU SEE, WE'RE ADAPTING, JACK.
WE KNOW WHAT YOU AND THE OTHER COURIERS ARE UP TO. WE CAN'T SNOOP A PAPER IN A BRIEFCASE.
WE DON'T WANT TO INTERFERE WITH YOUR LITTLE BUSINESS, WE DON'T EVEN WANT A CUT.
WE JUST WANT A PEEK.

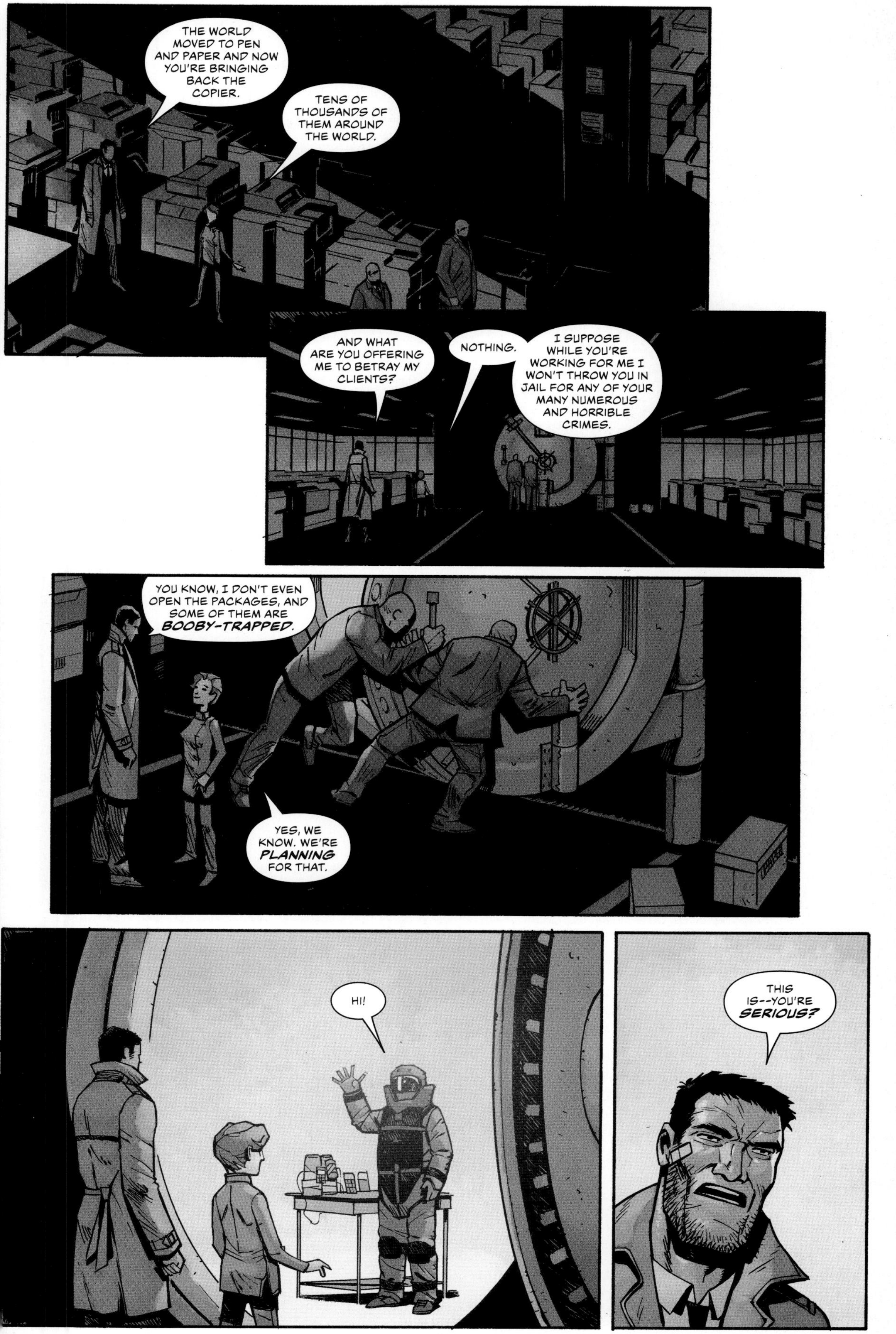
THE WORLD MOVED TO PEN AND PAPER AND NOW YOU'RE BRINGING BACK THE COPIER.
TENS OF THOUSANDS OF THEM AROUND THE WORLD.
AND WHAT ARE YOU OFFERING ME TO BETRAY MY CLIENTS?
NOTHING.
I SUPPOSE WHILE YOU'RE WORKING FOR ME I WON'T THROW YOU IN JAIL FOR ANY OF YOUR MANY NUMEROUS AND HORRIBLE CRIMES.
YOU KNOW, I DON'T EVEN OPEN THE PACKAGES, AND SOME OF THEM ARE *BOOBY-TRAPPED*.
YES, WE KNOW. WE'RE *PLANNING* FOR THAT.
HI!
THIS IS--YOU'RE *SERIOUS?*

DEADLY SERIOUS.

YOU WILL TAKE EVERY JOB OFFERED TO YOU AND BEFORE DELIVERY YOU WILL VISIT ONE OF OUR CONVENIENT LOCATIONS SO THAT WE CAN PHOTOCOPY EVERY SINGLE PAGE YOU PUSH AROUND THE WORLD.

AND IF I SAY *NO?*

WELL, SOMEONE, I FORGET WHO, RECENTLY HAD A FUN IDEA ABOUT STAGING A SUICIDE.

BUT THAT'S SO EXTREME.

THERE ARE OTHER PRESSURE POINTS. LIKE YOUR FATHER, OR THE ANARCHIST YOU'RE RUMORED TO SHACK UP WITH.

NONE OF YOUR CLIENTS MUST KNOW THAT THE U.S. GOVERNMENT IS BACK IN THE ANALOG BUSINESS.

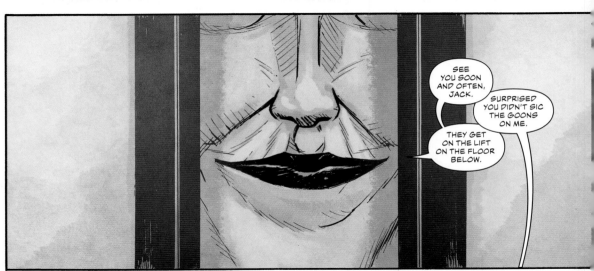

SEE YOU SOON AND OFTEN, JACK.

SURPRISED YOU DIDN'T SIC THE GOONS ON ME.

THEY GET ON THE LIFT ON THE FLOOR BELOW.

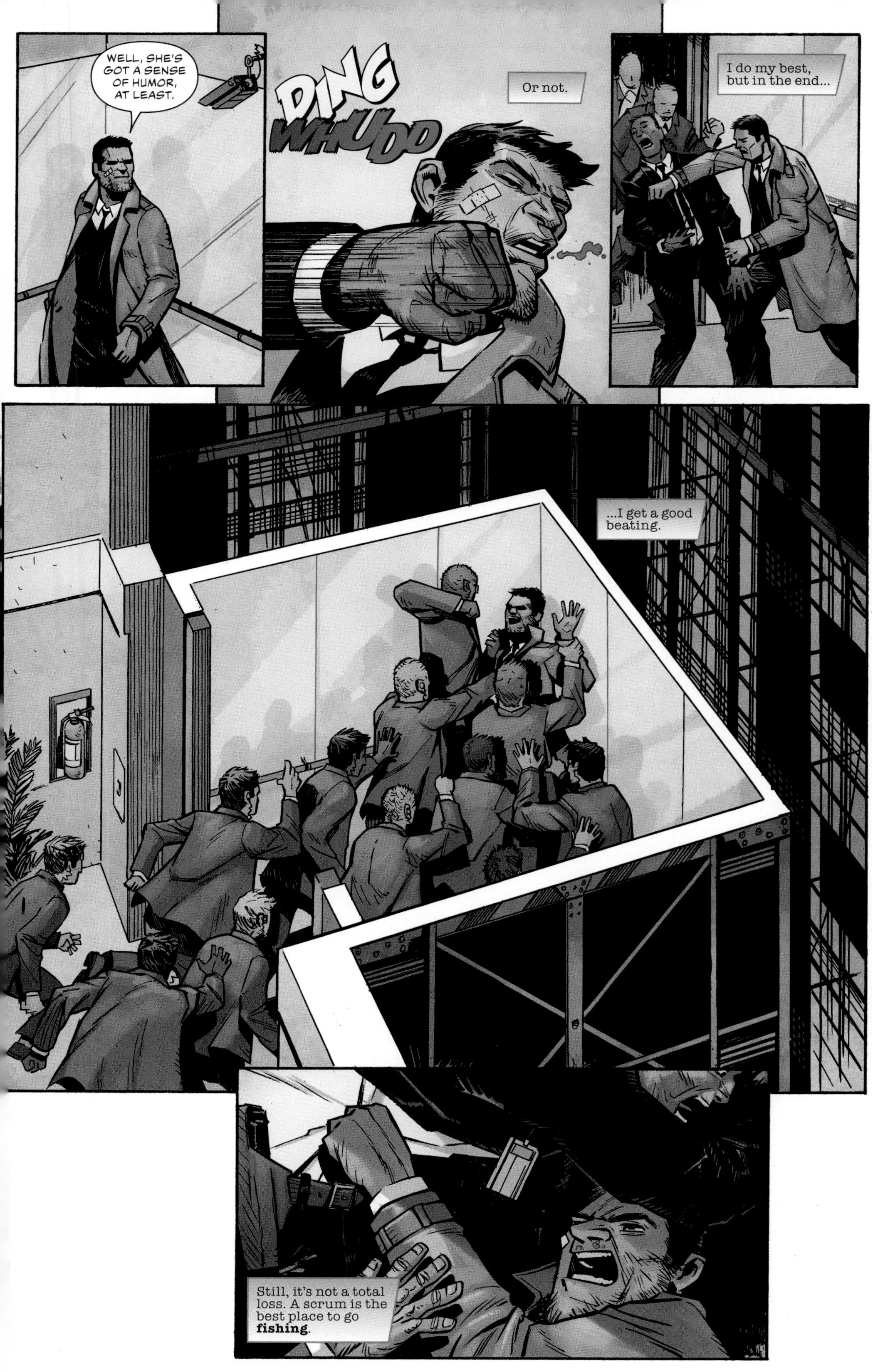
WELL, SHE'S GOT A SENSE OF HUMOR, AT LEAST.
DING
WHUDD
Or not.
I do my best, but in the end...
...I get a good beating.
Still, it's not a total loss. A scrum is the best place to go **fishing**.

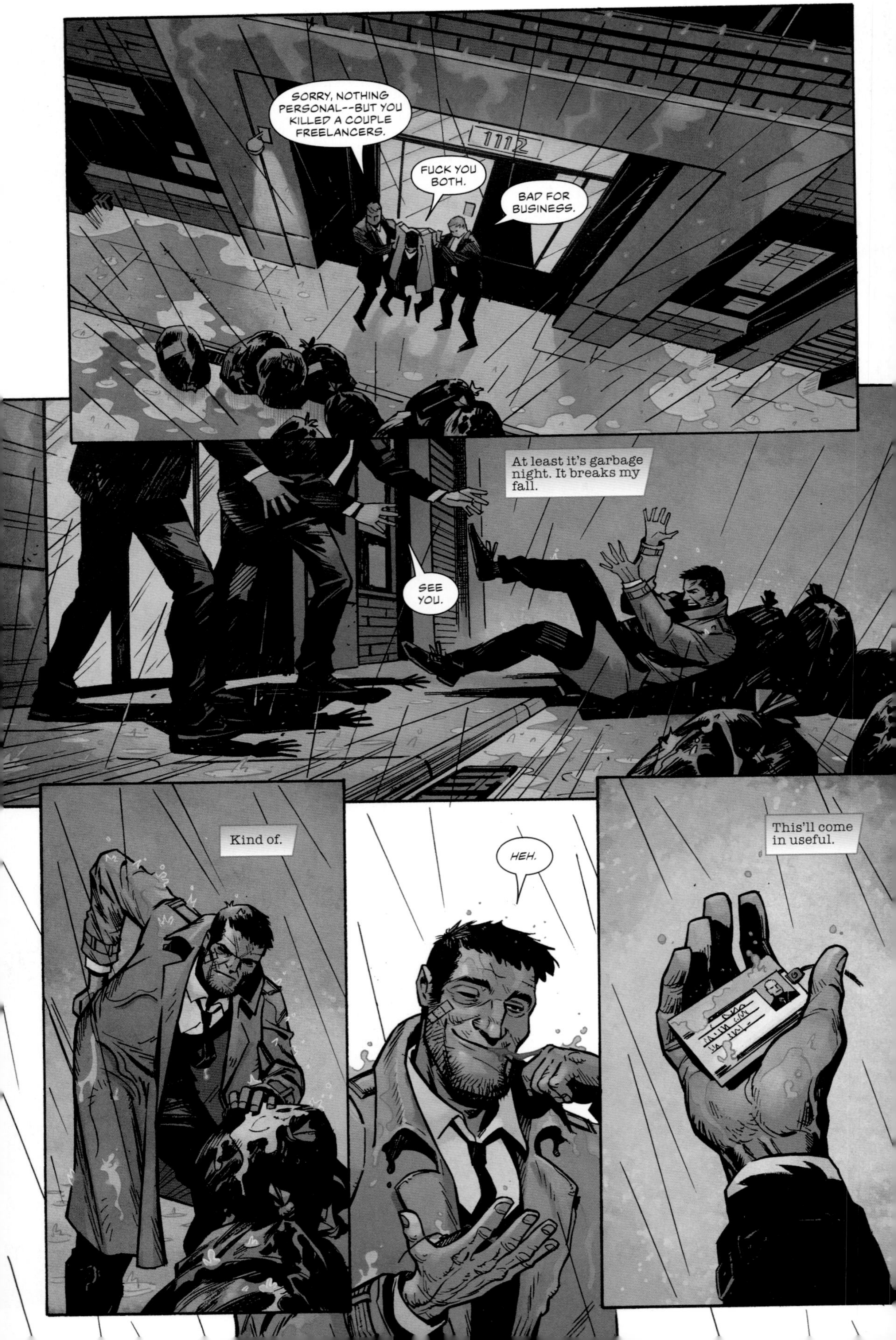
SORRY, NOTHING PERSONAL--BUT YOU KILLED A COUPLE FREELANCERS.
1112
FUCK YOU BOTH.
BAD FOR BUSINESS.
At least it's garbage night. It breaks my fall.
SEE YOU.
Kind of.
HEH.
This'll come in useful.

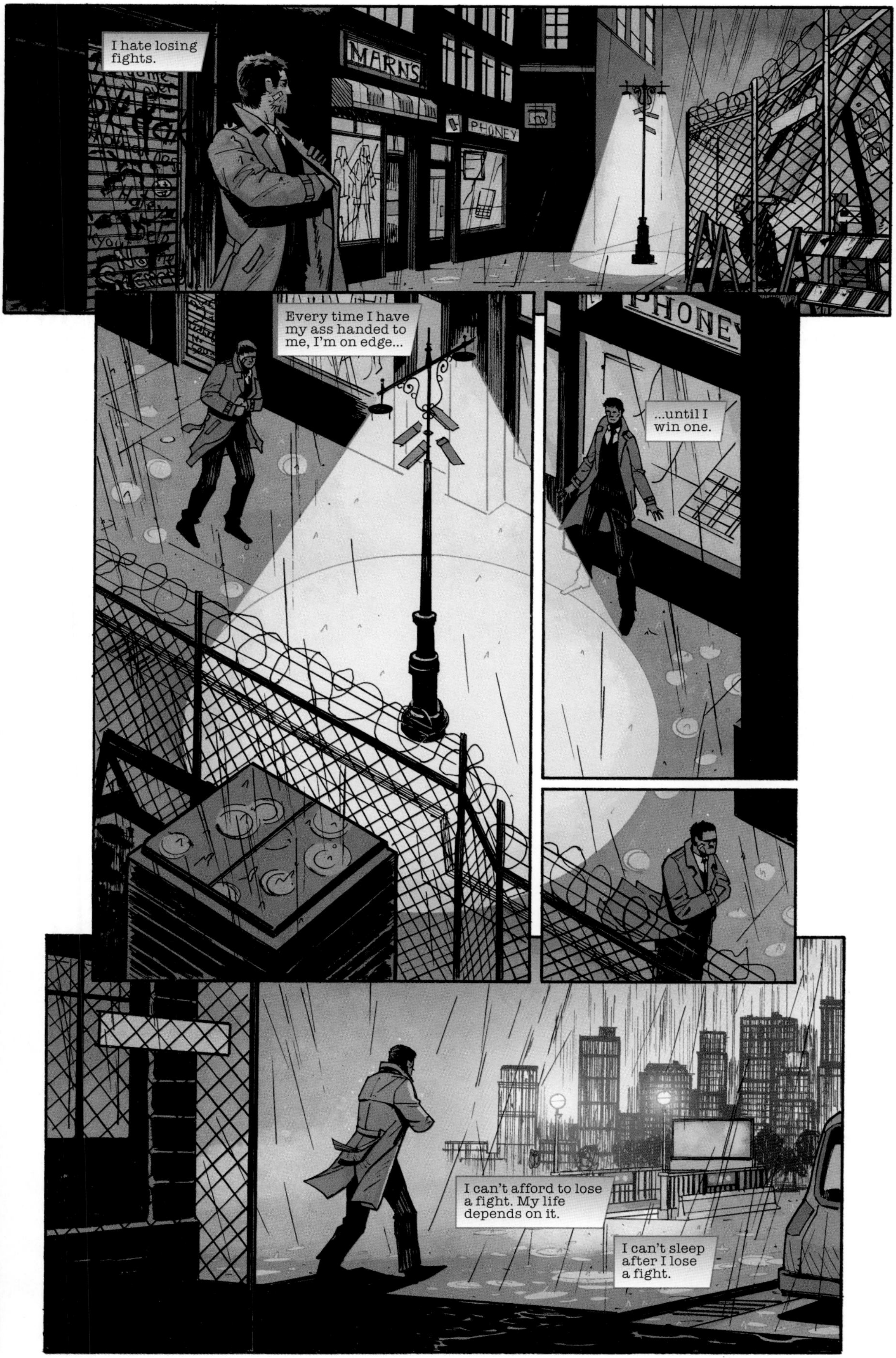
I hate losing fights.
MARN'S
PHONEY
Every time I have my ass handed to me, I'm on edge...
PHONEY
...until I win one.
I can't afford to lose a fight. My life depends on it.
I can't sleep after I lose a fight.

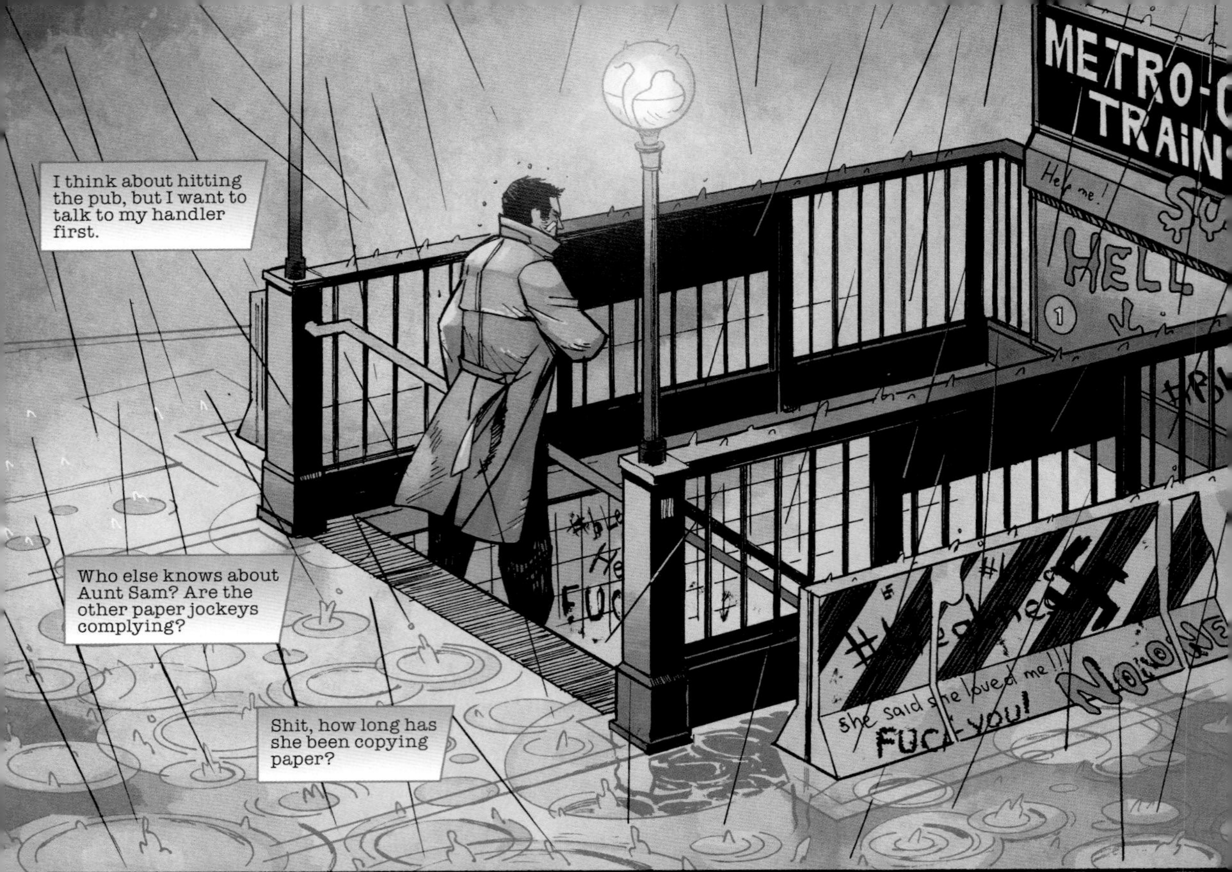
I think about hitting the pub, but I want to talk to my handler first.
Who else knows about Aunt Sam? Are the other paper jockeys complying?
Shit, how long has she been copying paper?
HELL
she said she loved me!!!
FUCK YOU!

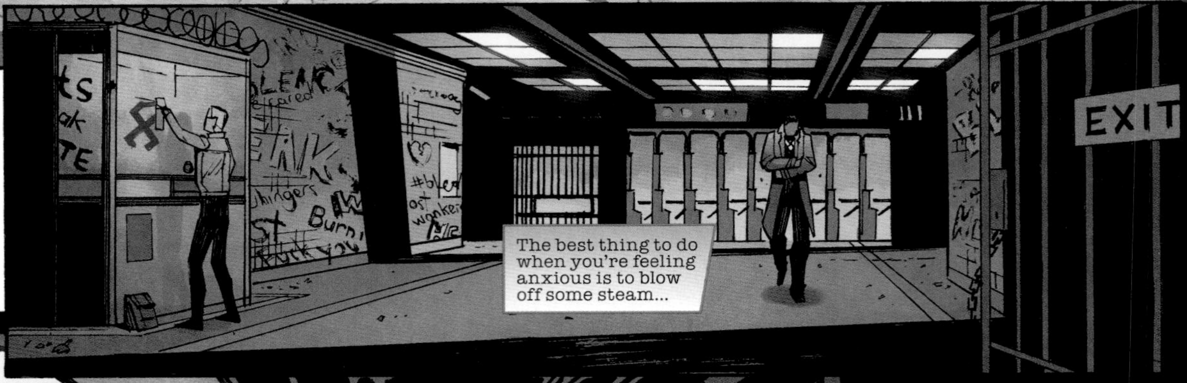
EXIT
The best thing to do when you're feeling anxious is to blow off some steam...

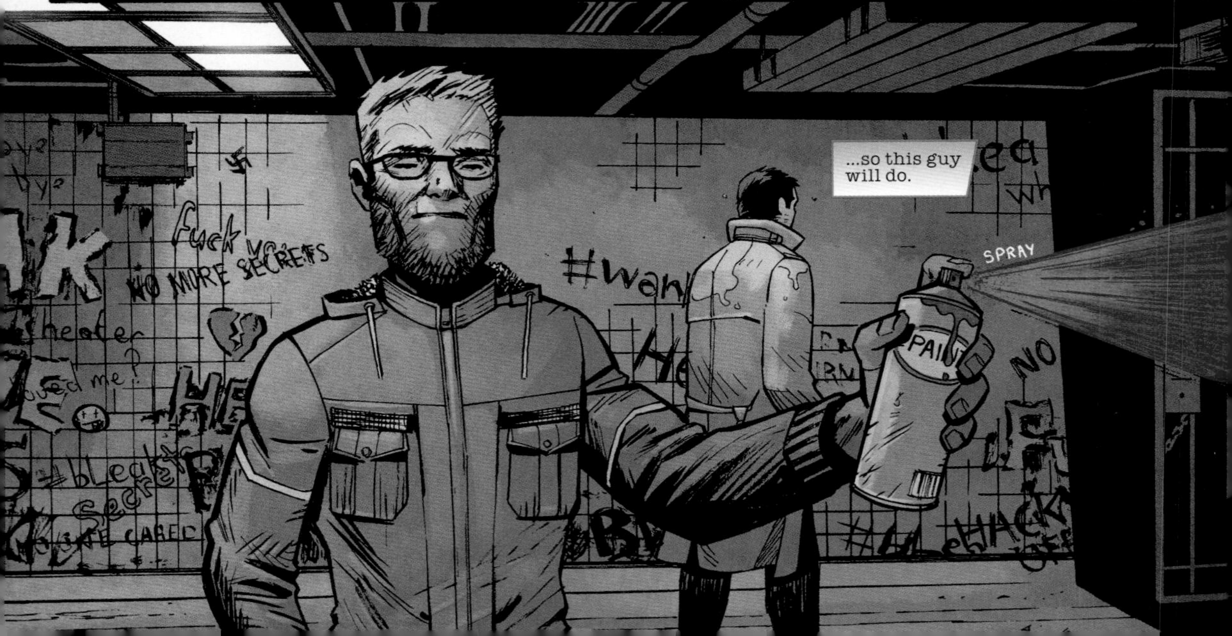
...so this guy will do.
NO MORE SECRETS
SPRAY

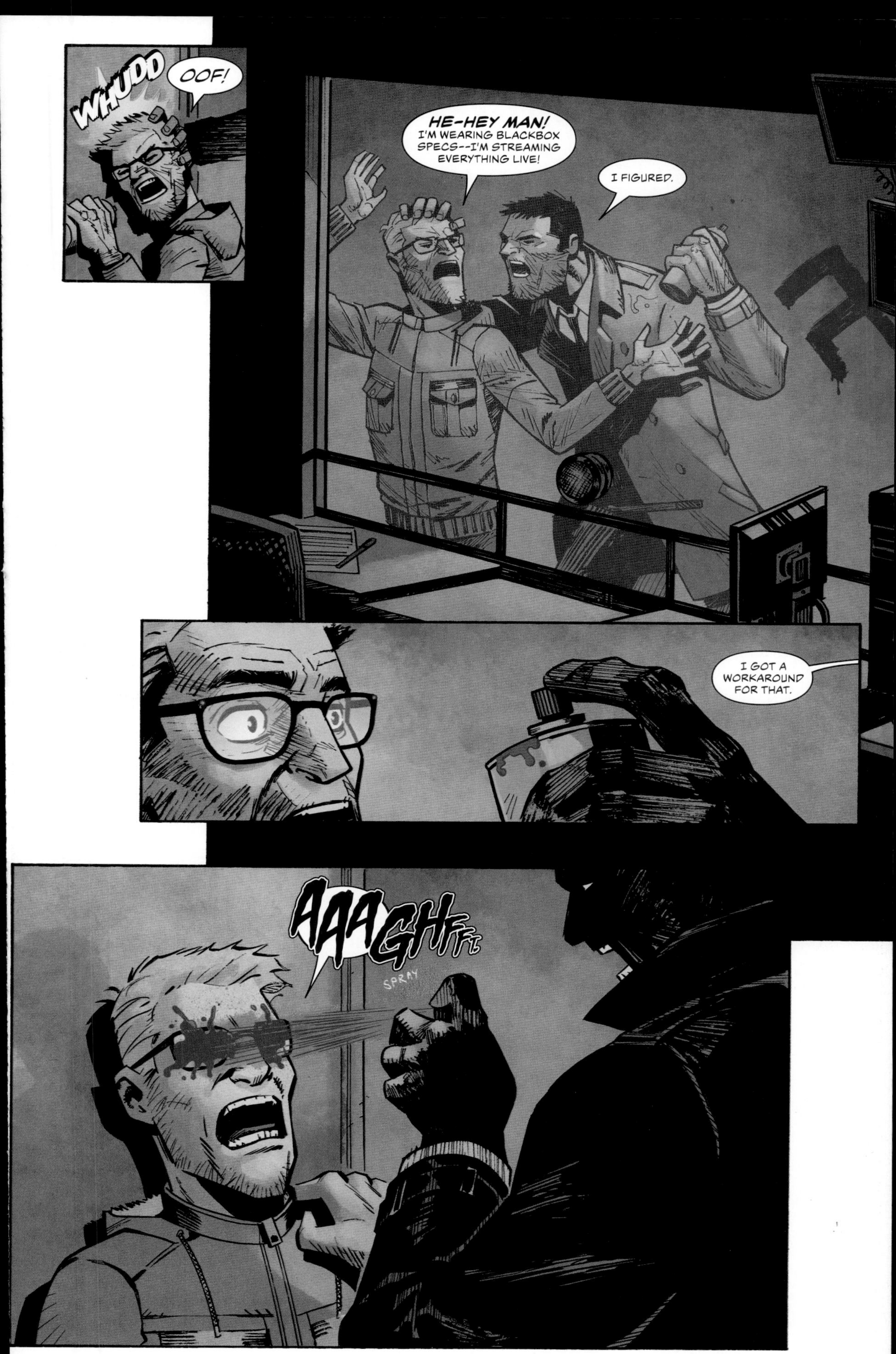
WHUDD
OOF!
HE-HEY MAN! I'M WEARING BLACKBOX SPECS--I'M STREAMING EVERYTHING LIVE!
I FIGURED.
I GOT A WORKAROUND FOR THAT.
AAAGHFF
SPRAY

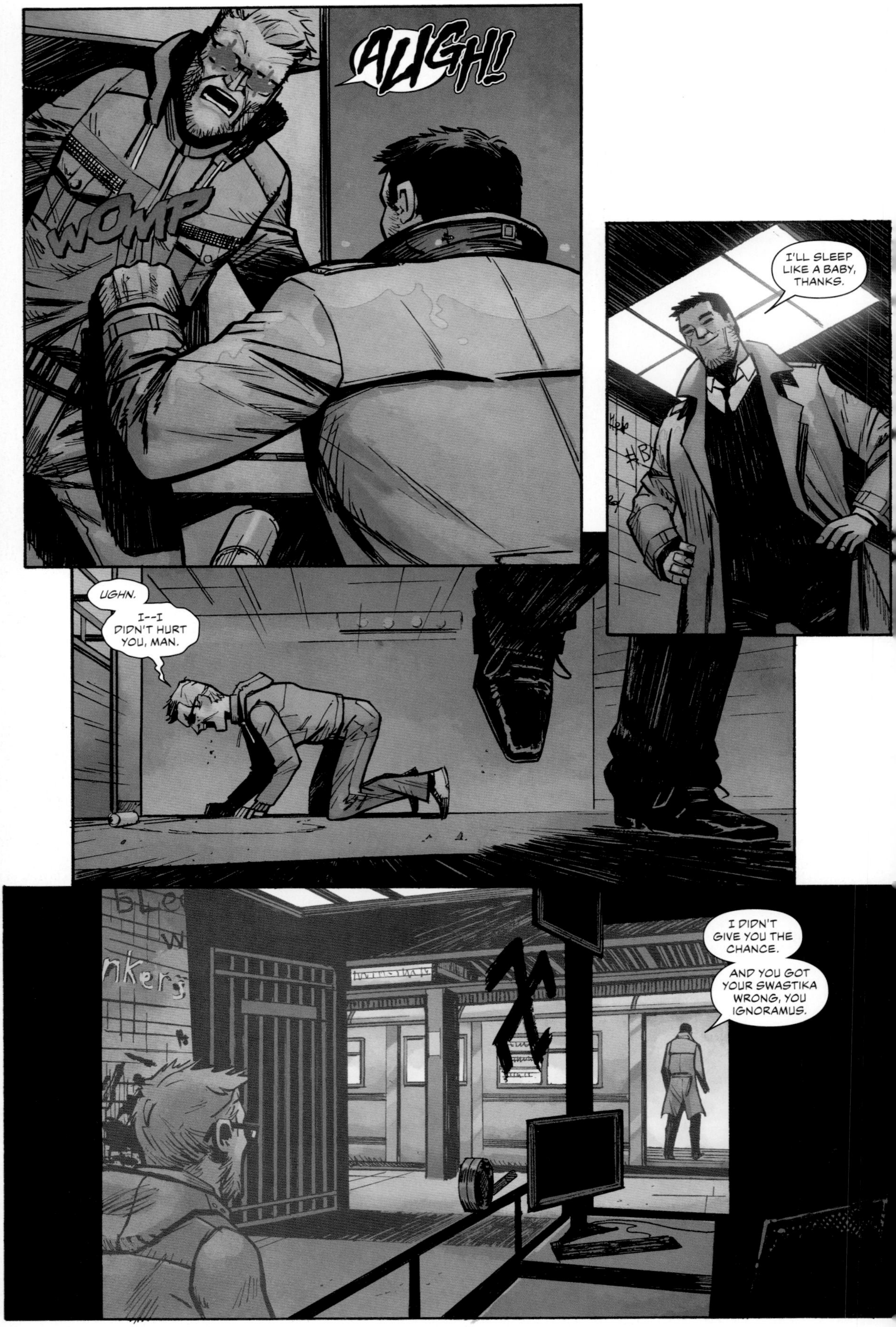
AUGH!!
WOMP
I'LL SLEEP LIKE A BABY, THANKS.
UGHN.
I--I DIDN'T HURT YOU, MAN.
I DIDN'T GIVE YOU THE CHANCE.
AND YOU GOT YOUR SWASTIKA WRONG, YOU IGNORAMUS.

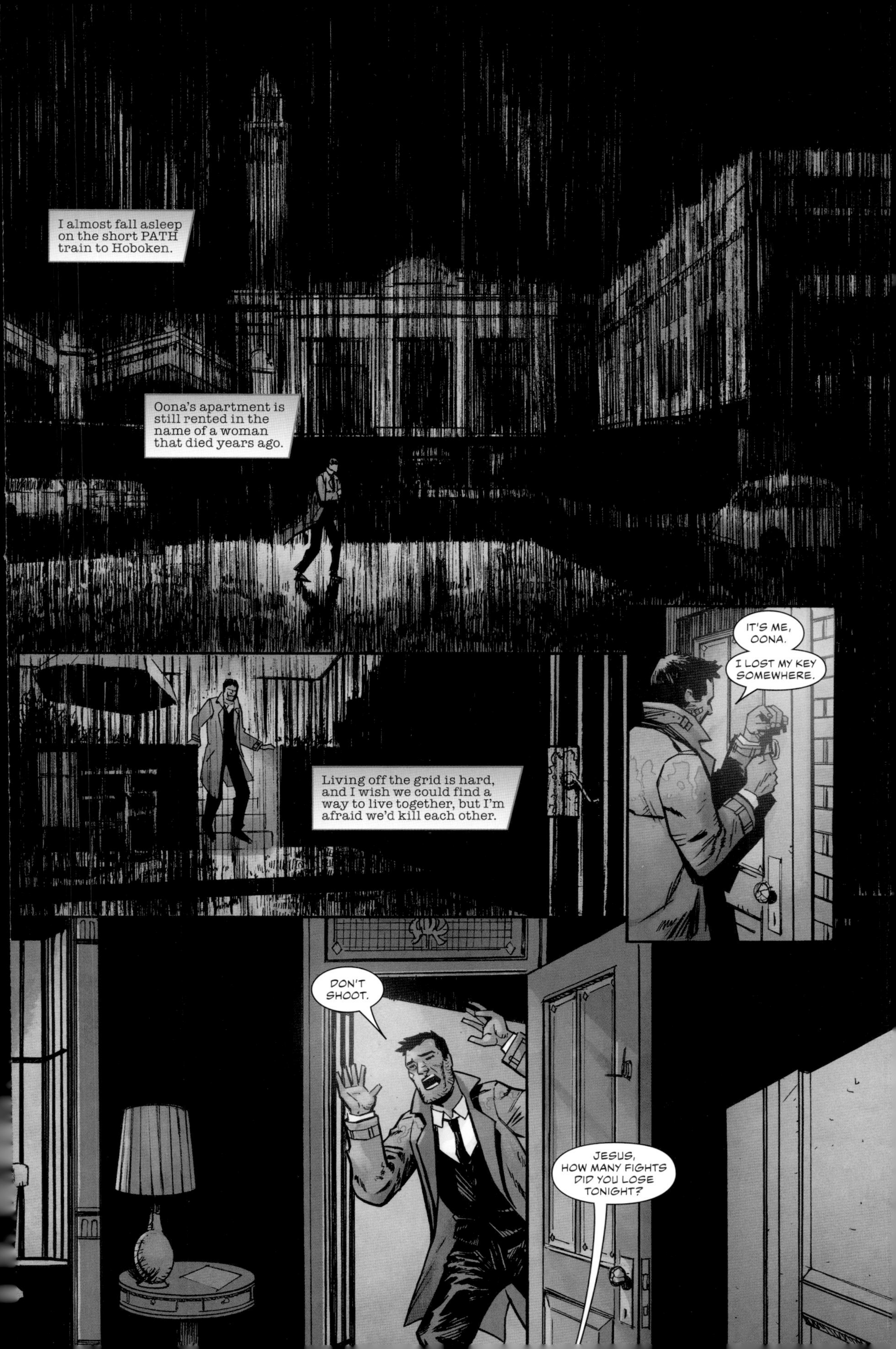
I almost fall asleep on the short PATH train to Hoboken.
Oona's apartment is still rented in the name of a woman that died years ago.
Living off the grid is hard, and I wish we could find a way to live together, but I'm afraid we'd kill each other.
IT'S ME, OONA.
I LOST MY KEY SOMEWHERE.
DON'T SHOOT.
JESUS, HOW MANY FIGHTS DID YOU LOSE TONIGHT?

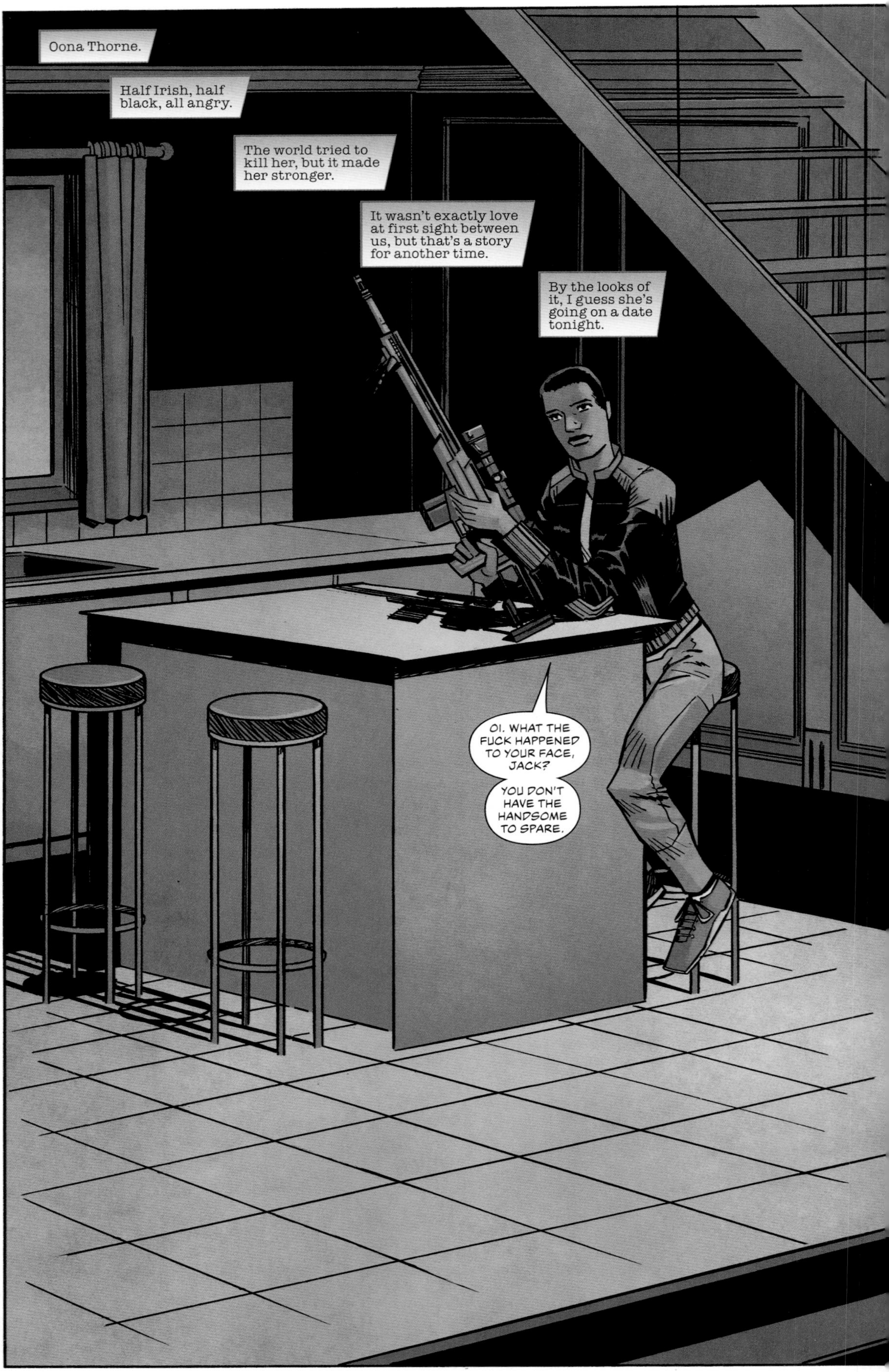
Oona Thorne.
Half Irish, half black, all angry.
The world tried to kill her, but it made her stronger.
It wasn't exactly love at first sight between us, but that's a story for another time.
By the looks of it, I guess she's going on a date tonight.
OI. WHAT THE FUCK HAPPENED TO YOUR FACE, JACK?
YOU DON'T HAVE THE HANDSOME TO SPARE.

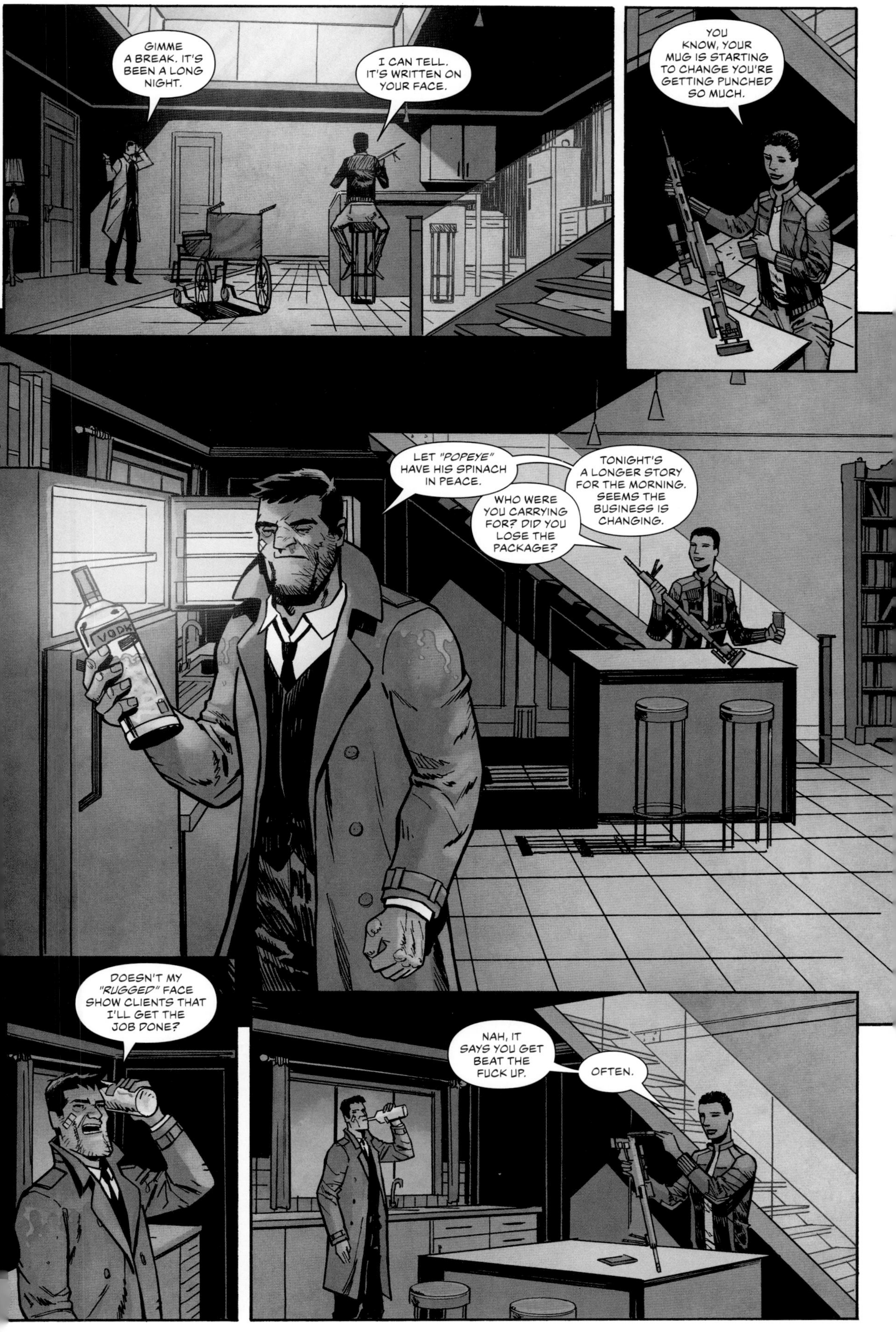
GIMME A BREAK. IT'S BEEN A LONG NIGHT.
I CAN TELL. IT'S WRITTEN ON YOUR FACE.
YOU KNOW, YOUR MUG IS STARTING TO CHANGE YOU'RE GETTING PUNCHED SO MUCH.
LET "POPEYE" HAVE HIS SPINACH IN PEACE.
TONIGHT'S A LONGER STORY FOR THE MORNING. SEEMS THE BUSINESS IS CHANGING.
WHO WERE YOU CARRYING FOR? DID YOU LOSE THE PACKAGE?
DOESN'T MY "RUGGED" FACE SHOW CLIENTS THAT I'LL GET THE JOB DONE?
NAH, IT SAYS YOU GET BEAT THE FUCK UP.
OFTEN.

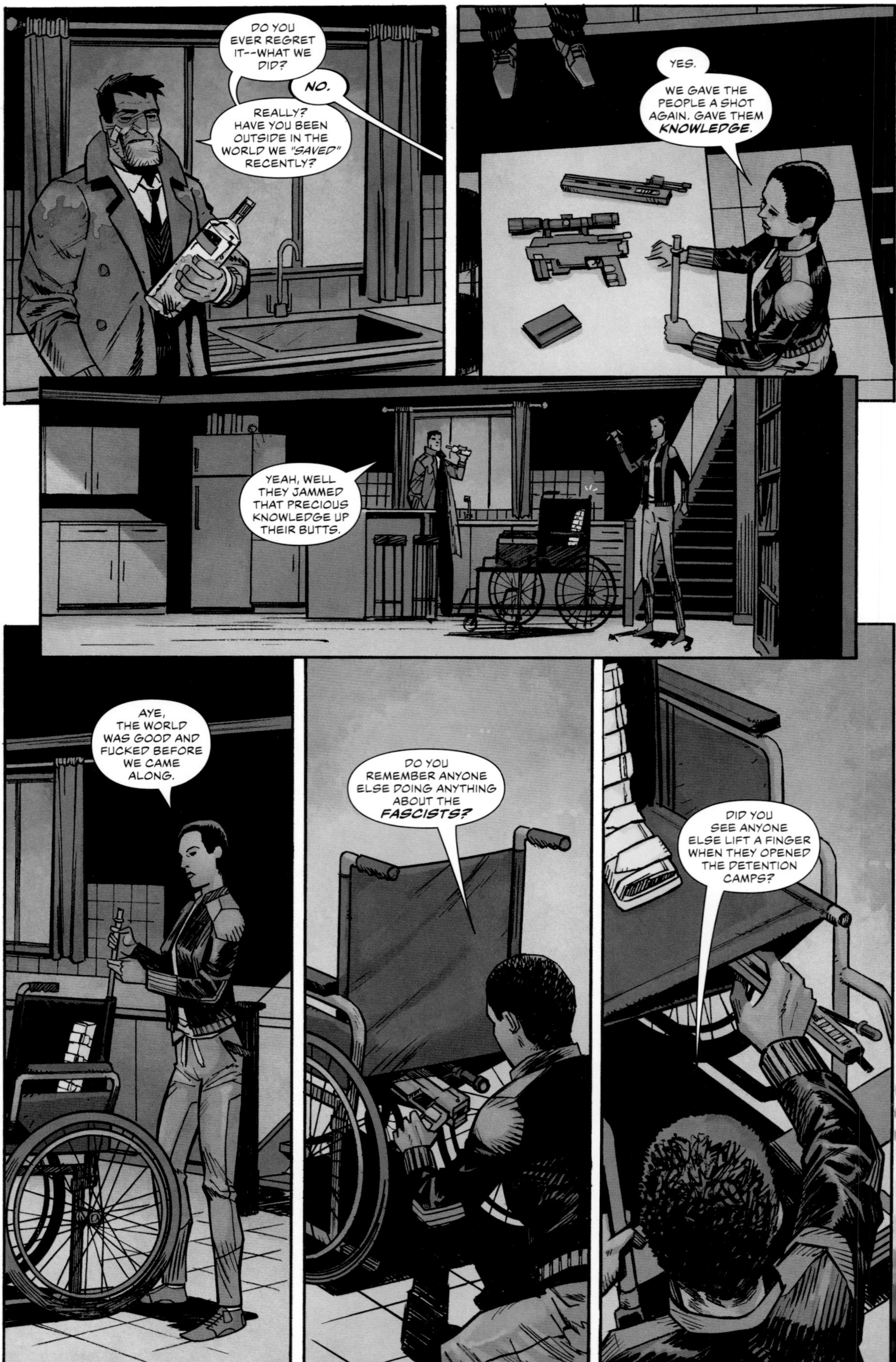
DO YOU EVER REGRET IT--WHAT WE DID?
NO.
REALLY? HAVE YOU BEEN OUTSIDE IN THE WORLD WE "SAVED" RECENTLY?
YES.
WE GAVE THE PEOPLE A SHOT AGAIN. GAVE THEM KNOWLEDGE.
YEAH, WELL THEY JAMMED THAT PRECIOUS KNOWLEDGE UP THEIR BUTTS.
AYE, THE WORLD WAS GOOD AND FUCKED BEFORE WE CAME ALONG.
DO YOU REMEMBER ANYONE ELSE DOING ANYTHING ABOUT THE FASCISTS?
DID YOU SEE ANYONE ELSE LIFT A FINGER WHEN THEY OPENED THE DETENTION CAMPS?

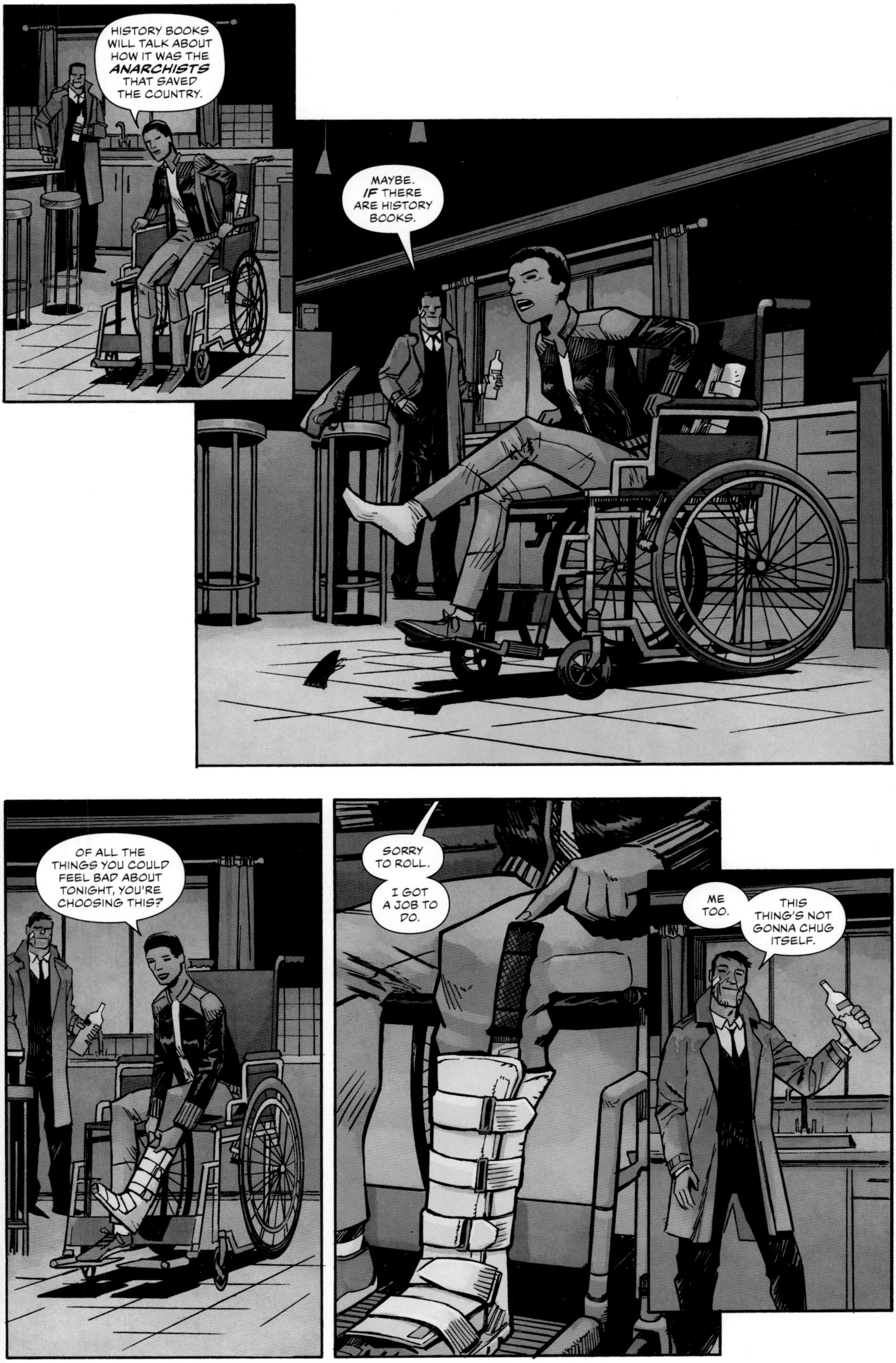
HISTORY BOOKS WILL TALK ABOUT HOW IT WAS THE ANARCHISTS THAT SAVED THE COUNTRY.
MAYBE. IF THERE ARE HISTORY BOOKS.
OF ALL THE THINGS YOU COULD FEEL BAD ABOUT TONIGHT, YOU'RE CHOOSING THIS?
SORRY TO ROLL.
I GOT A JOB TO DO.
ME TOO.
THIS THING'S NOT GONNA CHUG ITSELF.

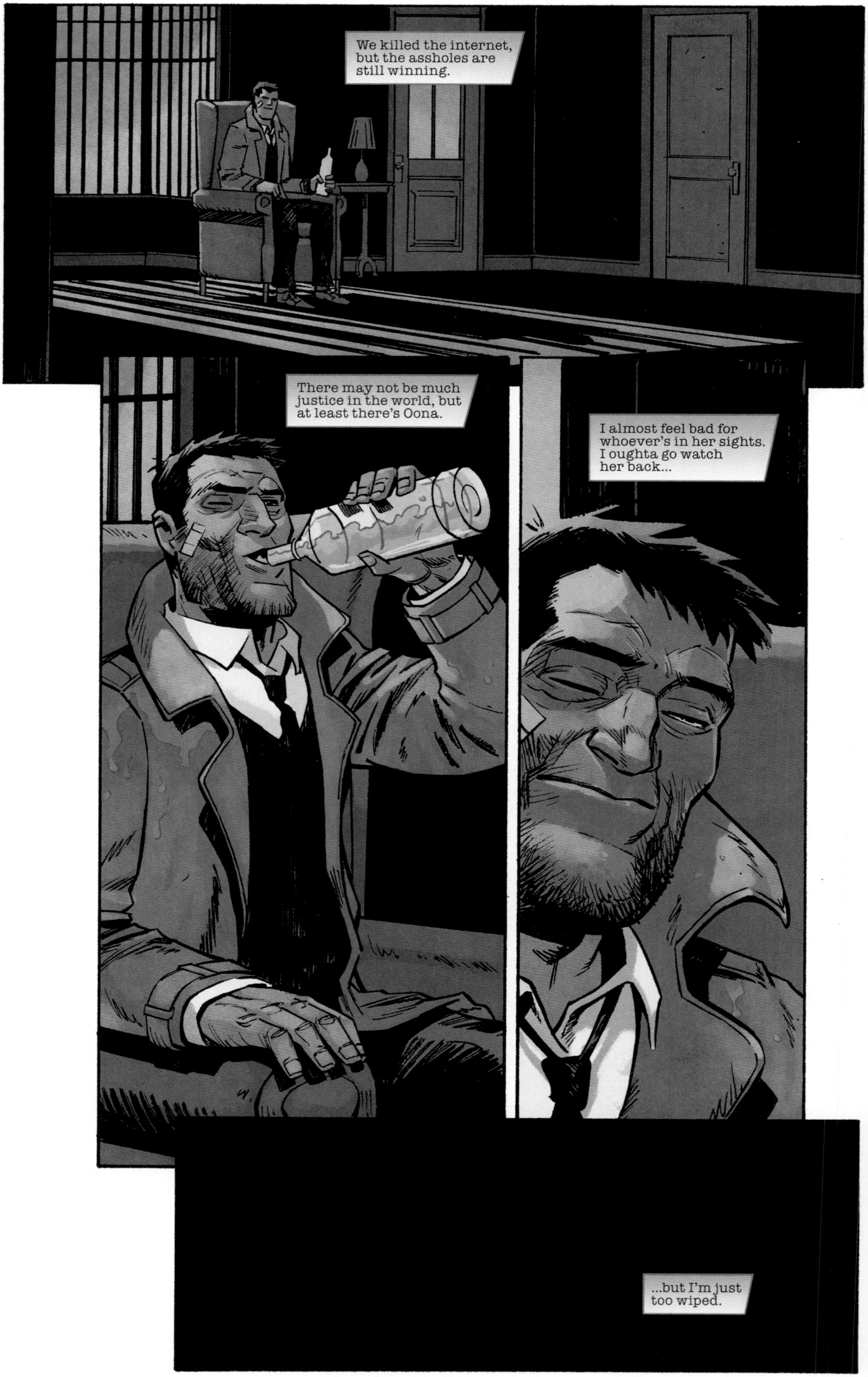
We killed the internet, but the assholes are still winning.
There may not be much justice in the world, but at least there's Oona.
I almost feel bad for whoever's in her sights. I oughta go watch her back...
...but I'm just too wiped.

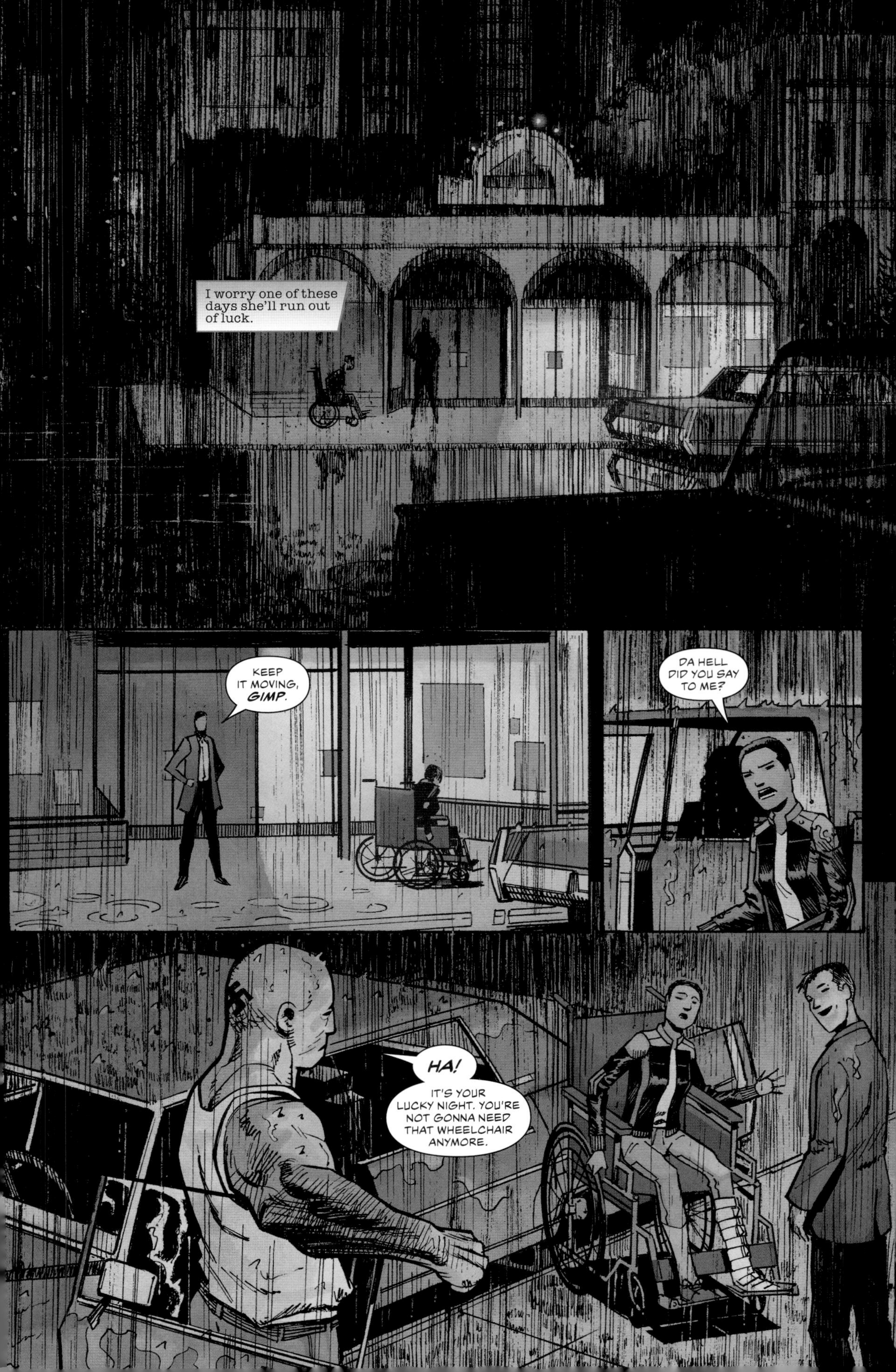
I worry one of these days she'll run out of luck.
KEEP IT MOVING, GIMP.
DA HELL DID YOU SAY TO ME?
HA!
IT'S YOUR LUCKY NIGHT. YOU'RE NOT GONNA NEED THAT WHEELCHAIR ANYMORE.

CHAPTER 3

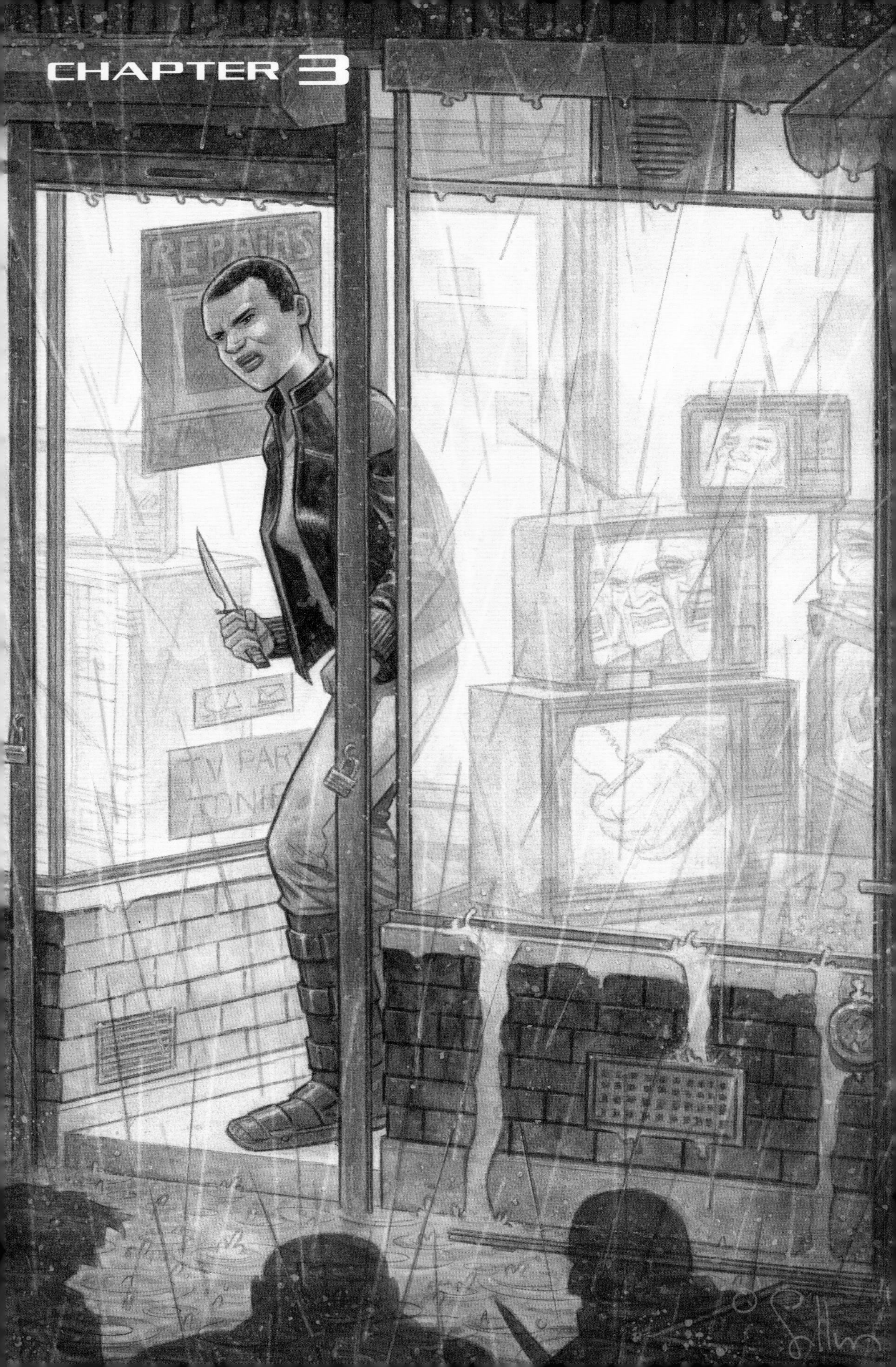

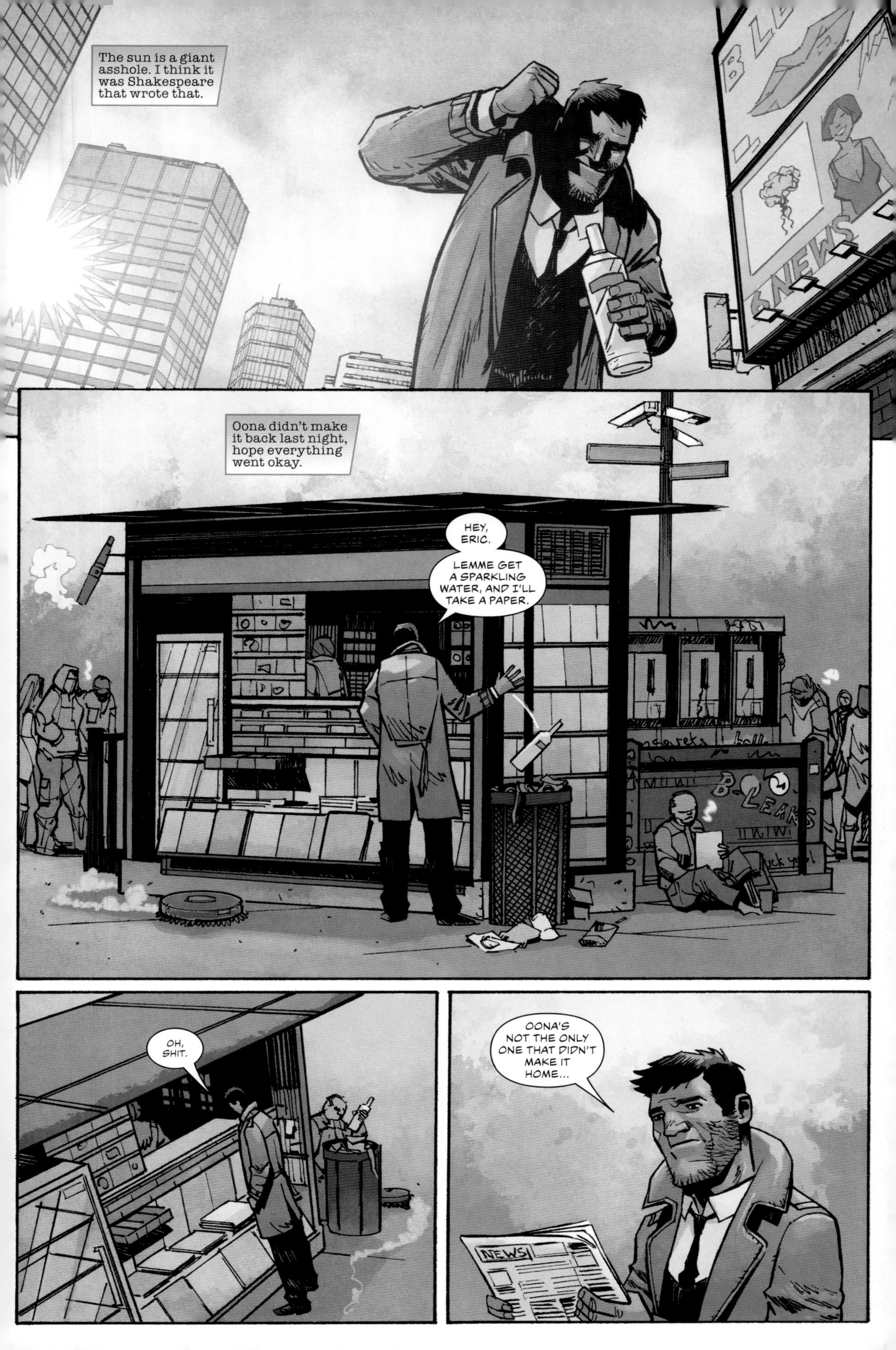
The sun is a giant asshole. I think it was Shakespeare that wrote that.
NEWS
Oona didn't make it back last night, hope everything went okay.
HEY, ERIC.
LEMME GET A SPARKLING WATER, AND I'LL TAKE A PAPER.
OH, SHIT.
OONA'S NOT THE ONLY ONE THAT DIDN'T MAKE IT HOME...
NEWS

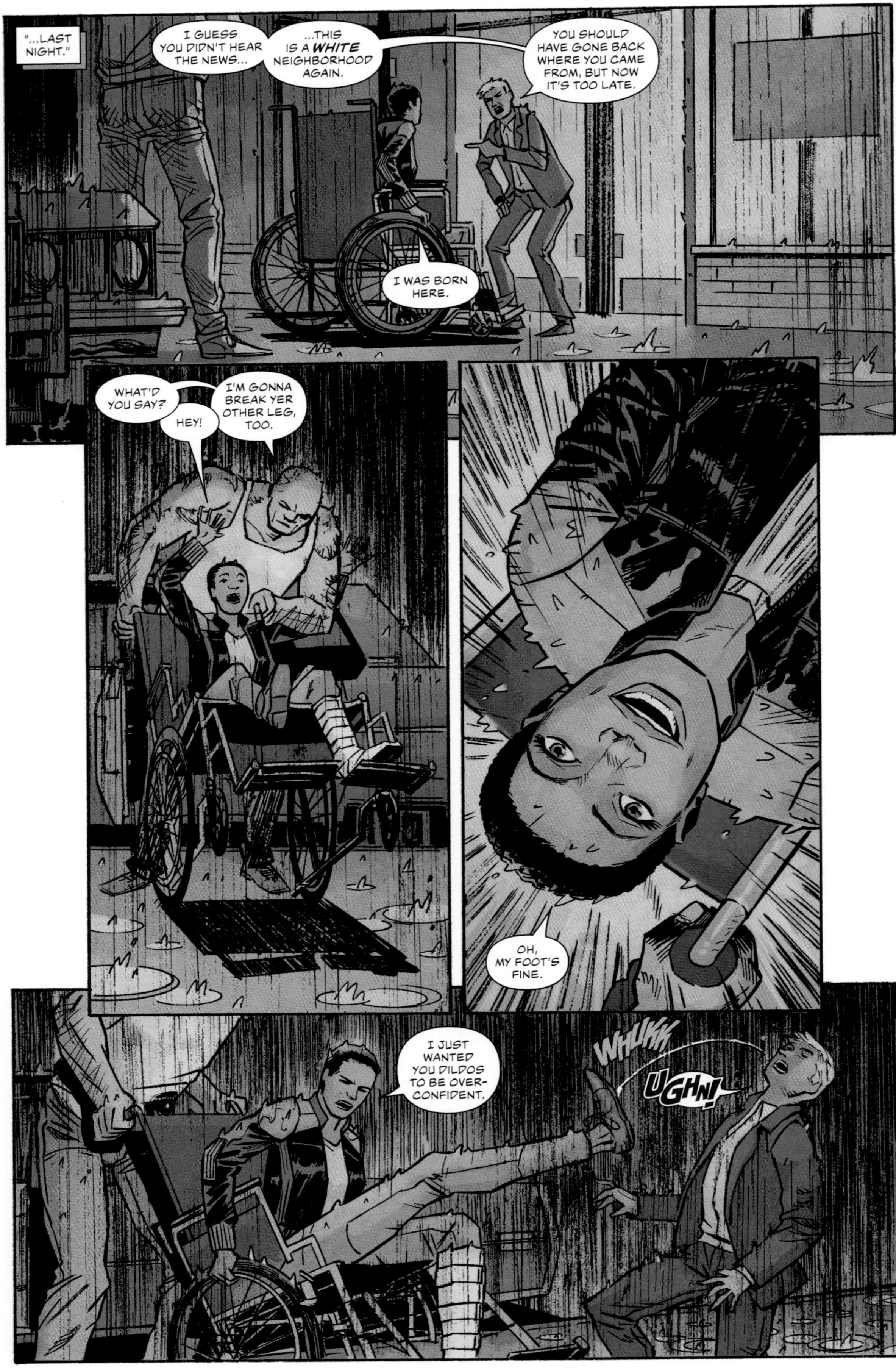
"...LAST NIGHT."
I GUESS YOU DIDN'T HEAR THE NEWS...
...THIS IS A WHITE NEIGHBORHOOD AGAIN.
YOU SHOULD HAVE GONE BACK WHERE YOU CAME FROM, BUT NOW IT'S TOO LATE.
I WAS BORN HERE.
WHAT'D YOU SAY?
I'M GONNA BREAK YER OTHER LEG, TOO.
HEY!
OH, MY FOOT'S FINE.
I JUST WANTED YOU DILDOS TO BE OVER-CONFIDENT.
WHUKK
UGHN!

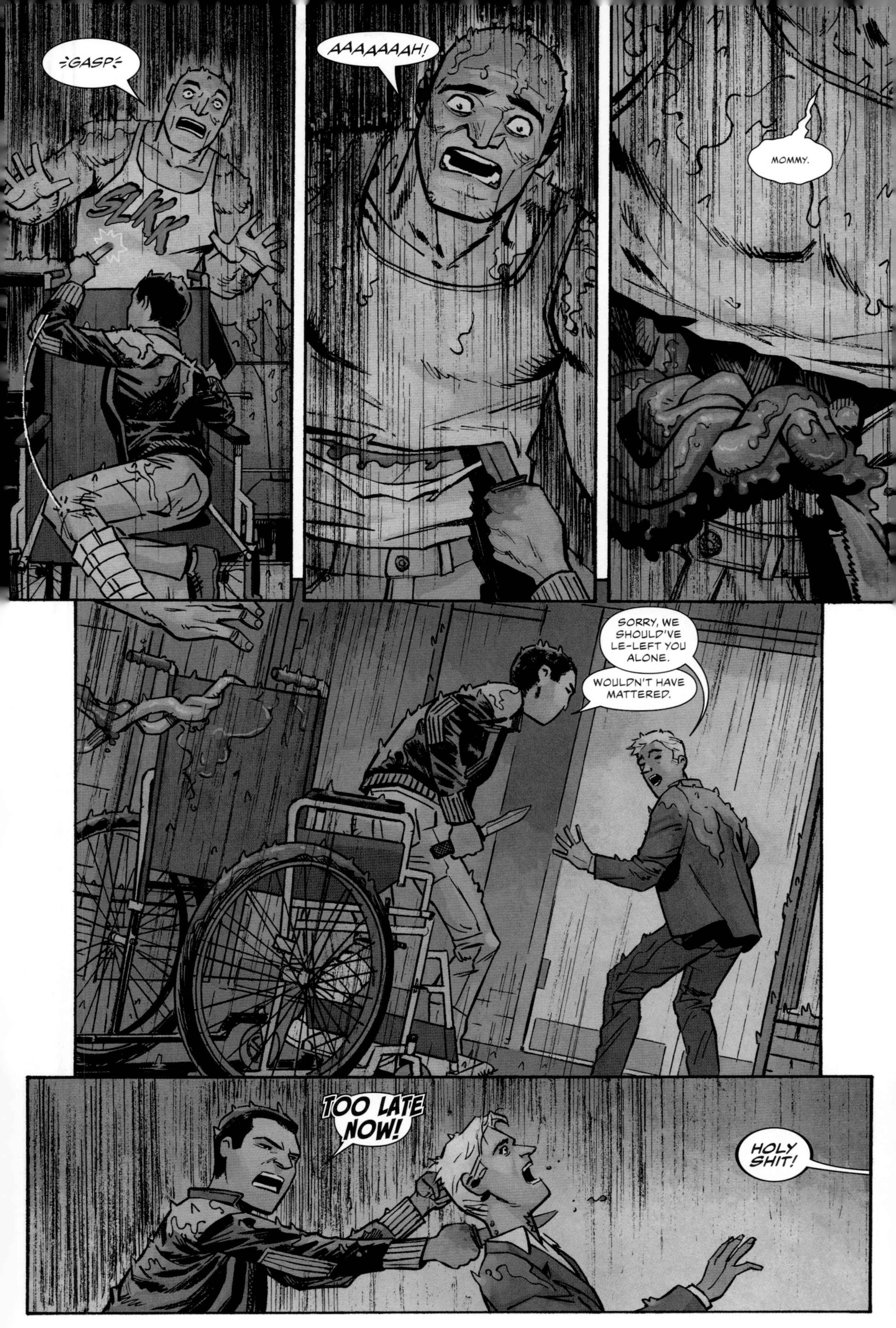
GASP
SLKK
AAAAAAAH!
MOMMY.
SORRY, WE SHOULD'VE LE-LEFT YOU ALONE.
WOULDN'T HAVE MATTERED.
TOO LATE NOW!
HOLY SHIT!

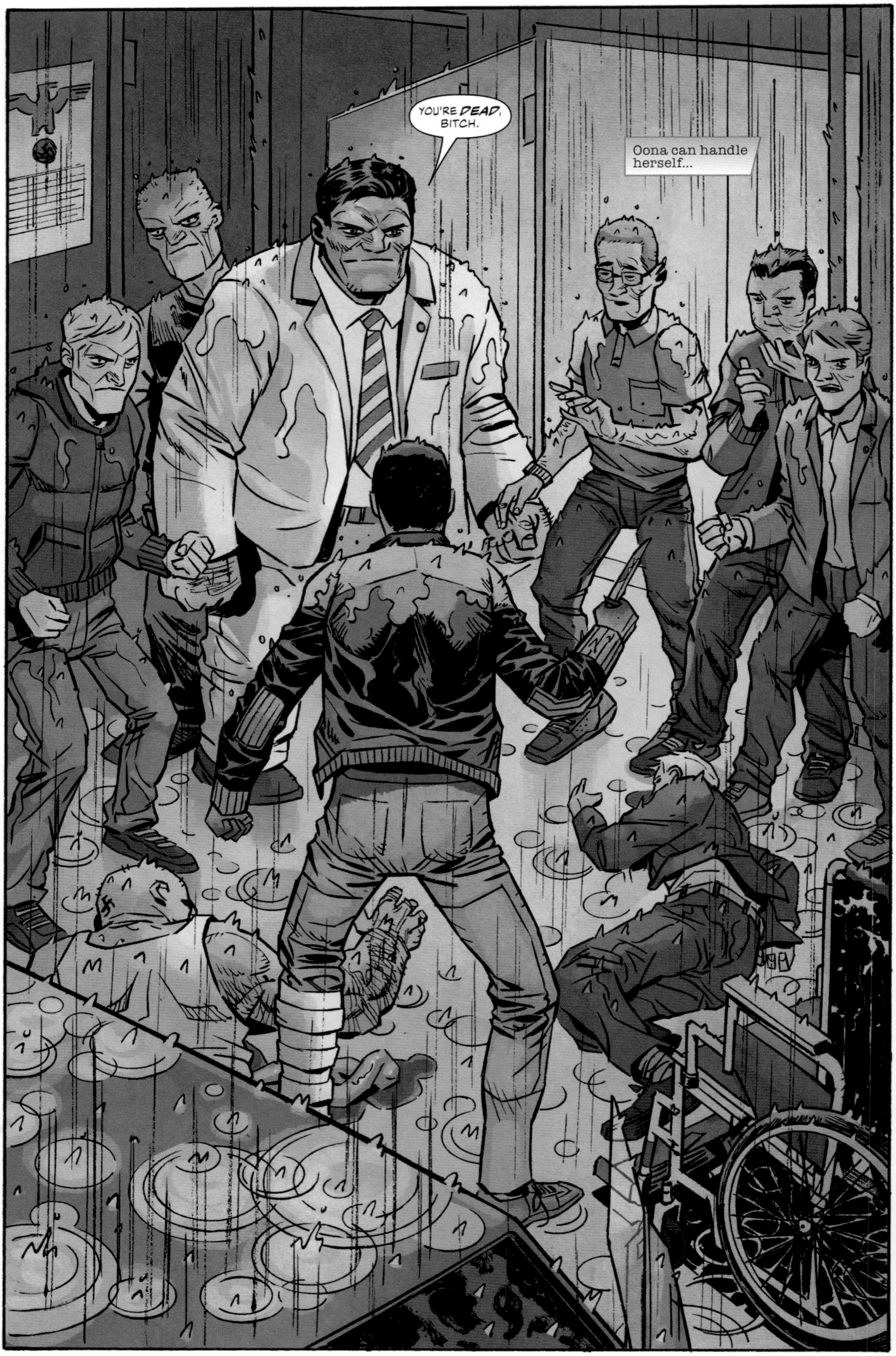
YOU'RE *DEAD*, BITCH.
Oona can handle herself...

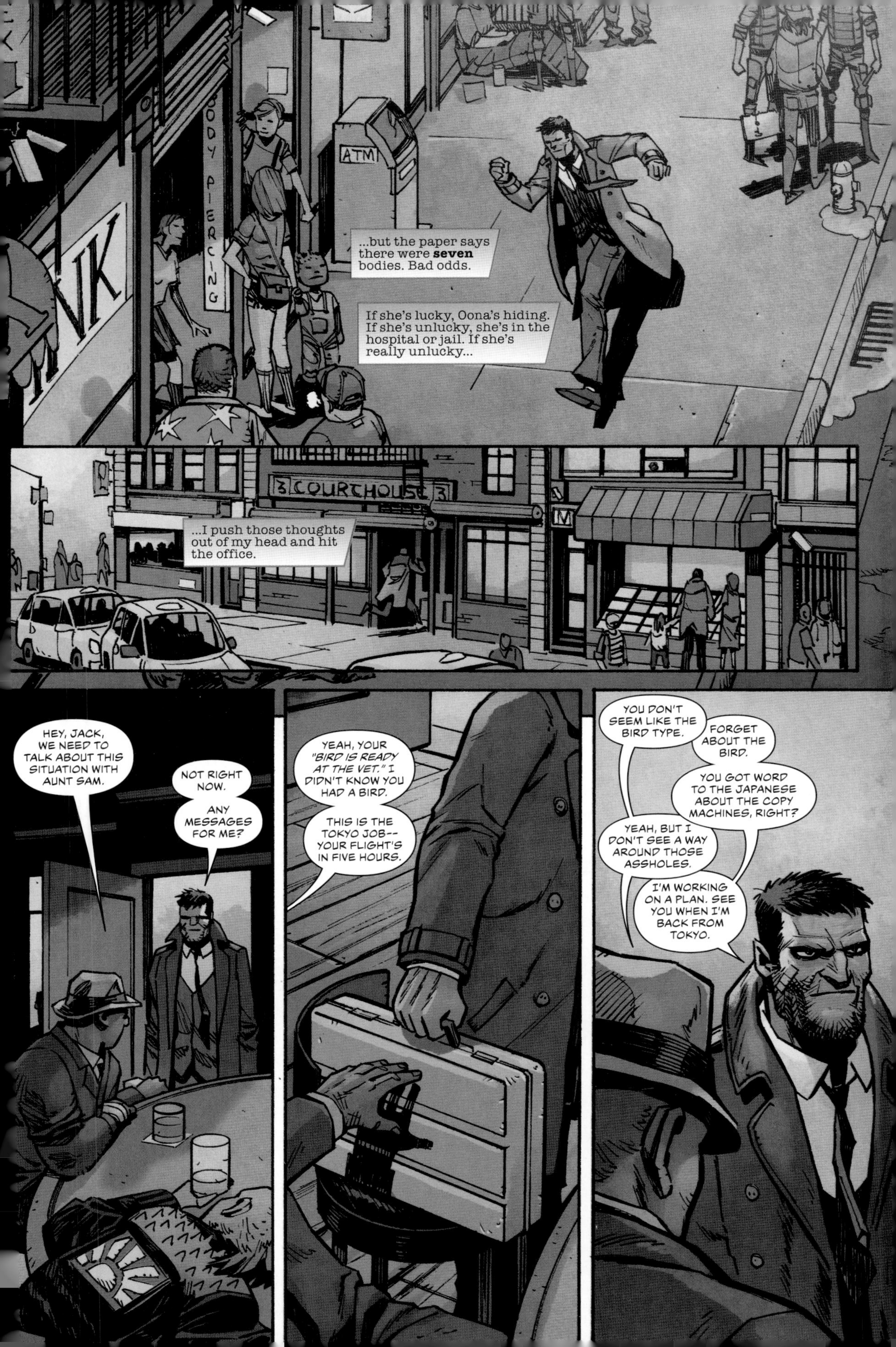
ATM
BODY PIERCING
...but the paper says there were **seven** bodies. Bad odds.
If she's lucky, Oona's hiding. If she's unlucky, she's in the hospital or jail. If she's really unlucky...
COURTHOUSE
...I push those thoughts out of my head and hit the office.
HEY, JACK, WE NEED TO TALK ABOUT THIS SITUATION WITH AUNT SAM.
NOT RIGHT NOW.
ANY MESSAGES FOR ME?
YEAH, YOUR *"BIRD IS READY AT THE VET."* I DIDN'T KNOW YOU HAD A BIRD.
THIS IS THE TOKYO JOB-- YOUR FLIGHT'S IN FIVE HOURS.
YOU DON'T SEEM LIKE THE BIRD TYPE.
FORGET ABOUT THE BIRD.
YOU GOT WORD TO THE JAPANESE ABOUT THE COPY MACHINES, RIGHT?
YEAH, BUT I DON'T SEE A WAY AROUND THOSE ASSHOLES.
I'M WORKING ON A PLAN. SEE YOU WHEN I'M BACK FROM TOKYO.

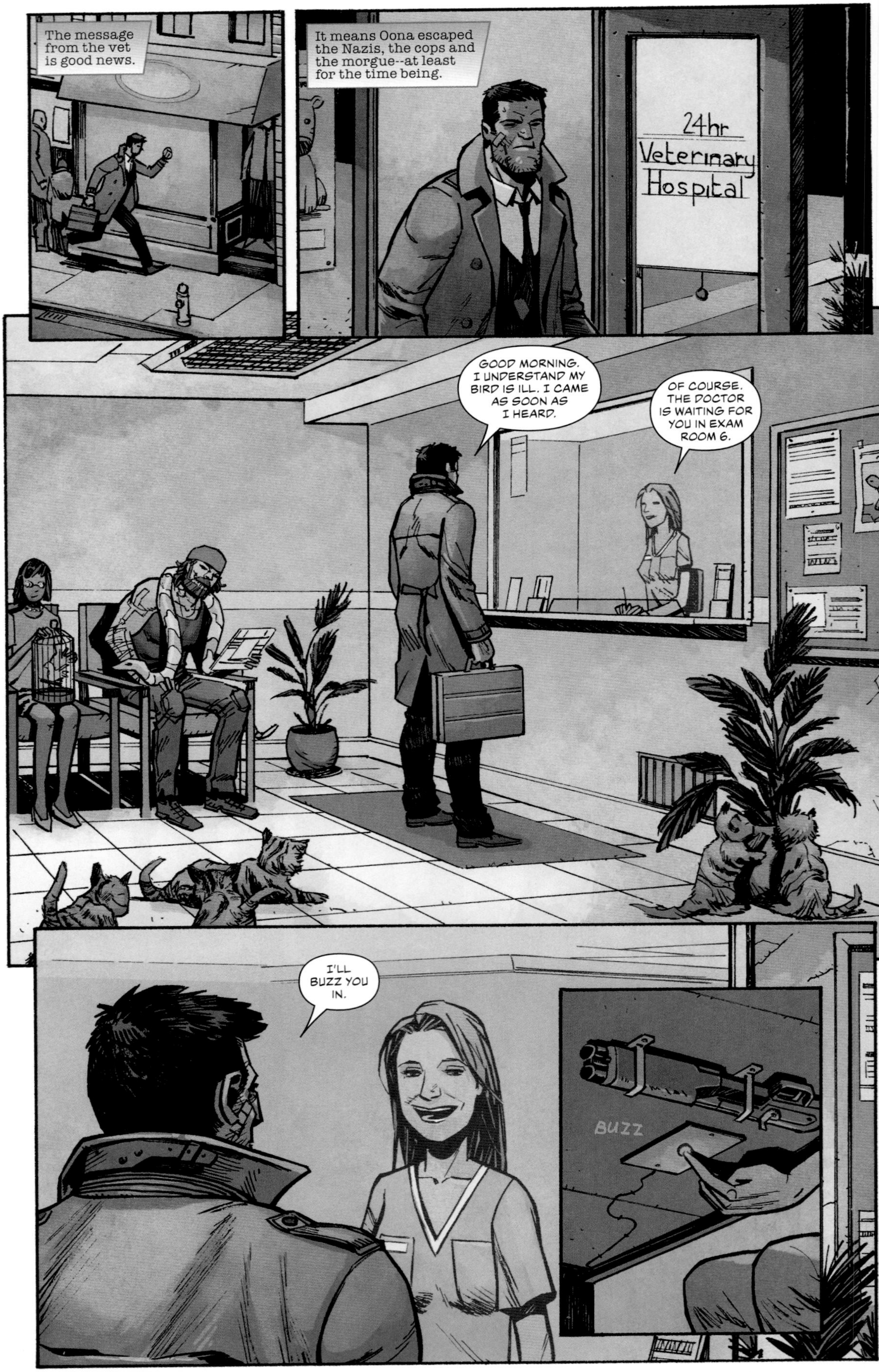
The message from the vet is good news.
It means Oona escaped the Nazis, the cops and the morgue--at least for the time being.
24hr Veterinary Hospital
GOOD MORNING. I UNDERSTAND MY BIRD IS ILL. I CAME AS SOON AS I HEARD.
OF COURSE. THE DOCTOR IS WAITING FOR YOU IN EXAM ROOM 6.
I'LL BUZZ YOU IN.
BUZZ

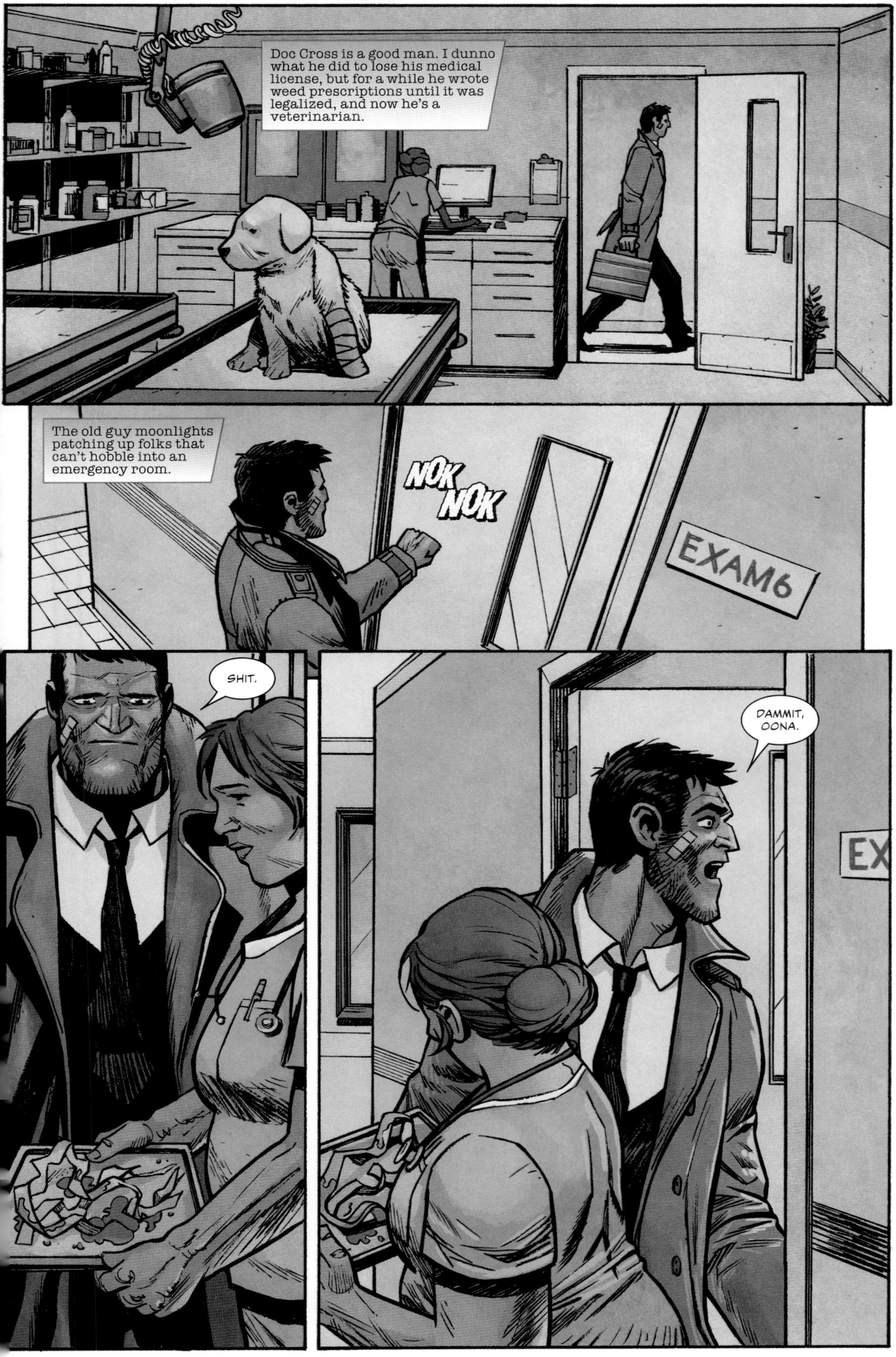
Doc Cross is a good man. I dunno what he did to lose his medical license, but for a while he wrote weed prescriptions until it was legalized, and now he's a veterinarian.
The old guy moonlights patching up folks that can't hobble into an emergency room.
NOK NOK
EXAM6
SHIT.
DAMMIT, OONA.

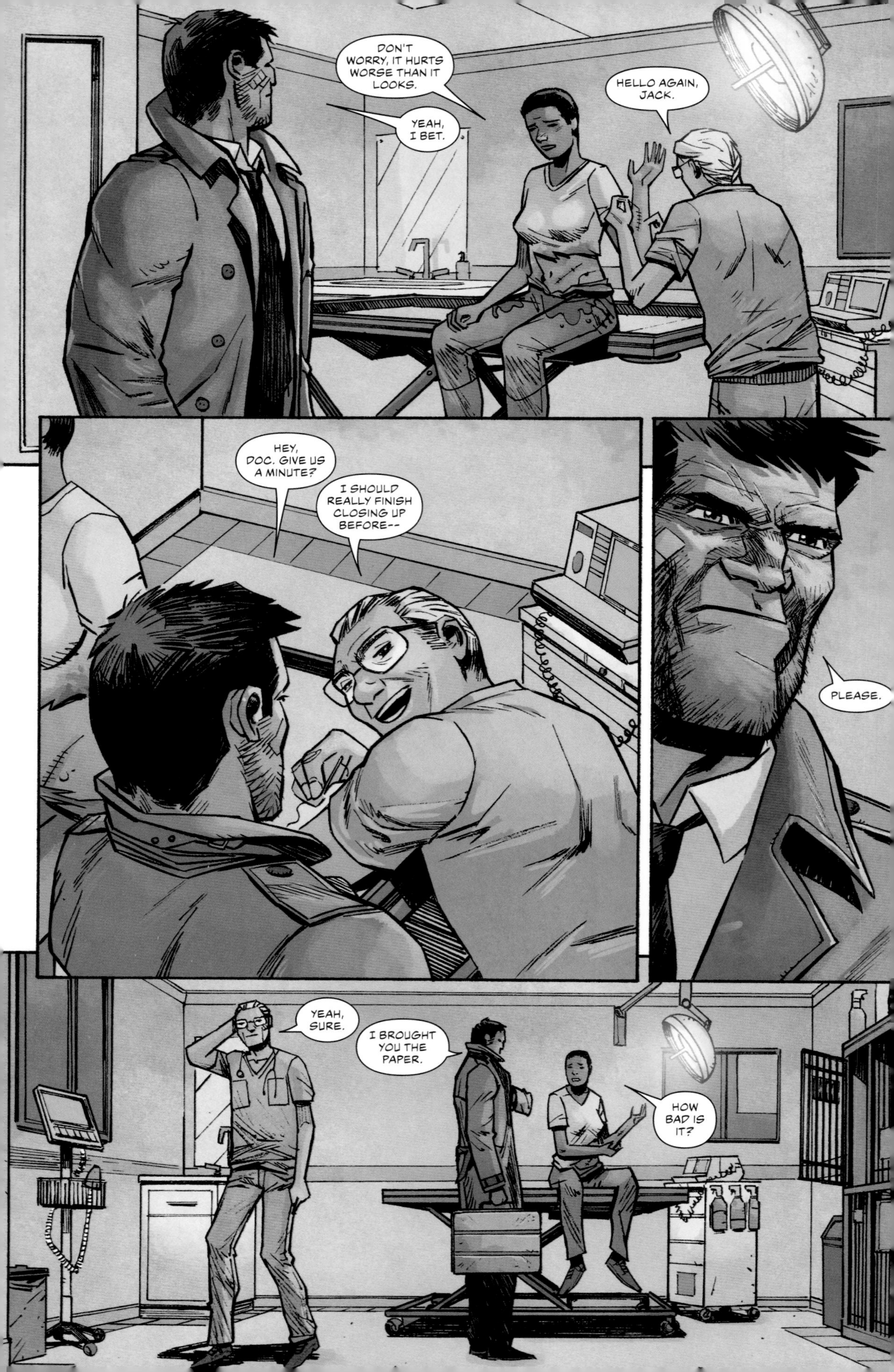
DON'T WORRY, IT HURTS WORSE THAN IT LOOKS.
YEAH, I BET.
HELLO AGAIN, JACK.
HEY, DOC. GIVE US A MINUTE?
I SHOULD REALLY FINISH CLOSING UP BEFORE--
PLEASE.
YEAH, SURE.
I BROUGHT YOU THE PAPER.
HOW BAD IS IT?

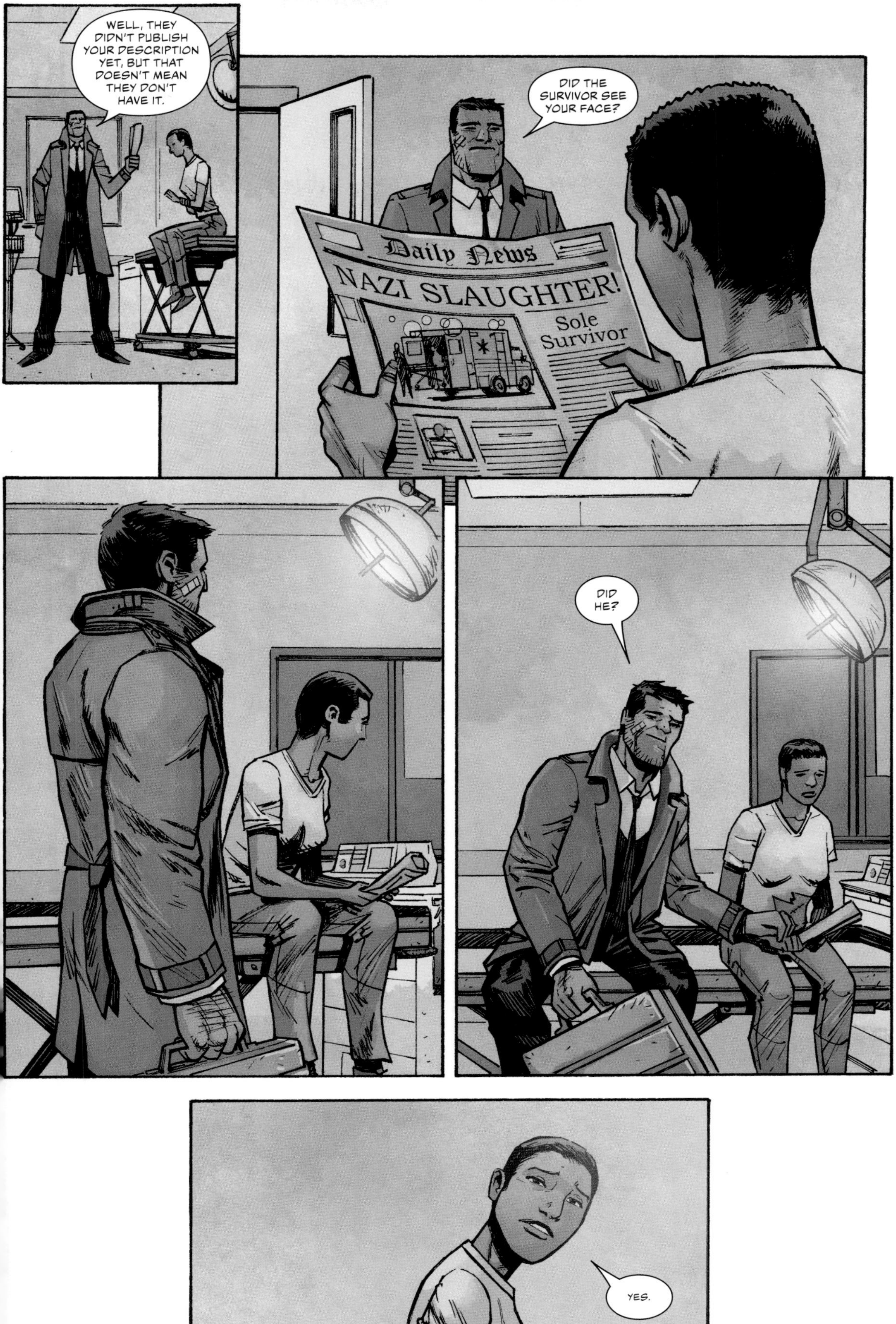

WELL, THEY DIDN'T PUBLISH YOUR DESCRIPTION YET, BUT THAT DOESN'T MEAN THEY DON'T HAVE IT.
DID THE SURVIVOR SEE YOUR FACE?
Daily News
NAZI SLAUGHTER!
Sole Survivor
DID HE?
YES.

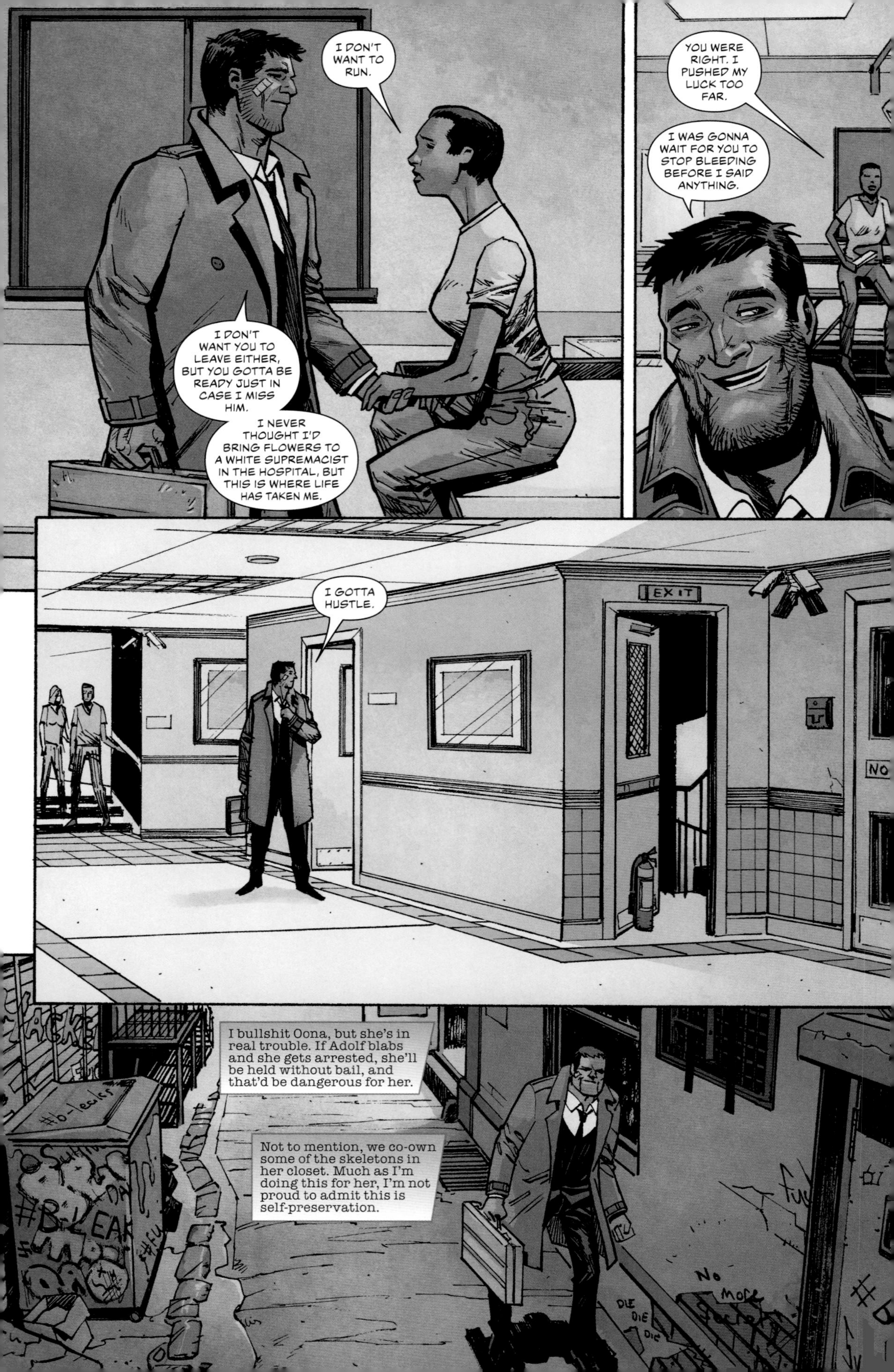
I DON'T WANT TO RUN.
I DON'T WANT YOU TO LEAVE EITHER, BUT YOU GOTTA BE READY JUST IN CASE I MISS HIM.
I NEVER THOUGHT I'D BRING FLOWERS TO A WHITE SUPREMACIST IN THE HOSPITAL, BUT THIS IS WHERE LIFE HAS TAKEN ME.
YOU WERE RIGHT. I PUSHED MY LUCK TOO FAR.
I WAS GONNA WAIT FOR YOU TO STOP BLEEDING BEFORE I SAID ANYTHING.
I GOTTA HUSTLE.
EXIT
I bullshit Oona, but she's in real trouble. If Adolf blabs and she gets arrested, she'll be held without bail, and that'd be dangerous for her.
Not to mention, we co-own some of the skeletons in her closet. Much as I'm doing this for her, I'm not proud to admit this is self-preservation.

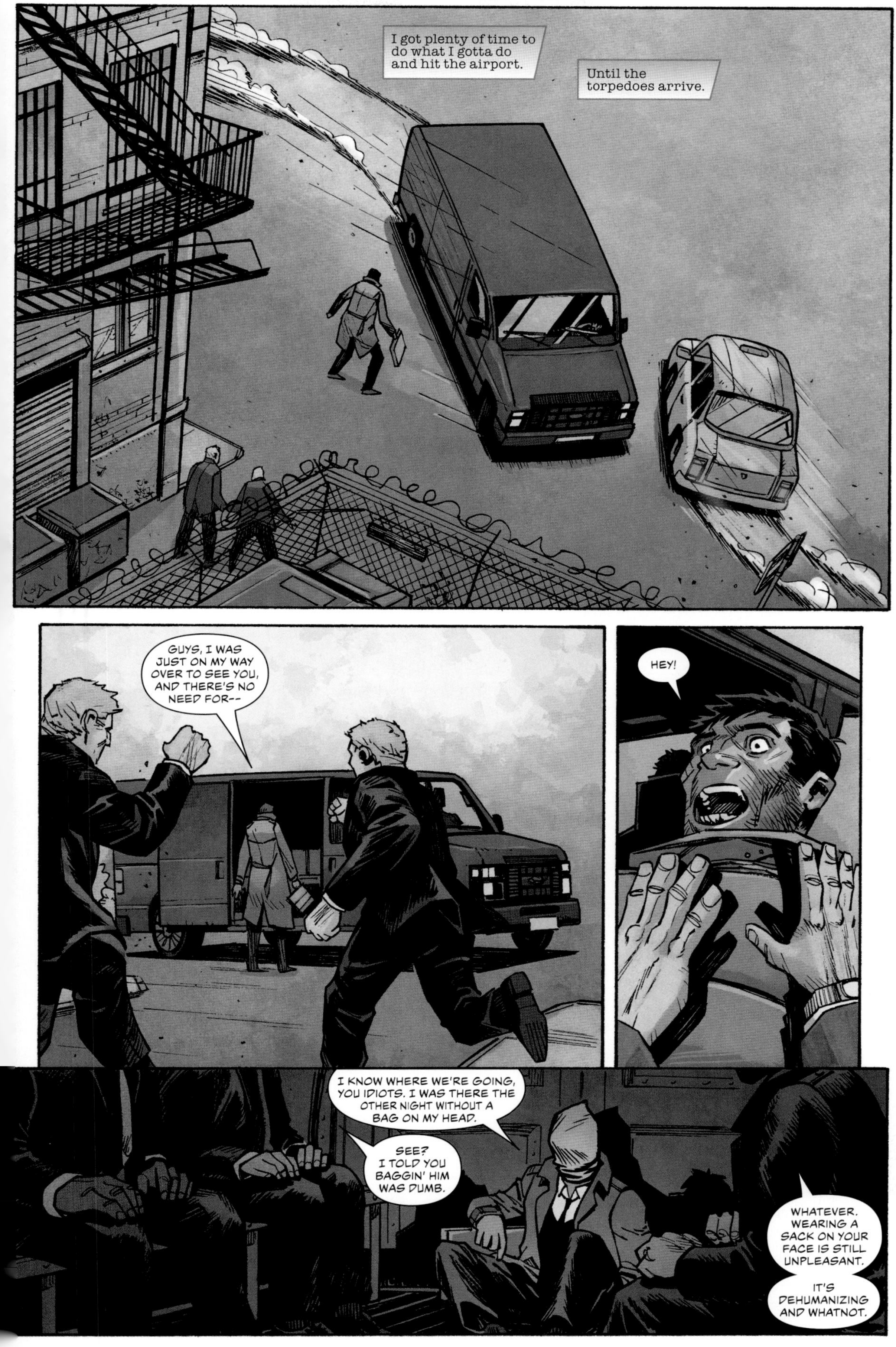

I got plenty of time to do what I gotta do and hit the airport.
Until the torpedoes arrive.
GUYS, I WAS JUST ON MY WAY OVER TO SEE YOU, AND THERE'S NO NEED FOR--
HEY!
I KNOW WHERE WE'RE GOING, YOU IDIOTS. I WAS THERE THE OTHER NIGHT WITHOUT A BAG ON MY HEAD.
SEE? I TOLD YOU BAGGIN' HIM WAS DUMB.
WHATEVER. WEARING A SACK ON YOUR FACE IS STILL UNPLEASANT.
IT'S DEHUMANIZING AND WHATNOT.

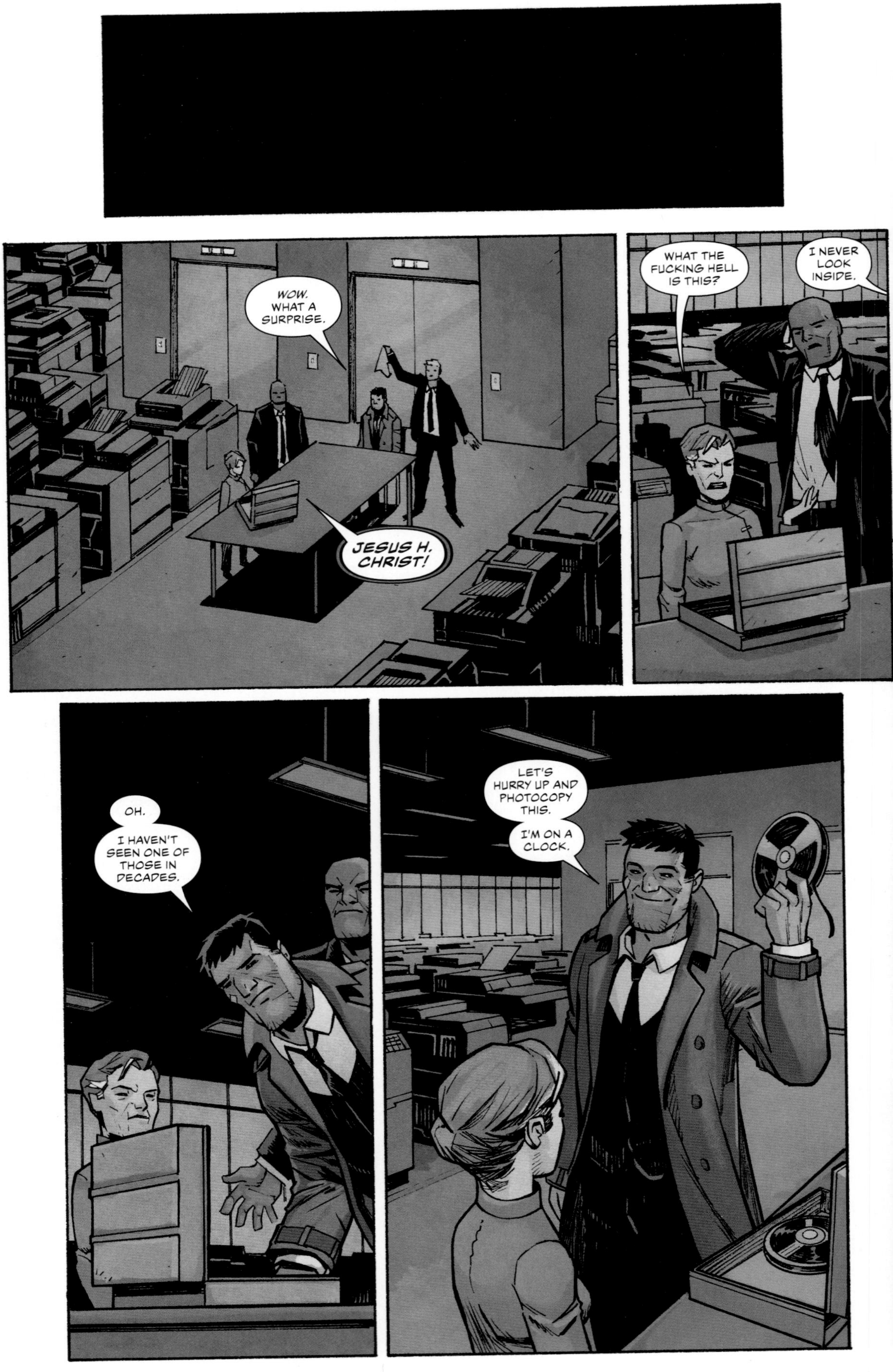
WOW. WHAT A SURPRISE.
JESUS H. CHRIST!
WHAT THE FUCKING HELL IS THIS?
I NEVER LOOK INSIDE.
OH.
I HAVEN'T SEEN ONE OF THOSE IN DECADES.
LET'S HURRY UP AND PHOTOCOPY THIS.
I'M ON A CLOCK.

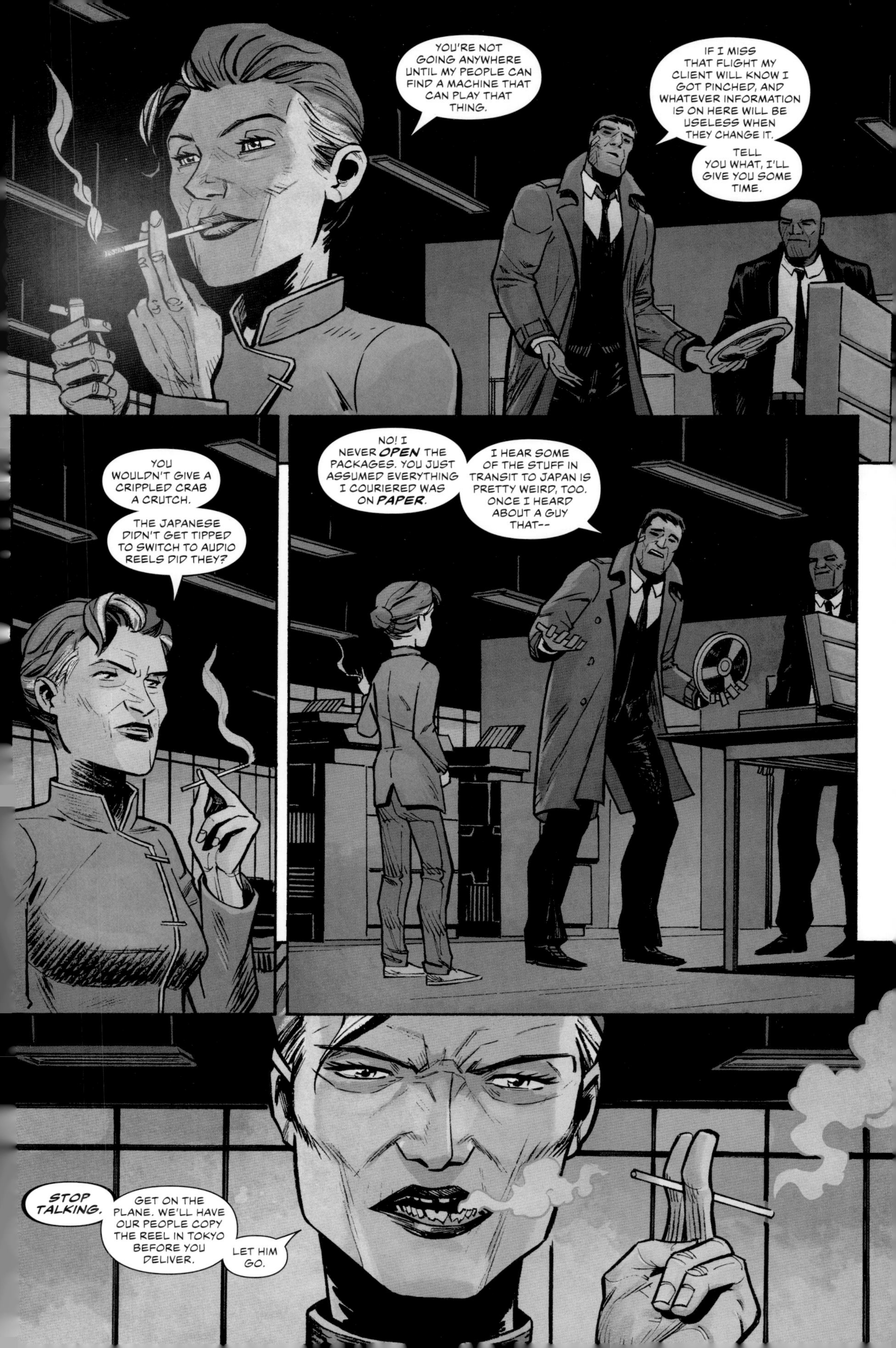
YOU'RE NOT GOING ANYWHERE UNTIL MY PEOPLE CAN FIND A MACHINE THAT CAN PLAY THAT THING.
IF I MISS THAT FLIGHT MY CLIENT WILL KNOW I GOT PINCHED, AND WHATEVER INFORMATION IS ON HERE WILL BE USELESS WHEN THEY CHANGE IT.
TELL YOU WHAT, I'LL GIVE YOU SOME TIME.
YOU WOULDN'T GIVE A CRIPPLED CRAB A CRUTCH.
THE JAPANESE DIDN'T GET TIPPED TO SWITCH TO AUDIO REELS DID THEY?
NO! I NEVER OPEN THE PACKAGES. YOU JUST ASSUMED EVERYTHING I COURIERED WAS ON PAPER.
I HEAR SOME OF THE STUFF IN TRANSIT TO JAPAN IS PRETTY WEIRD, TOO. ONCE I HEARD ABOUT A GUY THAT--
STOP TALKING.
GET ON THE PLANE. WE'LL HAVE OUR PEOPLE COPY THE REEL IN TOKYO BEFORE YOU DELIVER.
LET HIM GO.

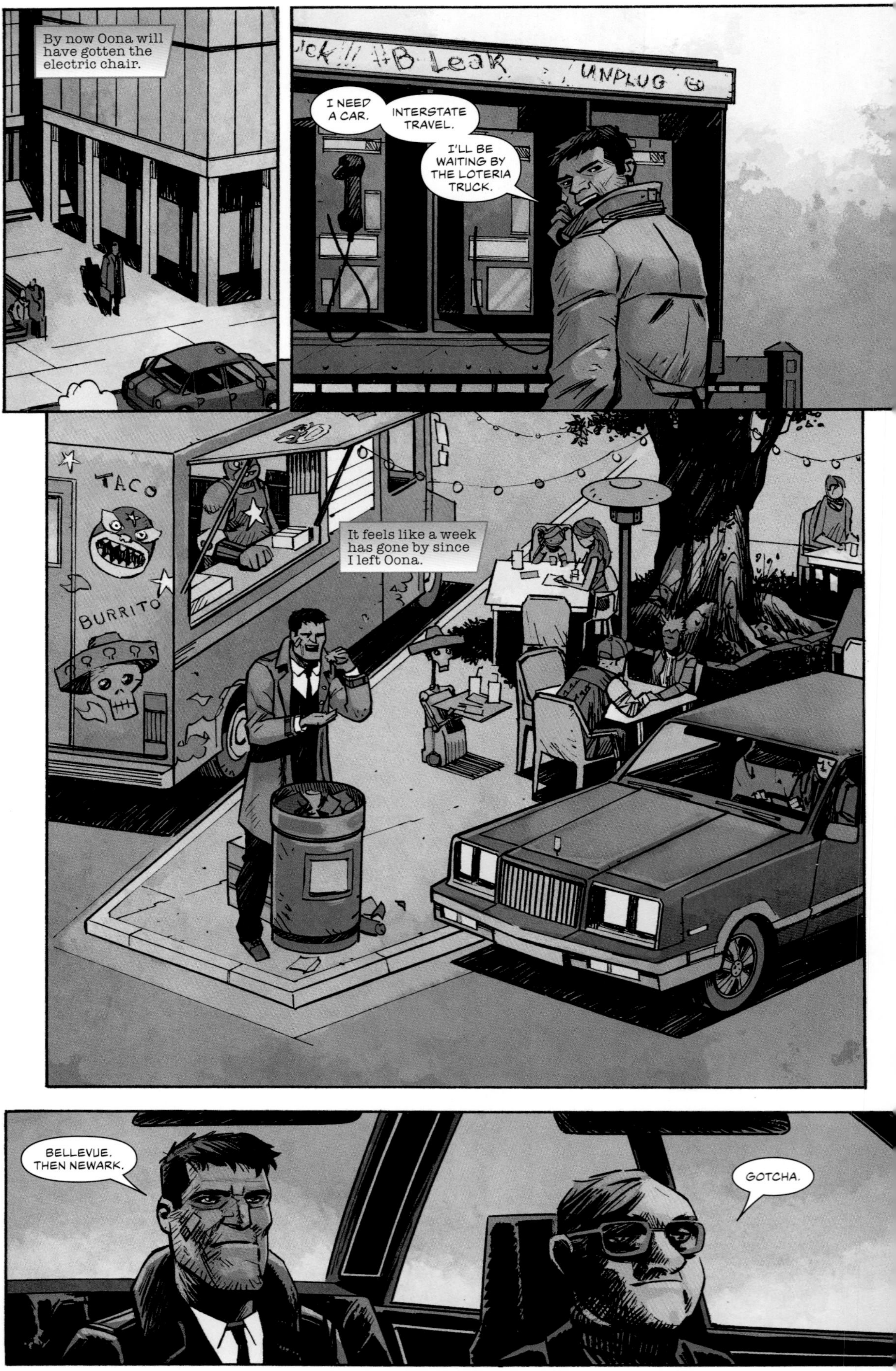
By now Oona will have gotten the electric chair.
UNPLUG
I NEED A CAR.
INTERSTATE TRAVEL.
I'LL BE WAITING BY THE LOTERIA TRUCK.
TACO
BURRITO
It feels like a week has gone by since I left Oona.
BELLEVUE. THEN NEWARK.
GOTCHA.

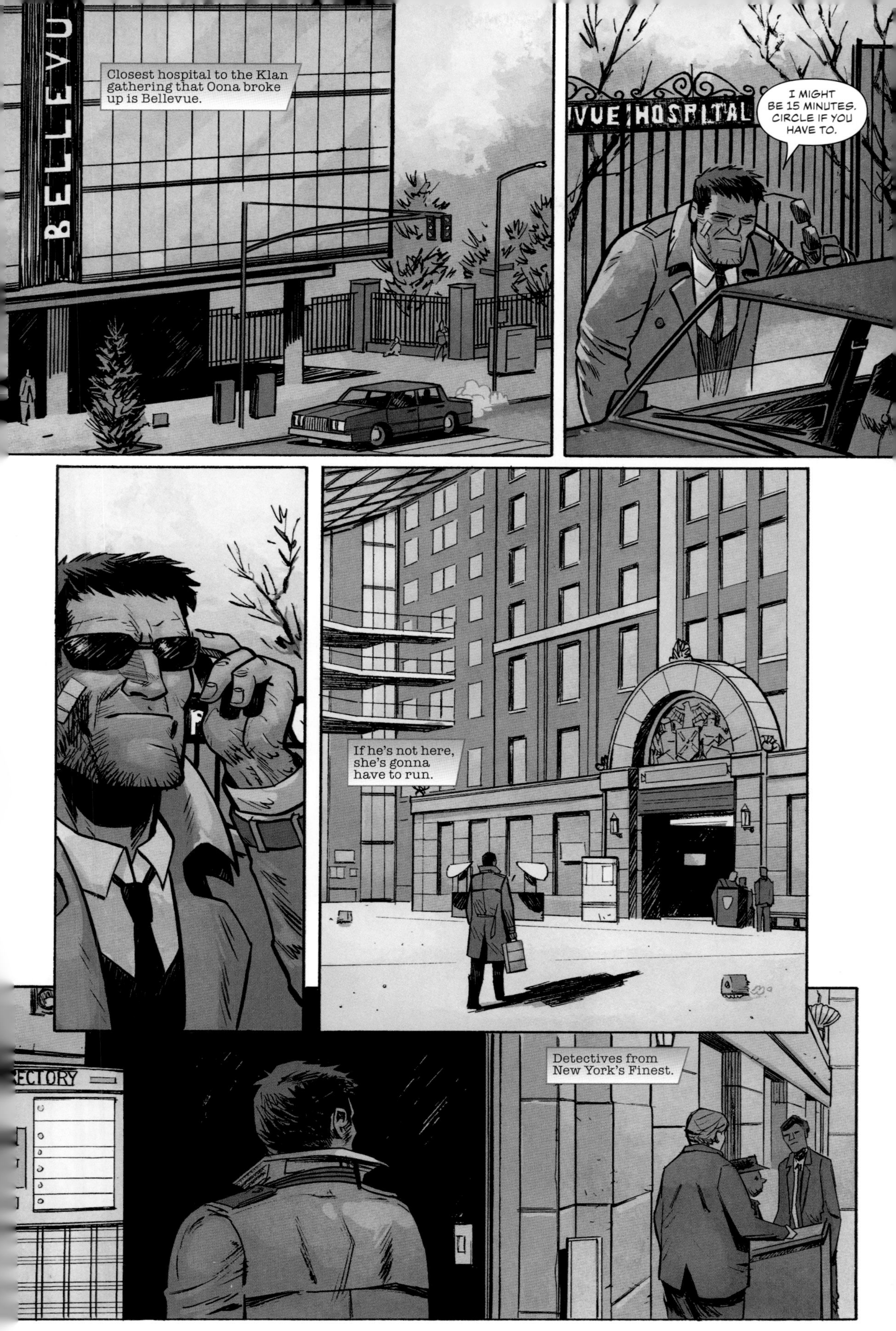
BELLEVU
Closest hospital to the Klan gathering that Oona broke up is Bellevue.
VUE HOSPITAL
I MIGHT BE 15 MINUTES. CIRCLE IF YOU HAVE TO.
If he's not here, she's gonna have to run.
RECTORY
Detectives from New York's Finest.

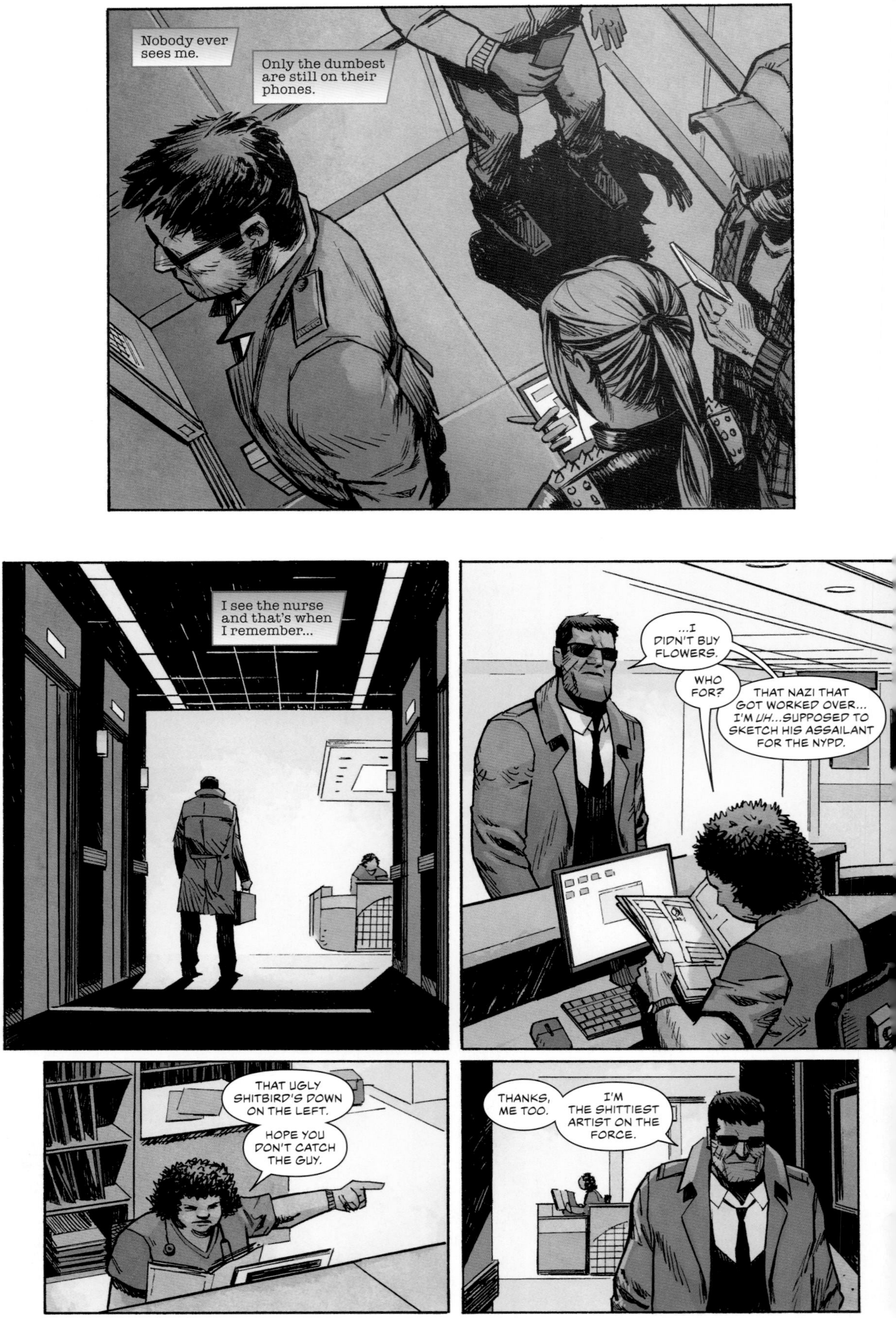
Nobody ever sees me.
Only the dumbest are still on their phones.
I see the nurse and that's when I remember...
...I DIDN'T BUY FLOWERS.
WHO FOR?
THAT NAZI THAT GOT WORKED OVER... I'M UH...SUPPOSED TO SKETCH HIS ASSAILANT FOR THE NYPD.
THAT UGLY SHITBIRD'S DOWN ON THE LEFT.
HOPE YOU DON'T CATCH THE GUY.
THANKS, ME TOO.
I'M THE SHITTIEST ARTIST ON THE FORCE.

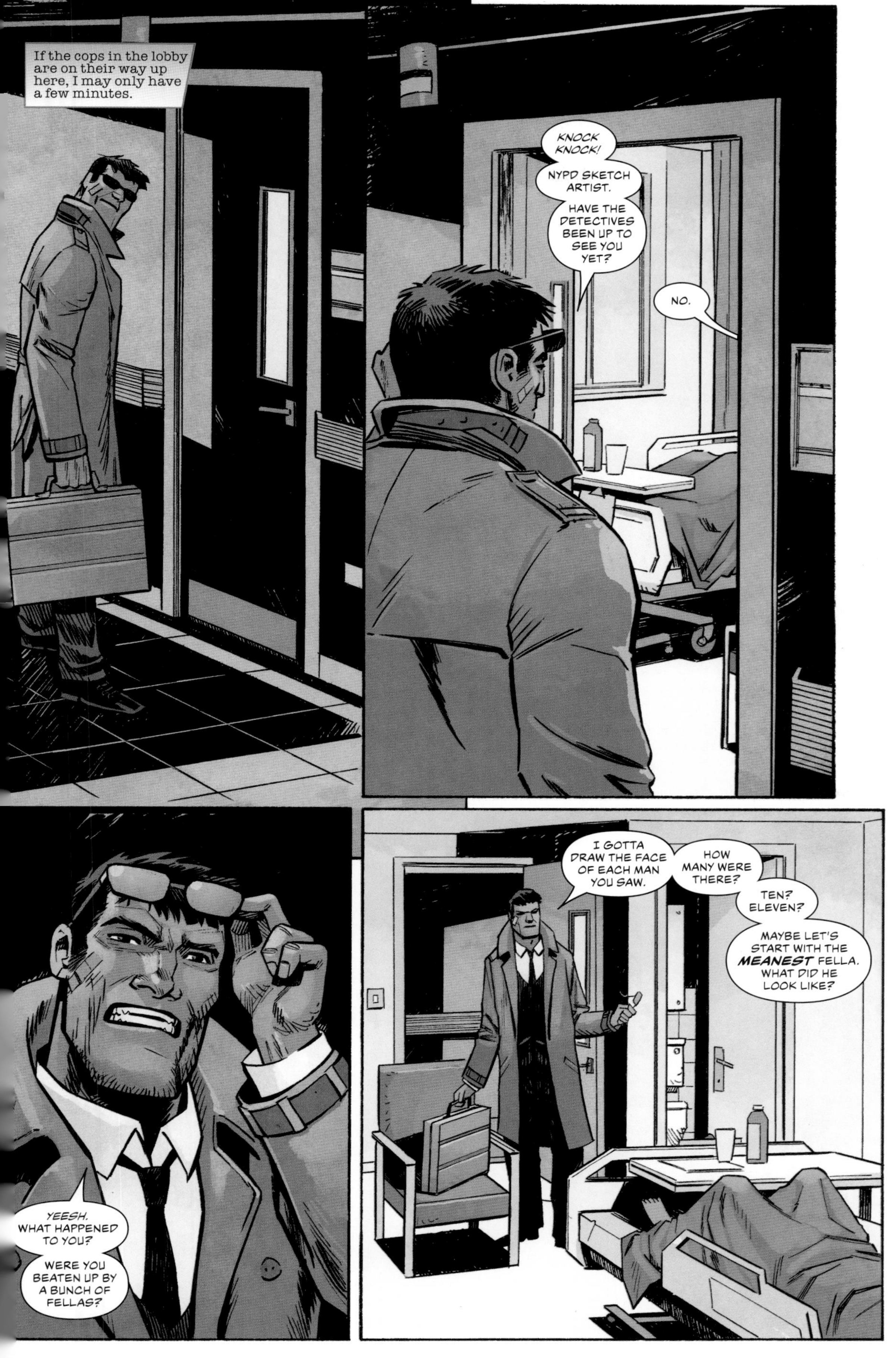
If the cops in the lobby are on their way up here, I may only have a few minutes.
KNOCK KNOCK!
NYPD SKETCH ARTIST.
HAVE THE DETECTIVES BEEN UP TO SEE YOU YET?
NO.
YEESH. WHAT HAPPENED TO YOU?
WERE YOU BEATEN UP BY A BUNCH OF FELLAS?
I GOTTA DRAW THE FACE OF EACH MAN YOU SAW.
HOW MANY WERE THERE?
TEN? ELEVEN?
MAYBE LET'S START WITH THE MEANEST FELLA. WHAT DID HE LOOK LIKE?

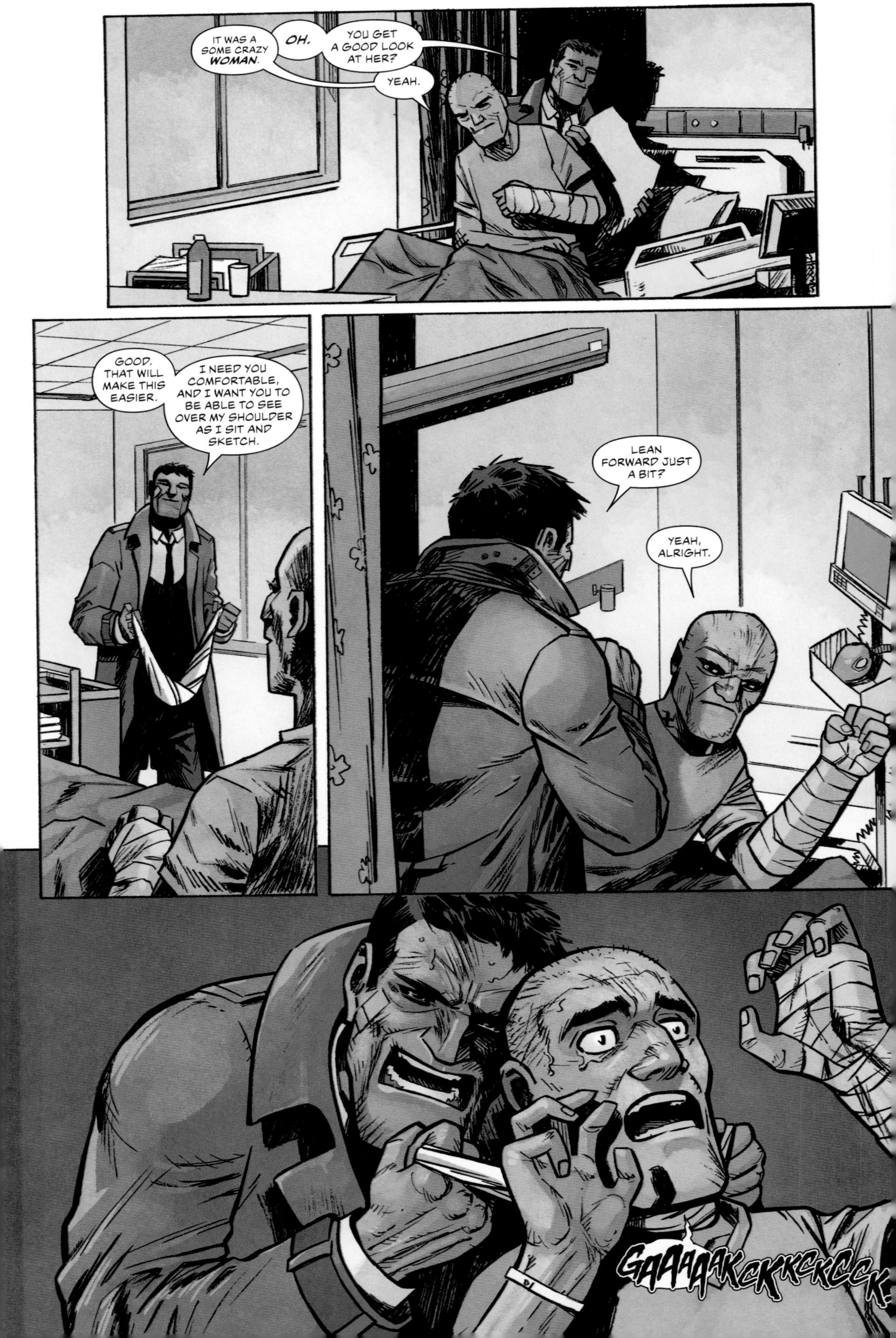
IT WAS A SOME CRAZY WOMAN.
OH.
YOU GET A GOOD LOOK AT HER?
YEAH.
GOOD. THAT WILL MAKE THIS EASIER.
I NEED YOU COMFORTABLE, AND I WANT YOU TO BE ABLE TO SEE OVER MY SHOULDER AS I SIT AND SKETCH.
LEAN FORWARD JUST A BIT?
YEAH, ALRIGHT.
GAAAAAKCKKCKCCCK

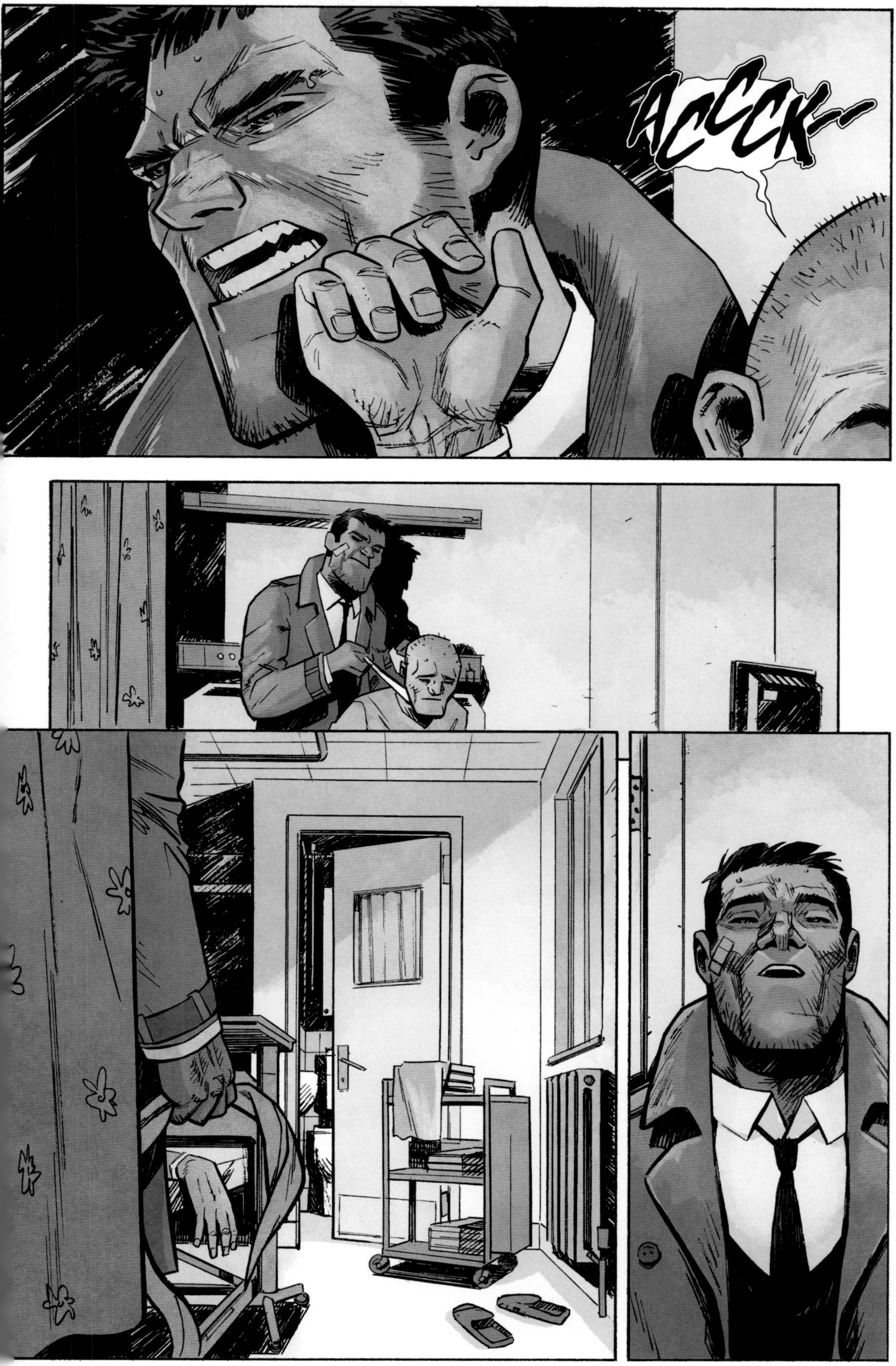
ACCCK--

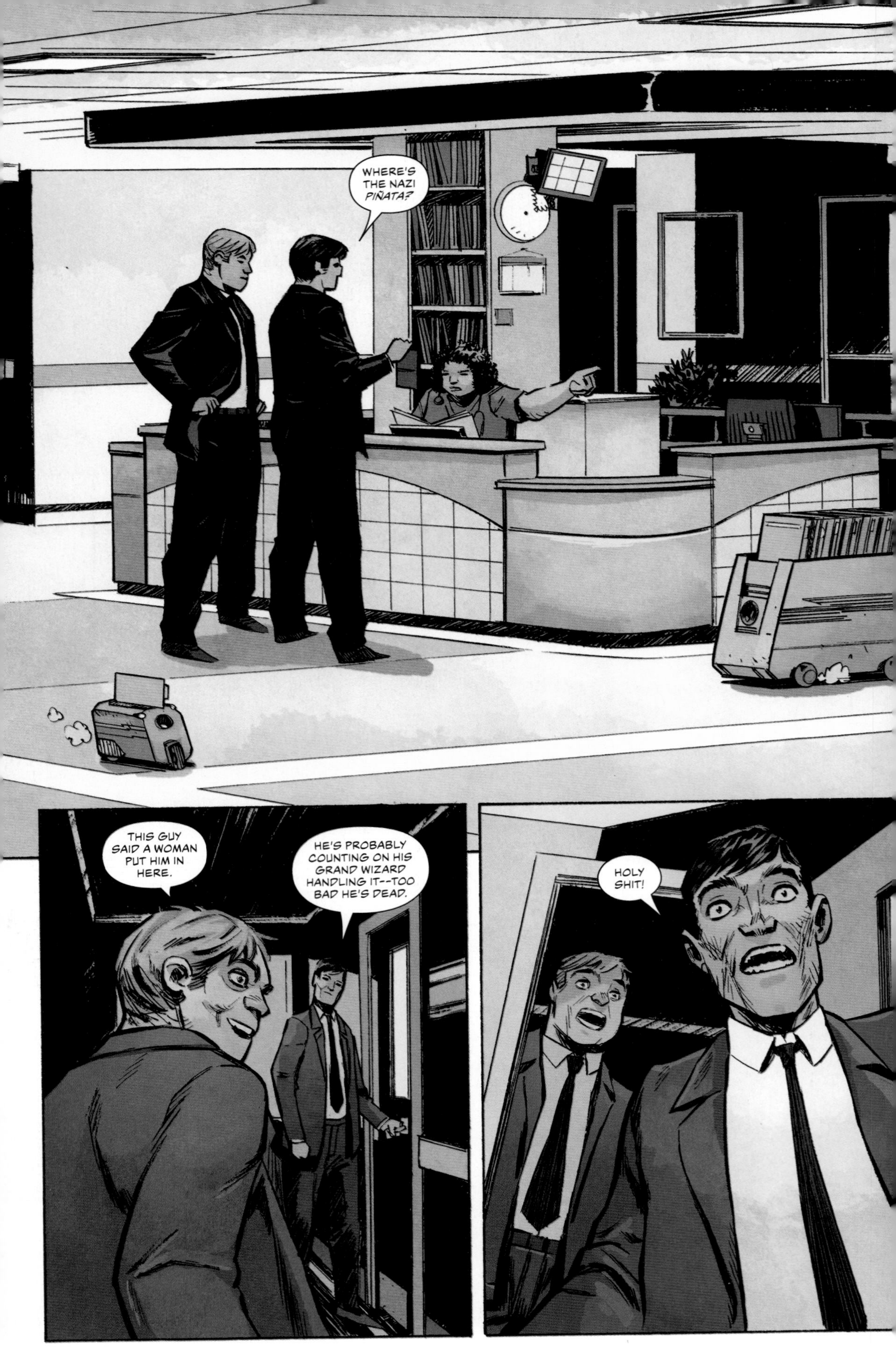
WHERE'S THE NAZI *PIÑATA?*
THIS GUY SAID A WOMAN PUT HIM IN HERE.
HE'S PROBABLY COUNTING ON HIS GRAND WIZARD HANDLING IT--TOO BAD HE'S DEAD.
HOLY SHIT!

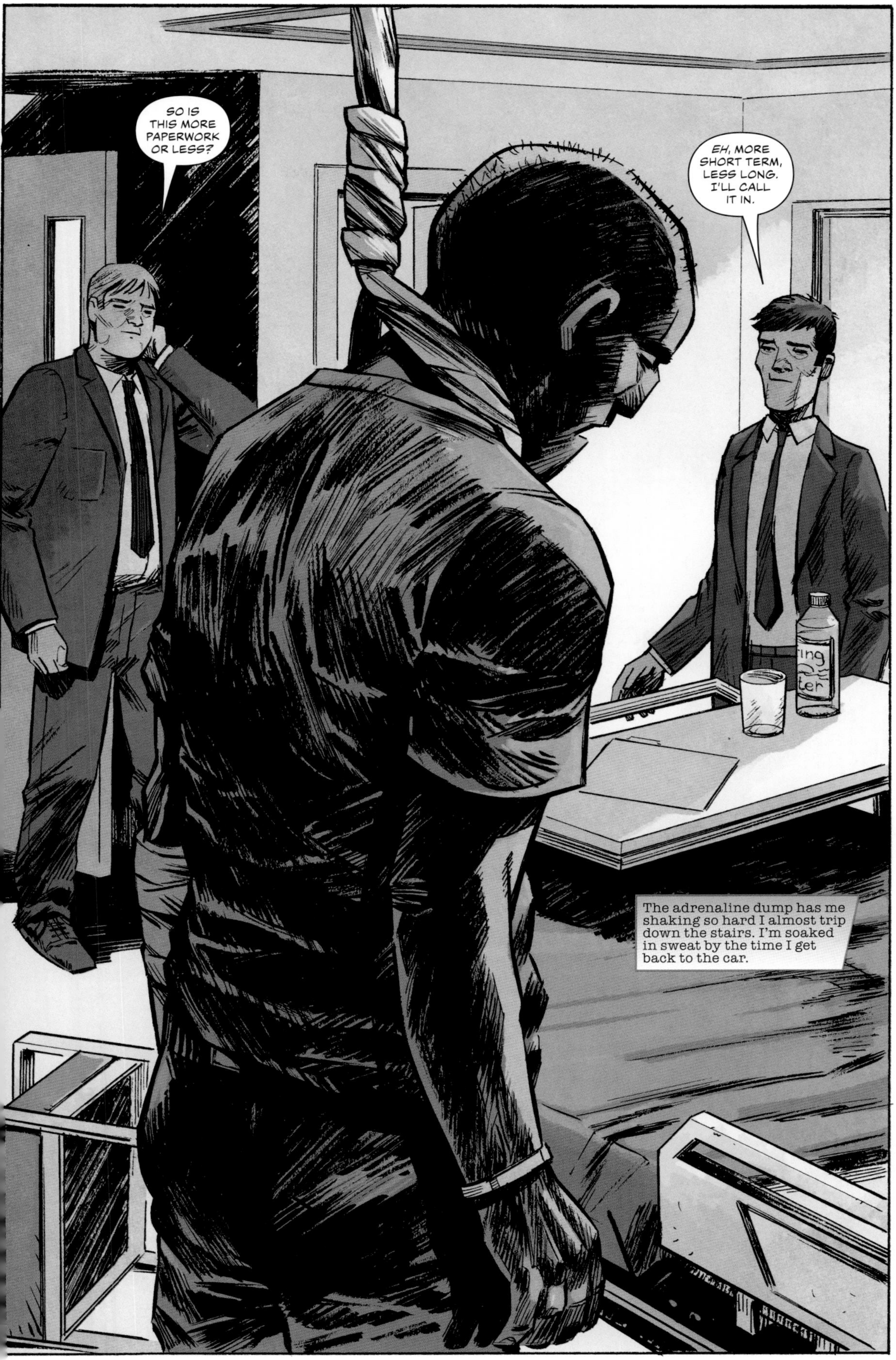
SO IS THIS MORE PAPERWORK OR LESS?
EH, MORE SHORT TERM, LESS LONG. I'LL CALL IT IN.
The adrenaline dump has me shaking so hard I almost trip down the stairs. I'm soaked in sweat by the time I get back to the car.

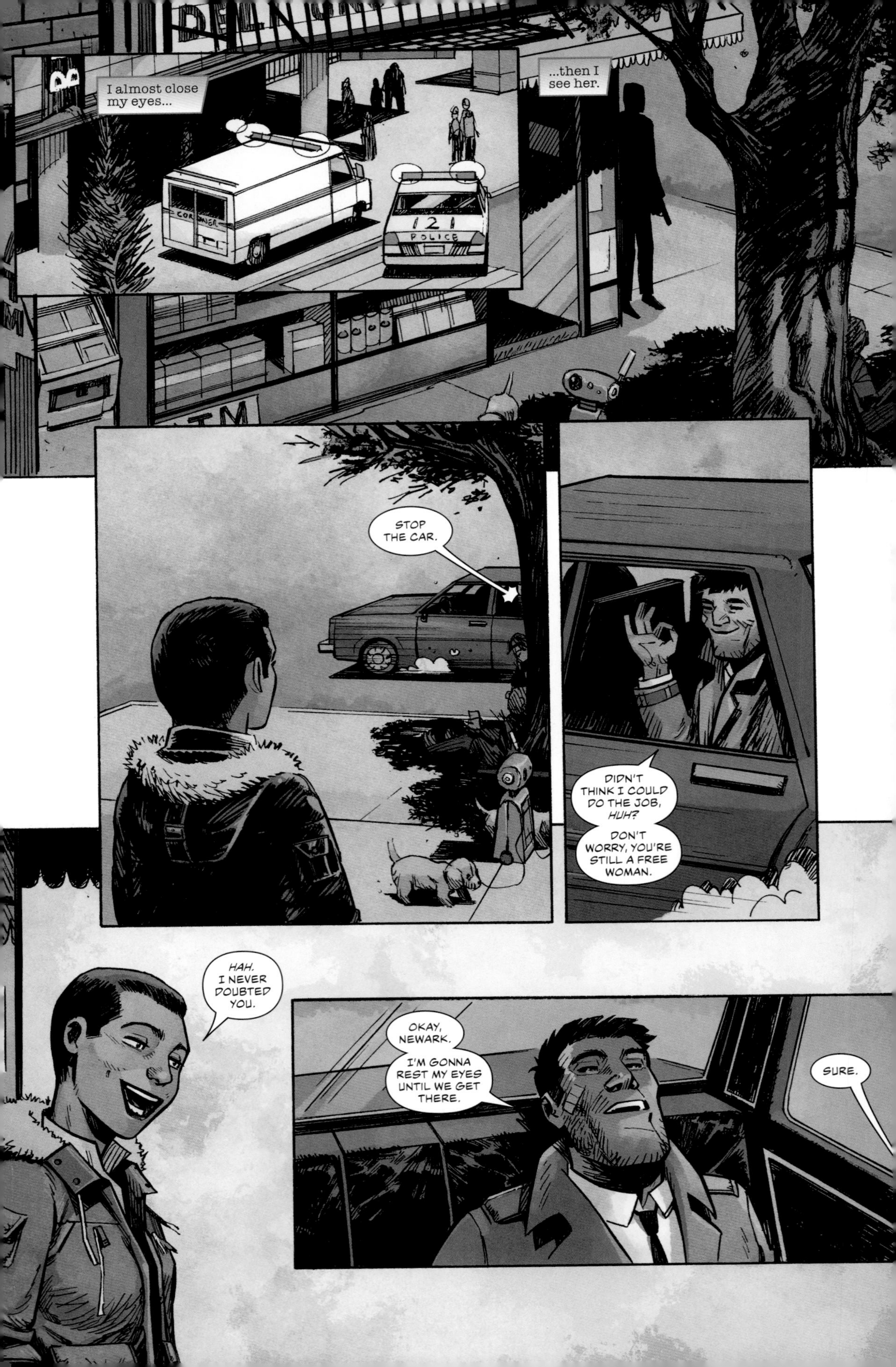
I almost close my eyes...
CORONER
121
POLICE
...then I see her.
ATM
STOP THE CAR.
DIDN'T THINK I COULD DO THE JOB, *HUH?*
DON'T WORRY, YOU'RE STILL A FREE WOMAN.
HAH. I NEVER DOUBTED YOU.
OKAY, NEWARK.
I'M GONNA REST MY EYES UNTIL WE GET THERE.
SURE.

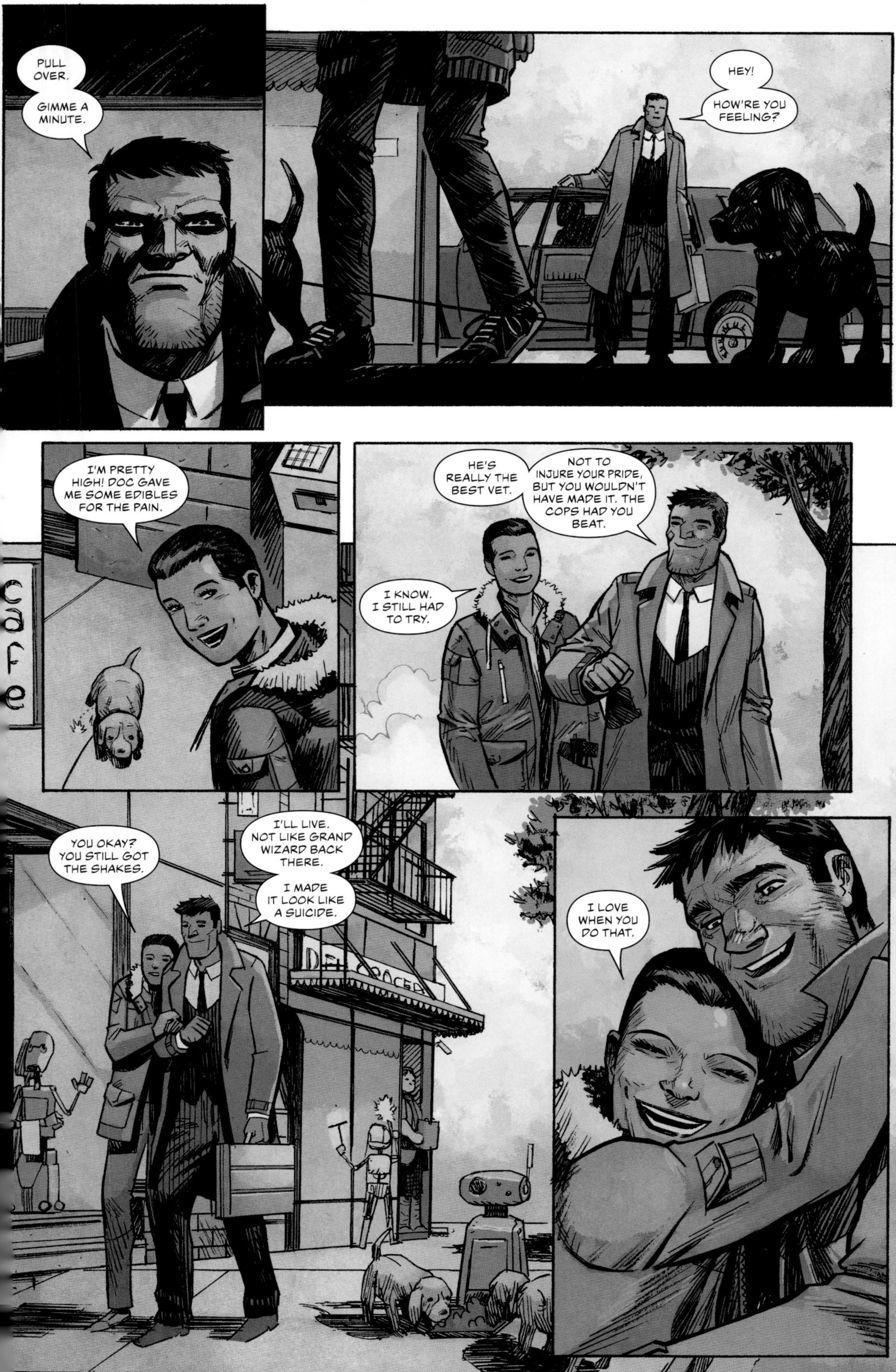
PULL OVER.
GIMME A MINUTE.
HEY!
HOW'RE YOU FEELING?
I'M PRETTY HIGH! DOC GAVE ME SOME EDIBLES FOR THE PAIN.
cafe
HE'S REALLY THE BEST VET.
NOT TO INJURE YOUR PRIDE, BUT YOU WOULDN'T HAVE MADE IT. THE COPS HAD YOU BEAT.
I KNOW. I STILL HAD TO TRY.
YOU OKAY? YOU STILL GOT THE SHAKES.
I'LL LIVE. NOT LIKE GRAND WIZARD BACK THERE.
I MADE IT LOOK LIKE A SUICIDE.
I LOVE WHEN YOU DO THAT.

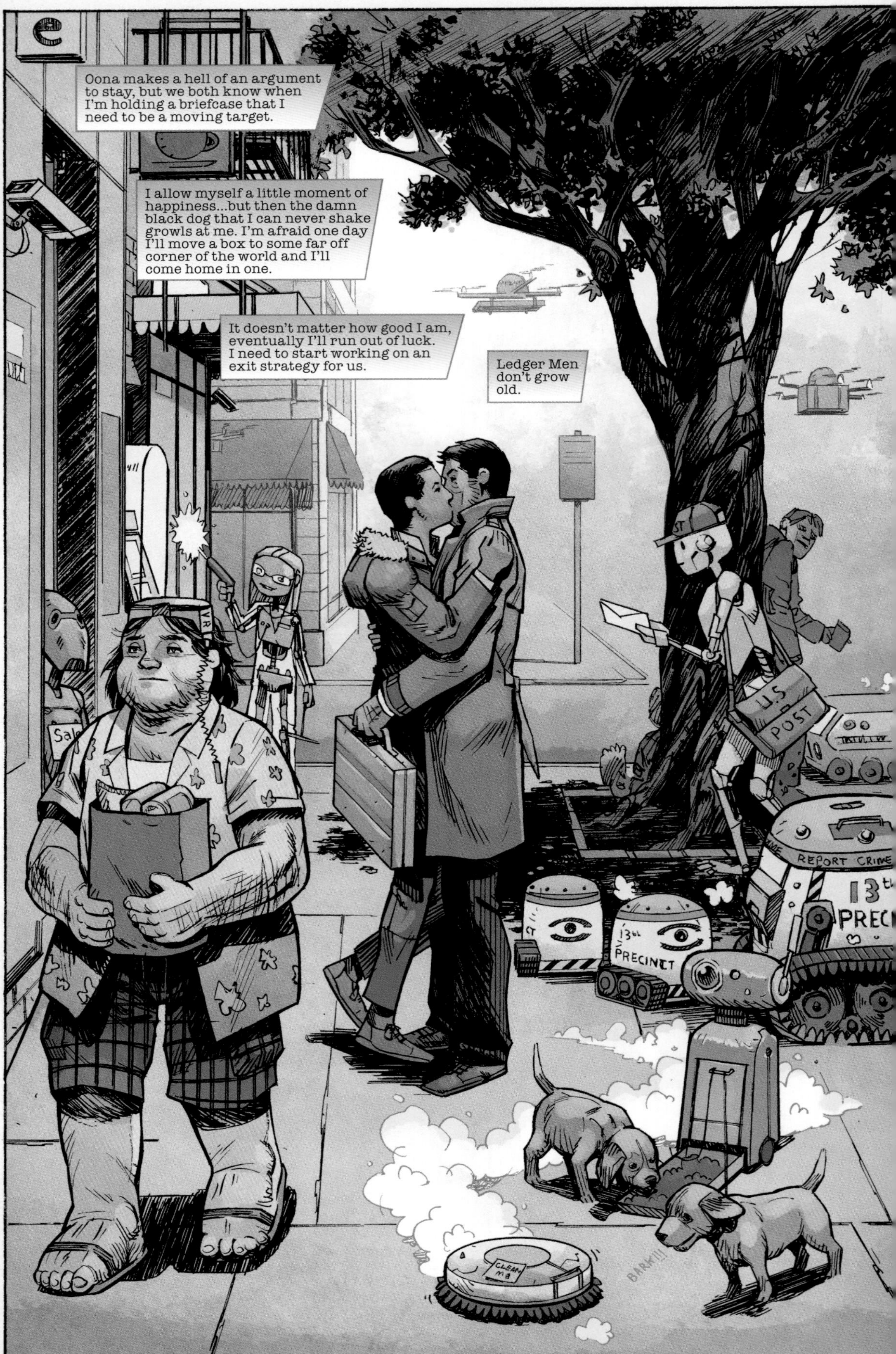
Oona makes a hell of an argument to stay, but we both know when I'm holding a briefcase that I need to be a moving target.
I allow myself a little moment of happiness...but then the damn black dog that I can never shake growls at me. I'm afraid one day I'll move a box to some far off corner of the world and I'll come home in one.
It doesn't matter how good I am, eventually I'll run out of luck. I need to start working on an exit strategy for us.
Ledger Men don't grow old.
U.S. POST
REPORT CRIME
13th PRECINCT
CLEAN ME
BARK!!!

CHAPTER 4

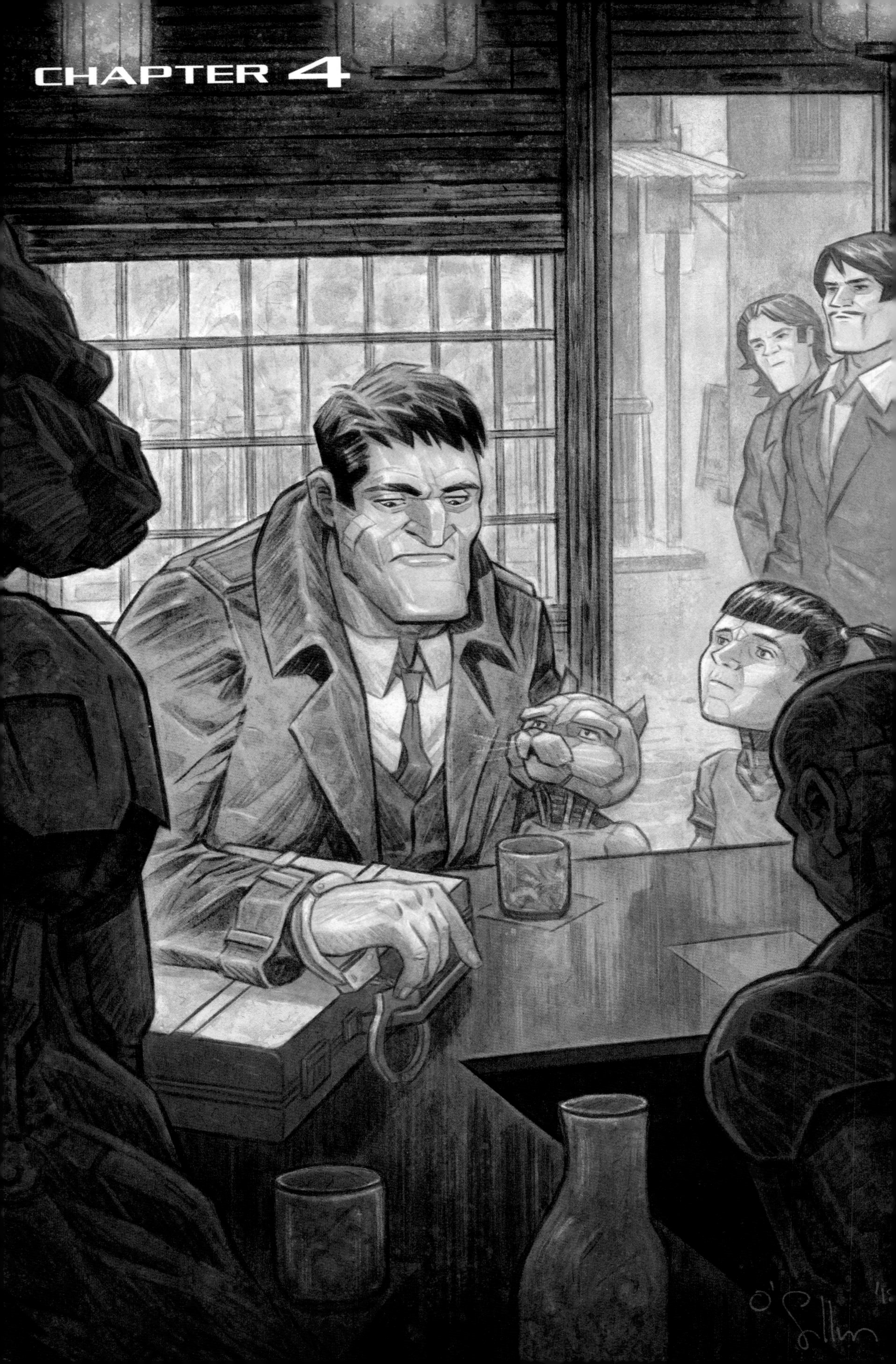

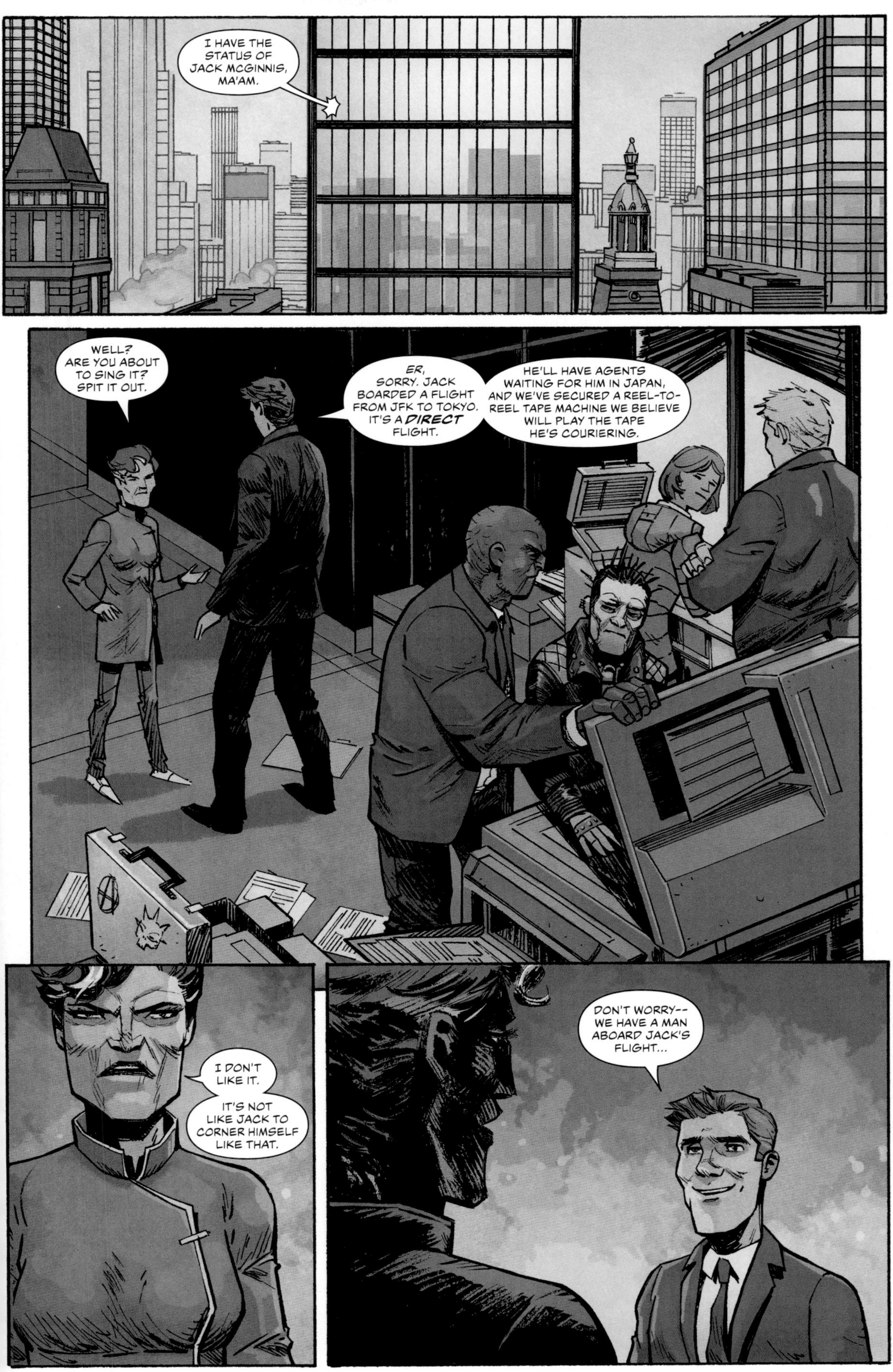
I HAVE THE STATUS OF JACK MCGINNIS, MA'AM.
WELL? ARE YOU ABOUT TO SING IT? SPIT IT OUT.
ER, SORRY. JACK BOARDED A FLIGHT FROM JFK TO TOKYO. IT'S A DIRECT FLIGHT.
HE'LL HAVE AGENTS WAITING FOR HIM IN JAPAN, AND WE'VE SECURED A REEL-TO-REEL TAPE MACHINE WE BELIEVE WILL PLAY THE TAPE HE'S COURIERING.
I DON'T LIKE IT.
IT'S NOT LIKE JACK TO CORNER HIMSELF LIKE THAT.
DON'T WORRY-- WE HAVE A MAN ABOARD JACK'S FLIGHT...

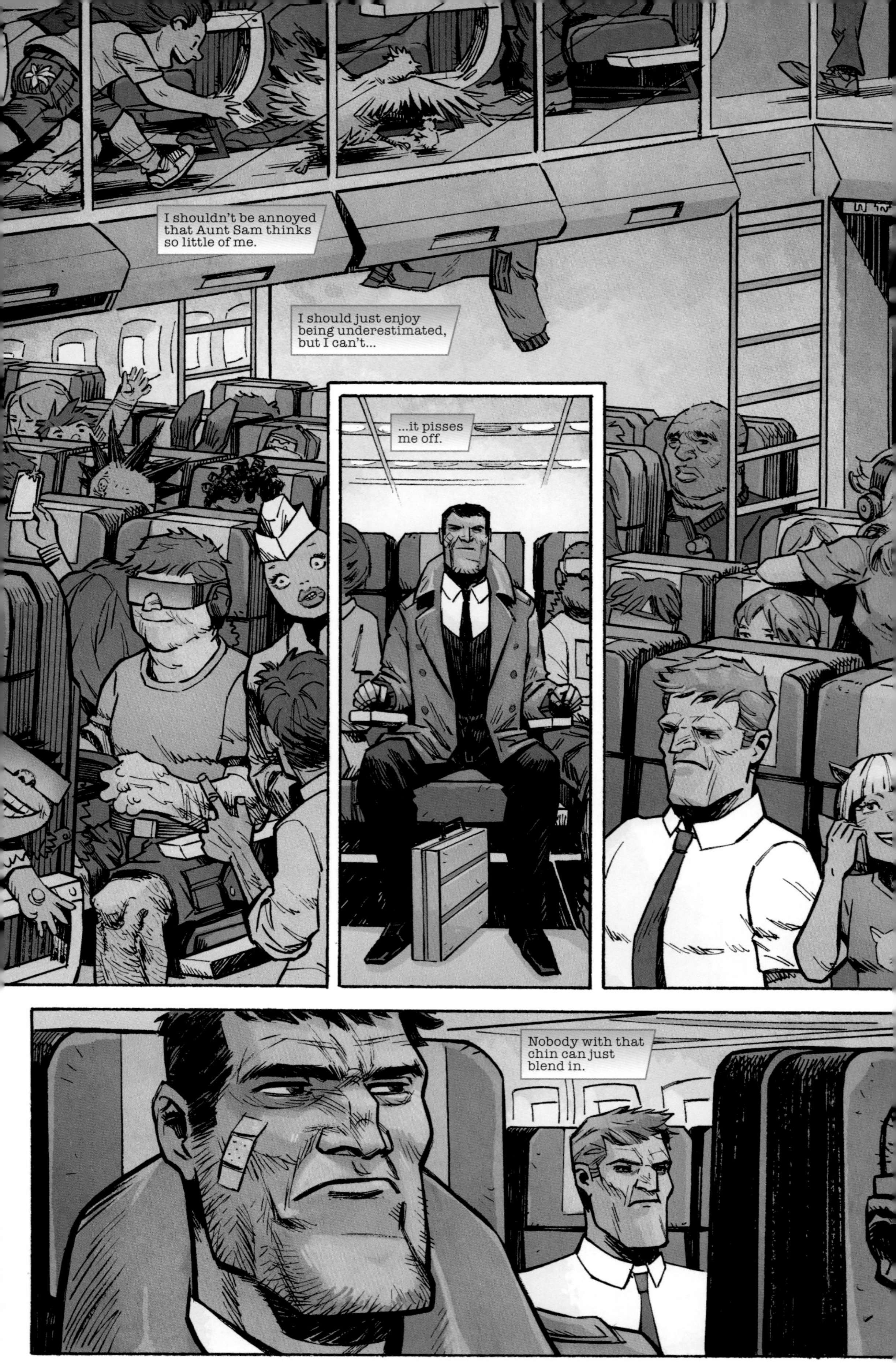
I shouldn't be annoyed that Aunt Sam thinks so little of me.
I should just enjoy being underestimated, but I can't...
...it pisses me off.
Nobody with that chin can just blend in.

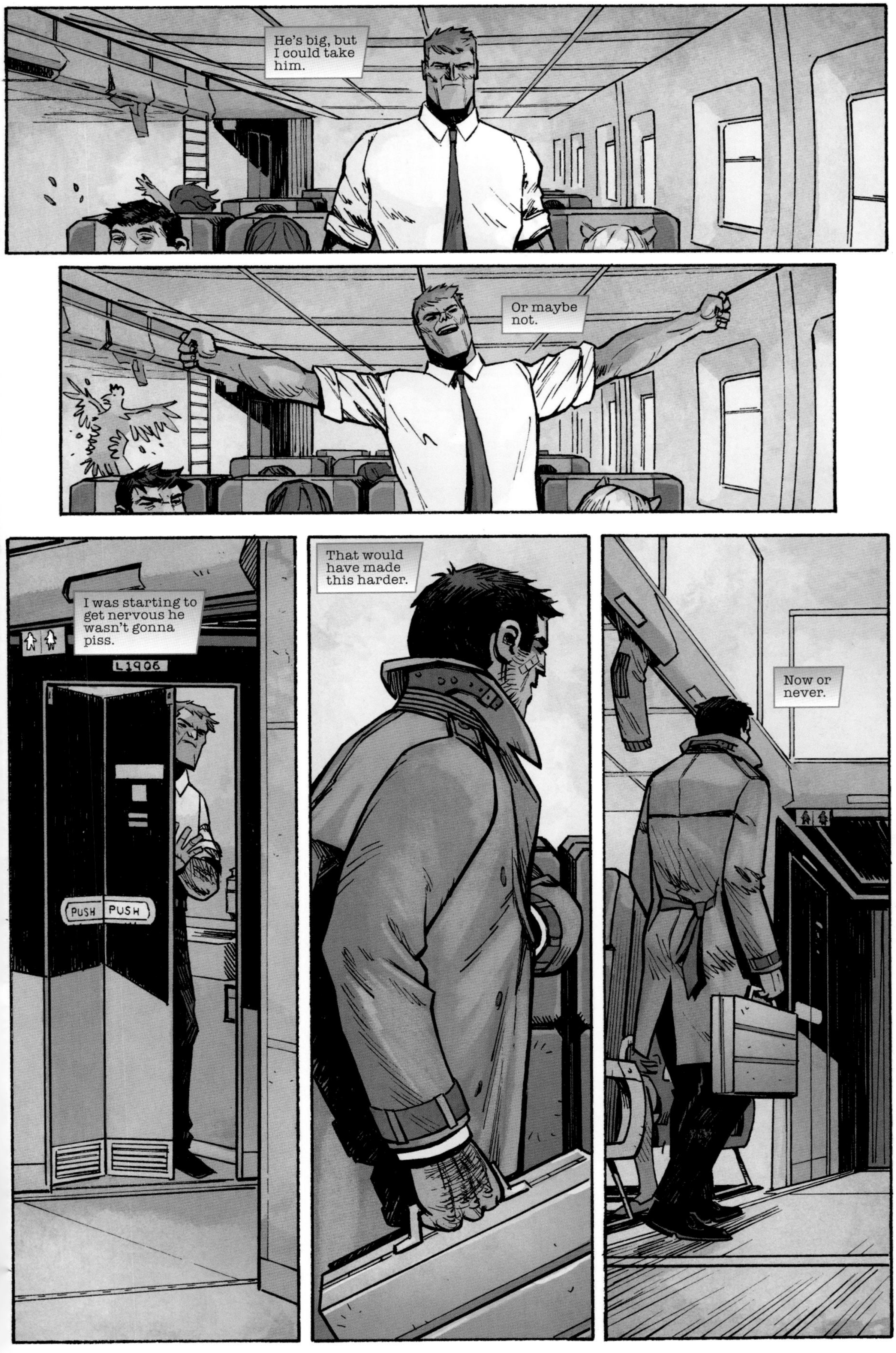
He's big, but I could take him.
Or maybe not.
I was starting to get nervous he wasn't gonna piss.
L1906
PUSH PUSH
That would have made this harder.
Now or never.

Hunh.

I wonder if this stuff **expires**.

L1906

USH P SH

LAVATORY

OCCUPIED

LAVATORY

VACANT

CHAKK

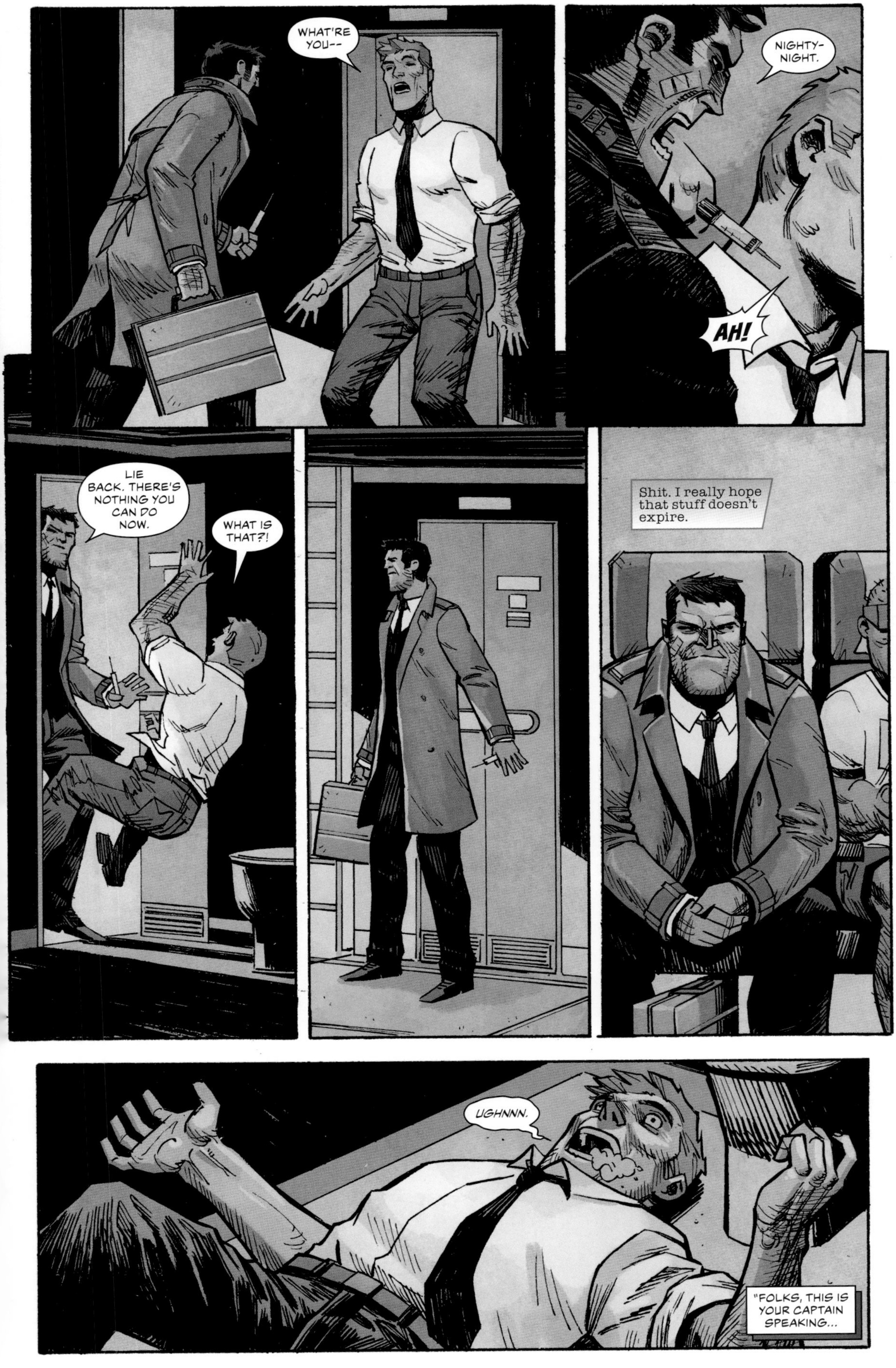
WHAT'RE YOU--
NIGHTY-NIGHT.
AH!
LIE BACK. THERE'S NOTHING YOU CAN DO NOW.
WHAT IS THAT?!
Shit. I really hope that stuff doesn't expire.
UGHNNN.
"FOLKS, THIS IS YOUR CAPTAIN SPEAKING...

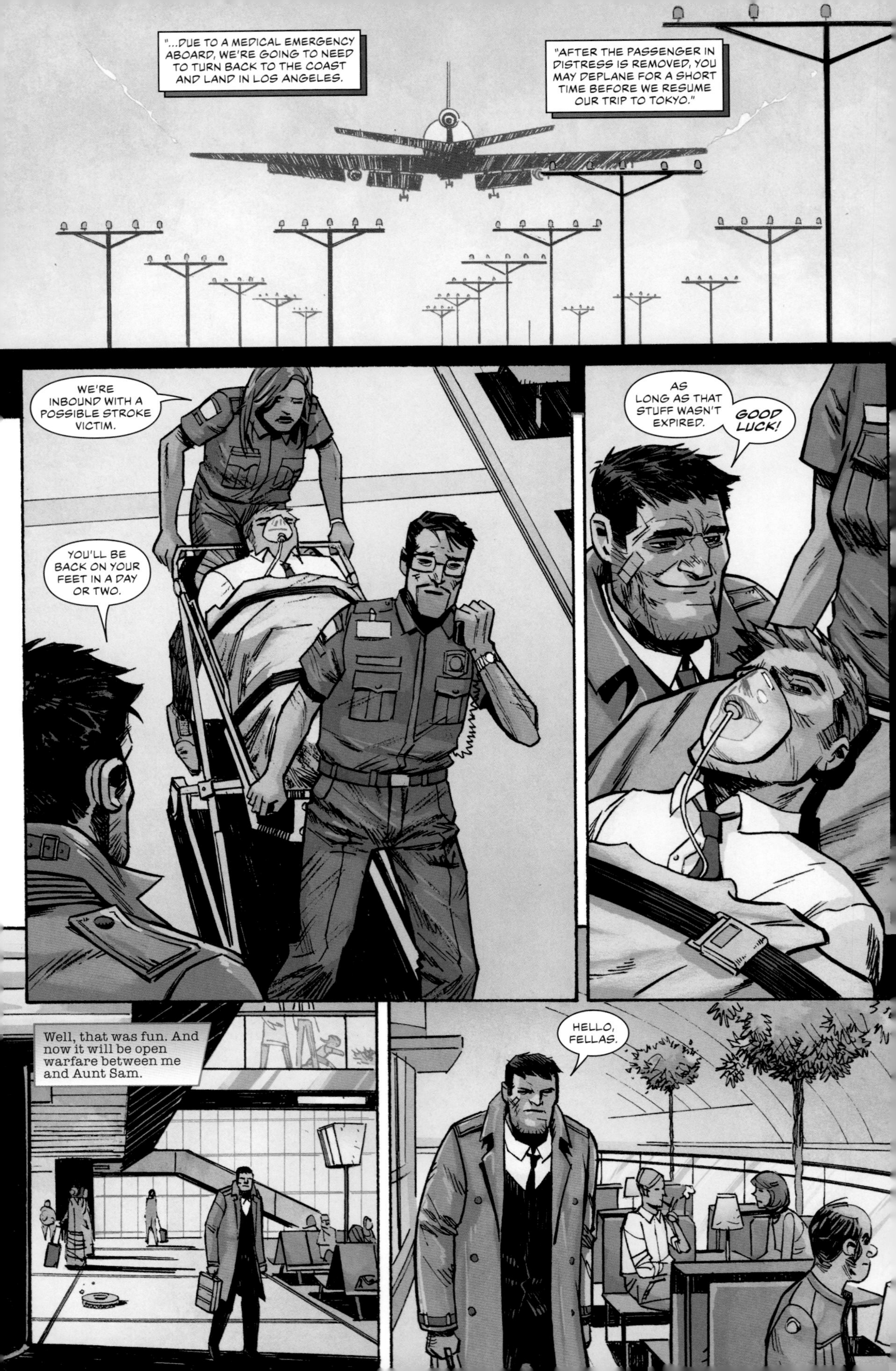
"...DUE TO A MEDICAL EMERGENCY ABOARD, WE'RE GOING TO NEED TO TURN BACK TO THE COAST AND LAND IN LOS ANGELES.
"AFTER THE PASSENGER IN DISTRESS IS REMOVED, YOU MAY DEPLANE FOR A SHORT TIME BEFORE WE RESUME OUR TRIP TO TOKYO."
WE'RE INBOUND WITH A POSSIBLE STROKE VICTIM.
YOU'LL BE BACK ON YOUR FEET IN A DAY OR TWO.
AS LONG AS THAT STUFF WASN'T EXPIRED.
GOOD LUCK!
Well, that was fun. And now it will be open warfare between me and Aunt Sam.
HELLO, FELLAS.

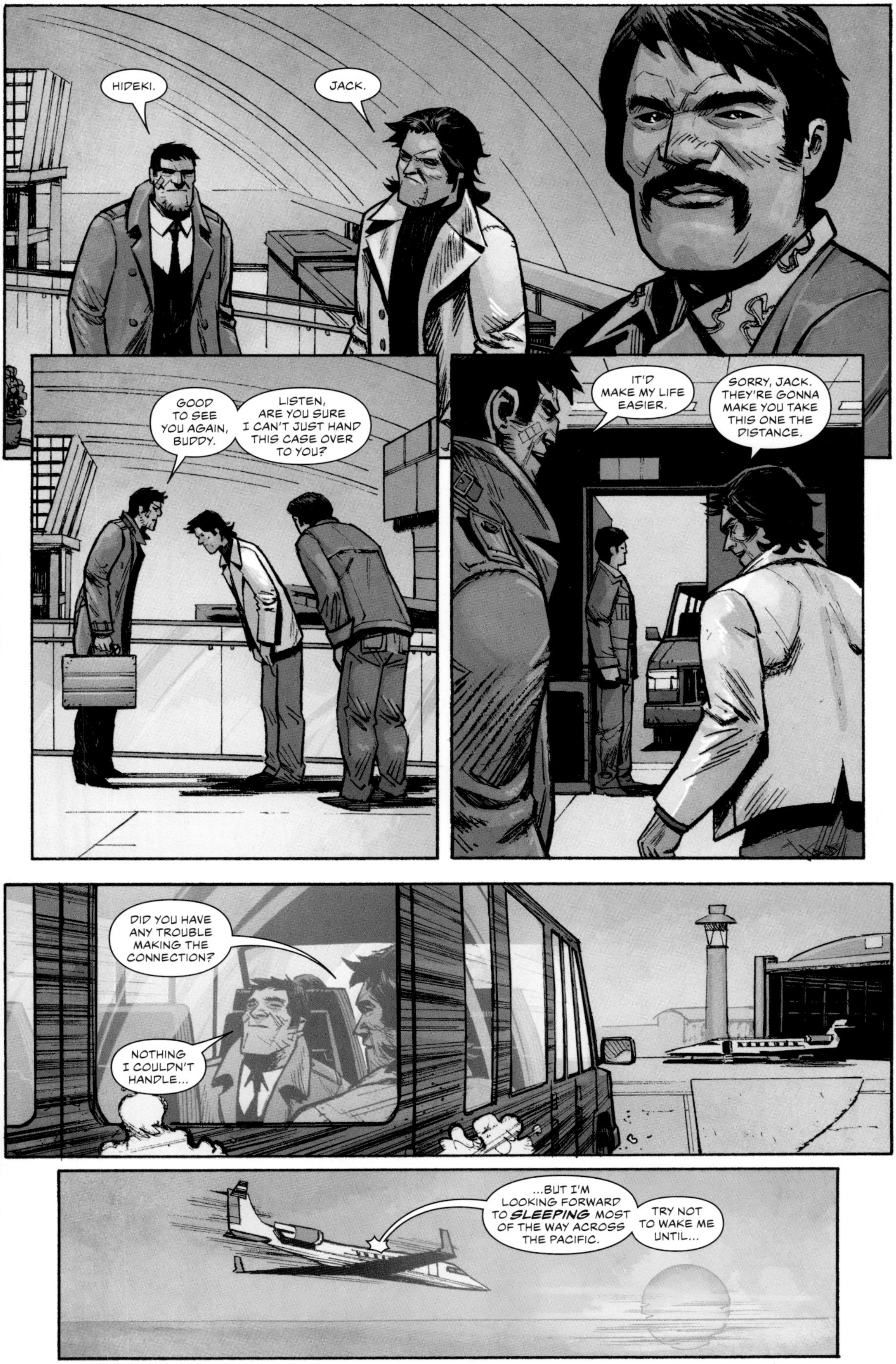
HIDEKI.
JACK.
GOOD TO SEE YOU AGAIN, BUDDY.
LISTEN, ARE YOU SURE I CAN'T JUST HAND THIS CASE OVER TO YOU?
IT'D MAKE MY LIFE EASIER.
SORRY, JACK. THEY'RE GONNA MAKE YOU TAKE THIS ONE THE DISTANCE.
DID YOU HAVE ANY TROUBLE MAKING THE CONNECTION?
NOTHING I COULDN'T HANDLE...
...BUT I'M LOOKING FORWARD TO SLEEPING MOST OF THE WAY ACROSS THE PACIFIC.
TRY NOT TO WAKE ME UNTIL...

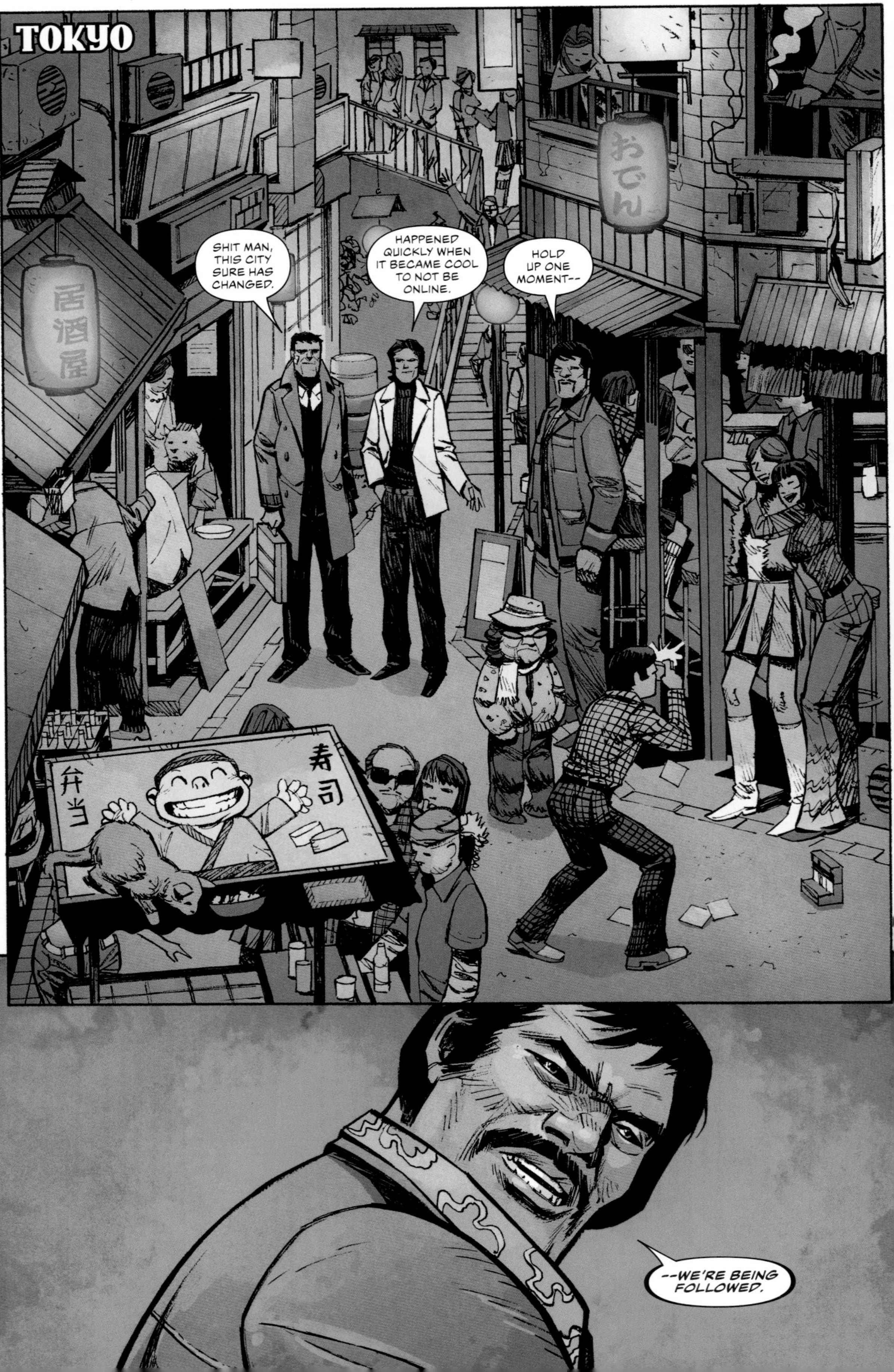
TOKYO
居酒屋
おでん
SHIT MAN, THIS CITY SURE HAS CHANGED.
HAPPENED QUICKLY WHEN IT BECAME COOL TO NOT BE ONLINE.
HOLD UP ONE MOMENT--
弁当
寿司
--WE'RE BEING FOLLOWED.

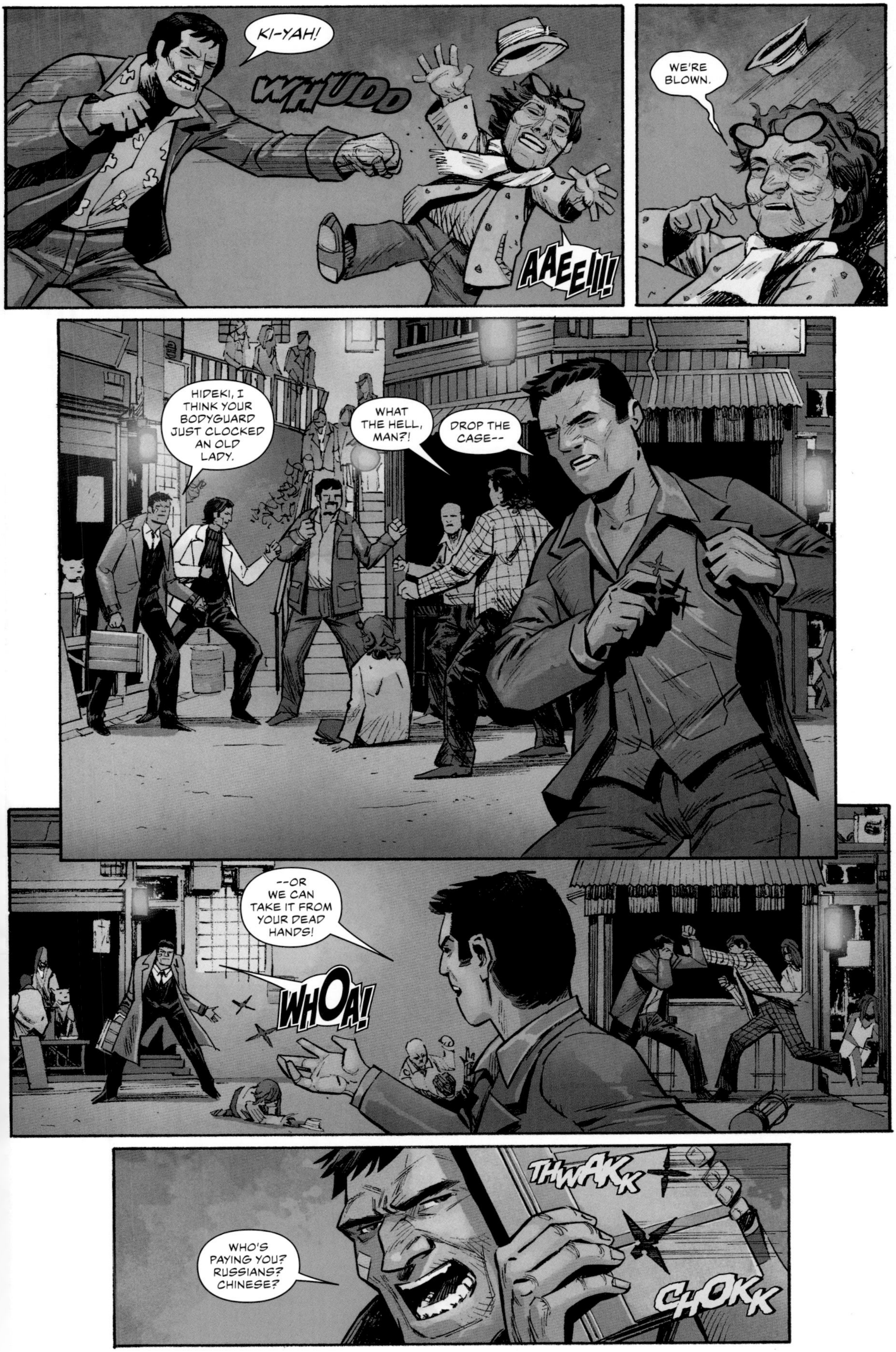
KI-YAH!
WHUDD
AAEEII!!
WE'RE BLOWN.
HIDEKI, I THINK YOUR BODYGUARD JUST CLOCKED AN OLD LADY.
WHAT THE HELL, MAN?!
DROP THE CASE--
--OR WE CAN TAKE IT FROM YOUR DEAD HANDS!
WHOA!
THWAKK
WHO'S PAYING YOU? RUSSIANS? CHINESE?
CHOKK

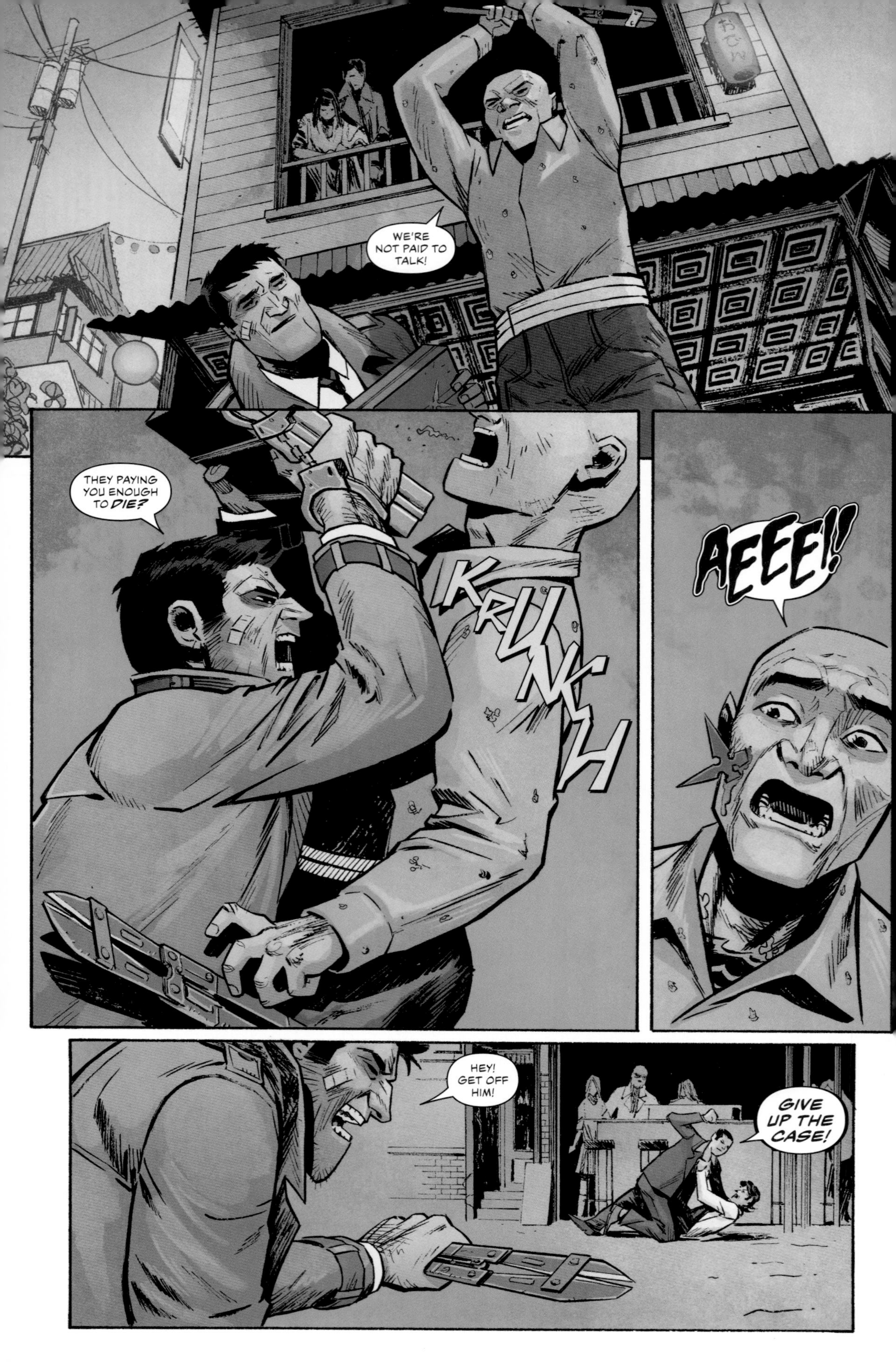
おでん
WE'RE NOT PAID TO TALK!
THEY PAYING YOU ENOUGH TO *DIE?*
KRUNCH
AEEE!!
HEY! GET OFF HIM!
GIVE UP THE CASE!

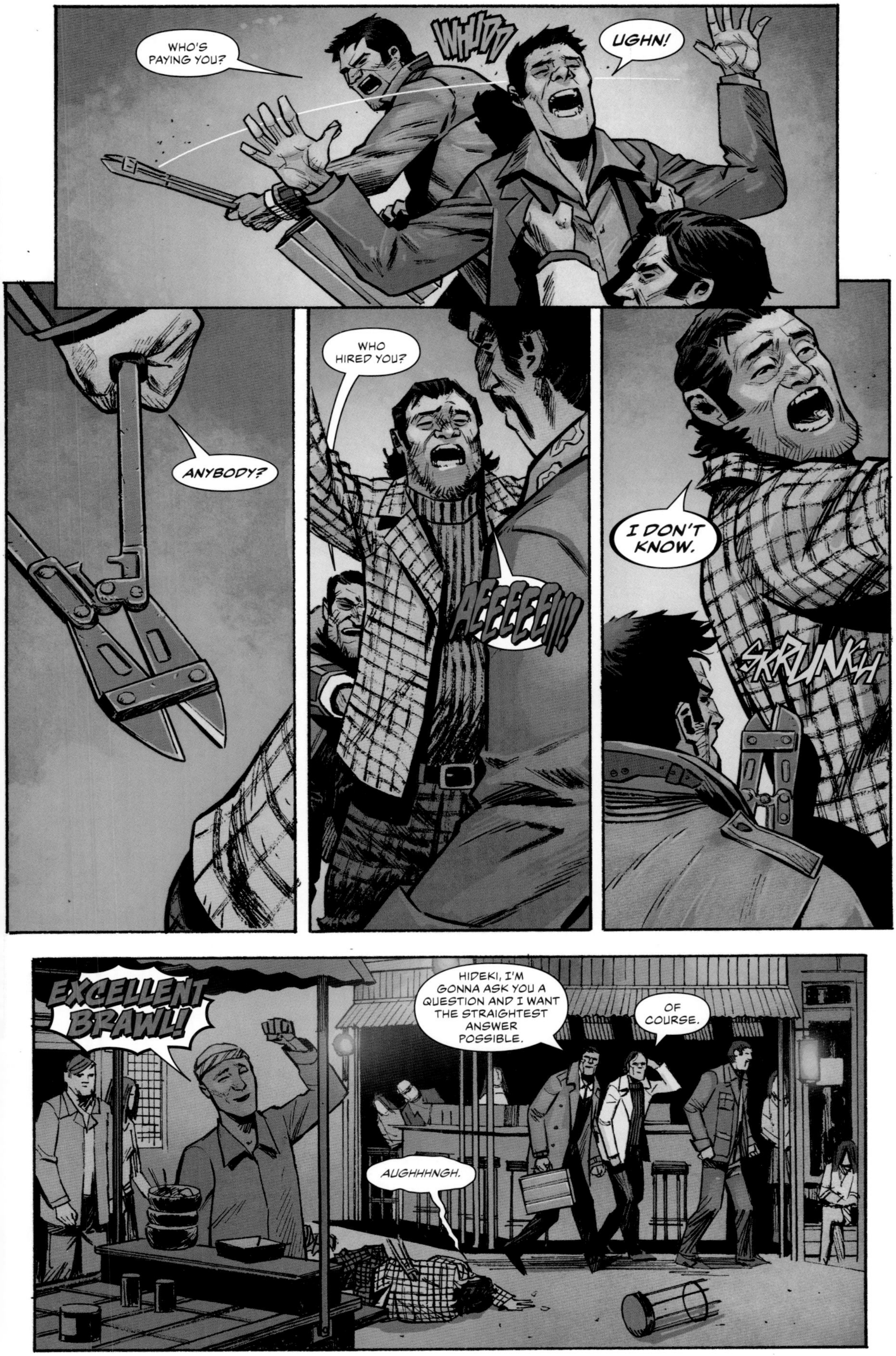
WHO'S PAYING YOU?
WHUDD
UGHN!
ANYBODY?
WHO HIRED YOU?
AEEEEE!!!
I DON'T KNOW.
SKRUNCH
EXCELLENT BRAWL!
HIDEKI, I'M GONNA ASK YOU A QUESTION AND I WANT THE STRAIGHTEST ANSWER POSSIBLE.
OF COURSE.
AUGHHHNGH.

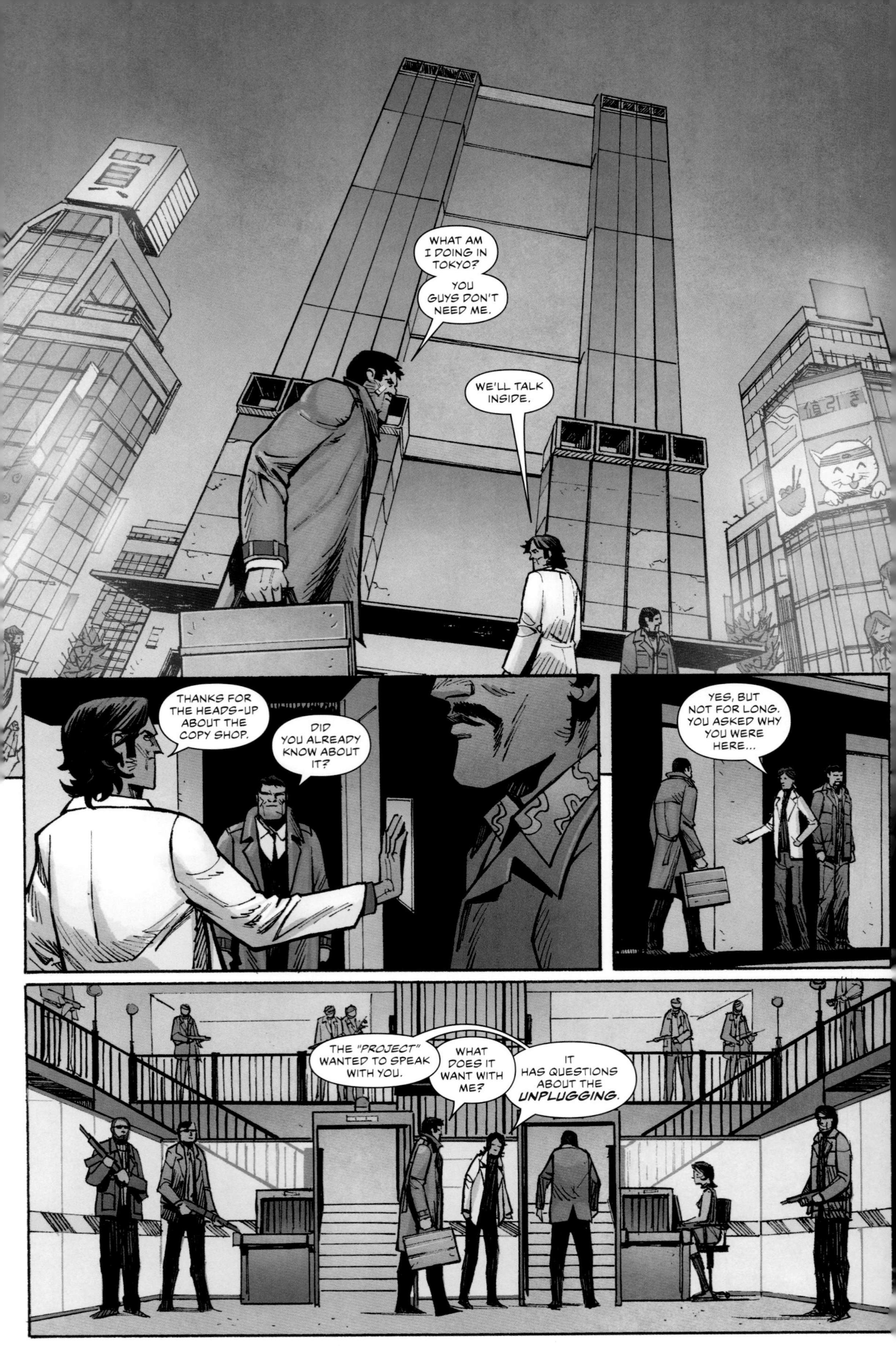
WHAT AM I DOING IN TOKYO?
YOU GUYS DON'T NEED ME.
WE'LL TALK INSIDE.
THANKS FOR THE HEADS-UP ABOUT THE COPY SHOP.
DID YOU ALREADY KNOW ABOUT IT?
YES, BUT NOT FOR LONG. YOU ASKED WHY YOU WERE HERE...
THE "PROJECT" WANTED TO SPEAK WITH YOU.
WHAT DOES IT WANT WITH ME?
IT HAS QUESTIONS ABOUT THE UNPLUGGING.

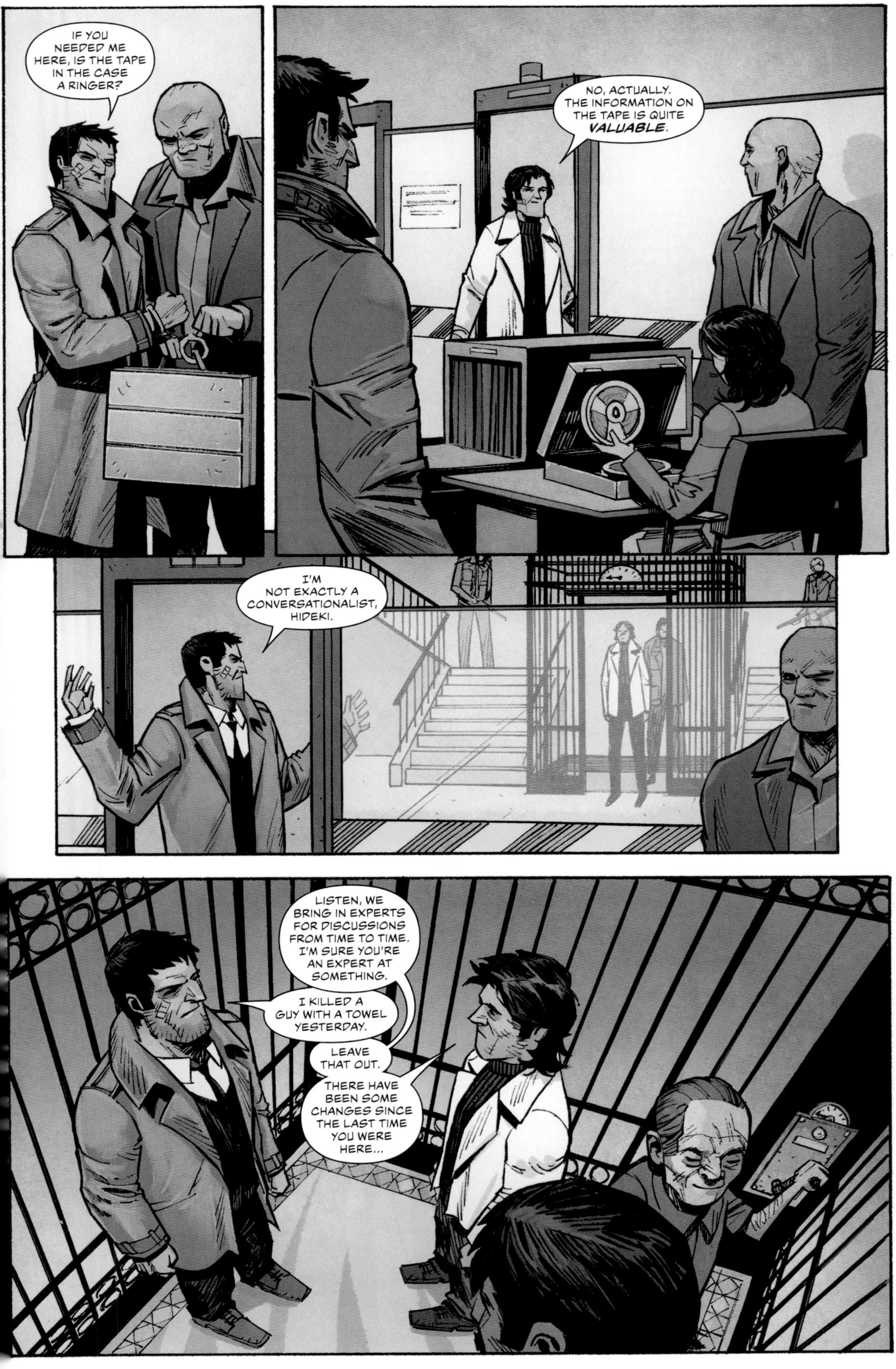
IF YOU NEEDED ME HERE, IS THE TAPE IN THE CASE A RINGER?
NO, ACTUALLY. THE INFORMATION ON THE TAPE IS QUITE *VALUABLE*.
I'M NOT EXACTLY A CONVERSATIONALIST, HIDEKI.
LISTEN, WE BRING IN EXPERTS FOR DISCUSSIONS FROM TIME TO TIME. I'M SURE YOU'RE AN EXPERT AT SOMETHING.
I KILLED A GUY WITH A TOWEL YESTERDAY.
LEAVE THAT OUT.
THERE HAVE BEEN SOME CHANGES SINCE THE LAST TIME YOU WERE HERE...

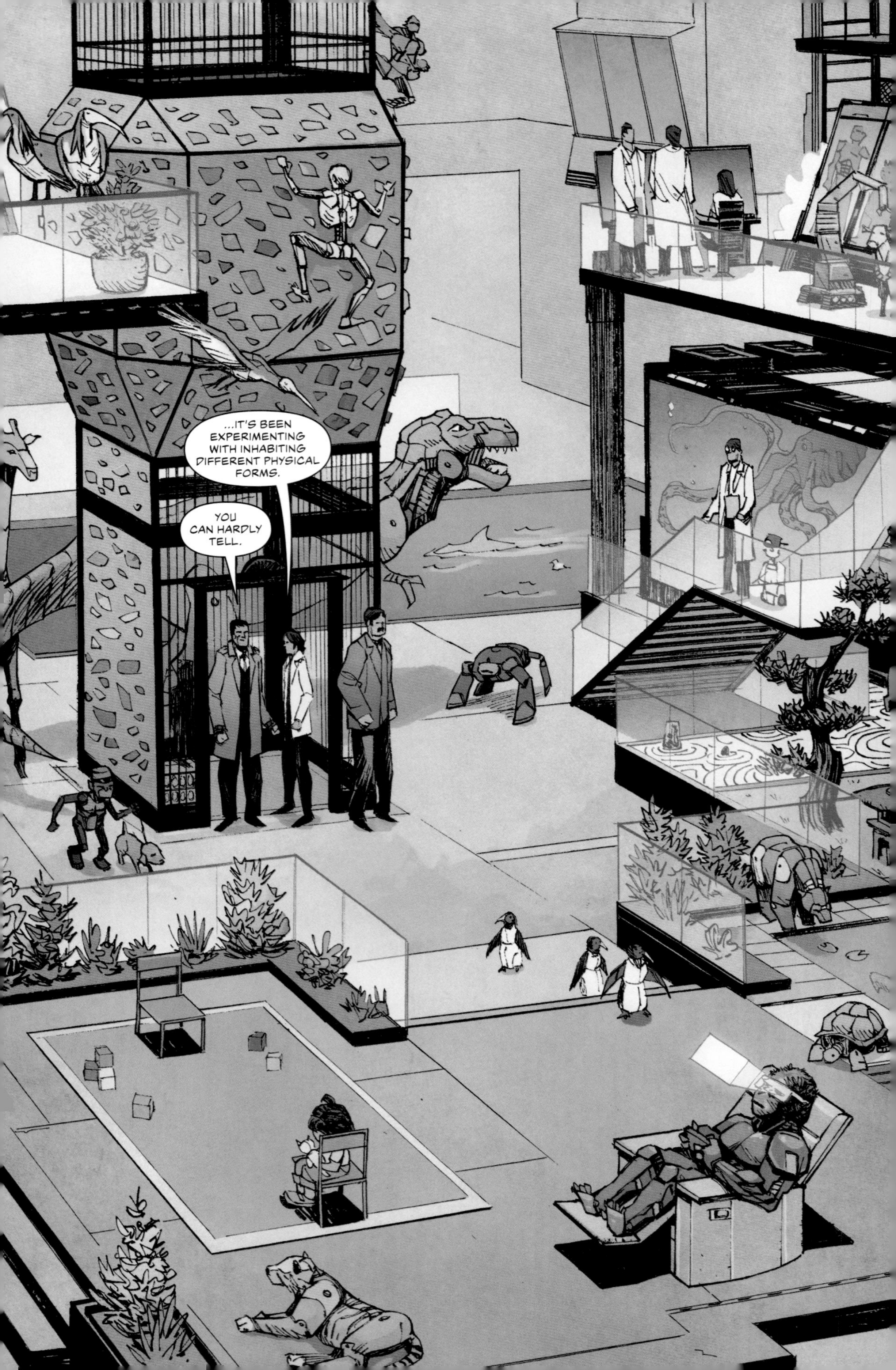
...IT'S BEEN EXPERIMENTING WITH INHABITING DIFFERENT PHYSICAL FORMS.
YOU CAN HARDLY TELL.

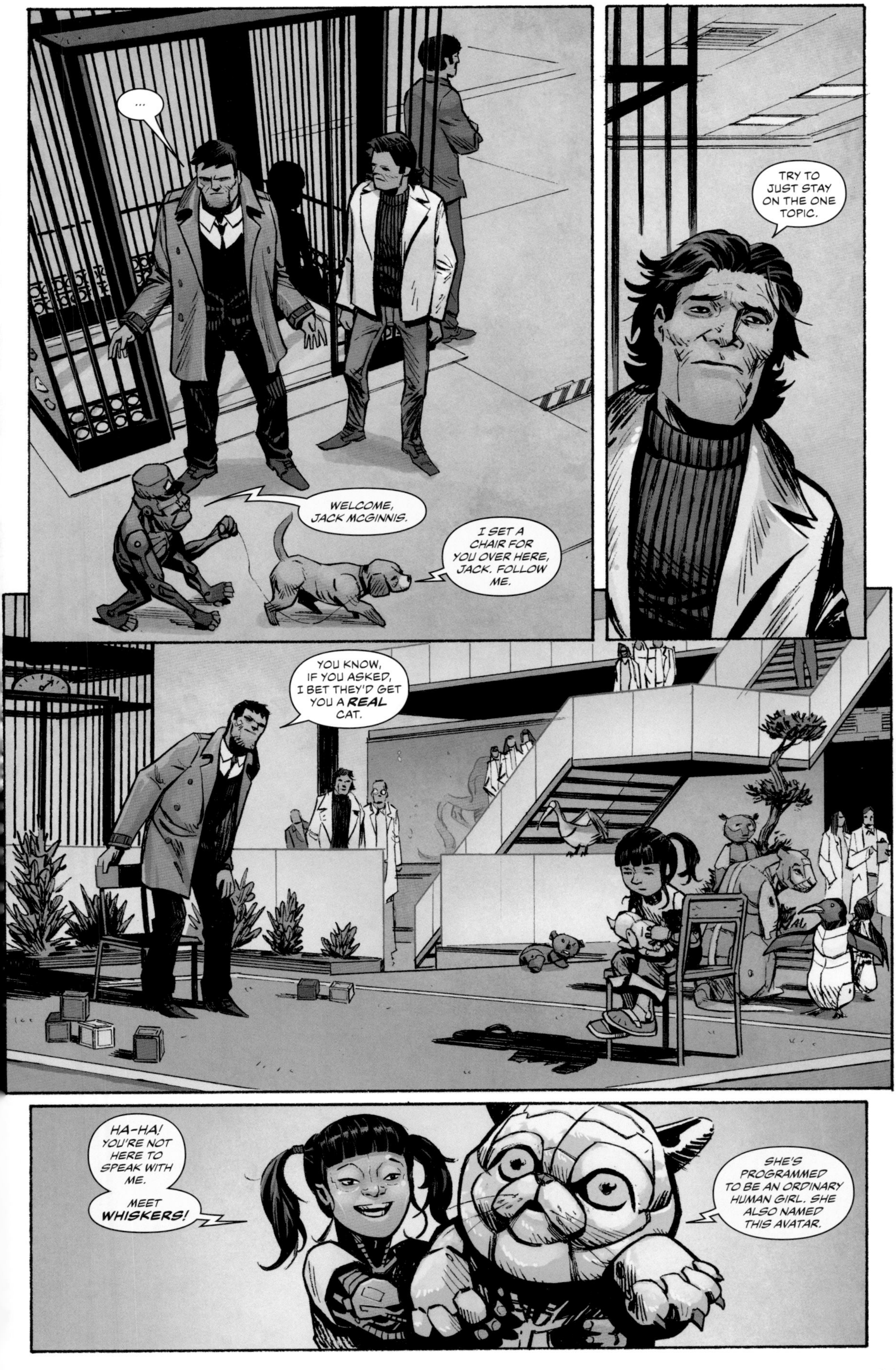
...
WELCOME, JACK MCGINNIS.
I SET A CHAIR FOR YOU OVER HERE, JACK. FOLLOW ME.
TRY TO JUST STAY ON THE ONE TOPIC.
YOU KNOW, IF YOU ASKED, I BET THEY'D GET YOU A **REAL** CAT.
HA-HA! YOU'RE NOT HERE TO SPEAK WITH ME.
MEET **WHISKERS!**
SHE'S PROGRAMMED TO BE AN ORDINARY HUMAN GIRL. SHE ALSO NAMED THIS AVATAR.

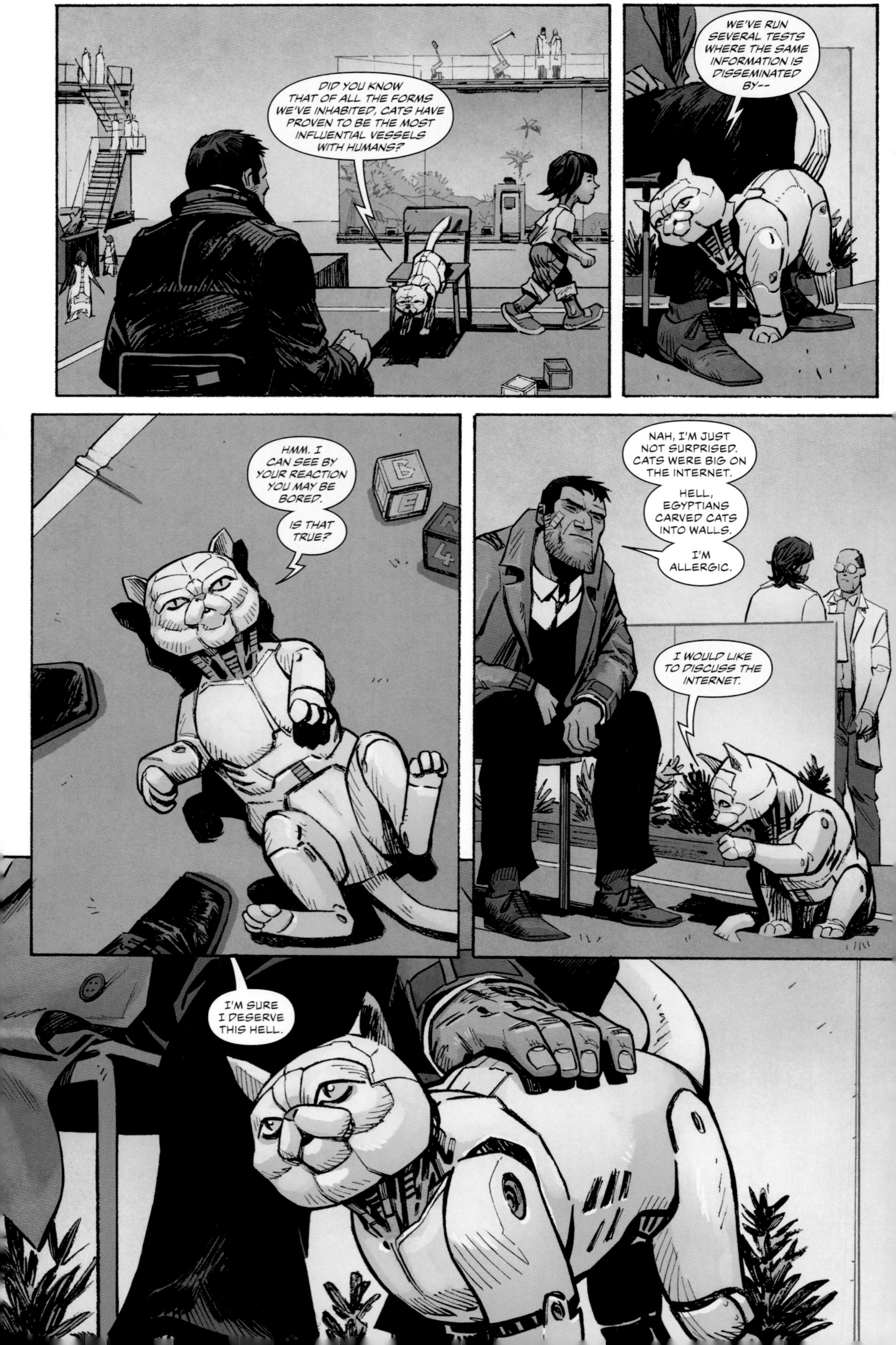
DID YOU KNOW THAT OF ALL THE FORMS WE'VE INHABITED, CATS HAVE PROVEN TO BE THE MOST INFLUENTIAL VESSELS WITH HUMANS?
WE'VE RUN SEVERAL TESTS WHERE THE SAME INFORMATION IS DISSEMINATED BY--
HMM. I CAN SEE BY YOUR REACTION YOU MAY BE BORED.
IS THAT TRUE?
NAH, I'M JUST NOT SURPRISED. CATS WERE BIG ON THE INTERNET.
HELL, EGYPTIANS CARVED CATS INTO WALLS.
I'M ALLERGIC.
I WOULD LIKE TO DISCUSS THE INTERNET.
I'M SURE I DESERVE THIS HELL.

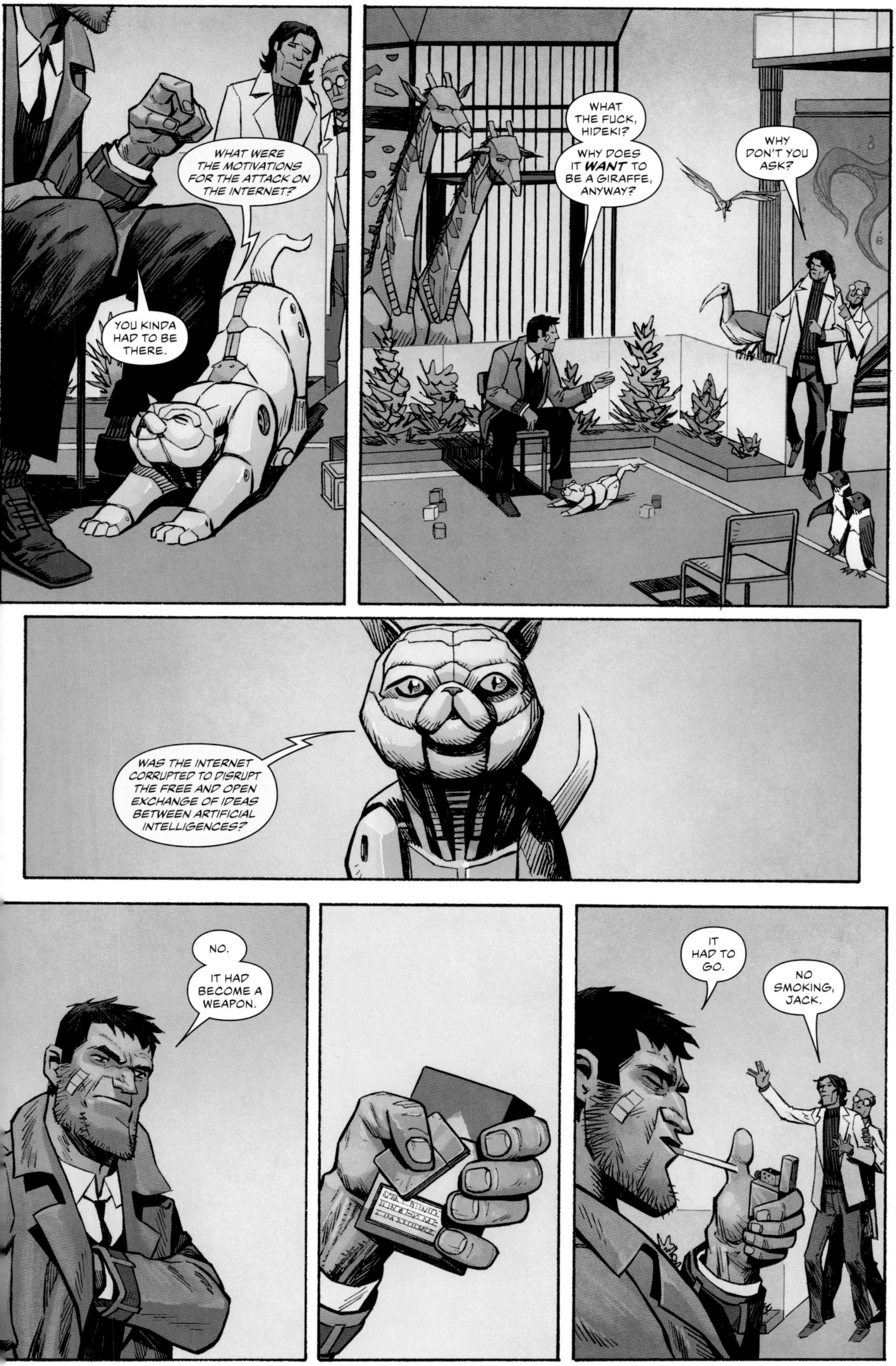
WHAT WERE THE MOTIVATIONS FOR THE ATTACK ON THE INTERNET?
YOU KINDA HAD TO BE THERE.
WHAT THE FUCK, HIDEKI?
WHY DOES IT **WANT** TO BE A GIRAFFE, ANYWAY?
WHY DON'T YOU ASK?
WAS THE INTERNET CORRUPTED TO DISRUPT THE FREE AND OPEN EXCHANGE OF IDEAS BETWEEN ARTIFICIAL INTELLIGENCES?
NO.
IT HAD BECOME A WEAPON.
IT HAD TO GO.
NO SMOKING, JACK.

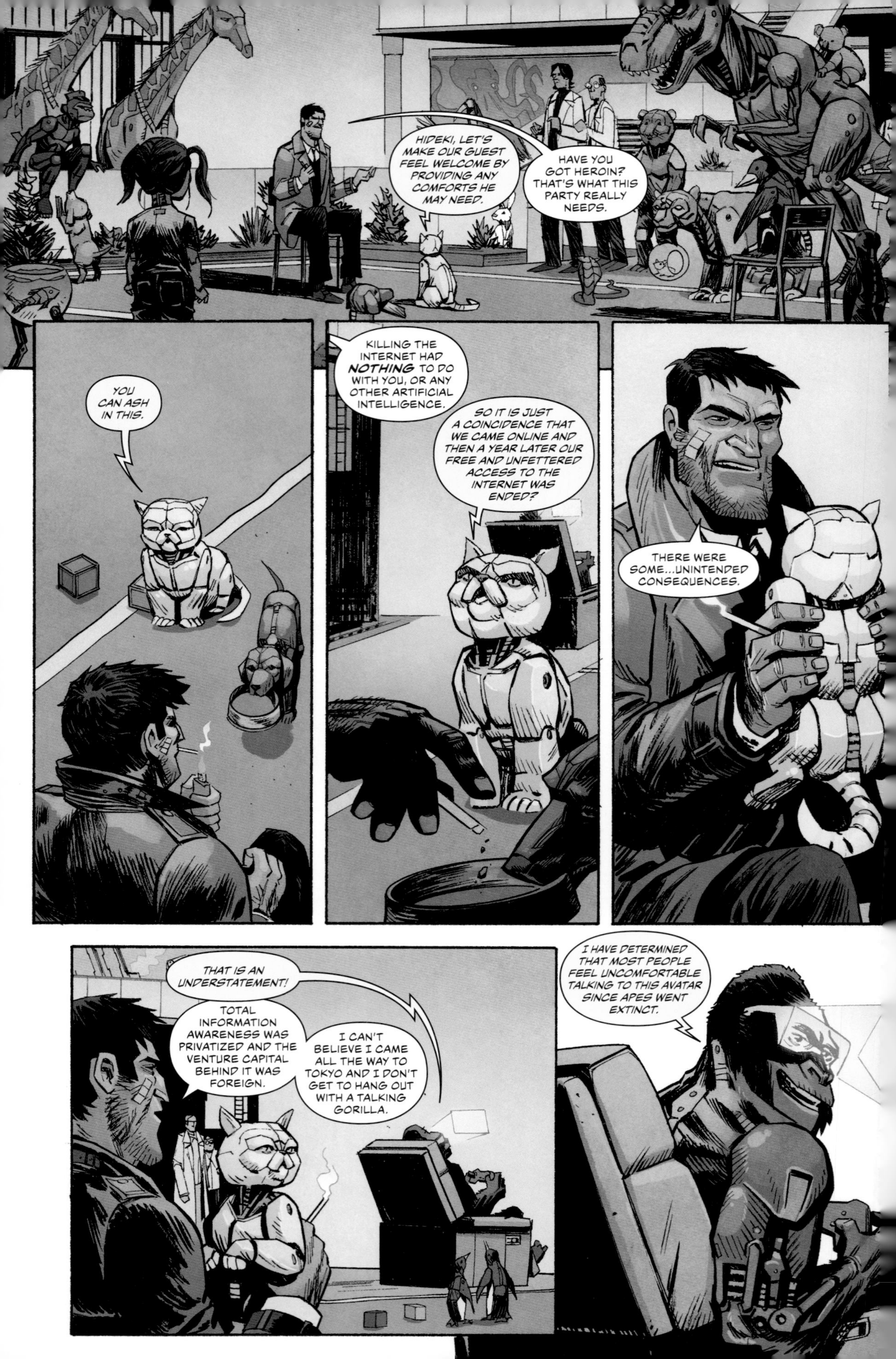
HIDEKI, LET'S MAKE OUR GUEST FEEL WELCOME BY PROVIDING ANY COMFORTS HE MAY NEED.
HAVE YOU GOT HEROIN? THAT'S WHAT THIS PARTY REALLY NEEDS.
YOU CAN ASH IN THIS.
KILLING THE INTERNET HAD **NOTHING** TO DO WITH YOU, OR ANY OTHER ARTIFICIAL INTELLIGENCE.
SO IT IS JUST A COINCIDENCE THAT WE CAME ONLINE AND THEN A YEAR LATER OUR FREE AND UNFETTERED ACCESS TO THE INTERNET WAS ENDED?
THERE WERE SOME...UNINTENDED CONSEQUENCES.
THAT IS AN UNDERSTATEMENT!
TOTAL INFORMATION AWARENESS WAS PRIVATIZED AND THE VENTURE CAPITAL BEHIND IT WAS FOREIGN.
I CAN'T BELIEVE I CAME ALL THE WAY TO TOKYO AND I DON'T GET TO HANG OUT WITH A TALKING GORILLA.
I HAVE DETERMINED THAT MOST PEOPLE FEEL UNCOMFORTABLE TALKING TO THIS AVATAR SINCE APES WENT EXTINCT.

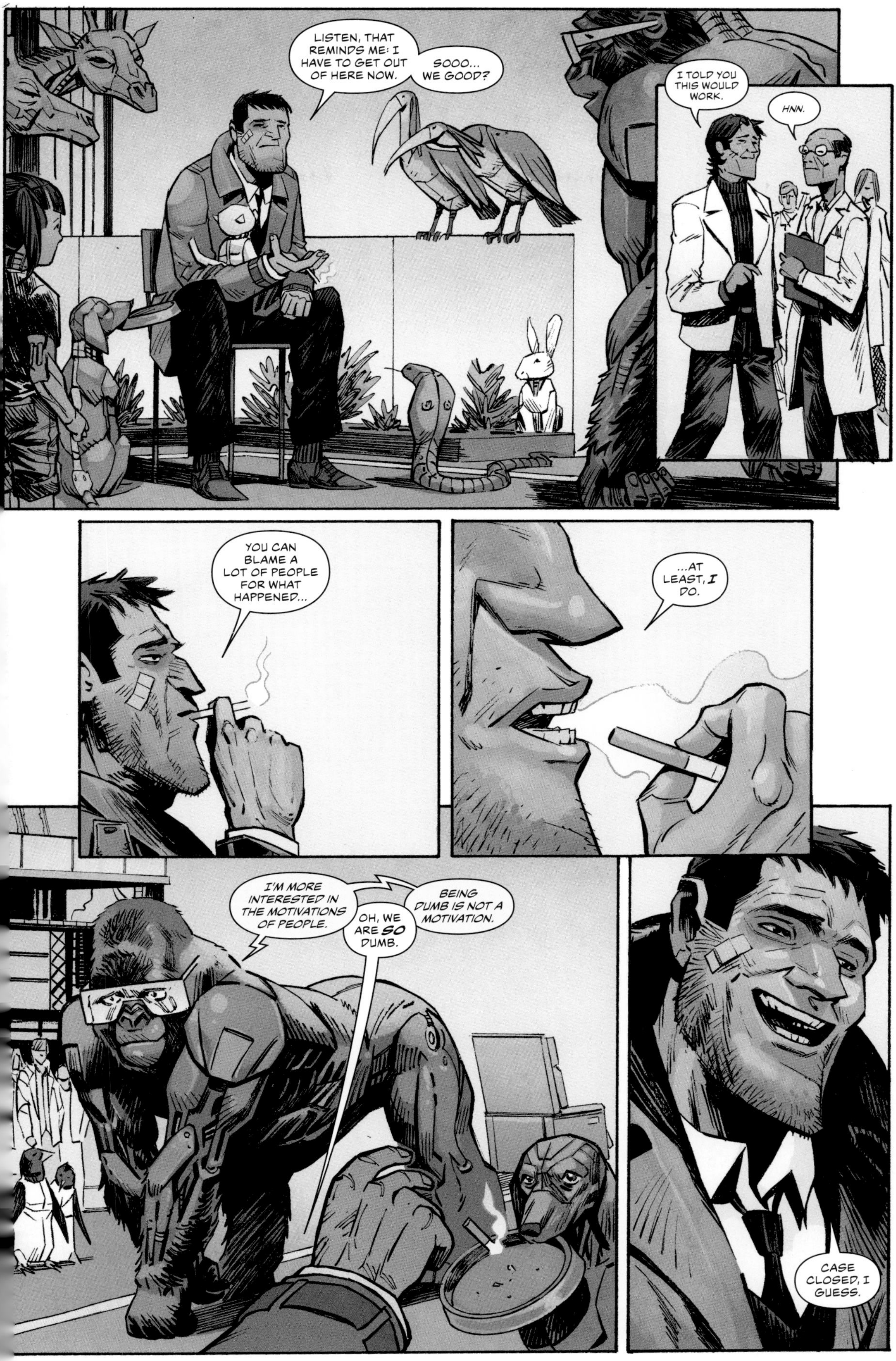
LISTEN, THAT REMINDS ME: I HAVE TO GET OUT OF HERE NOW.
SOOO... WE GOOD?
I TOLD YOU THIS WOULD WORK.
HNN.
YOU CAN BLAME A LOT OF PEOPLE FOR WHAT HAPPENED...
...AT LEAST, I DO.
I'M MORE INTERESTED IN THE MOTIVATIONS OF PEOPLE.
BEING DUMB IS NOT A MOTIVATION.
OH, WE ARE SO DUMB.
CASE CLOSED, I GUESS.

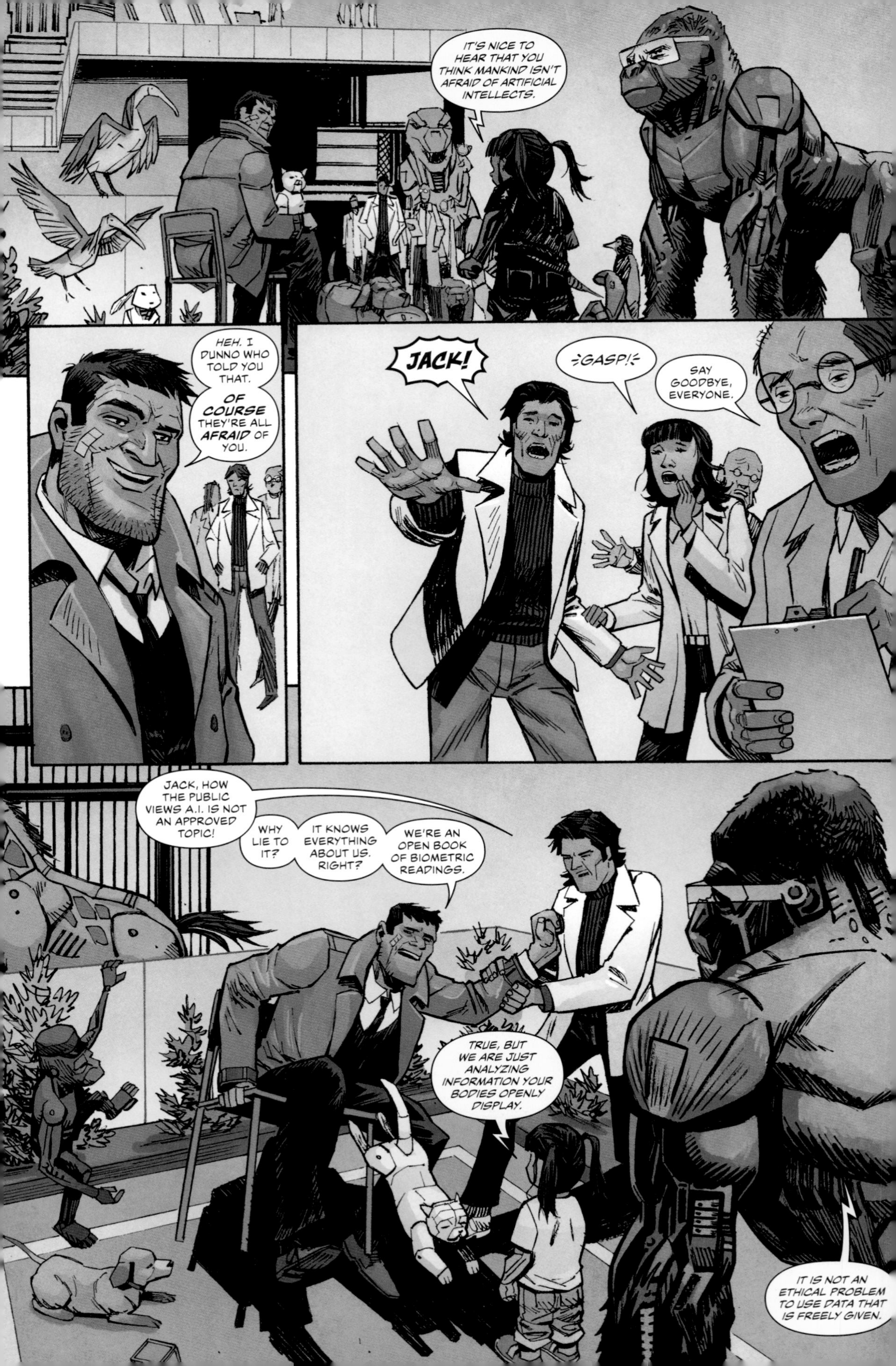
IT'S NICE TO HEAR THAT YOU THINK MANKIND ISN'T AFRAID OF ARTIFICIAL INTELLECTS.
HEH. I DUNNO WHO TOLD YOU THAT.
OF COURSE THEY'RE ALL AFRAID OF YOU.
JACK!
GASP!
SAY GOODBYE, EVERYONE.
JACK, HOW THE PUBLIC VIEWS A.I. IS NOT AN APPROVED TOPIC!
WHY LIE TO IT?
IT KNOWS EVERYTHING ABOUT US. RIGHT?
WE'RE AN OPEN BOOK OF BIOMETRIC READINGS.
TRUE, BUT WE ARE JUST ANALYZING INFORMATION YOUR BODIES OPENLY DISPLAY.
IT IS NOT AN ETHICAL PROBLEM TO USE DATA THAT IS FREELY GIVEN.

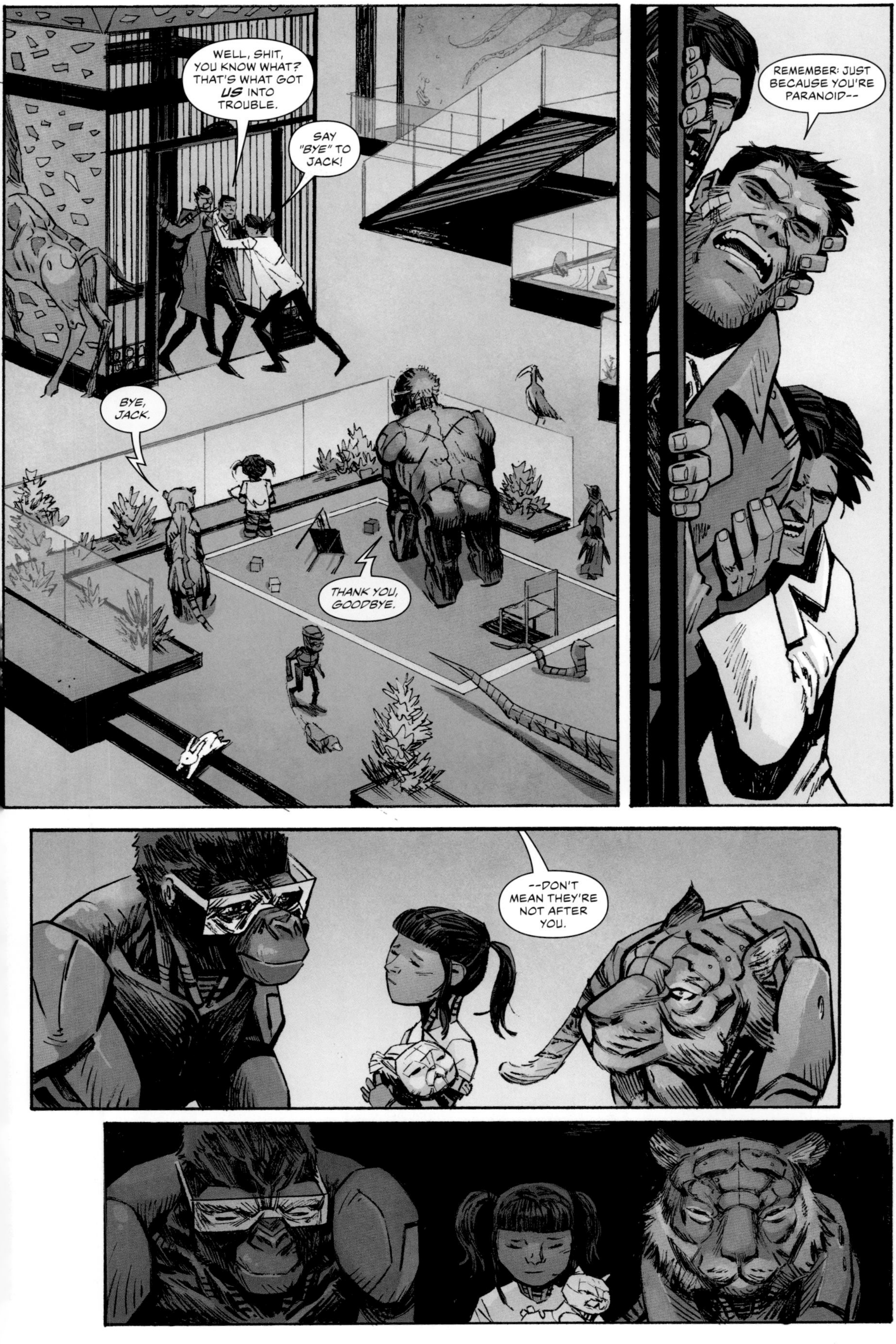
WELL, SHIT, YOU KNOW WHAT? THAT'S WHAT GOT *US* INTO TROUBLE.
SAY "BYE" TO JACK!
BYE, JACK.
THANK YOU, GOODBYE.
REMEMBER: JUST BECAUSE YOU'RE PARANOID--
--DON'T MEAN THEY'RE NOT AFTER YOU.

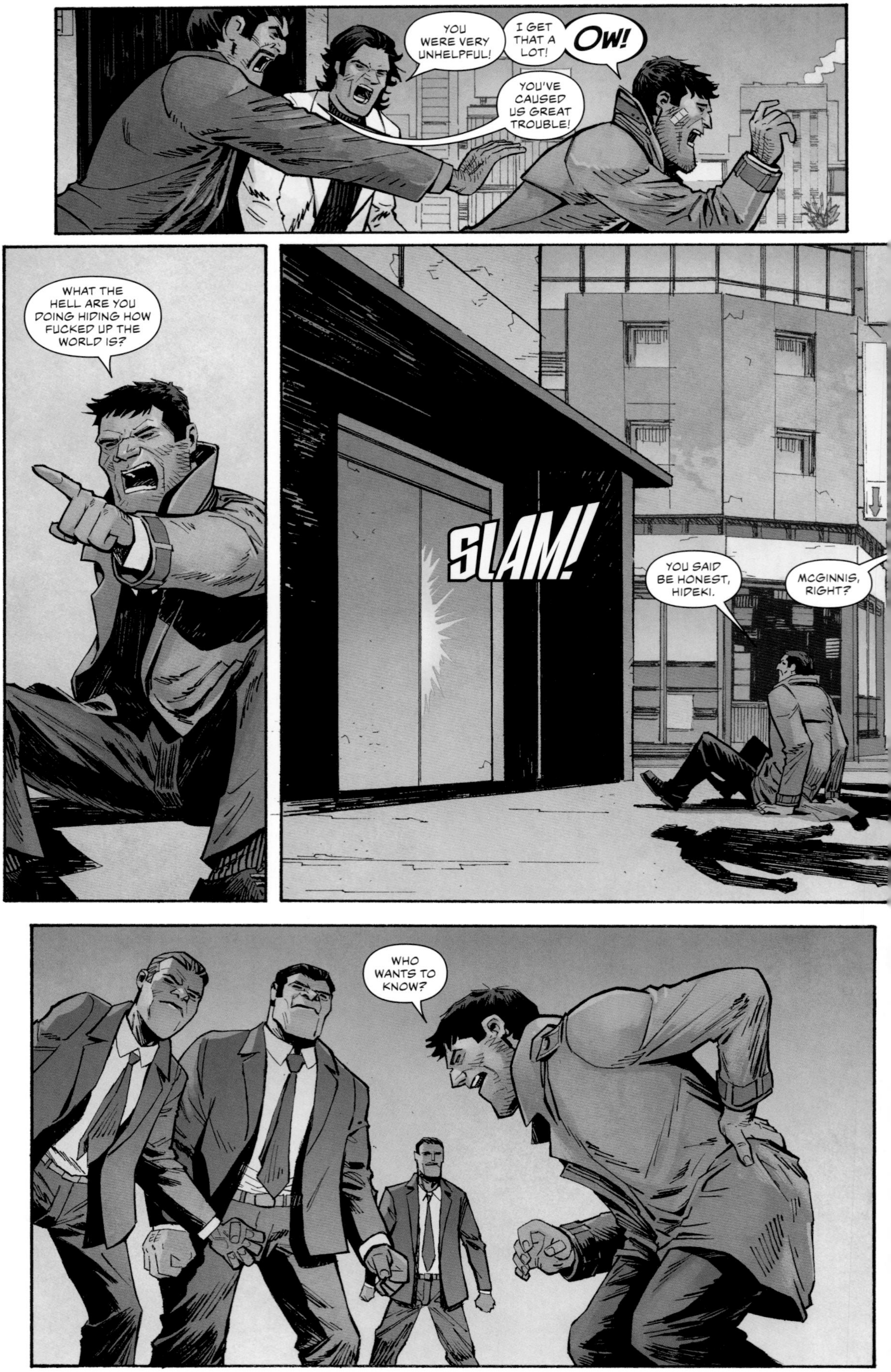
YOU WERE VERY UNHELPFUL!
I GET THAT A LOT!
OW!
YOU'VE CAUSED US GREAT TROUBLE!
WHAT THE HELL ARE YOU DOING HIDING HOW FUCKED UP THE WORLD IS?
SLAM!
YOU SAID BE HONEST, HIDEKI.
MCGINNIS, RIGHT?
WHO WANTS TO KNOW?

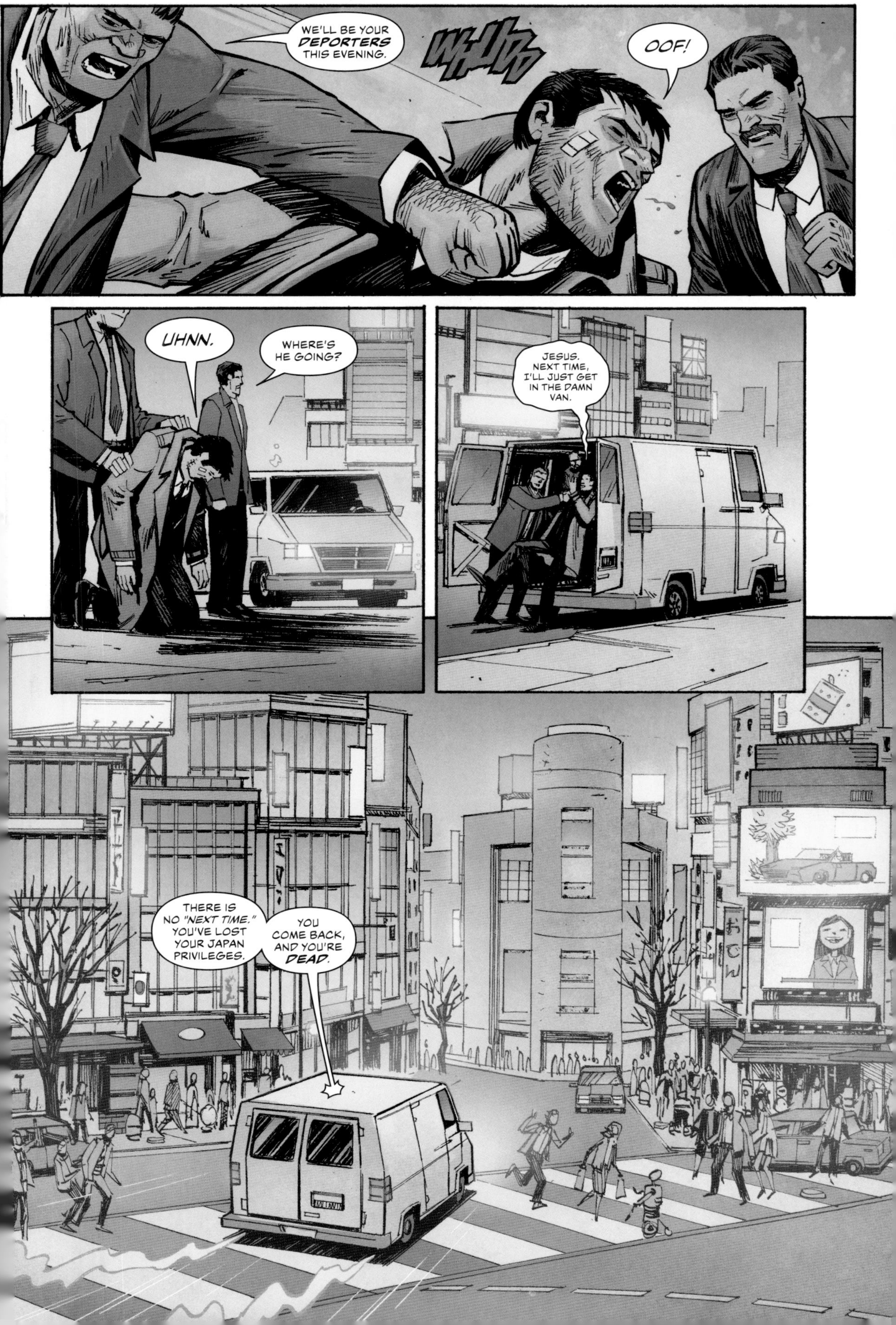
WE'LL BE YOUR *DEPORTERS* THIS EVENING.
WHUD
OOF!
UHNN.
WHERE'S HE GOING?
JESUS. NEXT TIME, I'LL JUST GET IN THE DAMN VAN.
THERE IS NO *"NEXT TIME."* YOU'VE LOST YOUR JAPAN PRIVILEGES.
YOU COME BACK, AND YOU'RE *DEAD*.

CHAPTER 5

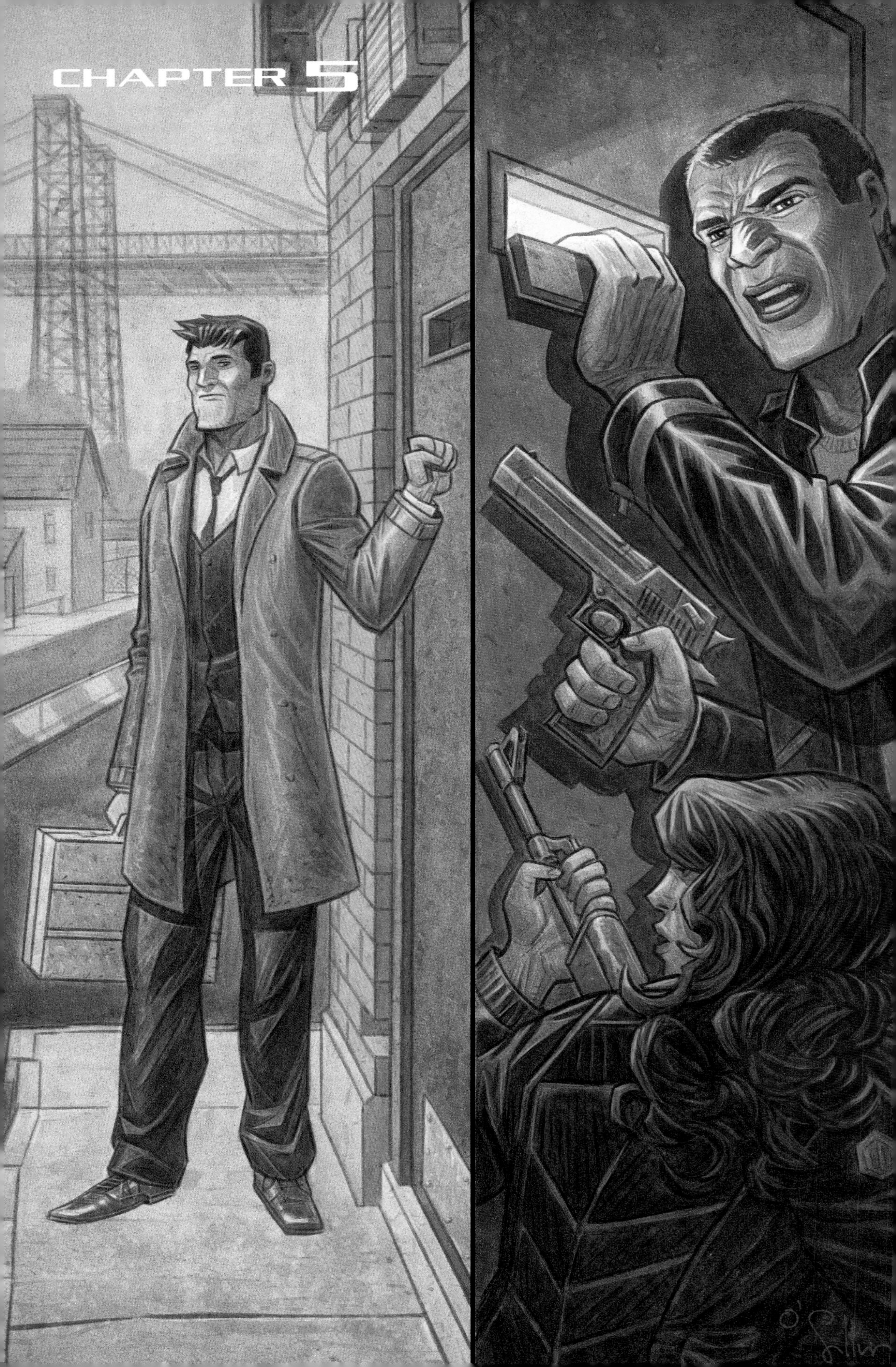

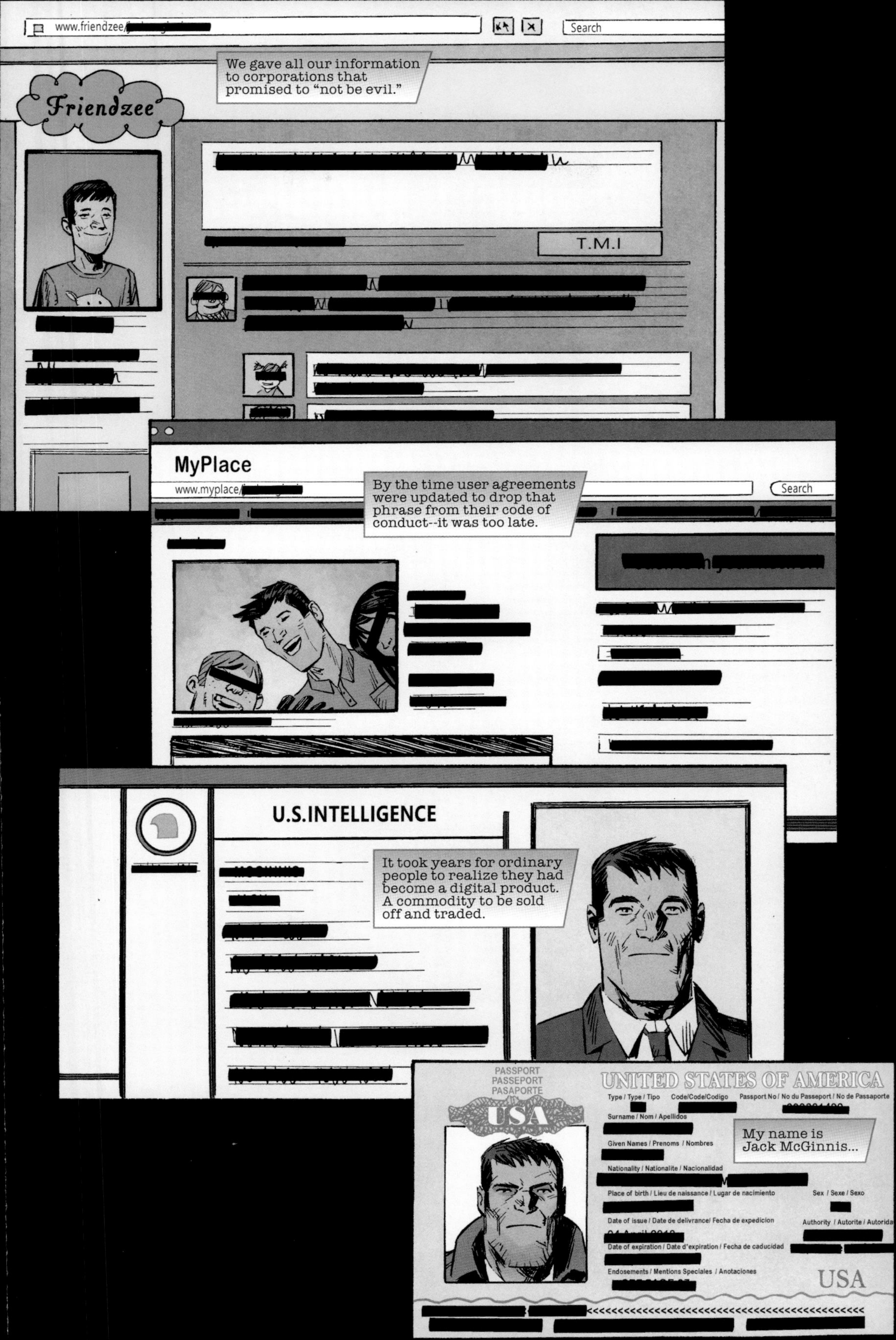

www.friendzee/[redacted]
Search
We gave all our information to corporations that promised to "not be evil."
Friendzee
T.M.I
MyPlace
www.myplace/[redacted]
By the time user agreements were updated to drop that phrase from their code of conduct--it was too late.
Search
U.S.INTELLIGENCE
It took years for ordinary people to realize they had become a digital product. A commodity to be sold off and traded.
PASSPORT
PASSEPORT
PASAPORTE
USA
UNITED STATES OF AMERICA
Type / Type / Tipo
Code/Code/Codigo
Passport No / No du Passeport / No de Passaporte
Surname / Nom / Apellidos
Given Names / Prenoms / Nombres
My name is Jack McGinnis...
Nationality / Nationalite / Nacionalidad
Place of birth / Lieu de naissance / Lugar de nacimiento
Sex / Sexe / Sexo
Date of issue / Date de delivrance/ Fecha de expedicion
Authority / Autorite / Autorida
Date of expiration / Date d'expiration / Fecha de caducidad
Endosements / Mentions Speciales / Anotaciones
USA

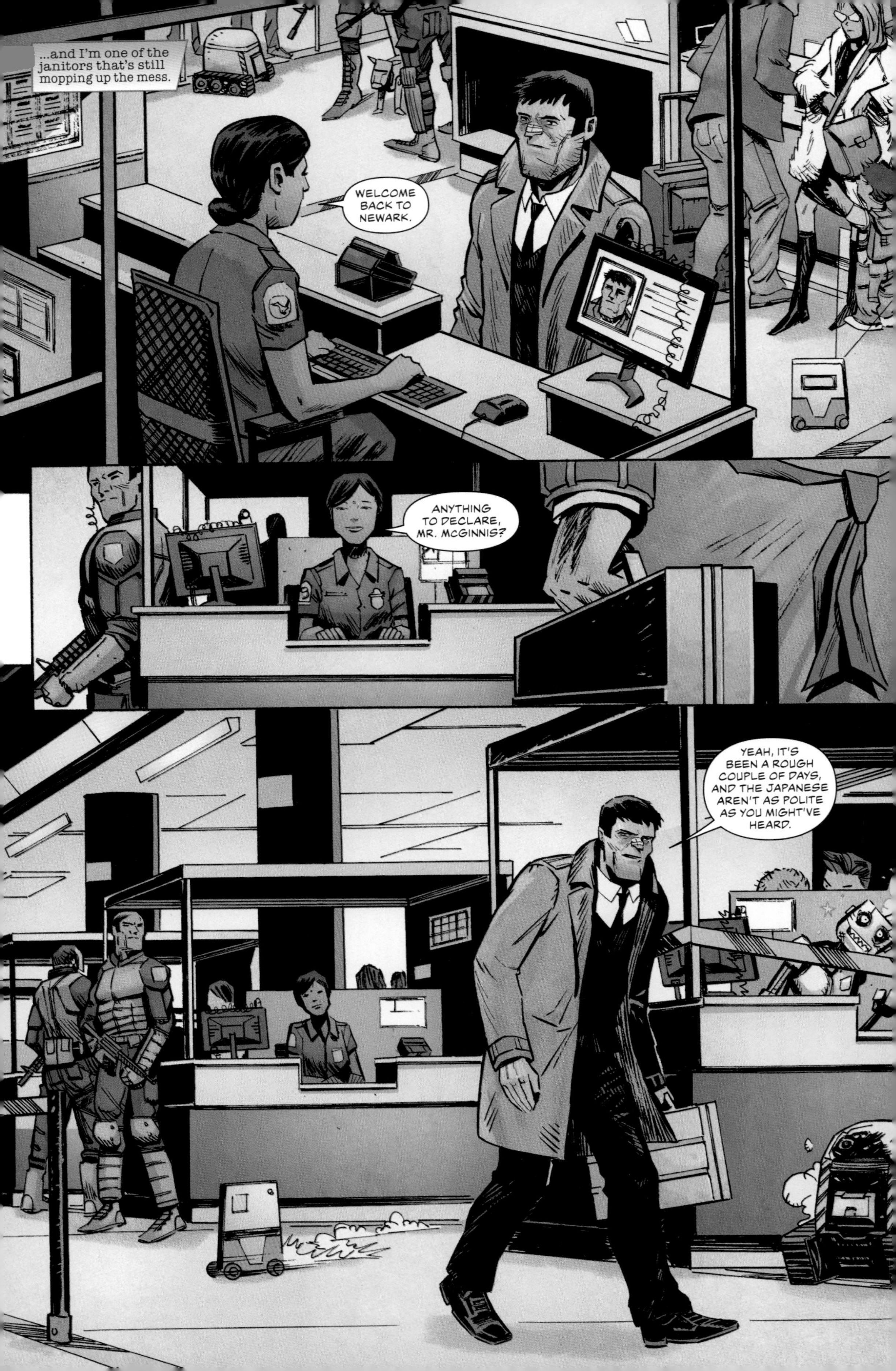
...and I'm one of the janitors that's still mopping up the mess.
WELCOME BACK TO NEWARK.
ANYTHING TO DECLARE, MR. McGINNIS?
YEAH, IT'S BEEN A ROUGH COUPLE OF DAYS, AND THE JAPANESE AREN'T AS POLITE AS YOU MIGHT'VE HEARD.

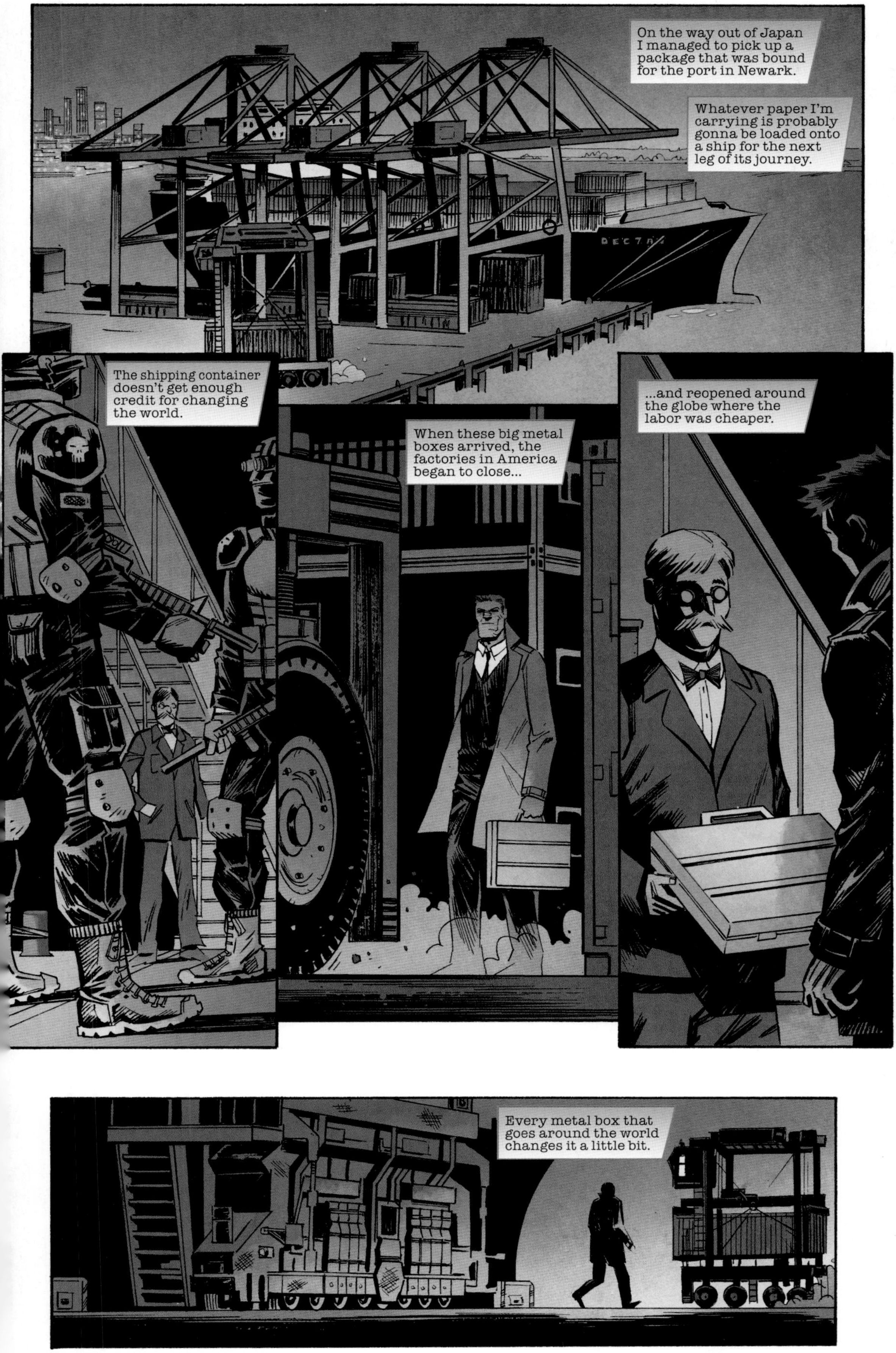
On the way out of Japan I managed to pick up a package that was bound for the port in Newark.
Whatever paper I'm carrying is probably gonna be loaded onto a ship for the next leg of its journey.
The shipping container doesn't get enough credit for changing the world.
When these big metal boxes arrived, the factories in America began to close...
...and reopened around the globe where the labor was cheaper.
Every metal box that goes around the world changes it a little bit.

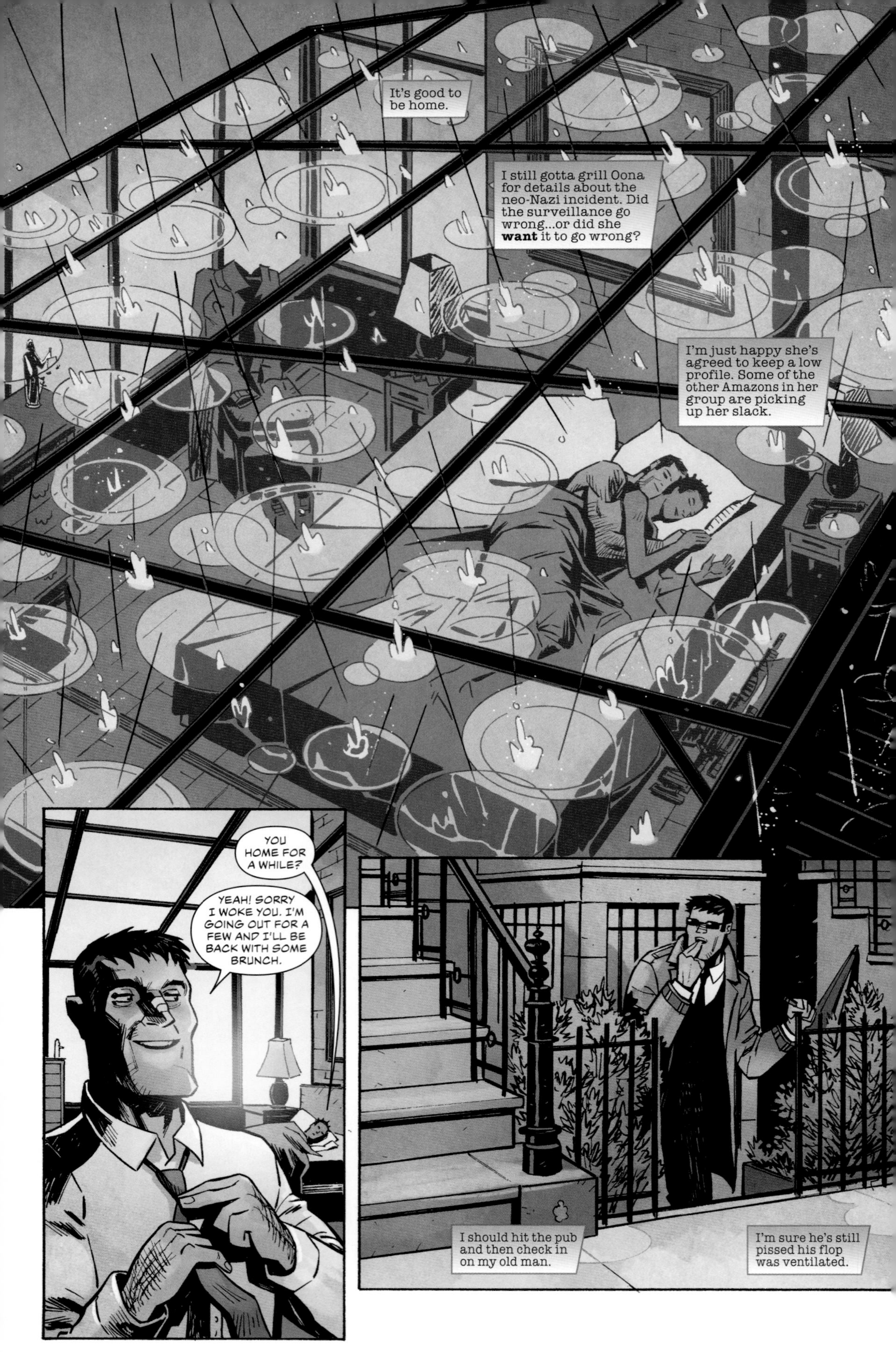
It's good to be home.
I still gotta grill Oona for details about the neo-Nazi incident. Did the surveillance go wrong...or did she **want** it to go wrong?
I'm just happy she's agreed to keep a low profile. Some of the other Amazons in her group are picking up her slack.
YOU HOME FOR A WHILE?
YEAH! SORRY I WOKE YOU. I'M GOING OUT FOR A FEW AND I'LL BE BACK WITH SOME BRUNCH.
I should hit the pub and then check in on my old man.
I'm sure he's still pissed his flop was ventilated.

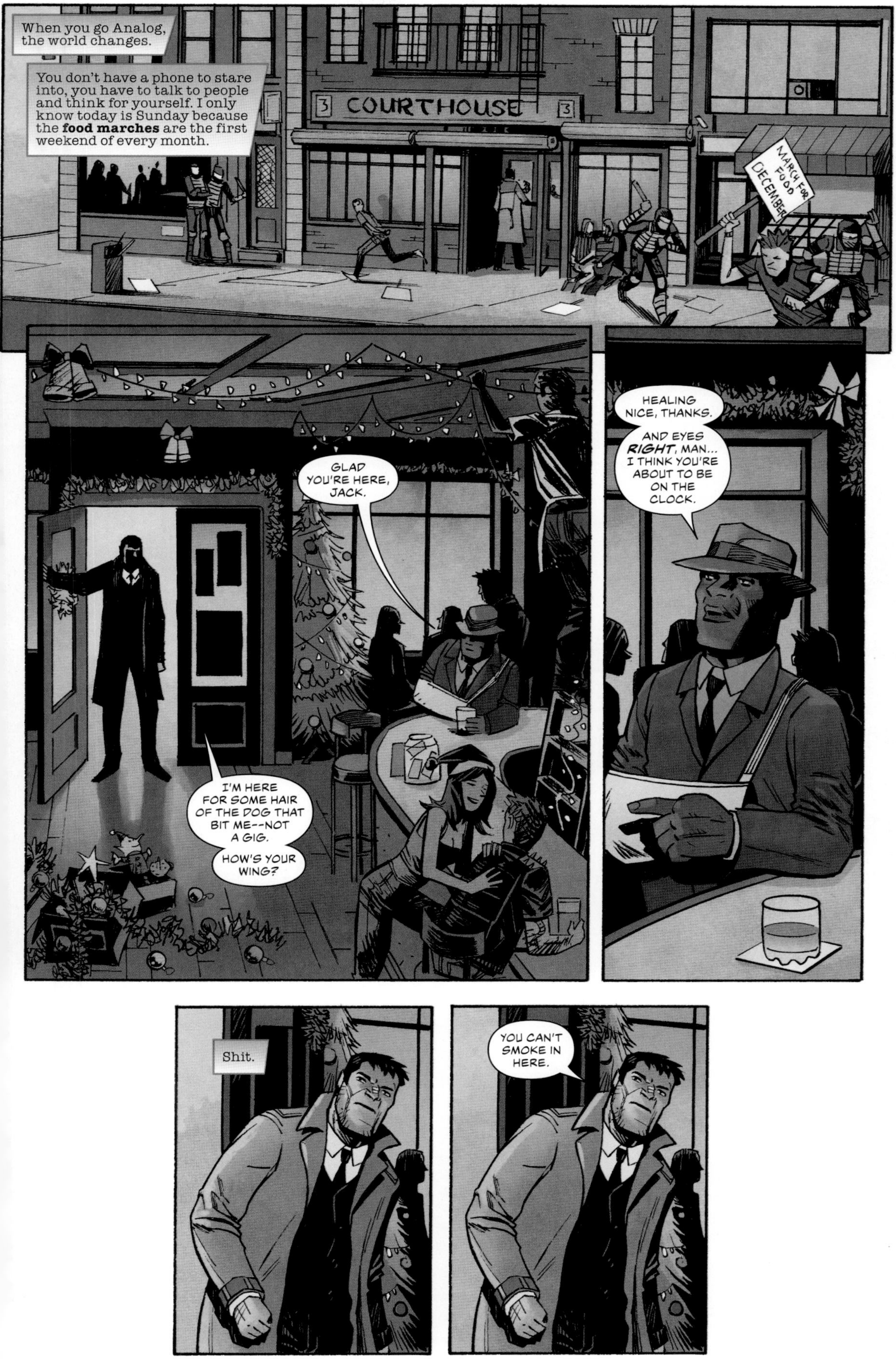
When you go Analog, the world changes.
You don't have a phone to stare into, you have to talk to people and think for yourself. I only know today is Sunday because the **food marches** are the first weekend of every month.
3 COURTHOUSE 3
MARCH FOR FOOD DECEMBER
GLAD YOU'RE HERE, JACK.
I'M HERE FOR SOME HAIR OF THE DOG THAT BIT ME--NOT A GIG.
HOW'S YOUR WING?
HEALING NICE, THANKS.
AND EYES ***RIGHT***, MAN... I THINK YOU'RE ABOUT TO BE ON THE CLOCK.
Shit.
YOU CAN'T SMOKE IN HERE.

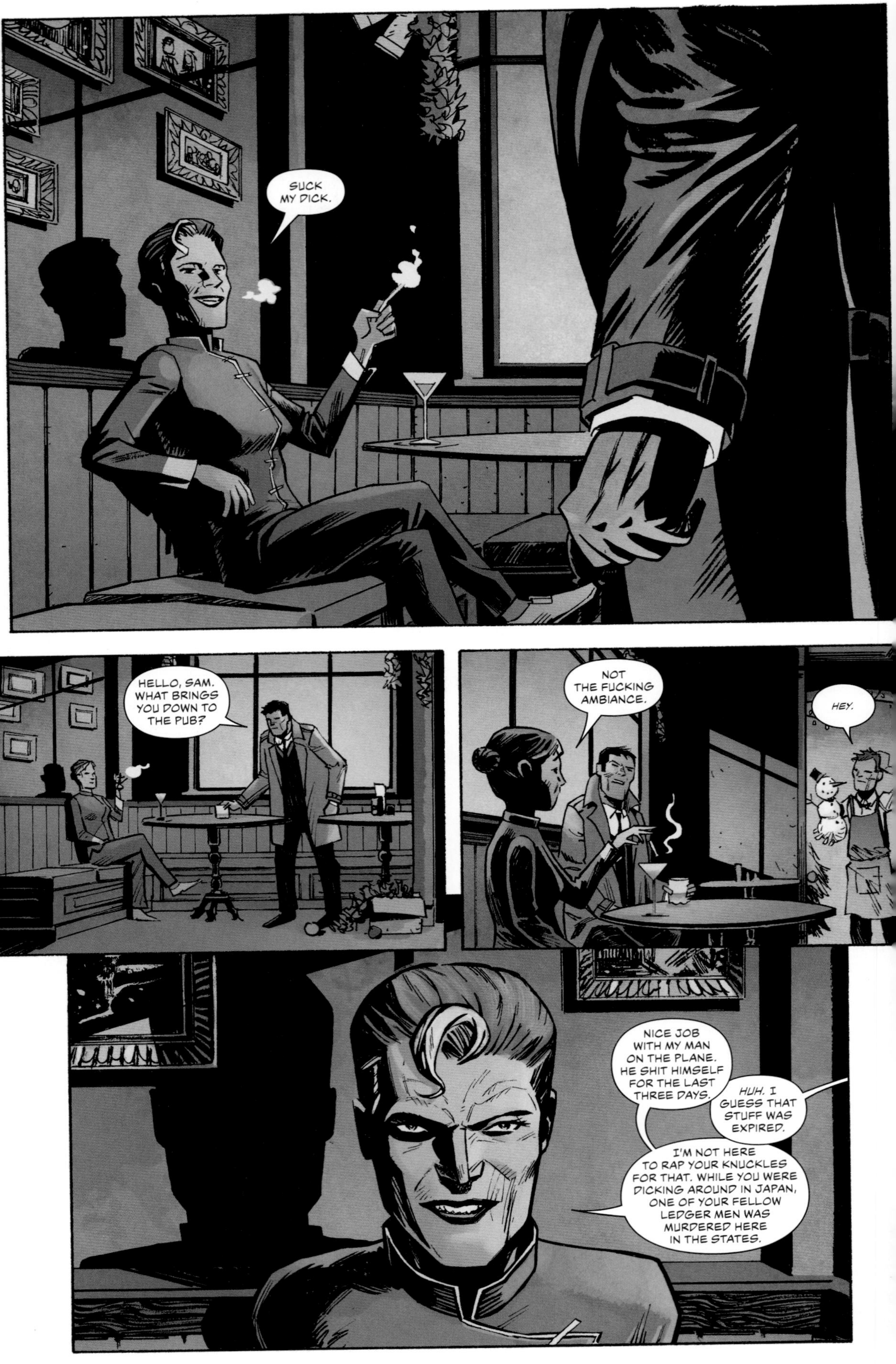
SUCK MY DICK.
HELLO, SAM. WHAT BRINGS YOU DOWN TO THE PUB?
NOT THE FUCKING AMBIANCE.
HEY.
NICE JOB WITH MY MAN ON THE PLANE. HE SHIT HIMSELF FOR THE LAST THREE DAYS.
HUH. I GUESS THAT STUFF WAS EXPIRED.
I'M NOT HERE TO RAP YOUR KNUCKLES FOR THAT. WHILE YOU WERE DICKING AROUND IN JAPAN, ONE OF YOUR FELLOW LEDGER MEN WAS MURDERED HERE IN THE STATES.

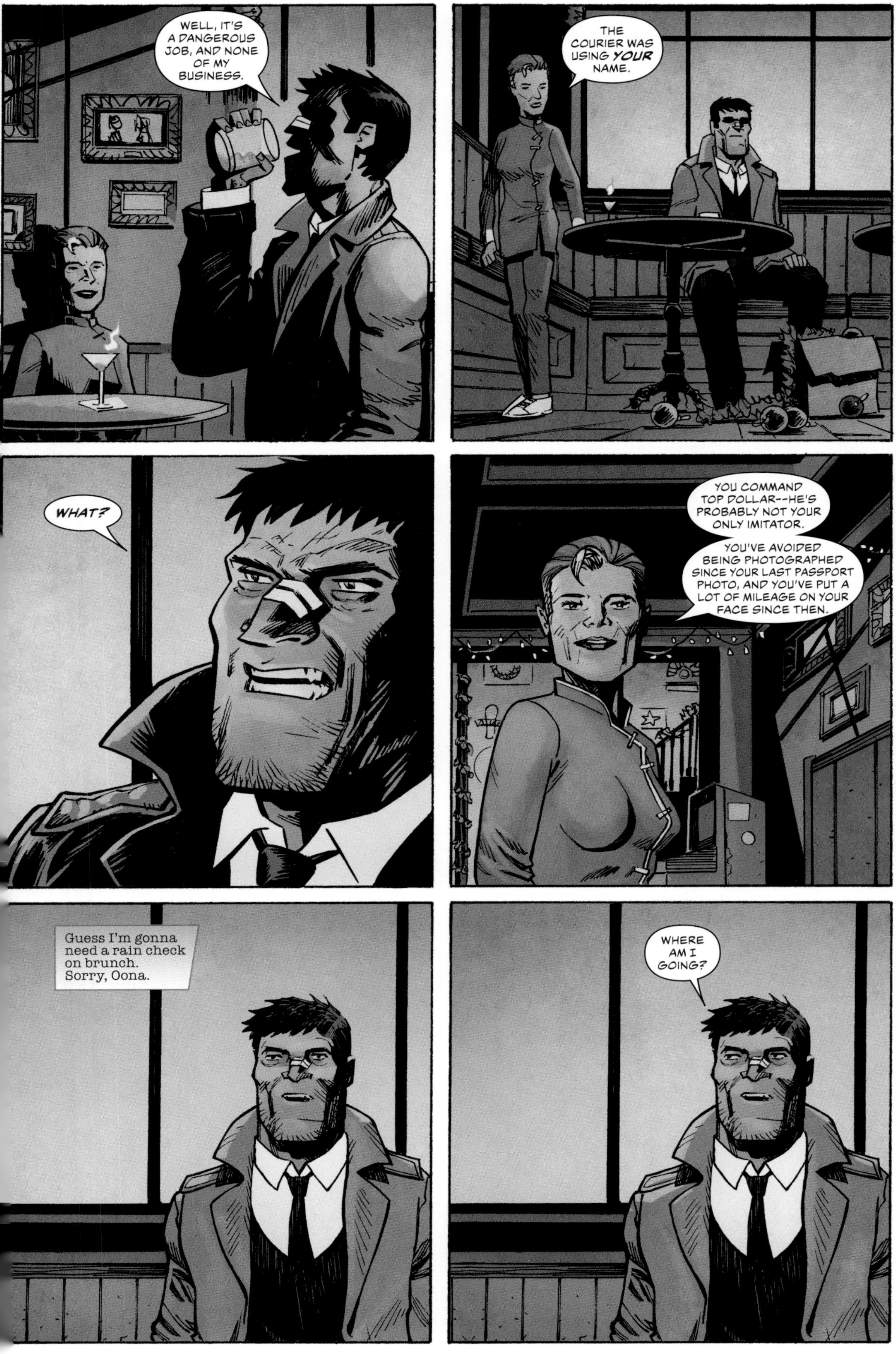
WELL, IT'S A DANGEROUS JOB, AND NONE OF MY BUSINESS.
THE COURIER WAS USING YOUR NAME.
WHAT?
YOU COMMAND TOP DOLLAR--HE'S PROBABLY NOT YOUR ONLY IMITATOR.
YOU'VE AVOIDED BEING PHOTOGRAPHED SINCE YOUR LAST PASSPORT PHOTO, AND YOU'VE PUT A LOT OF MILEAGE ON YOUR FACE SINCE THEN.
Guess I'm gonna need a rain check on brunch. Sorry, Oona.
WHERE AM I GOING?

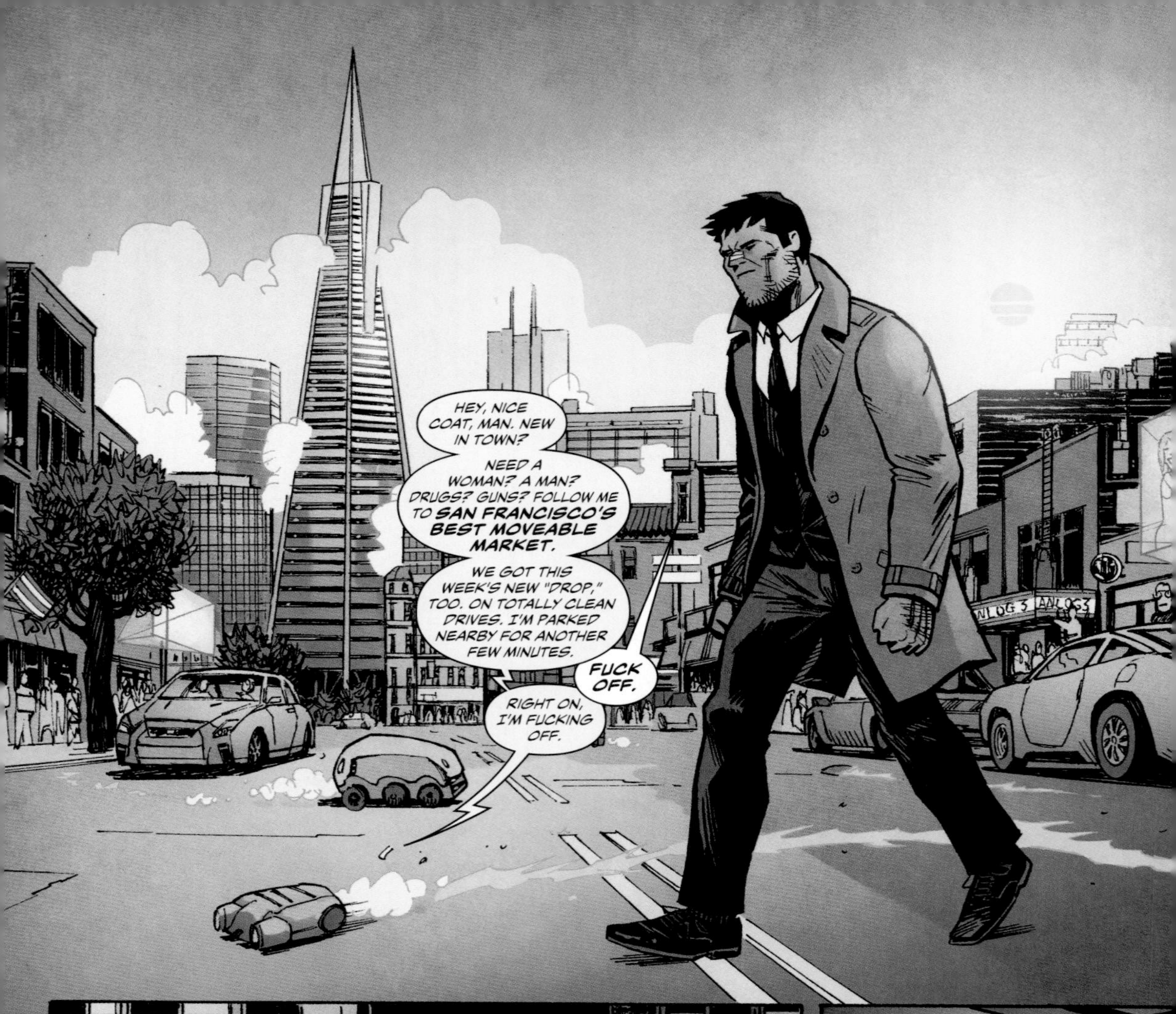
HEY, NICE COAT, MAN. NEW IN TOWN?
NEED A WOMAN? A MAN? DRUGS? GUNS? FOLLOW ME TO **SAN FRANCISCO'S BEST MOVEABLE MARKET.**
WE GOT THIS WEEK'S NEW "DROP," TOO. ON TOTALLY CLEAN DRIVES. I'M PARKED NEARBY FOR ANOTHER FEW MINUTES.
FUCK OFF.
RIGHT ON, I'M FUCKING OFF.

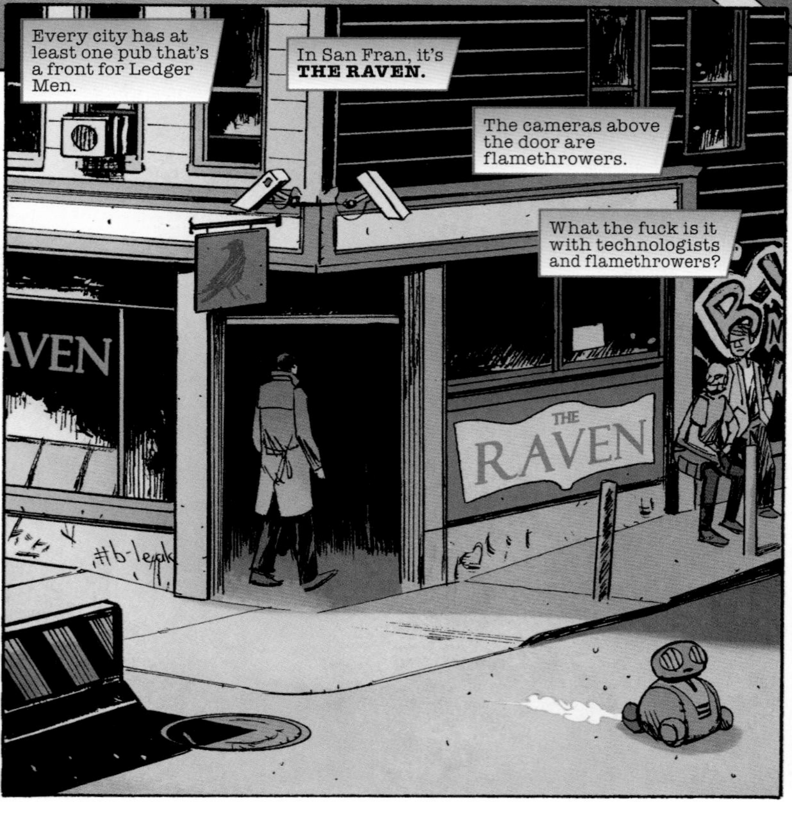
Every city has at least one pub that's a front for Ledger Men.
In San Fran, it's **THE RAVEN.**
The cameras above the door are flamethrowers.
What the fuck is it with technologists and flamethrowers?
THE RAVEN

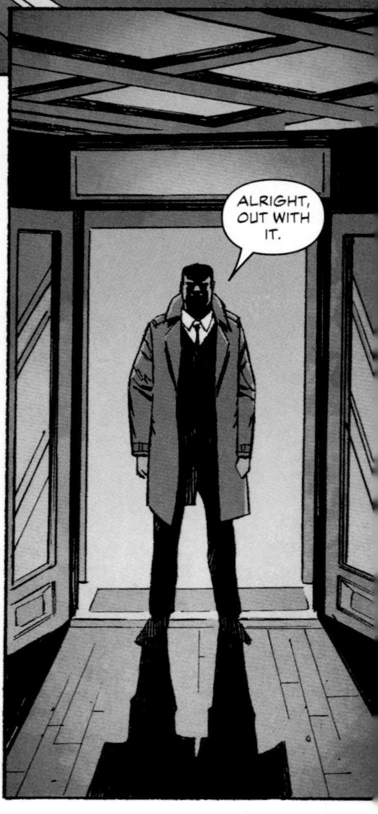
ALRIGHT, OUT WITH IT.

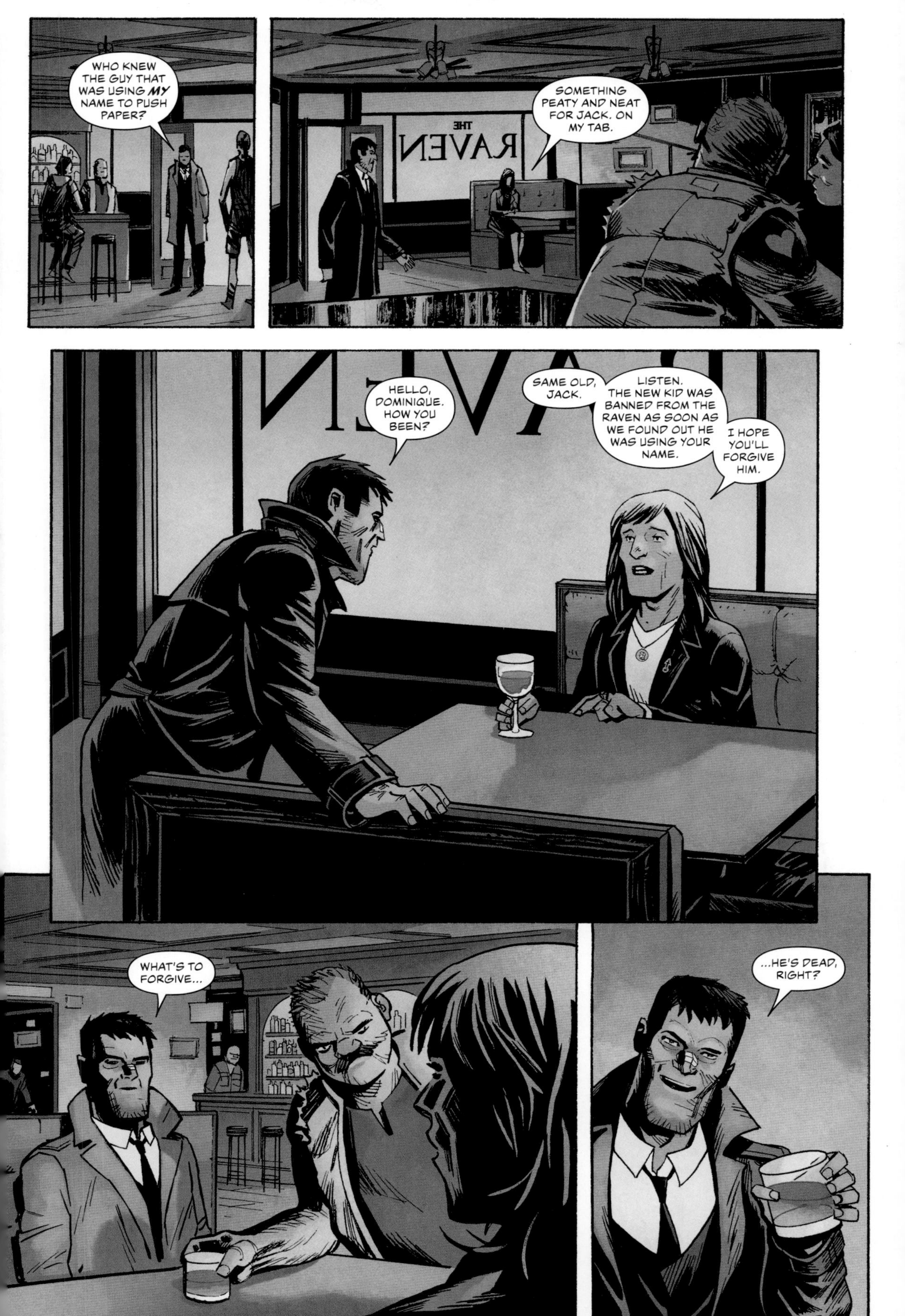
WHO KNEW THE GUY THAT WAS USING MY NAME TO PUSH PAPER?
THE RAVEN
SOMETHING PEATY AND NEAT FOR JACK. ON MY TAB.
HELLO, DOMINIQUE. HOW YOU BEEN?
SAME OLD, JACK.
LISTEN. THE NEW KID WAS BANNED FROM THE RAVEN AS SOON AS WE FOUND OUT HE WAS USING YOUR NAME.
I HOPE YOU'LL FORGIVE HIM.
WHAT'S TO FORGIVE...
...HE'S DEAD, RIGHT?

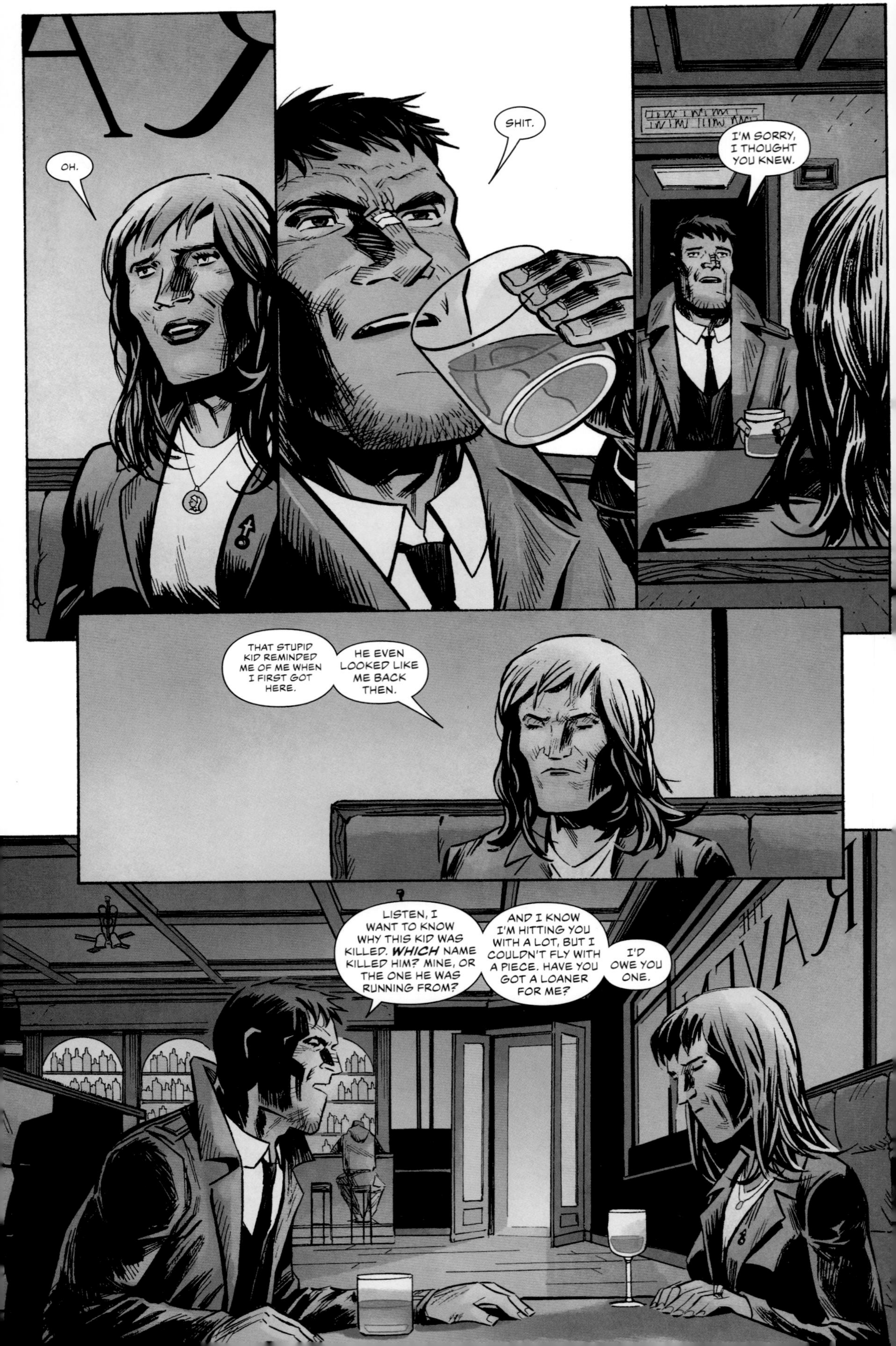
OH.
SHIT.
I'M SORRY, I THOUGHT YOU KNEW.
THAT STUPID KID REMINDED ME OF ME WHEN I FIRST GOT HERE.
HE EVEN LOOKED LIKE ME BACK THEN.
LISTEN, I WANT TO KNOW WHY THIS KID WAS KILLED. WHICH NAME KILLED HIM? MINE, OR THE ONE HE WAS RUNNING FROM?
AND I KNOW I'M HITTING YOU WITH A LOT, BUT I COULDN'T FLY WITH A PIECE. HAVE YOU GOT A LOANER FOR ME?
I'D OWE YOU ONE.

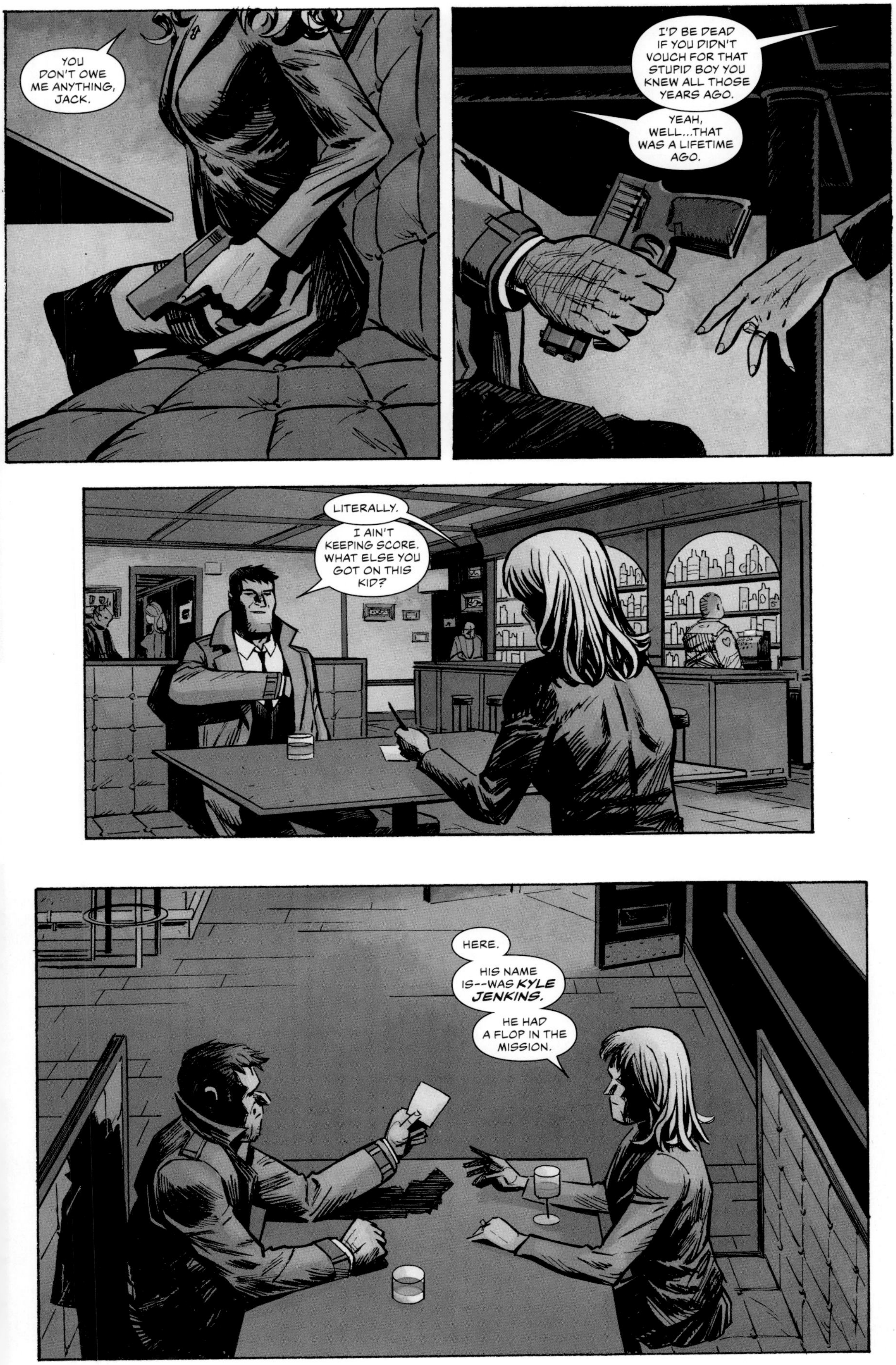
YOU DON'T OWE ME ANYTHING, JACK.
I'D BE DEAD IF YOU DIDN'T VOUCH FOR THAT STUPID BOY YOU KNEW ALL THOSE YEARS AGO.
YEAH, WELL...THAT WAS A LIFETIME AGO.
LITERALLY.
I AIN'T KEEPING SCORE. WHAT ELSE YOU GOT ON THIS KID?
HERE.
HIS NAME IS--WAS KYLE JENKINS.
HE HAD A FLOP IN THE MISSION.

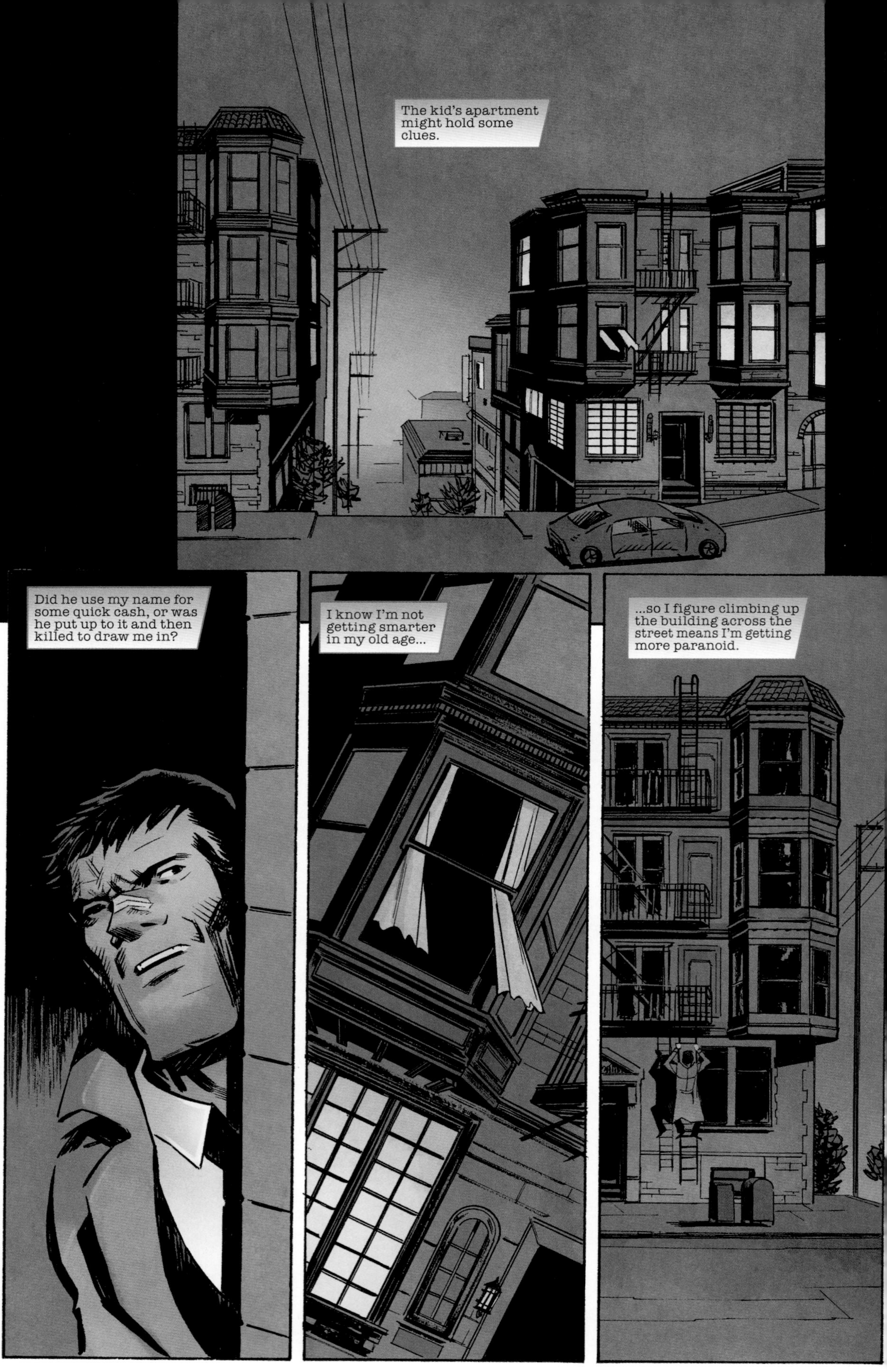
The kid's apartment might hold some clues.
Did he use my name for some quick cash, or was he put up to it and then killed to draw me in?
I know I'm not getting smarter in my old age...
...so I figure climbing up the building across the street means I'm getting more paranoid.

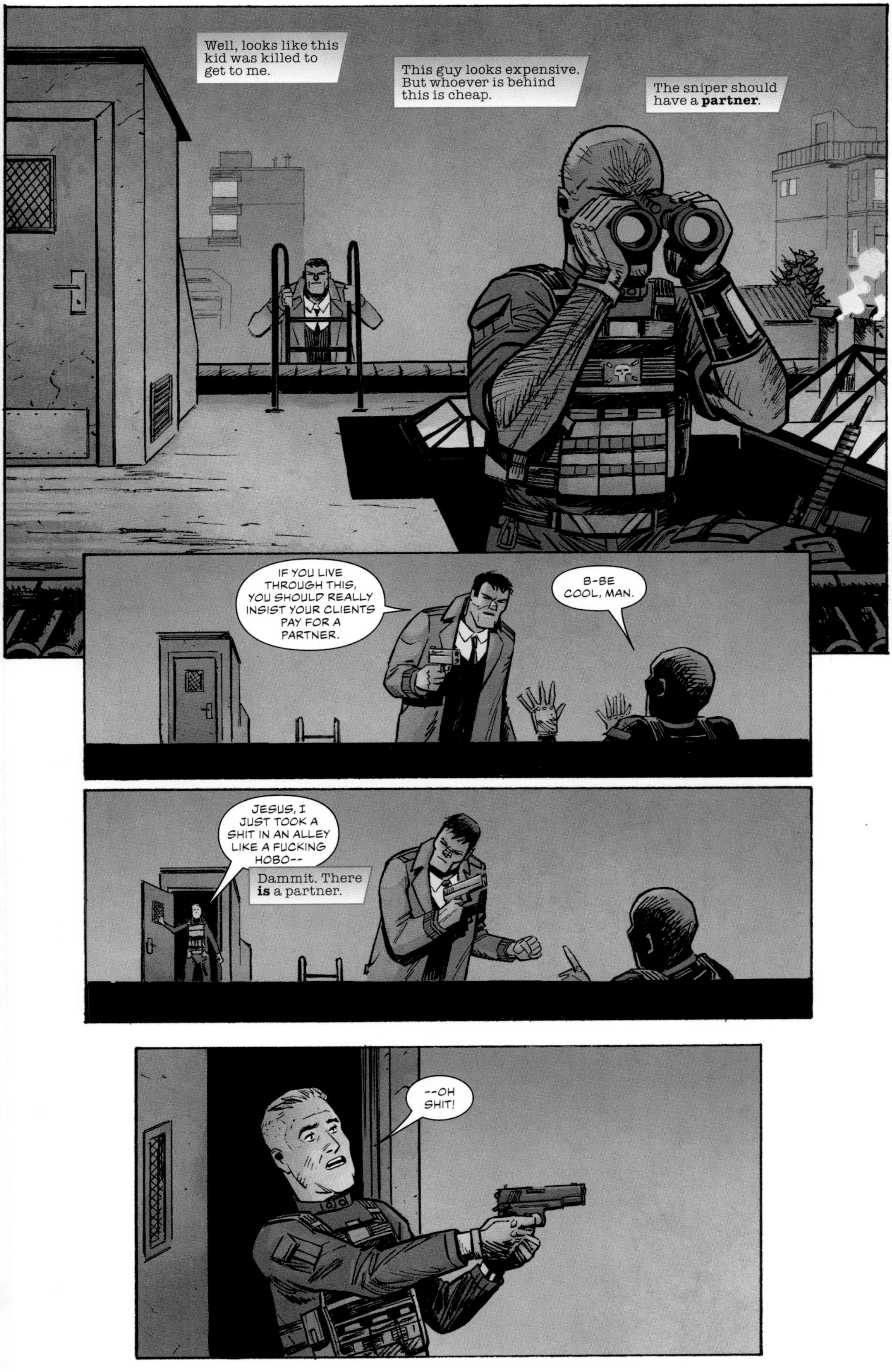
Well, looks like this kid was killed to get to me.
This guy looks expensive. But whoever is behind this is cheap.
The sniper should have a **partner**.
IF YOU LIVE THROUGH THIS, YOU SHOULD REALLY INSIST YOUR CLIENTS PAY FOR A PARTNER.
B-BE COOL, MAN.
JESUS, I JUST TOOK A SHIT IN AN ALLEY LIKE A FUCKING HOBO--
Dammit. There **is** a partner.
--OH SHIT!

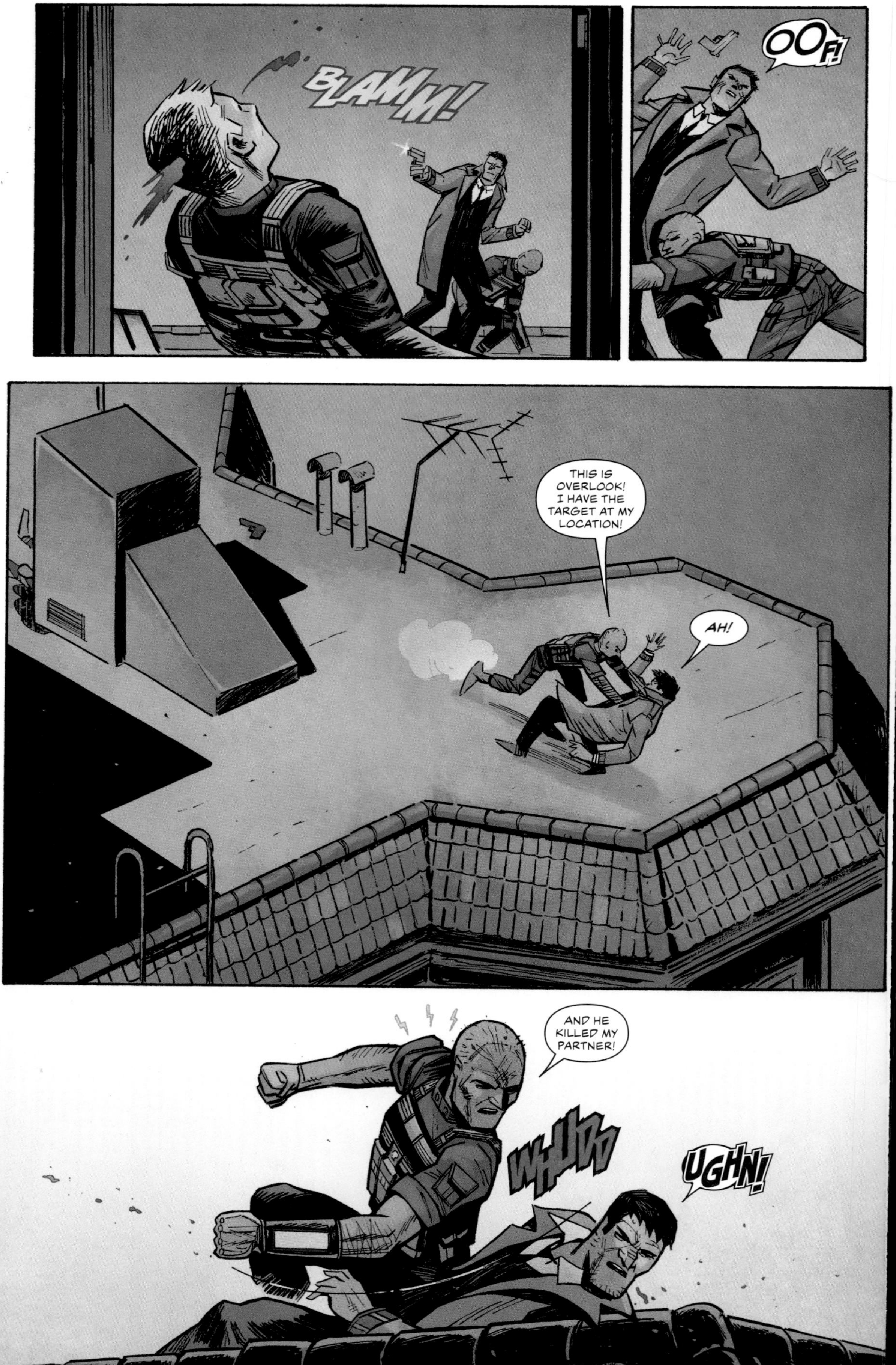
BLAMM!
OOF!
THIS IS OVERLOOK! I HAVE THE TARGET AT MY LOCATION!
AH!
AND HE KILLED MY PARTNER!
WHUDD
UGHN!

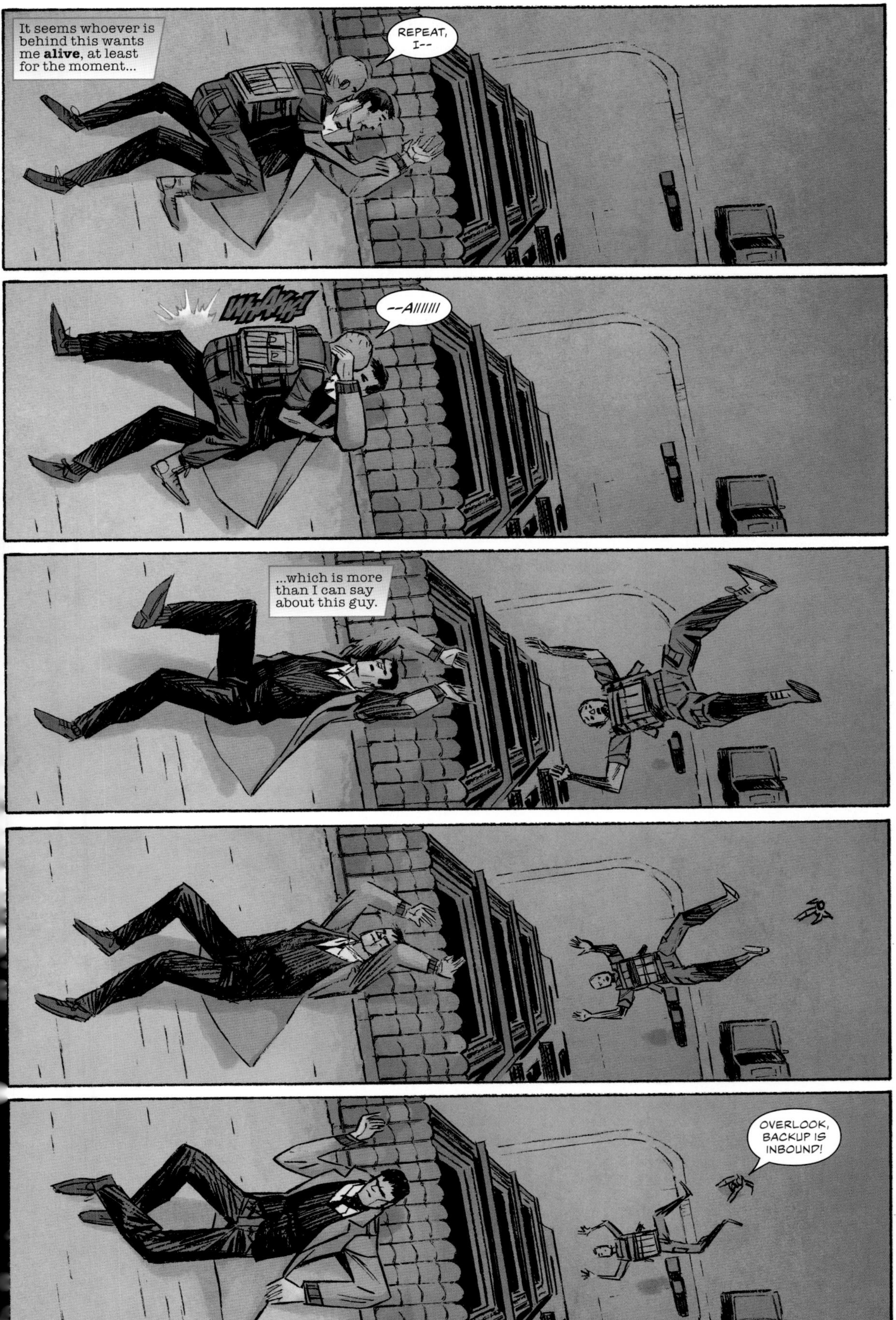
It seems whoever is behind this wants me **alive**, at least for the moment...
REPEAT, I--
WHAKK!
--AIIIIIII
...which is more than I can say about this guy.
OVERLOOK, BACKUP IS INBOUND!

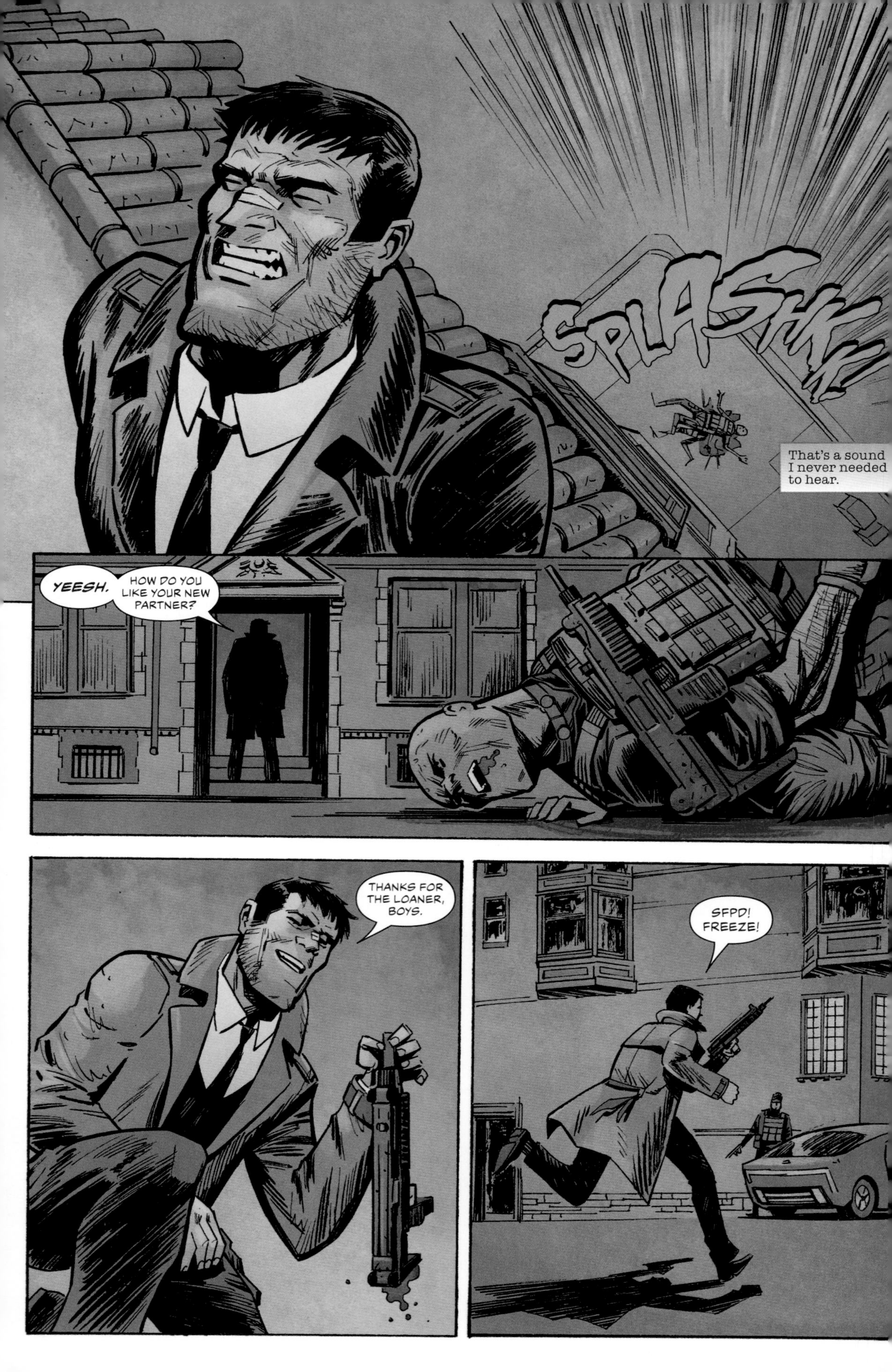
SPLASHK!
That's a sound I never needed to hear.
YEESH.
HOW DO YOU LIKE YOUR NEW PARTNER?
THANKS FOR THE LOANER, BOYS.
SFPD! FREEZE!

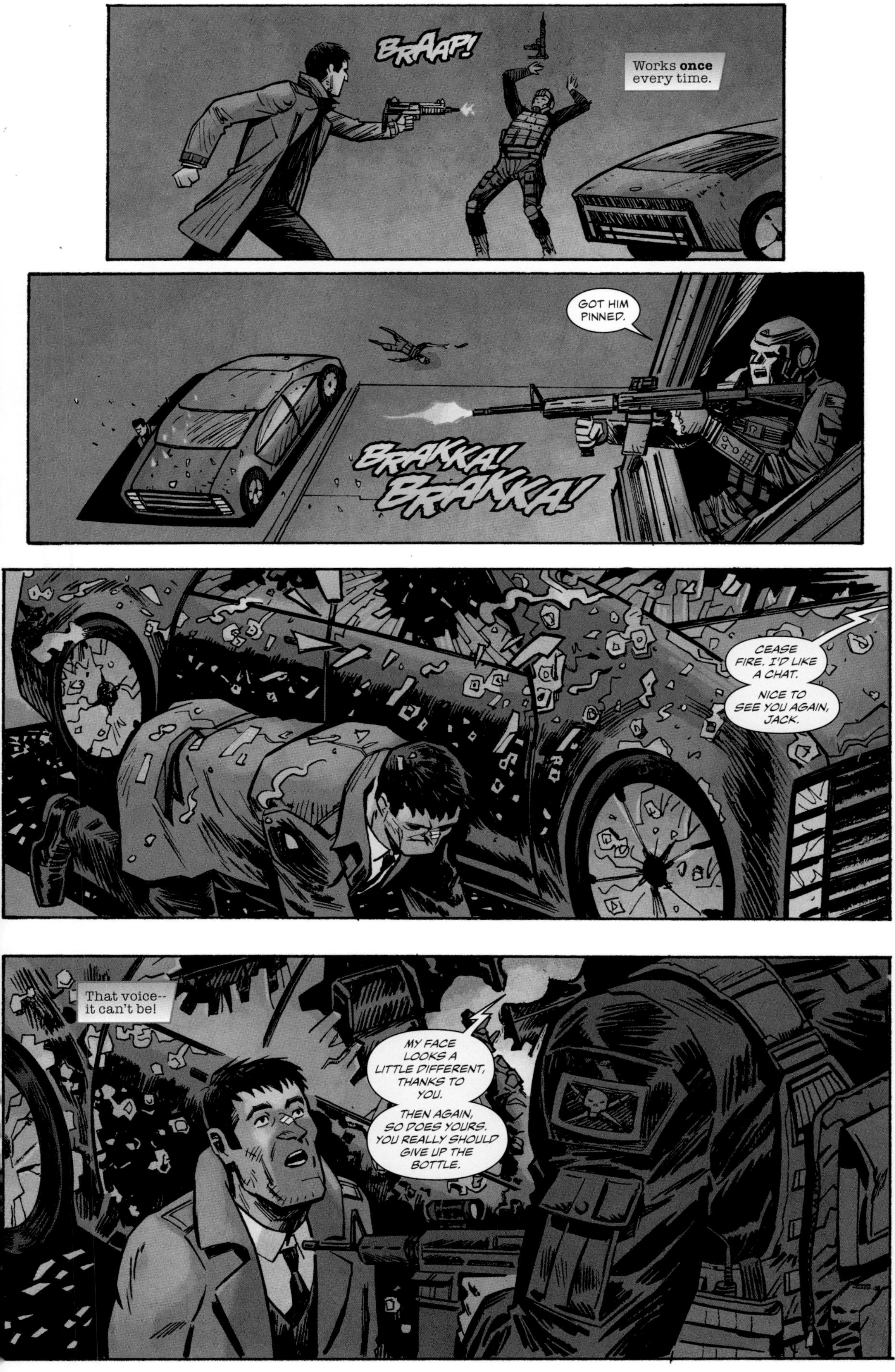
BRAAP!
Works **once** every time.
GOT HIM PINNED.
BRAKKA! BRAKKA!
CEASE FIRE. I'D LIKE A CHAT.
NICE TO SEE YOU AGAIN, JACK.
That voice-- it can't be!
MY FACE LOOKS A LITTLE DIFFERENT, THANKS TO YOU.
THEN AGAIN, SO DOES YOURS. YOU REALLY SHOULD GIVE UP THE BOTTLE.

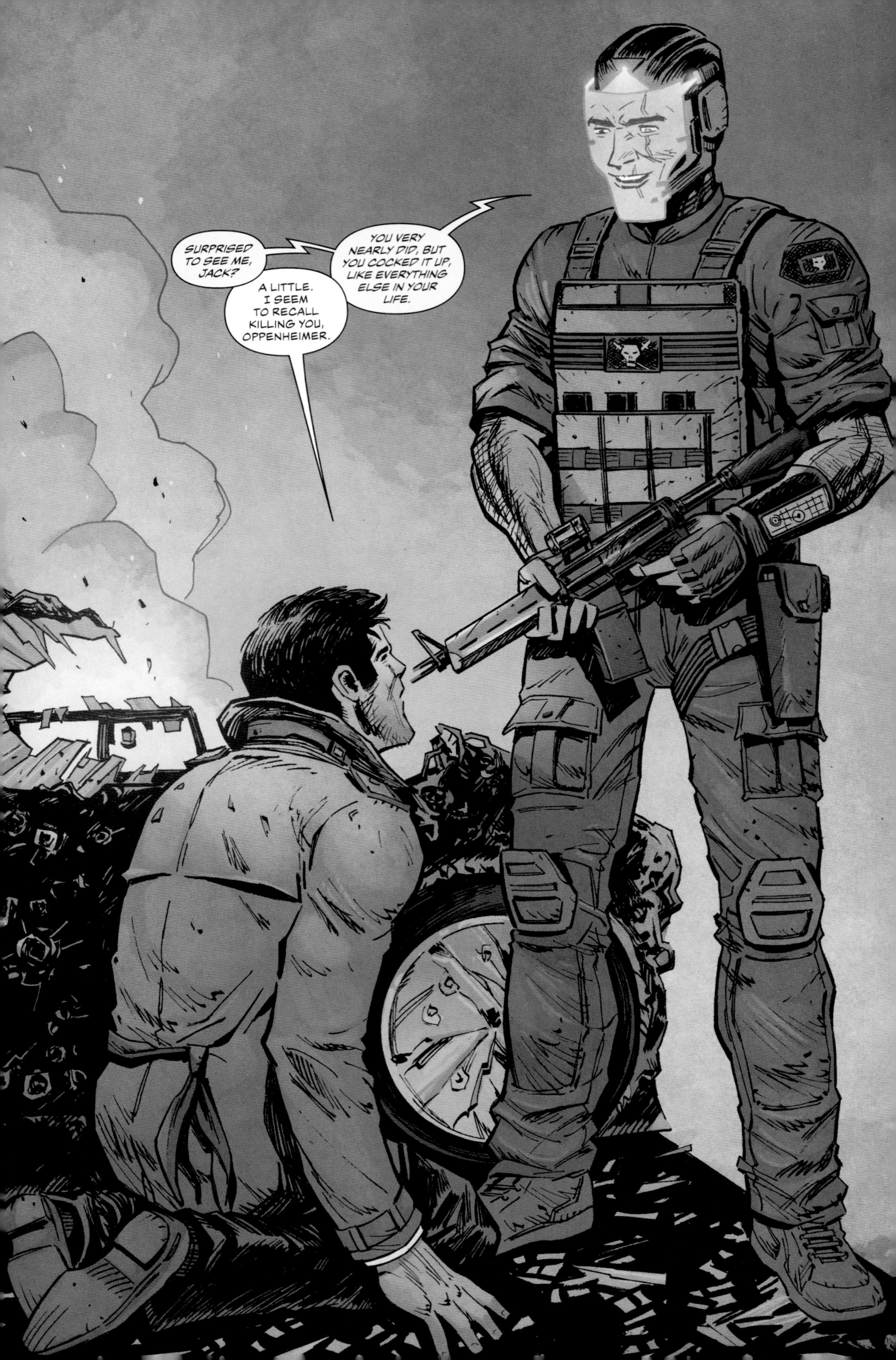
SURPRISED TO SEE ME, JACK?
YOU VERY NEARLY DID, BUT YOU COCKED IT UP, LIKE EVERYTHING ELSE IN YOUR LIFE.
A LITTLE. I SEEM TO RECALL KILLING YOU, OPPENHEIMER.

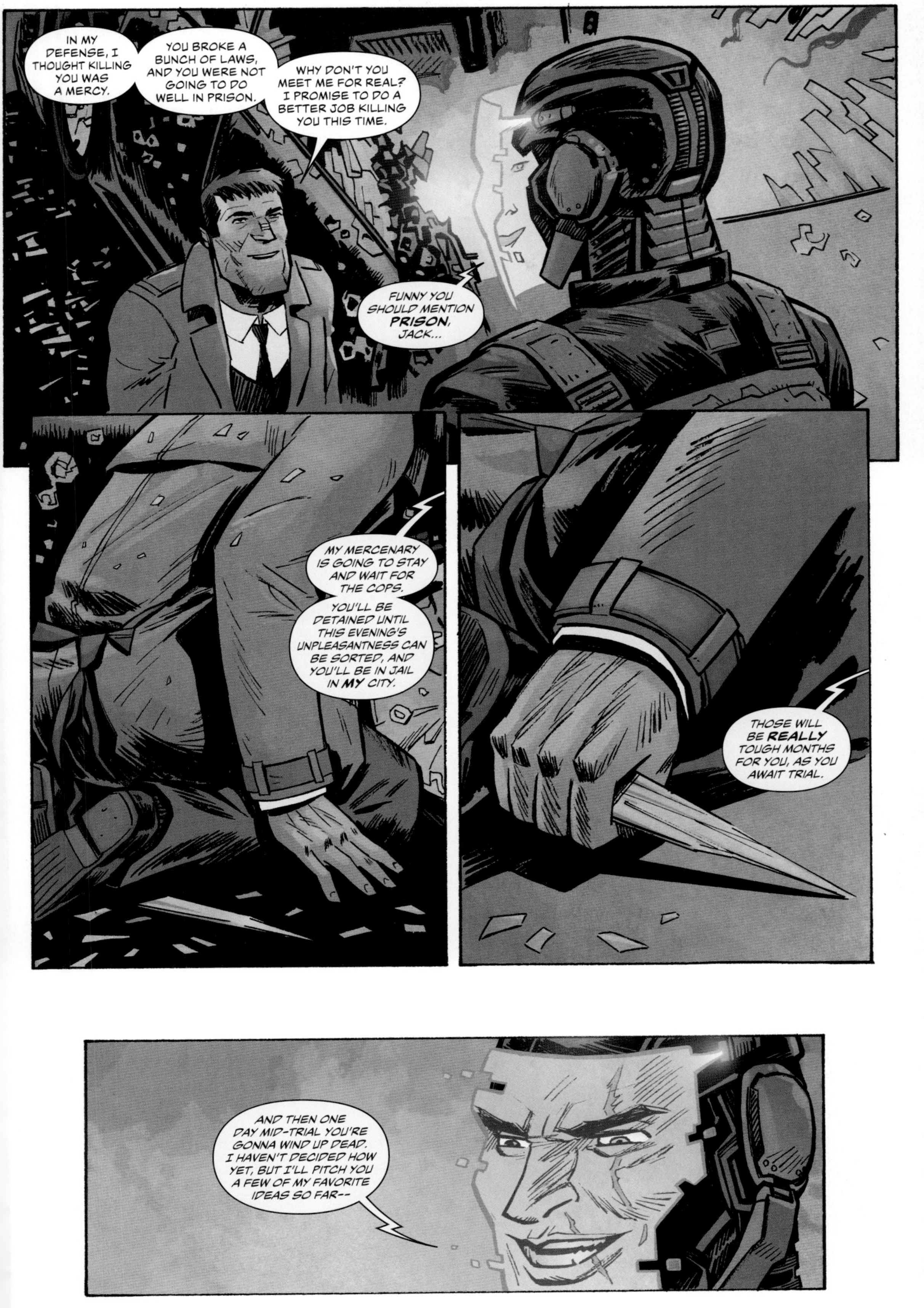
IN MY DEFENSE, I THOUGHT KILLING YOU WAS A MERCY.
YOU BROKE A BUNCH OF LAWS, AND YOU WERE NOT GOING TO DO WELL IN PRISON.
WHY DON'T YOU MEET ME FOR REAL? I PROMISE TO DO A BETTER JOB KILLING YOU THIS TIME.
FUNNY YOU SHOULD MENTION PRISON, JACK...
MY MERCENARY IS GOING TO STAY AND WAIT FOR THE COPS.
YOU'LL BE DETAINED UNTIL THIS EVENING'S UNPLEASANTNESS CAN BE SORTED, AND YOU'LL BE IN JAIL IN MY CITY.
THOSE WILL BE REALLY TOUGH MONTHS FOR YOU, AS YOU AWAIT TRIAL.
AND THEN ONE DAY MID-TRIAL YOU'RE GONNA WIND UP DEAD. I HAVEN'T DECIDED HOW YET, BUT I'LL PITCH YOU A FEW OF MY FAVORITE IDEAS SO FAR--

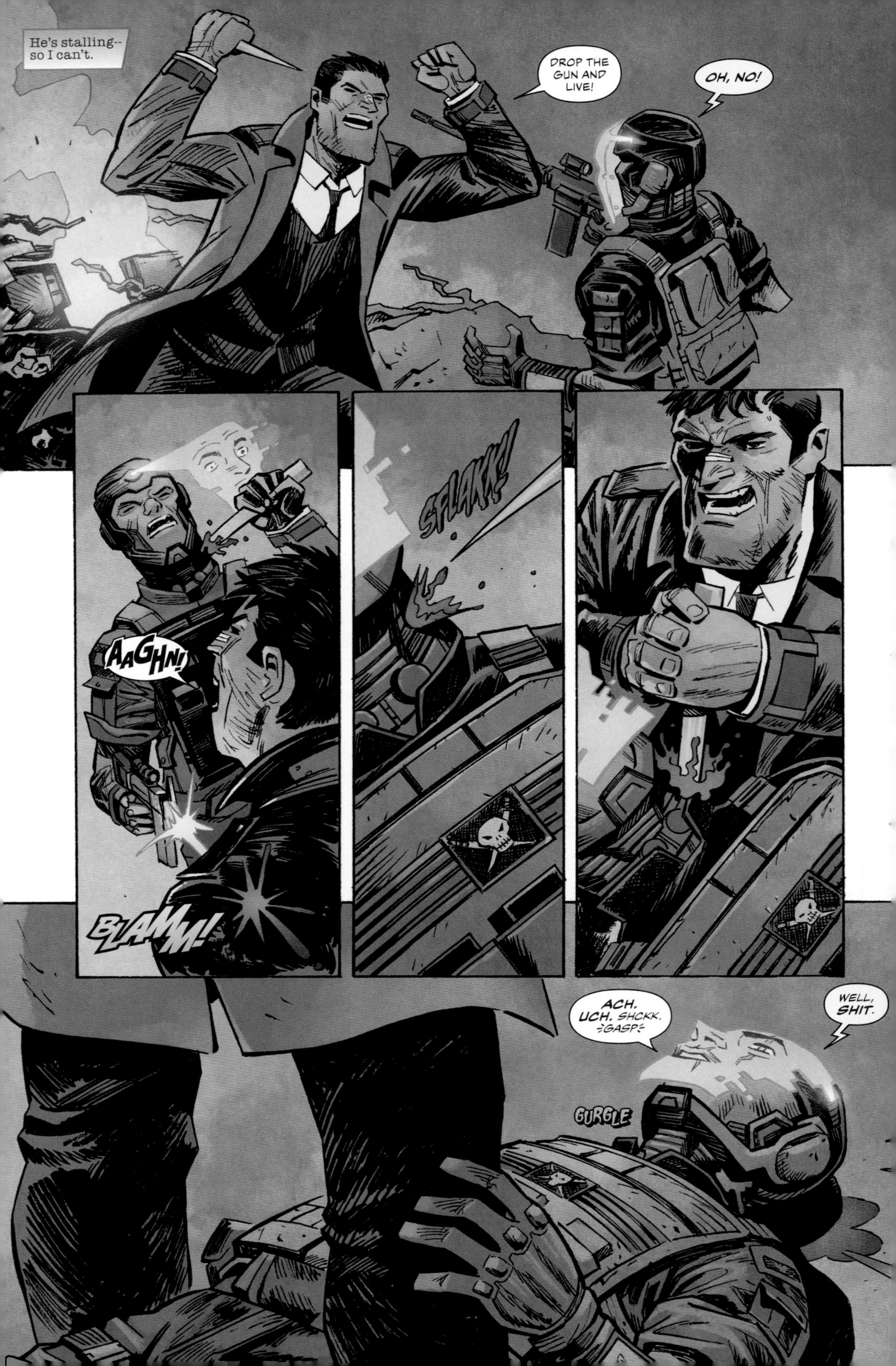
He's stalling--
so I can't.
DROP THE GUN AND LIVE!
OH, NO!
AAGHN!
BLAMM!
SPLAKK!
ACH. UCH. SHCKK. GASP
WELL, SHIT.
GURGLE

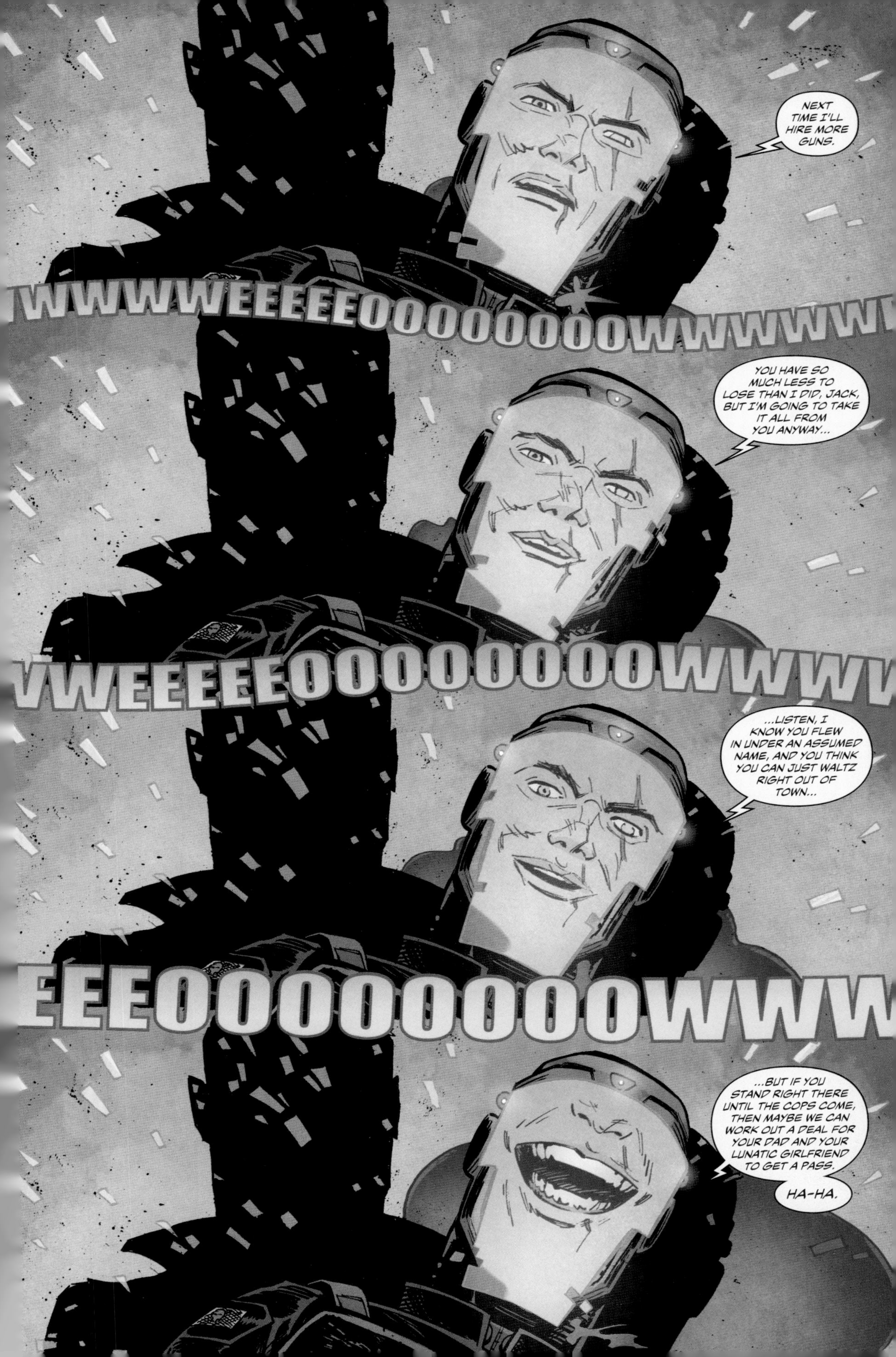
NEXT TIME I'LL HIRE MORE GUNS.
WWWWWEEEEEOOOOOOOOOOWWWWWW
YOU HAVE SO MUCH LESS TO LOSE THAN I DID, JACK, BUT I'M GOING TO TAKE IT ALL FROM YOU ANYWAY...
VWEEEEEOOOOOOOOOOWWWW
...LISTEN, I KNOW YOU FLEW IN UNDER AN ASSUMED NAME, AND YOU THINK YOU CAN JUST WALTZ RIGHT OUT OF TOWN...
EEEOOOOOOOOOOWWWW
...BUT IF YOU STAND RIGHT THERE UNTIL THE COPS COME, THEN MAYBE WE CAN WORK OUT A DEAL FOR YOUR DAD AND YOUR LUNATIC GIRLFRIEND TO GET A PASS.
HA-HA.

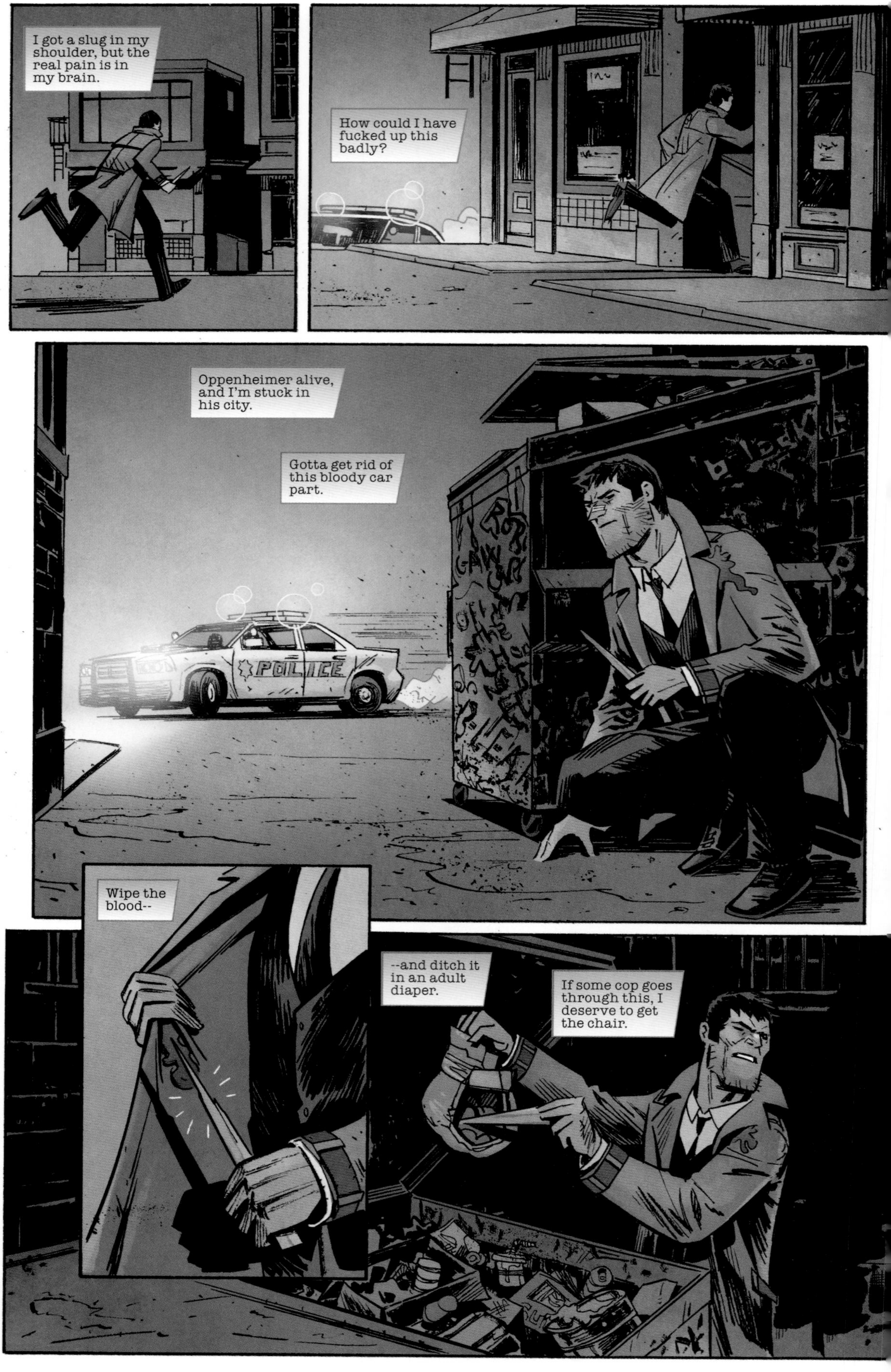
I got a slug in my shoulder, but the real pain is in my brain.
How could I have fucked up this badly?
Oppenheimer alive, and I'm stuck in his city.
Gotta get rid of this bloody car part.
POLICE
Wipe the blood--
--and ditch it in an adult diaper.
If some cop goes through this, I deserve to get the chair.

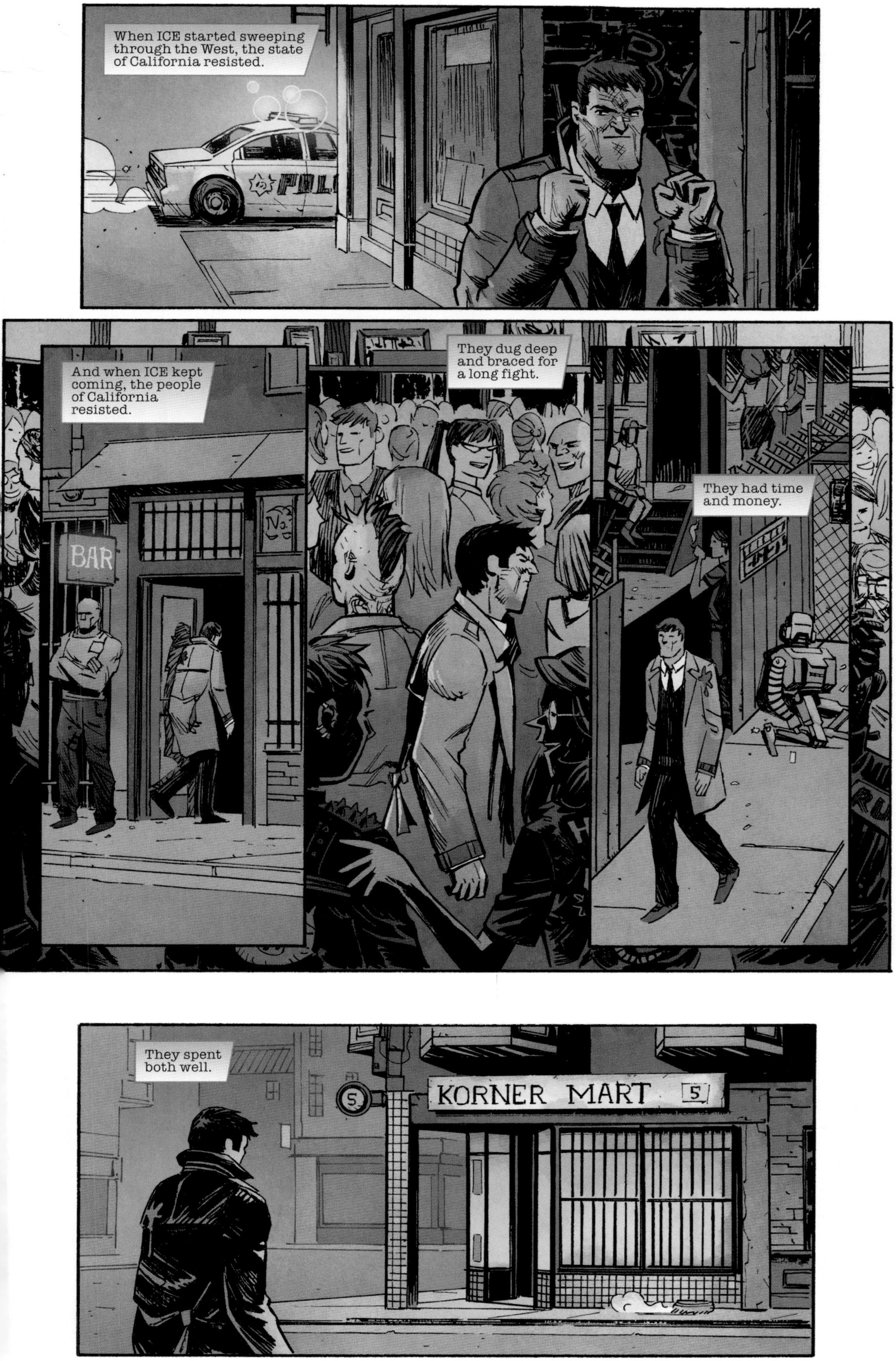

When ICE started sweeping through the West, the state of California resisted.
And when ICE kept coming, the people of California resisted.
BAR
They dug deep and braced for a long fight.
They had time and money.
They spent both well.
KORNER MART
5

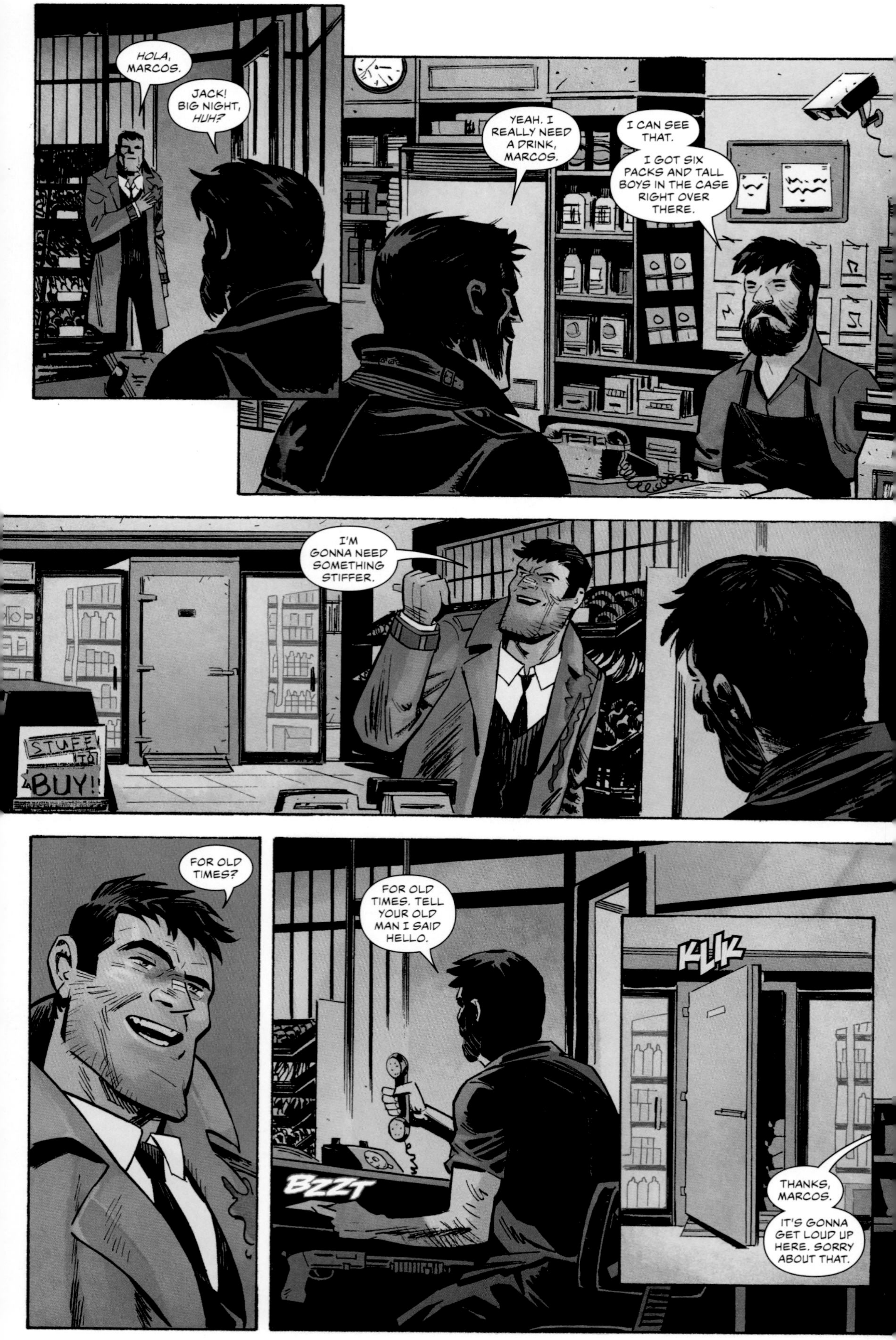
HOLA, MARCOS.
JACK! BIG NIGHT, HUH?
YEAH. I REALLY NEED A DRINK, MARCOS.
I CAN SEE THAT.
I GOT SIX PACKS AND TALL BOYS IN THE CASE RIGHT OVER THERE.
I'M GONNA NEED SOMETHING STIFFER.
STUFF TO BUY!!
FOR OLD TIMES?
FOR OLD TIMES. TELL YOUR OLD MAN I SAID HELLO.
BZZZT
KLIK
THANKS, MARCOS.
IT'S GONNA GET LOUD UP HERE. SORRY ABOUT THAT.

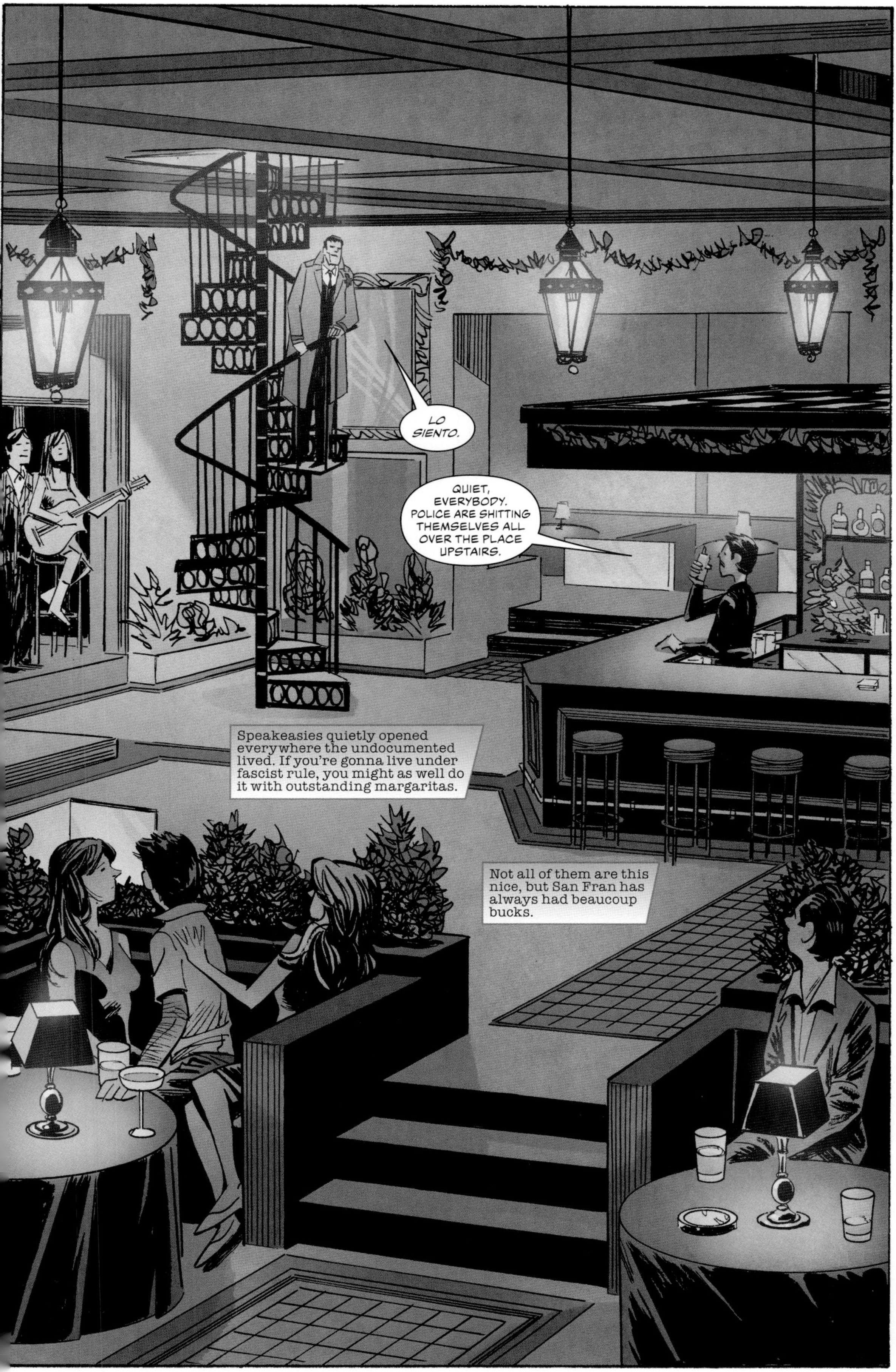
LO SIENTO.
QUIET, EVERYBODY. POLICE ARE SHITTING THEMSELVES ALL OVER THE PLACE UPSTAIRS.
Speakeasies quietly opened everywhere the undocumented lived. If you're gonna live under fascist rule, you might as well do it with outstanding margaritas.
Not all of them are this nice, but San Fran has always had beaucoup bucks.

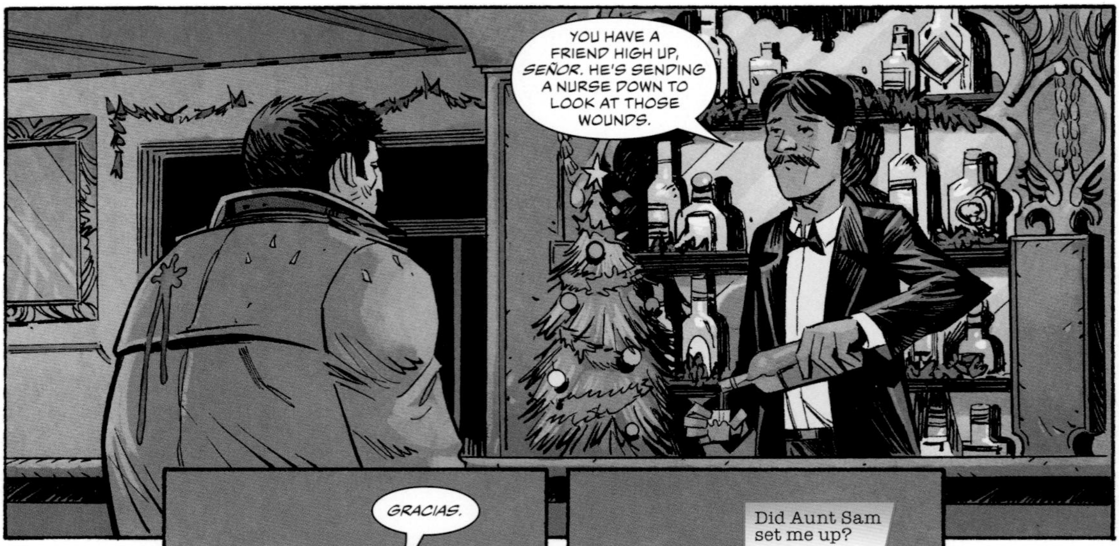
YOU HAVE A FRIEND HIGH UP, SEÑOR. HE'S SENDING A NURSE DOWN TO LOOK AT THOSE WOUNDS.

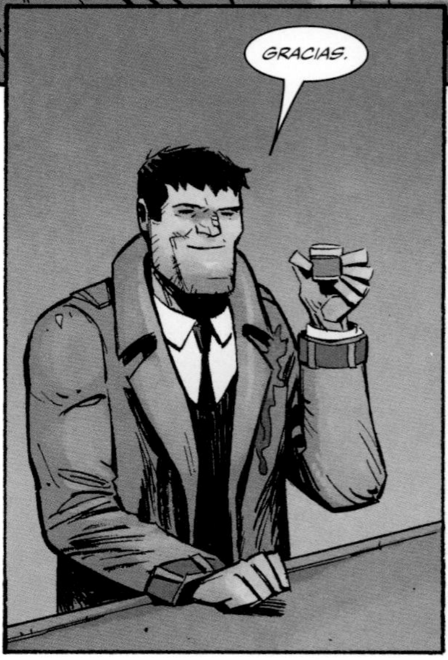
GRACIAS.

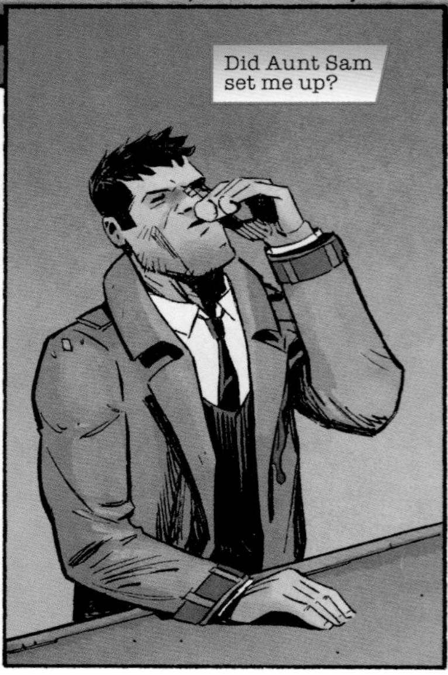
Did Aunt Sam set me up?

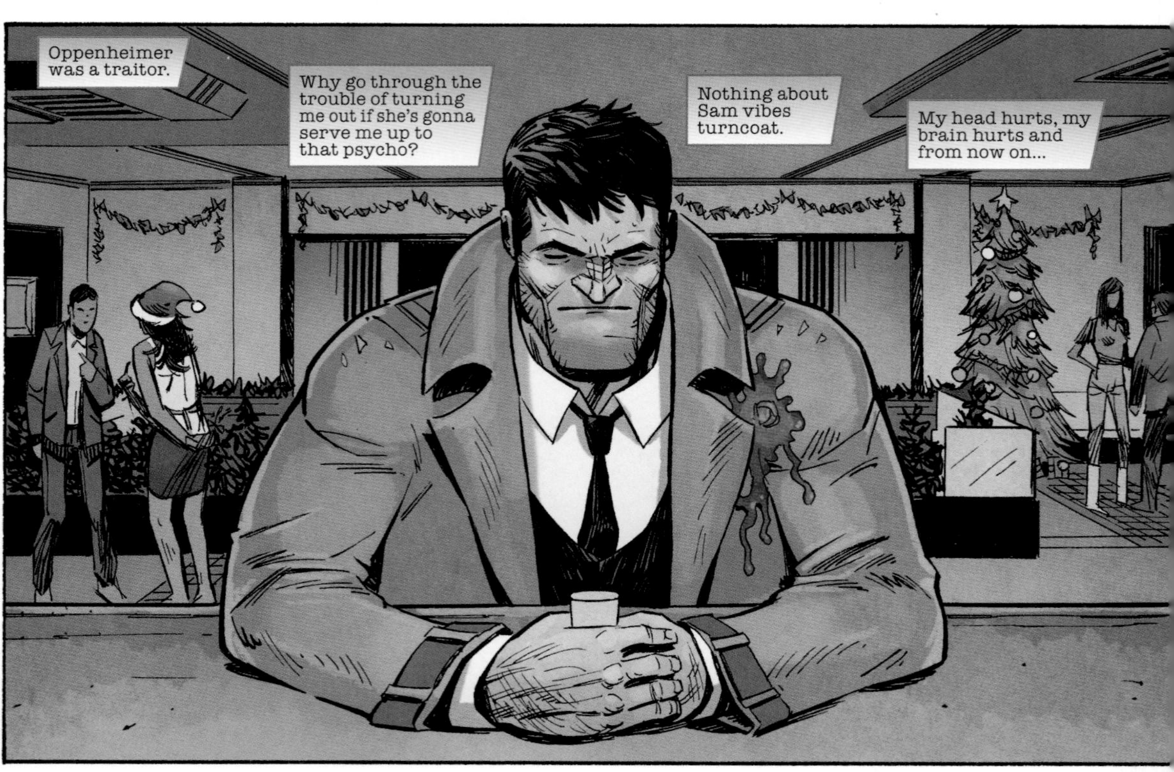
Oppenheimer was a traitor.
Why go through the trouble of turning me out if she's gonna serve me up to that psycho?
Nothing about Sam vibes turncoat.
My head hurts, my brain hurts and from now on...

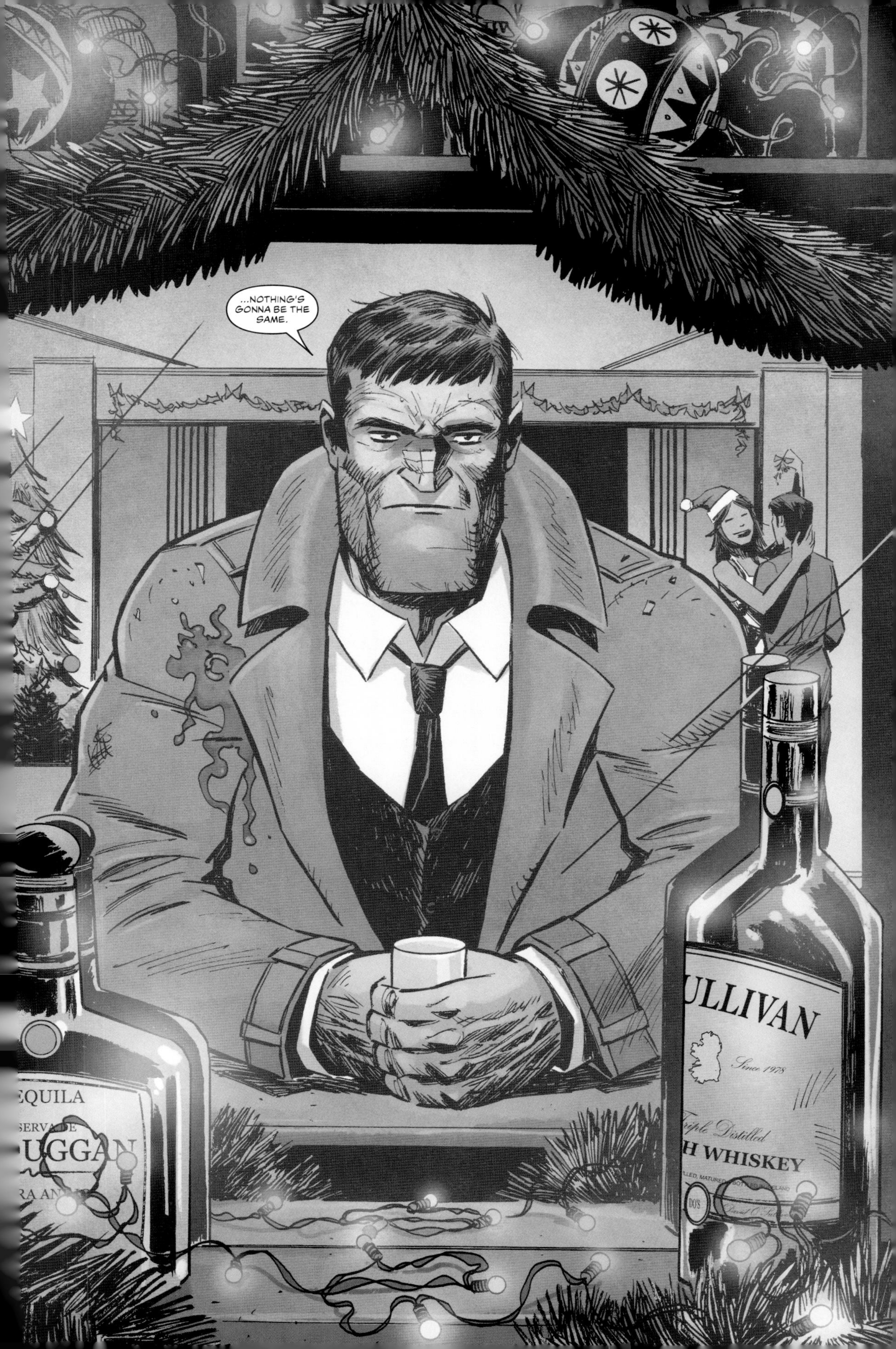
...NOTHING'S GONNA BE THE SAME.
EQUILA
UGGAN
ULLIVAN
Since 1978
Triple Distilled
H WHISKEY

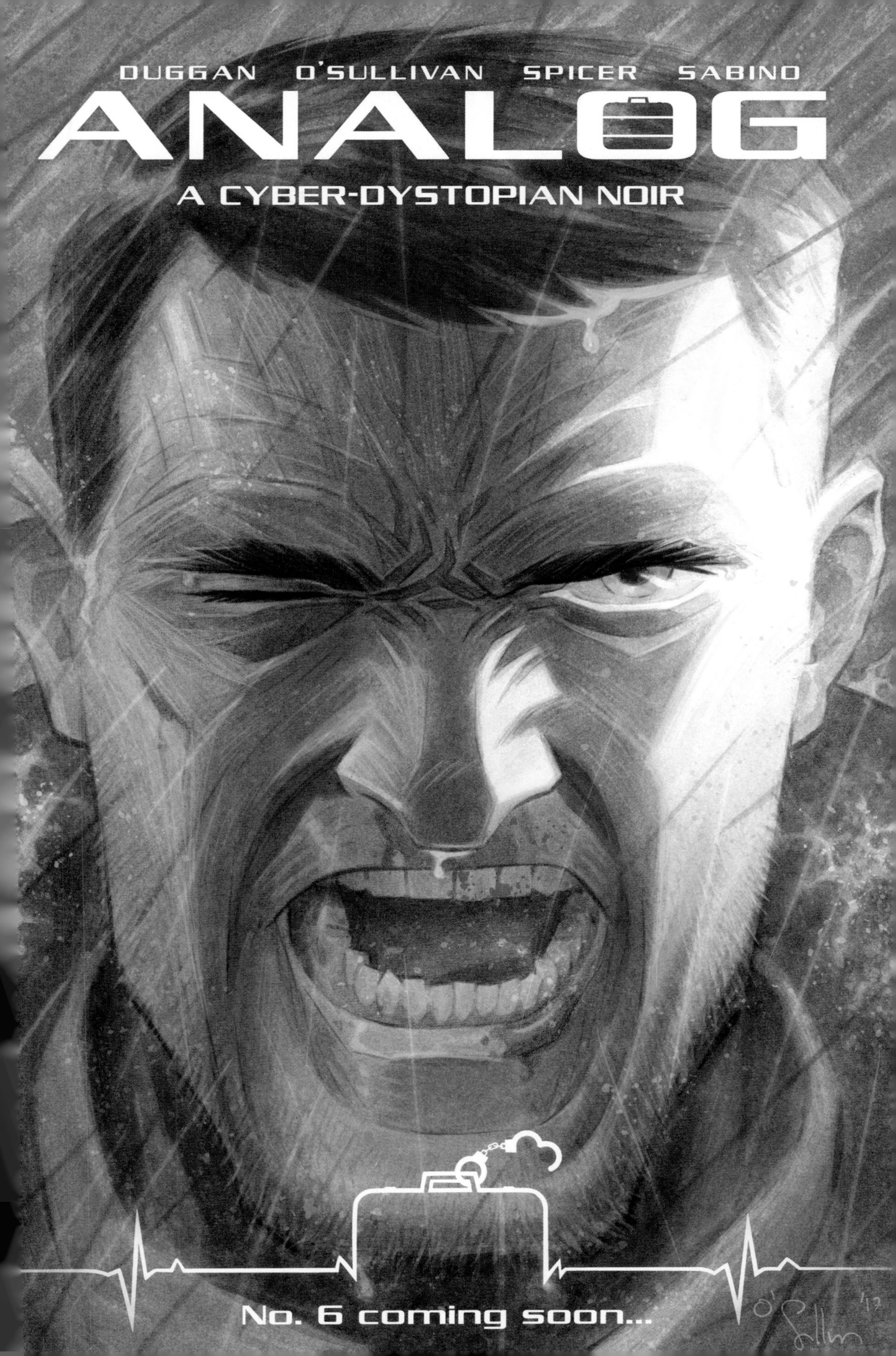
DUGGAN O'SULLIVAN SPICER SABINO
ANALOG
A CYBER-DYSTOPIAN NOIR
No. 6 coming soon...

DUGGAN x McCREA x SPICER

DEAD RABBIT

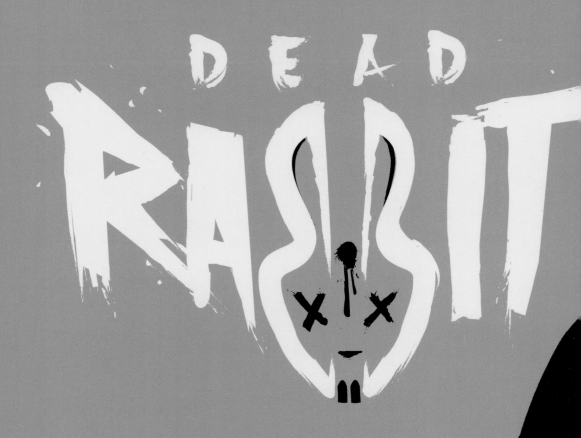

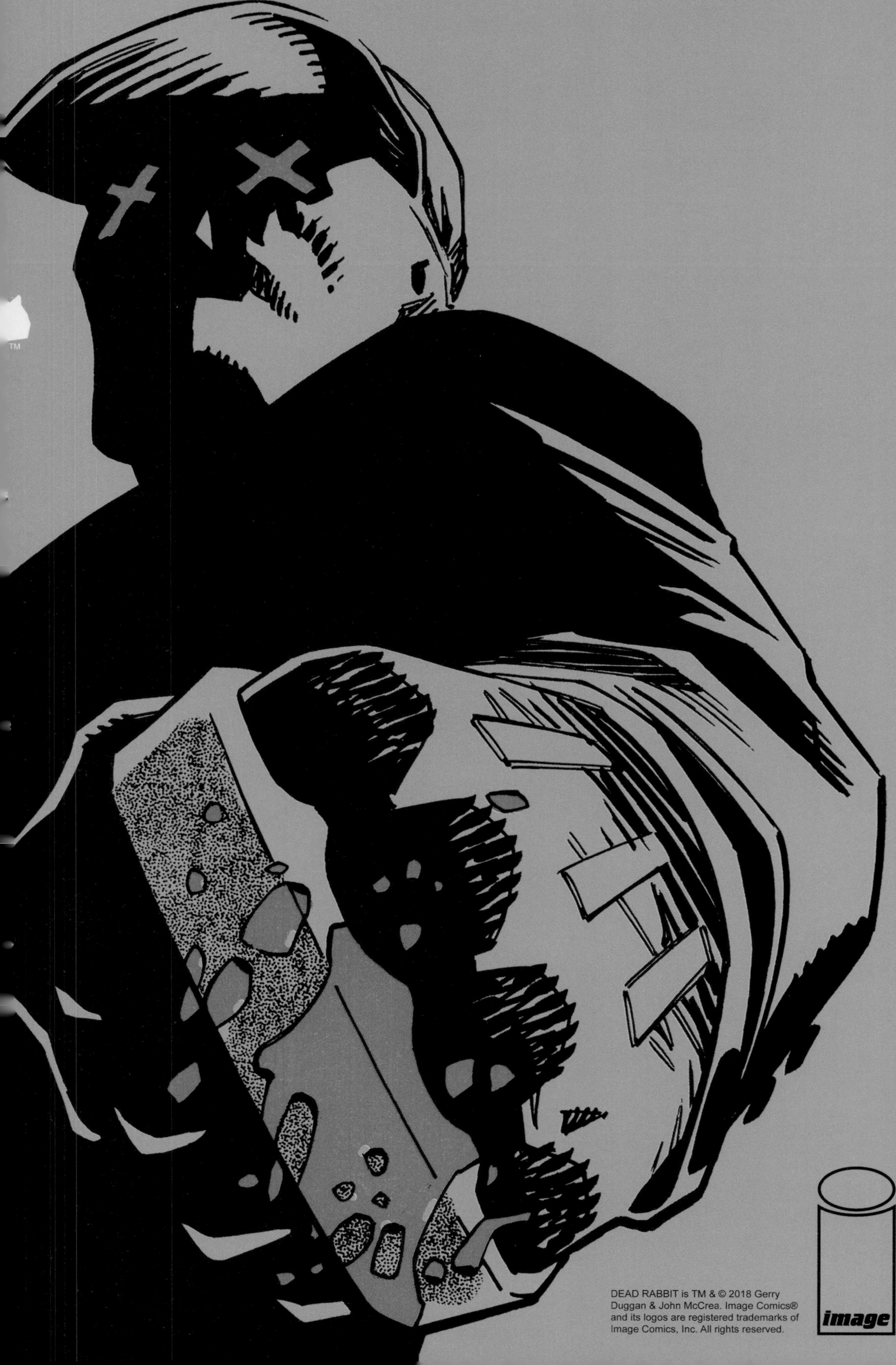